COYOTE HORIZON

Novels by Allen M. Steele

NEAR-SPACE SERIES
ORBITAL DECAY
CLARKE COUNTY, SPACE
LUNAR DESCENT
LABYRINTH OF NIGHT
A KING OF INFINITE SPACE

THE JERICHO ITERATION
THE TRANQUILLITY ALTERNATIVE
OCEANSPACE
CHRONOSPACE

COYOTE TRILOGY
COYOTE
COYOTE RISING
COYOTE FRONTIER

COYOTE CHRONICLES
COYOTE HORIZON

COYOTE UNIVERSE
SPINDRIFT
GALAXY BLUES

Collections by Allen M. Steele

RUDE ASTRONAUTS
ALL-AMERICAN ALIEN BOY
SEX AND VIOLENCE IN ZERO-G: THE COMPLETE "NEAR SPACE" STORIES
AMERICAN BEAUTY
THE LAST SCIENCE FICTION WRITER

Nonfiction by Allen M. Steele

PRIMARY IGNITION: ESSAYS 1997–2001

COYOTE HORIZON

A Novel of Interstellar Discovery

ALLEN M. STEELE

ACE BOOKS, NEW YORK

THE BERKLEY PUBLISHING GROUP
Published by the Penguin Group
Penguin Group (USA) Inc.
375 Hudson Street, New York, New York 10014, USA
Penguin Group (Canada), 90 Eglinton Avenue East, Suite 700, Toronto, Ontario M4P 2Y3, Canada
(a division of Pearson Penguin Canada Inc.)
Penguin Books Ltd., 80 Strand, London WC2R 0RL, England
Penguin Group Ireland, 25 St. Stephen's Green, Dublin 2, Ireland (a division of Penguin Books Ltd.)
Penguin Group (Australia), 250 Camberwell Road, Camberwell, Victoria 3124, Australia
(a division of Pearson Australia Group Pty. Ltd.)
Penguin Books India Pvt. Ltd., 11 Community Centre, Panchsheel Park, New Delhi—110 017, India
Penguin Group (NZ), 67 Apollo Drive, Rosedale, North Shore 0632, New Zealand
(a division of Pearson New Zealand Ltd.)
Penguin Books (South Africa) (Pty.) Ltd., 24 Sturdee Avenue, Rosebank, Johannesburg 2196,
South Africa

Penguin Books Ltd., Registered Offices: 80 Strand, London WC2R 0RL, England

This is an original publication of The Berkley Publishing Group.

This is a work of fiction. Names, characters, places, and incidents either are the product of the author's imagination or are used fictitiously, and any resemblance to actual persons, living or dead, business establishments, events, or locales is entirely coincidental. The publisher does not have any control over and does not assume any responsibility for author or third-party websites or their content.

FIRST EDITION: March 2009

Library of Congress Cataloging-in-Publication Data

Steele, Allen M.
    Coyote horizon : a novel of interstellar discovery / Allen M. Steele.—1st ed.
        p. cm.
    ISBN 978-0-441-01682-2
    1. Space colonies—Fiction.   2. Life on other planets—Fiction.   3. Outer space—Exploration—
Fiction.   4. Interplanetary voyages—Fiction.   I. Title.

PS3569.T338425C693 2009
813'.54—dc22

                                                                      2008049491

PRINTED IN THE UNITED STATES OF AMERICA

10   9   8   7   6   5   4   3   2   1

CONTENTS

FOREWORD

When I began writing *Coyote* in early 2000, I believed that the tale I wanted to tell—the story of the first starship from Earth and the first interstellar colony—could be done in one volume. I'd been researching and developing this particular novel through most of the previous decade; after a couple of false starts, the time had finally come to put it down on paper.

As things turned out, though, the story was too big for one novel, so I decided to write a sequel, *Coyote Rising*, which would tie up the threads left hanging at the end of the first book. Yet that wasn't enough, either; by the time I finished the second book, I'd come to realize that I still hadn't answered a lot of questions I myself had put forward. As a result, a third book became necessary, and thus I wrote *Coyote Frontier*.

Once the Coyote trilogy was finished, I turned my attention to other matters, including a couple of independent novels—*Spindrift* and *Galaxy Blues*—set in the same universe. Then something happened that I didn't expect.

When reviews of *Coyote Frontier* started coming in, quite a few critics expressed the opinion that, while it was obvious that I'd wrapped up the story line, there was more about Coyote that remained to be told. Then I began receiving fan mail from readers, with the majority asking me to write more. One reader used the maps Ron Miller and I had created to build a globe of Coyote; it now rests on my desk as a reference tool. Another took my description of the Coyote Federation flag to make one for me; it's taped to my notebook. Yet another went so far as to create an entire fan website that included interactive maps and lists of all the major characters, events, starships, and locales mentioned in the books (you can visit it at www.coyoteseries.com). Not long after that, *Coyote* entered the curriculum of university science-fiction courses, with one student emailing me to ask questions for a dissertation she was writing about the trilogy.

Motivated by the attention, I decided to write some short fiction about Coyote. The first story, "Walking Star," occurred after the events of *Coyote Frontier*; a slightly different version appears in this novel as Part Two. A second novella, "The River Horses," filled in the gap between *Coyote* and *Coyote Rising*. And a short story, "The War of Dogs and Boids," related an incident that didn't make its way into *Coyote*. I thought these stories would satisfy everyone, but they only added fuel to the fire. Readers continued to insist that I write more about the world I had created, and after a while I came to realize that, although the original story arc was complete, I wasn't finished with this place yet.

It should be pointed out that *Coyote Horizon* isn't the "fourth book of the trilogy" but rather the first volume of a duology; the second volume, *Coyote Destiny*, will conclude the story arc. Although astute readers of this series may notice that the events of *Coyote Horizon* are roughly concurrent with those depicted in *Galaxy Blues*, it isn't necessary to read the other book first in order to understand this novel.

This novel is dedicated to everyone who asked for more. Thank you for your support, and for demanding that I return to Coyote.

DRAMATIS PERSONAE

Montero Family

Carlos Montero—former president and diplomatic attaché, Coyote Federation

Wendy Gunther—former president, Coyote Federation

Susan Montero—naturalist, Colonial University

Jonathan Parson—captain, CFS *Ted LeMare*

Jorge Montero II—Susan and Jon's son

Hawk Thompson—customs inspector

Melissa Sanchez—prostitute

Sawyer Lee—wilderness guide

Joseph Walking Star Cassidy—equerry

Morgan Goldstein—CEO, Janus Ltd.

Mike Kennedy—Goldstein's bodyguard

Grey Rice—Dominionist missionary

Alberto Consenza—Dominionist deacon

Joe Bains—parole officer

Lynn Hu—journalist

Barry Dreyfus—pilot and first mate, CFS *Ted LeMare*

David Laird—member, Living Earth

"Hurricane Dave" Peck—bartender

Charlie Banks—gyro pilot

Owen McKay—innkeeper

Bess Cole—barmaid

Yuri Scklovskii—drover

Anastasia Tereshkova—commodore, Coyote Federation Navy
Russell Heflin—chief petty officer, CFSS *Robert E. Lee*
Tomas Conseco—aide to Wendy Gunther
Dieter Vogel—ambassador, European Alliance
Mahamatasja Jas Sa-Fhadda—*hjadd* Prime Emissary
Jasahajahd Taf Sa-Fhadda—*hjadd* Cultural Ambassador

PROLOGUE

Traveler's Rest, the home of two former presidents of the Coyote Federation, was located on top of the Eastern Divide, the granite wall that separated the savannas of New Florida from the broad expanse of the East Channel. Built of sturdy blackwood imported from Great Dakota, with a slate roof cantilevered at a forty-five-degree angle, the manor overlooked the channel and the port town of Bridgeton and, on the other side of the Divide, the grassy flatlands that lay southwest of Liberty. The residence had its own wind turbine, a slender pylon on which three blades slowly rotated in the early-spring breeze, as well as a satellite dish perched on a corner of the roof. Although visible for many miles, the house could only be reached by a narrow dirt road that wound its way up the ridge.

President Gunther's personal aide had recommended that she come ahead of time, so Lynn Hu made sure that she arrived at Traveler's Rest an hour before her scheduled appointment. It wasn't until the cab she'd hired in Liberty came to a halt at the front gate at the bottom of the ridge, though, that she knew why. An iron-barred arch eight feet tall, the gate was the sole point of entry through the chain-link fence surrounding the estate. Although the bluff was steep enough to challenge even the most dedicated of climbers, the fence extended all up the side of the Divide, prohibiting anyone from climbing over. If that weren't enough, solar-powered floodlights and surveillance cameras were positioned on posts within the fence.

To be sure, the couple who lived here had good reason to guard their privacy. Yet in the three weeks that she'd been on Coyote, Lynn hadn't seen this measure of protection since going through customs at the New Brighton spaceport. Even Government House was remarkably accessible;

all she'd had to do to arrange a meeting with the current president was present her credentials and have a brief chat with a couple of bureaucrats before she was escorted upstairs to his office.

Despite his colorful past—an uncle who'd been a hero of the Revolution, teenage years spent as a member of the Rigil Kent Brigade, being elected mayor of Clarksburg despite having a notorious brother who was murdered by his own son—Garth Thompson had given her a boring interview, with little worth quoting save as background material. Yet in the end, he'd come through with what Lynn really wanted: a satphone call to Traveler's Rest, setting up an appointment for her to see the very person whom she'd traveled forty-six light-years to meet.

And so here she was. Lynn paid the driver *C*10, adding a couple of colonials as a tip. He pocketed the money without so much as a word, then reached up to shut the gullwing door; the coupe rose on its skirts and turned around to glide back down Swamp Road toward town. Stepping closer to the gate, Lynn noticed a small metal box on a post next to the gate. Raising its hinged cover, she found an intercom.

She pressed its button, bent closer. "Hello?"

"Yes?" The voice from the speaker was male, with the Hispanic accent of someone born in the Western Hemisphere Union back on Earth. *"Who's calling, please?"*

"Lynn Hu . . . Pan News Service. I have an appointment with . . ."

"Of course, senorita. We've been expecting you." A brief buzz, then the right half of the gate slowly swung open. *"Please come up."*

"Thank you." Lynn started to step through the gate, then stopped as something occurred to her. "Umm . . . come up, you said?"

"Yes."

She stared at the dirt road leading up the ridge and swallowed. No signs that any vehicles had recently come this way. Nothing that looked like a tram. She heard the chitter of small birds—grasshoarders, she'd learned they were called—within the high grass on either side of the road; a skeeter buzzed past her face, and she swatted it away.

"Walk, you mean," she added.

No response from the intercom, yet as she strolled through the gate, it silently closed behind her, locking with a definitive click. Realizing that argument was pointless, she took a deep breath, then set out to climb the rest of the way to Traveler's Rest.

The ascent was less difficult than it appeared. The house was only about three hundred yards from the bottom of the bluffs, with the road cut in a series of switchbacks that afforded an easy grade. Yet, although someone born and raised on Coyote probably would have considered it little more than morning exercise, Lynn had only recently become acclimated to the thin atmosphere; when she'd left the inn in Liberty, she hadn't expected to go hiking. So her linen business suit was drenched with sweat and her sandals filled with sand by the time she arrived, out of breath and gasping, at the top of the ridge.

Traveler's Rest was magnificent. Tall cathedral windows looked out upon carefully cultivated gardens, their beds planted with flowers both native to Coyote and imported from Earth, lending color to a place where it was least expected. Wooden stairs led her up a low retaining wall to a semicircular veranda upon which Adirondack chairs and potted shrubs had been set out; she noticed a small refractor telescope on a tripod, its capped lens pointed toward the sky. As she came closer, Lynn was startled to hear a horse whinny; looking around, she spotted a chestnut mare peering at her from the half door of a shed beneath the wind turbine. Horses were still scarce on this world, and most were working animals, yet this one was obviously a pet, something a rich person would ride every now and then.

She was about to walk over to the shed when a carved blackwood door opened on the veranda. A young man, not much older than herself and wearing a homespun tunic and trousers, stepped out. "Ms. Hu? I'm Tomas Conseco, the president's personal aide. Would you follow me, please?"

The foyer was cool after the unseasonal warmth of the morning, the lighting subdued. "You may leave your shoes there," Tomas said, motioning to a row of boots and moccasins carefully arranged on the tile floor beside the door. As Lynn gratefully slipped off her sandals, he offered her a hempcloth towel. "It's a long walk here," he added. "If you'd like to freshen up a bit, the guest bath is just over here."

"No, thank you. This will be fine." She ran the towel across her face and neck, mopping her sweat. Suddenly, her business suit felt too warm. "Is there any place where I may . . . ?" She plucked at her jacket lapel.

"Of course." Tomas gallantly extended a hand, and Lynn shrugged out of the jacket and surrendered it to him.

"Just one thing, though," she said, reaching for its inside pocket. "I need my pad . . ."

"Sorry. No pads." Tomas shook his head as he draped her jacket across his arm. "Not until the president gives permission."

"You don't understand. I'm here to interview . . ."

"The president scheduled a time for you to meet with her." Tomas turned to walk up a short flight of stairs. "Whether she consents to an interview is another matter entirely."

Irritated, but with no choice but to comply, Lynn followed Tomas as he escorted her through the house. Much of the ground floor was taken up by a large living room, with overstuffed cat-skin furniture arranged around a fieldstone hearth whose chimney rose nearly twenty feet above the polished wooden floor. The sun shone brightly through the cathedral windows, illuminating a framed portrait of the two presidents that hung upon a wall above a handcrafted cabinet. A miniature globe of Coyote, positioned within a semicircular arc carried upon the shoulders of a pewter boid, stood upon a glass-topped center table; scattered here and there were books, delicate ceramic sculptures, finely woven blankets. A place of splendid isolation, inhabited by a couple who'd earned a dignified retirement after a lifetime of labor and sacrifice.

At the back of the living room was another row of windows, shorter than the ones that faced west. Tomas opened a glass door, then stepped aside to let Lynn pass through. She found herself on an open balcony that ran the length of the house, with only a railing separating her from a sheer escarpment that plunged several hundred feet to the rocky shores of the West Channel. And it was here that she found the former president of the Coyote Federation.

Wendy Gunther didn't appear much older than she did when she and her husband, Carlos Montero, traveled to Earth as Coyote's emissaries to the United Nations. With pale blond hair turned silver with age and braided into a slender rope that hung down her back from beneath a straw sun hat, she remained slender and almost sensuously regal, with only crow's-feet at the corners of her eyes and the wrinkled skin on the backs of her hands giving evidence of her age. There was a certain strength to her, though, that hinted at a sense of belonging to this place; Lynn would later reflect that it was as if she'd become part of Coyote, as native to this world as any of the creatures that had evolved here.

An easel had been set up on the balcony, a broad canvas perched upon the tripod. President Gunther stood before it, wearing a smock smeared with flecks of gumtree-oil paint. She didn't look around as Tomas escorted Lynn onto the balcony but instead continued to gently daub at the canvas with a small shagshair brush, using brief, gentle strokes to add minute details to the landscape she was creating.

"Ms. Hu, yes?" she said softly, her voice almost too quiet to hear. "Welcome. I'll just be a minute." She nodded toward a nearby pair of wingback wicker chairs. "Have a seat, please. Tomas . . . I believe there's some ice tea in the kitchen. Would you be so kind?"

"Of course, Madam President." Tomas gestured Lynn toward a chair, then disappeared through the glass door. Yet Lynn didn't sit down yet. Instead, she stepped closer to the easel to see what President Gunther was painting.

The Garcia Narrows Bridge, as seen from the top of the Eastern Divide. Not a realistic depiction, though, but rather an impressionist image, its two-mile span rendered in muted, slightly unfocused earth tones, the reddish brown colors of the wooden trusswork contrasted against the blue waters of the West Channel and the dark tan of the Midland Rise on the opposite side. Certainly not a masterpiece, yet nonetheless the work of a talented amateur.

"Please don't tell me it's good." The president added a dash of magenta to the leaves of the faux-birch trees in the foreground, then sighed in frustration as she stepped back from the canvas. "An old lady's hobby, nothing more. Something to while away the time."

"Well . . . it is pleasant." Lynn gazed over the balcony rail at the view below. The Garcia Narrows Bridge rose high above the channel, its long roadway joining New Florida with the subcontinent of Midland to the east. If she correctly remembered the history of Coyote colonies, the bridge had been erected during the Union occupation, shortly before the Revolution. Although sabotaged by its own architect, James Alonzo Garcia, the bridge was rebuilt after the war, and now served as the major conduit between the two landmasses.

From the distance, she could see traffic moving along its roadway, with sleek hovercoupes recently imported from Earth competing with riders on horseback and farm wagons hauled by massive shags. Beneath the bridge lay Bridgeton's commercial port; dozens of vessels were tied up to the pier, while people and animals unloaded freight from barges that had recently sailed up the channel from the Great Equatorial River and carried it to warehouses along the nearby wharf.

"Flattery will get you nowhere . . . except here." President Gunther dropped her brush in a jar of grain alcohol, then picked up a rag next to the palette and wiped her hands. "So . . . from what I've been told, you're a journalist from the old world, come out here to write about what you've found in the new."

"Yes, ma'am. I—"

"Don't 'ma'am' me, young lady." The president's chin lifted slightly as she turned toward her. "I have a daughter about your age, and I wouldn't take that from her." Lynn couldn't tell she was joking until she glanced toward the door. "Tomas insists on formality," the president added, smiling as she lowered her voice in a conspiratorial manner. "He's been with me a long time, so I let him do that . . . but between you and me, I wish he'd call me by my first name."

"Umm . . . Wendy?"

"At your service." She offered her hand. "Pleased to meet you, Ms. Hu . . . or may I call you Lynn?"

"Lynn is fine." Surprised by the unexpected familiarity, Lynn accepted Wendy's hand. Her grasp was almost mannishly firm, her callused palm like old suede. "Yes, I'm writing a story . . . a series of stories, really . . . about the colonies. Trying to find out what's going on here, for my readers back on . . ."

" 'Trying to find out what's going on here.' Fascinating." Wendy glided over to the wicker chairs. "Please sit . . . ah, and here's Tomas with our drinks."

Lynn looked around just as Tomas opened the balcony door and stepped out, carrying two tall glasses filled with dark brown tea. He silently handed one to each of the women, then walked over to the railing and settled against it, arms folded against his chest. "Forgive the sarcasm," Wendy said as she sat down, "but I've been on Coyote for most of my life, and I'm still trying to find out 'what's going on here.' What makes you think you're going to do any better?"

Again, it was hard to tell if the former president of the colonies was serious or not. "I have a hard time believing that. I mean, one of the reasons why I want to interview you is because of your memoirs . . ."

"You've read my book?" Wendy's face expressed mild astonishment. "All of it?"

"Yes." Lynn couldn't help but grin. "You don't know that it's been a bestseller back home? Takes several minutes to download . . . and forget about trying to buy a hard copy in a bookstore. The waiting list is . . ."

"I had no idea." The president shrugged. "I should have a word with my editor. My royalty statements seem to be in arrears." She gave Lynn a sidelong glance. "Not that I'll see any money from the book. I've put it in my contract that all royalties are to be contributed to the Colonial University medical school. The Kuniko Okada Scholarship, named for . . ."

"Your adoptive mother, who taught you how to become a physician yourself." Lynn caught the annoyed look on Wendy's face and shook her head. "Sorry. Didn't mean to interrupt."

"Not at all. I'm afraid I'm the one who keeps interrupting." Wendy took a sip from her tea, then placed her glass on a table between them. Taking off her sun hat, she stood up for a moment to untie her smock, revealing the light summer dress she wore beneath it. "But the question still stands," she continued, sitting down again. "What makes you think you can do any better?"

Lynn had lost the train of conversation. "Umm . . . at what?"

Wendy gazed at her for a moment, then turned her eyes toward the unfinished painting. "I've written my memoirs, and lately I've taken up art, and still I find that I'm unable to express . . . or even understand . . . what this has all been about. And I've been here since I was little more than a child. This place . . ." She shook her head. "I'm sorry, but you've come to the wrong person. I'm afraid I can't help you."

"Perhaps if you just spoke." Lynn glanced at Tomas. "If I could have my pad, we could do an interview. Get it all down, in your own words."

She hesitated. "Or perhaps I could speak with your husband, if you'd rather not."

"Carlos is in Liberty, visiting our grandson and attending to some business. I'm afraid he won't be back for a few days."

"I see." Lynn picked up her glass of tea, took a sip. "I understand he's become the official liaison to the *hjadd*. Is that where he is now? Visiting their consulate, I mean."

Wendy said nothing for a moment. Lynn wondered if she'd pried a little further than she should. "His dealings with the *hjadd* are matters of state," Wendy said at last, "and not open for discussion. Was the walk up here difficult? I can't help but notice that you're sweating."

"Not really. Just getting used to the thin air." Lynn cast her gaze across the balcony. "This is a beautiful house. Interesting place to build . . ."

"But a little off the beaten path, right?" Again, the guarded smile. "After I finished my second term in office, my husband's sister had it built for us. We considered remaining in Liberty, but . . . well, considering that both Carlos and I had served as president, it became difficult for us to extricate ourselves from politics. Too many people seem to believe that, because they once voted for one or both of us, they're entitled to a few minutes of our time. So we moved out here and made it as hard as possible for anyone to reach us."

"Uh-huh." If Lynn's recollection was correct, that would be Carlos Montero's younger sister Marie, who had married into the family that owned the Thompson Wood Company, one of the largest private enterprises on this world. Indeed, it was the current president's older brother, Lars Thompson, who'd been Marie's husband before he was murdered; with the recent death of Molly Thompson, the family patriarch, it had fallen to Marie to run the family business. How interesting that the two families, the Monteros and the Thompsons, had come to command so much of the wealth and political power on Coyote. "Well, it is hard to get to."

"Our original house still stands in Liberty, if you care to visit it. Built shortly after he and I married. My daughter and her family live there now, but there's talk about having it turned into a historical monument. I'd sooner have it razed first, but"—an offhand shrug—"sometimes places are like people. They become legendary whether they want to or not."

"That's what I wanted to talk to you about." Lynn leaned a little closer, resting her elbows on her knees. "You and President Montero . . ."

"Carlos." Wendy smiled. "If he were here, he'd insist."

"Oh . . . yes, of course." Lynn struggled to keep the conversation on track. "You and Carlos have been here since you were teenagers . . . children, really. You were among the first to step foot on Coyote. You witnessed the establishment of the Liberty colony. Fought in the Revolution. Explored the planet. Became leaders of the Federation, then led the first delegation to the United Nations. You participated in the first contact between humankind and the *hjadd* . . ."

"No." Wendy briefly closed her eyes and wagged a finger. "Give credit where credit is due. That was the *Galileo* expedition . . . We only greeted the survivors after they returned from Rho Coronae Borealis."

"My apologies . . . but, as president, you did welcome the first *hjadd* ambassador, and saw to it that land was set aside in Liberty for them to build an embassy." She paused. "Just as Carlos later volunteered to become their Federation liaison."

"What else should I have done? Tell them to mind their own business and go home?" A quiet smile as Wendy sipped her ice tea. "No doubt there are some on Earth who wished I'd done just that. The Dominionists, for one . . . not to mention the Living Earth fanatics."

More than ever, Lynn wished that she had her pad, if only to catch such remarks on the record. But perhaps that was why Wendy had spoken so freely in the first place; she knew that this was a private chat and no more. "So what is it that you want from me?" Wendy went on, absently letting the ice rattle around her glass. "A few pithy remarks from a former president to spruce up your article? A few pictures?" She nodded toward the easel. "I can pose over there. Former President Gunther in retirement, beginning a new career as an artist. 'I like to paint,' she says. 'It makes me feel good . . .'"

She was getting nowhere, and Lynn was tired of being patronized. "Thank you for sparing a few minutes of your time, Madam President," she said, putting down her glass and standing up. "If you'd be gracious enough to have your assistant call me a cab, I'll be on my—"

"Your objection has been noted, Ms. Hu. Now sit down." When Lynn remained on her feet, Wendy lowered her voice. "No, really . . . sit with me, please. If you want that interview, you may have it. Only don't ask me to reiterate everything you've already read in my memoirs, or talk about me and Carlos as if we're relics who have nothing more to offer. Give us our dignity, and I'll tell you anything you want." She favored her with a sly wink. "And then some . . . provided you ask the right questions."

Lynn hesitated, then resumed her seat. As she sat down again, she felt something prod her shoulder: her pad, silently offered to her by Tomas. She took it from him, flipped it open, and placed it on the table between her and Wendy. The former president crossed her legs and nodded, and Lynn posed the question she wanted most to have answered:

"Where do we go from here?"

Wendy blinked. "Pardon me?"

Lynn tried not to smile. "You wanted a hard question. Well, here it is. Where do we go from here?" While her words were still sinking in, she went on. "Nearly three-quarters of Coyote is still unsettled, let alone explored, and yet the Coyote Federation continues to restrict immigration from Earth. This despite the fact that Earth's environment has collapsed and the solar system colonies are overpopulated."

"Well, I can't speak for . . ."

"In the meantime, the *hjadd* have established an embassy on Coyote while refusing to deal directly with Earth. And even then, there is very little that we know about them. Although they've recently opened trade negotiations with us, none of our ships has been allowed to travel to their world through the starbridge. Indeed, very few people have even seen what they look like inside the environment suits they wear when they go outside their compound . . . which is seldom, at best."

"Well, I . . ."

"Just a moment, please." Lynn glanced at the pad's screen to check her notes. "And, as you mentioned earlier, there has also been resistance from various groups, notably the Dominionist Christians and Living Earth, whom you described earlier as fanatics—"

"That was off the record."

"Of course." Lynn placed a finger across her lips to hide her smile. "Where was I? Oh, yes . . . certain organizations have objected to humankind's contact with alien races. Or, indeed, to the very idea of Coyote's becoming a refuge for the human race, when they believe our efforts should be devoted to saving what's left of Earth itself." She lifted her eyes to gaze at Wendy. "So . . ."

She stopped. The former president of the Coyote Federation stared back at her. "So?"

"So . . . where do we go from here?" Lynn crossed her legs as she settled back in her chair. "Or would you rather let me take pictures of you at your easel? I'm sure my readers would be interested in your hobby, as a sidebar."

The question hung in midair, an invisible wall between them. Wendy said nothing for a moment, then eased herself out of her chair. "I wish I could tell you," she said, walking over to the railing to gaze out at the channel, "but one thing that I've learned is that life seldom takes the turns you expect it to take. The future is unknowable, and any attempt to divine the shapes of things to come from studying the present is doomed to failure. And I, for one, do not believe in predestination."

"That's not much of an answer."

"It's the best I can give. But see here . . ."

Stepping over to the easel, Wendy laid a hand upon the canvas's frame. "This is a work in progress. I've rendered a pencil sketch of what I wish to depict, then used my oils and brushes in an attempt to bring that vision to life. But my skills are limited, and my eyes aren't what they used to be. Although I could avail myself of gene therapy to recover some of my youth, both my husband and I have decided that we'd rather let nature take its course and grow old gracefully. So I have to make do with what I have."

She picked up a dry brush. "In art, as in life, every action carries consequences. If my hand falters, if I select the wrong pigment"—she made a careless slash across the canvas, not touching the painting—"then the work is ruined and I have to start again." She dropped the brush on the table. "But life isn't so simple, is it? There's no fresh canvas, nor can it be discarded."

Wendy turned away from the painting. "Coyote is a work in progress. At first, we were only a handful of people, trying to survive on a world where every day had the potential to kill us. But those who came here first aboard the *Alabama* are in the winter of their lives, and even the

youngest . . . Carlos and his sister, me, a few of our friends . . . are seeing autumn closing in. Even those who arrived aboard the Union Astro-
nautica ships are getting old." She glanced at her aide. "Tomas was only
a boy when he came here with his family . . . aboard the *Spirit*, wasn't it,
Tom?"

"Yes, ma'am." Tomas nodded. *"The Spirit of Social Collectivism Carried to
the Stars* . . . the last starship built by the Union."

"And he's already an adult." Wendy smiled at him. "Carlos and I are
trying to groom him for political life, but he doesn't seem to have that
ambition." Tomas gave a noncommittal shrug, and she went on. "So the
future of this world belongs to those who came after us, the ones who've
taken advantage of the starbridge to make the journey here from Earth."

"So you do believe that your generation's time has come and gone?"

Wendy shrugged. "I'm painting that bridge because it was built by
people who are already old. Those who've come after them take it for
granted as something that existed before they set foot on this world.
One day, someone may decide that it's hopelessly antiquated and, therefore, see the necessity of tearing it down and replacing it with something more modern."

"Or it could stand for another hundred years." Lynn stood up, walked
over to the railing. "I rather hope so."

"So do I . . . but that won't be my decision to make, nor will it be
yours." Wendy gazed at her painting. "Maybe that's one of the reasons
why I'm doing this . . . to preserve, in some small way, what it looked
like, so that my grandson will have something to show his children."

She looked at Lynn again. "I think you've answered your own
question. Where do we go from here? We've made contact with an
alien race, but they're still reluctant to let us visit their world. We've
settled a new world, yet most of it remains unexplored . . . although
my good friend Morgan Goldstein has some ideas about that." Wendy
pointed toward the distant wharf. "Down there . . . see that ship being built?"

Lynn peered in the direction she indicated. She hadn't noticed it earlier, but an enormous sailship was under construction within a dry
dock. It was still little more than a skeleton; the keel had been laid, and
carpenters were working on the outer hull. "The *Ted LeMare*," Wendy

said. "Once it's finished next year, the Colonial University will use it to make the first circumnavigation of the Great Equatorial River."

"I've heard something about this, yes. And Morgan is paying for it?"

"Yes, he is . . . although I should mention that, unlike Carlos and me, he doesn't like to be called by his first name. Something to remember if you have a chance to interview him."

"I'll try to keep that in mind." Lynn hadn't planned to interview Goldstein, but now that Wendy had mentioned it, she realized that it might be a good idea. "That's awfully generous of him."

Wendy frowned. "Generosity has little to do with it. Earth looks to Coyote as its salvation. Sure, the Western Hemisphere Union still refuses to recognize our sovereignty, but despite that and our own efforts to control immigration, every ship that comes here brings more settlers. Sooner or later, the colonies are going to run out of room. Morgan knows this. He may pretend to be interested in exploration for its own sake, but the fact of the matter is that he wants to locate new real estate."

Lynn looked at her askance. "Sounds like you disapprove."

A wry smile. "At one time, my biggest worry in life was whether I'd be killed by a boid . . . but it's been years since I last saw one." The smile disappeared. "Now my greatest concern is whether someone will come up the road and ask me or my husband to do something we'd regret, because I know we'd have trouble turning them down. Like this damned expedition. Carlos . . ."

Wendy stopped herself, making Lynn wonder what she was about to say. "That's enough," the president murmured, lifting a weathered hand to her face. "I'm sorry, but I think that's all I want to say for now."

Startled by the abrupt termination of the interview, Lynn stared at her and was surprised to see tears at the corners of her eyes. "Madam President, did I . . . ?"

"No, no. I'm just . . ." Wendy hastily turned away, but not before Lynn saw her wipe the tears from her face. "Thank you for coming by. My apologies for not being able to answer all your questions. Maybe we can continue this another time. Tomas . . . ?"

"Here, Madam President." He walked over to the door, opened it for her. Without another word, Wendy strolled down the porch and disappeared into the house.

Lynn watched her go, then sighed as she walked over to the table and picked up her pad. The readout told her that her interview had lasted little more than ten minutes. Out of that, she'd probably get no more than two or three usable quotes. Hardly worth the effort.

Or was it? Wendy Gunther was right. Despite the fact that Coyote was home to nearly a hundred thousand people, it was still an alien world. Not only that, but the presence of the *hjadd* had added another catalyst whose effect was still unknown. And she'd seen Dominionist missionaries aboard the ship that had carried her here; what would they have to say about all this?

Once again, her gaze wandered to the unfinished painting. A work in progress, Wendy had called it. One errant brushstroke, and it would all be ruined.

Where do we go from here? A good question, indeed. Lynn had a feeling that it would be answered only in the fullness of time.

Book 1

Knowledge of God

We are the end products of countless throws of genetic dice; never in the whole of time and space would that exact evolutionary sequence be repeated. From the engineering viewpoint, men and apes are virtually identical, yet we seldom confuse them. Even humanoid ETs would look far more—well, alien—than a gorilla. And most ETs may well be stranger in appearance than an octopus, a mantis, or a dinosaur.

This may be the reason that many people are opposed to SETI, because they realize that it is ticking like a time bomb at the foundations of our pride—and of many of our religions. They would applaud the old B-movie cliché "Such knowledge is not meant for man."

—**SIR ARTHUR C. CLARKE,**
Greetings, Carbon-Based Bipeds!

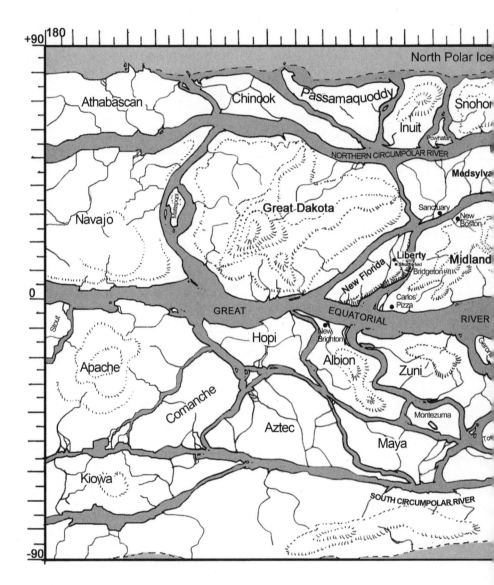

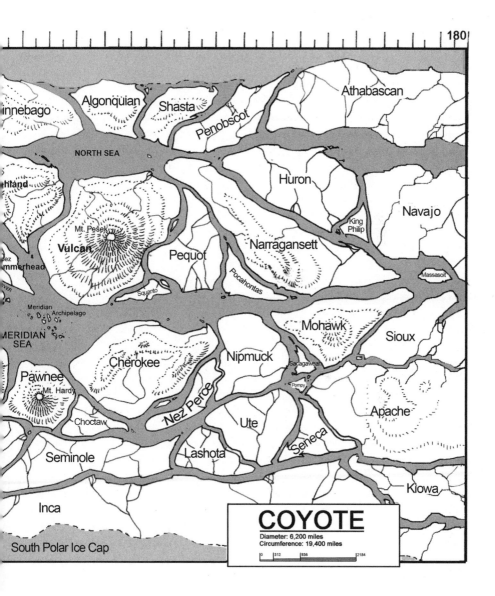

Athabascan

Algonquian Shasta
innebago   Penobscot

NORTH SEA   Huron

hland   Navajo

Mt. Pesek   King
Vulcan   Philip

ez   Pequot   Narragansett
mmerhead   Massasoit

Squanto   Pocahontas
Meridian
Archipelago

MERIDIAN   Mohawk   Sioux
SEA

Cherokee   Nipmuck
Pawnee   Sacagaweah
Mt. Hardy   Pompy

Nez Perce   Ute   Apache
Choctaw

Seneca
Seminole   Lashota

Kiowa

Inca

COYOTE
Diameter: 6,200 miles
Circumference: 19,400 miles

South Polar Ice Cap
0   312   936   2184

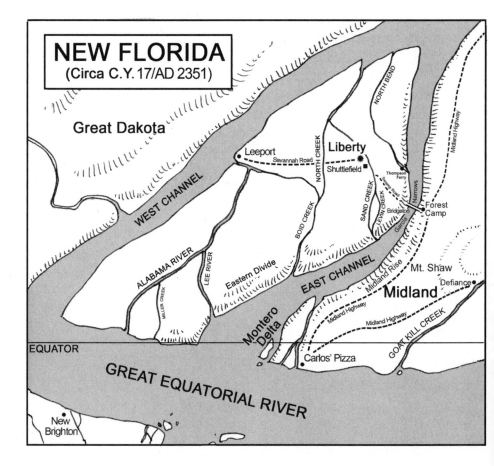

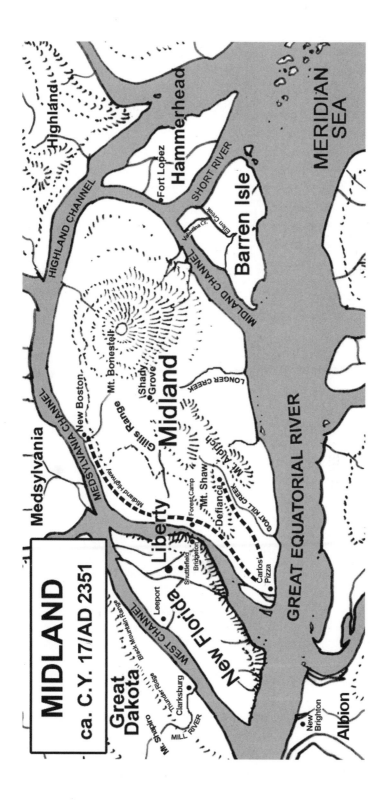

MIDLAND
ca. C.Y. 17/AD 2351

Highland

Hammerhead

Fort Lopez

SHORT RIVER

MERIDIAN SEA

Barren Isle

Valentina Cr.

Ellen Creek

MIDLAND CHANNEL

HIGHLAND CHANNEL

Mt. Bonestell

Shady Grove

New Boston

Gillis Range

LONGER CREEK

Midland

Medsylvania

MEDSYLVANIA CHANNEL

Midland Highway

Liberty

Forest Camp

Mt. Shaw

Mt. Aldrich

Defiance

GOAT KILL CREEK

Carlos' Pizza

GREAT EQUATORIAL RIVER

Shuttlefield

Bridgeton

New Florida

Leeport

WEST CHANNEL

Great Dakota

Black Mountain Range

Mt. Shapiro

Thumurghi Ripple

Clarksburg

MILL RIVER

New Brighton

Albion

Part 1

A MAN OF CONSTANT SORROW

The customs inspector sat at his desk, waiting to die.

His life was not in peril. In fact, of all the jobs one could have on Coyote, his was among the safest. Nor was he terminally ill; in his mid-twenties and reasonably healthy—at least in the physical sense—he would probably live sixty or seventy more years. No one had threatened him, and there was no reason for him to believe that tomorrow would be any different than today. His life was unremarkable, his existence dull and colorless.

Which was why he was waiting to die. He had nothing for which to live.

His desk was in a kiosk within the New Brighton spaceport, just past the entrance designated for arriving passengers. The desk measured four feet by two feet, and was clean except for a few items. A comp terminal, upon which abstract images swirled when it wasn't displaying data. A biometric scanner, its lens pointed toward the partition in the transparent cube that made up the kiosk walls. Several stacks of forms, carefully arranged according to purpose and separated into trays marked IN and OUT. Three pens, one of which was missing its cap. An electronic passport stamp. A small box of tissue paper. A plastic bottle of water.

Every morning when he came to work, the first thing the inspector did was make sure that everything was in its proper place. There was seldom any change in the appearance of his desk from when he'd last seen it, unless another inspector had borrowed a pen (which was why one of them was missing its cap) or swiped some tissue paper; nonetheless, it was a way of starting the day. Reassured that all was right in his world, he would open the lower-right drawer and place inside a brown paper bag containing his lunch: a ham-and-cheese sandwich, an apple, perhaps a chocolate brownie that he'd picked up at the deli down the street from his apartment. He would then take a seat in the hard, straight-backed chair and, folding his hands together, lift his gaze to the partition, through which he could see the broad windows overlooking the landing field.

Other customs inspectors sat in identical cubes, doing the same job as he did, or stood behind adjacent tables, ready to open suitcases, trunks, and bags in search of contraband: illegal drugs, unregistered firearms, explosive materials, invasive species of flora or fauna, or anything else that might pose a risk to the health and safety of the inhabitants of the new world. He seldom spoke to any of them, though, and they'd come to accept the fact that their coworker preferred to be left alone. But they'd all noticed the thick silver band on his left wrist and recognized it for what it was: a control bracelet, the kind issued to former criminals released on parole.

He'd never told anyone the reason he had to wear it, and their supervisors refused to divulge that information. But the other inspectors were as resourceful as they were curious, and it didn't take long for them to ferret out the background of their quiet colleague. During lunch-hour conversations in the break room—he almost always ate lunch by himself, so he was seldom among them—they sometimes discussed who he was and why he was here. And although they pitied him, or at least to the extent that anyone might express empathy for a young man with a troubled past, they also avoided him as someone who'd once committed an act of violence and who might well be provoked to do so again.

They didn't need to worry. The customs inspector would never again harm anyone. Those who were familiar with his case—his family; the superintendent of the rehabilitation farm where he'd lived for two and a half Coyote years; the psychiatrist who'd treated him; the magistrates who'd sentenced him and, later, approved his petition for conditional parole; the influential uncle who'd arranged for him to be assigned to a work-release program—agreed that he was not a dangerous individual, and that he should be given a chance to pay his debt to society.

So the bracelet was fastened around his wrist, and a parole officer was designated to handle his case. Then he was sent to New Brighton, where he became a faceless bureaucrat performing a routine and unimaginative task. And there he sat, waiting to see what would happen next, knowing that this day would be pretty much the same as yesterday and the day before that, and that someday in the future, many years from now, he would take his last breath, and his death would come as blessed relief from a life that had long since lost any spark or flavor.

His name was Hawk Thompson, and he'd killed his father. And now he was waiting to die.

The ships came from Earth.

Some days, there would be only one; others, there would be two or three. Every now and then, more would touch down, and the field would be crowded with spacecraft, parked so close together that it seemed as if their wingtips nearly touched one another. But seldom was there a time when the skies above New Brighton didn't thunder with a sonic boom, announcing the arrival of another vessel from Earth.

Most were passenger shuttles, ferrying people down from starships in low orbit above Coyote. The spaceport was also frequently visited by freighters, big cone-shaped craft that would land at the side of the spaceport where the warehouses were located. On rare occasion, the starships themselves would come down, usually when they needed to be dry-docked for major repair; when that happened, the ground itself seemed to shake, the windows of the terminal rattling gently within their frames, as the giant vessel slowly descended upon vertical thrusters to the steel-reinforced concrete of the field.

No matter their size, purpose, or registry, though, the ships all came from the same place. Their point of origin was Highgate, the international space colony in lunar orbit above the Moon. Upon departure, they'd make the short journey to Starbridge Earth, positioned at a Lagrange point nearly a quarter of a million miles away. Once traffic controllers aboard the starbridge gatehouse cleared the vessels for hyperspace transit, AIs would assume control of the craft from their pilots, and the ships would enter the artificial wormhole created within the center of the enormous silver ring. Five seconds later, in a burst of defocused light, they'd emerge from Starbridge Coyote, in trojan orbit around 47 Ursae Majoris-B, forty-six light-years from Earth.

A miracle of physics and engineering; Hawk was familiar with the details, but he hadn't experienced it for himself, nor was he likely ever to do so. Born and raised on Coyote, he'd never left the world his parents had come to call home. His mother, along with his uncle, had been among the 104 colonists who'd made the long voyage to 47 Uma aboard the URSS *Alabama*, while his father had been one of those who'd been aboard the first starship built by the Western Hemisphere Union, *Seeking Glorious Destiny Among the Stars for Greater Good of Social Collectivism*. His parents had been very young when they'd left Earth; the stories they'd told him about their early lives were based upon recollections that had faded with the years, until Earth had become little more than a vague childhood memory. To be sure, Uncle Carlos and Aunt Wendy had been back there, shortly after the starbridge was established, and they had served as Coyote's first emissaries to the United Nations. As far as Hawk was concerned, though, the place to which they'd gone was as mythical as Heaven, Asgard, or Nirvana.

So the ships from Earth would come, their arrival heralded by thunder and flame, and once the dust settled around the landing gear, their passengers would march down lowered gangway ramps and make their way to the terminal. The very first person they'd meet on Coyote would be the customs inspector who'd process them through passport control. And if they happened to pick the middle of three kiosks, that inspector would be Hawk himself.

Hawk would sit at his desk while the passengers, obeying multilingual holos floating above the floor, entered roped-off queues to take their turn at his kiosk. He kept his expression carefully neutral, showing neither pleasure nor disapproval, and once they approached his window, he'd ask the same set of questions.

Name, please?

Passport and visa?

Citizen of the Coyote Federation or nonresident?

And if it was the latter . . .

Reason for visiting?

Expected length of stay?

Are you bringing in any items valued above one hundred colonials?

And in the meantime, while he checked their papers and listened to their answers, the biometric scanner would examine their faces, matching their profiles against a database of known criminals. On the rare occasion that the database tagged someone as persona non grata, his comp would alert him and he'd surreptitiously press the small button beneath his desktop that would alert the proctor seated nearby that here was a person who needed to be pulled aside for questioning and possible arrest. But this seldom occurred; most of the time, the people who came off the ships had clean records, or at least so far as Earth's law-enforcement agencies were aware, and what they did after they had gone through passport control was none of his concern.

In the six months that he'd been at this job, Hawk had seen all kinds on the other side of his window. Indeed, it had become something of a private game, figuring out who they were and why they were here even before he asked his questions. If they wore expensive clothes and carried heavy suitcases, then they were tourists, usually wealthy, who'd come to Coyote for a vacation that might last anywhere between two weeks and a season. If they were well dressed, with only one or two light bags, then they were probably business travelers here for no more than six weeks, or however long it would take for them to conclude whatever deals they were trying to make. The ones who came off small, private ships and had a certain air of privilege were usually government officials—ambassadors, trade emissaries, general consuls, and the like—arriving to take up posts at embassies on New Florida. And every so often, he'd get someone who didn't fit one of the usual profiles. Celebrities, their entourages in tow, coming to make a vid, research a novel, or simply get away from the press for a while. Missionaries from one religion or another, determined to bring the word of God to the heathens of the new world. Now and then, nervous smugglers, trying hard to pass for normal while sweating out the drugs, liquor, or guns hidden in their bags.

More often than not, though, the people he met were immigrants.

They were the easiest to identify. Their clothes were plain, sometimes threadbare, and usually looked as if they'd been worn for days. Their bags and trunks were overstuffed, and Hawk knew that, if he were to watch them being unpacked at the nearby inspection tables, he'd see precious mementos and keepsakes from the life they'd left behind. And they were almost never alone, but were accompanied by husbands or wives, or children, or relatives, or lifelong friends.

But what really set them apart was the look in their eyes. Like everyone else on Coyote, Hawk had heard stories about how badly things on Earth had deteriorated. Not just environmental collapse—glaciers in northern Europe, desertification of the American heartland, catastrophic floods in the Middle East and Southeast Asia, widespread drought across much of Africa, Australia, and South America—but also the gradual breakdown of human civilization as a result of global climate change. The Western Hemisphere Union was crippled, its system of social collectivism buckling under the strain of having too many mouths to feed. The European Alliance wasn't faring much better; the great cities of London, Paris, Amsterdam, and Moscow were emptying out, their former residents fleeing south to places like Rome, Athens, and Istanbul, which themselves were struggling with the huge influx of refugees. The Pacific Coalition had all but lapsed into anarchy, with nearly a third of its population reduced to living on anchored ships and barges, while the nations of the southern hemisphere had become a patchwork of city-states, ranging from fundamentalist theocracies to military dictatorships.

So anyone who was able to do so was leaving Earth, sometimes with little more than the clothes on their backs. But the limited resources of the Moon and Mars colonies couldn't support so many people, and the Jovian moons were inhospitable to all but the most brave, adaptable, or crazy. Which left Coyote as the last, best refuge for the human race.

Day after day, Hawk saw the faces of those fortunate enough to buy passage to 47 Ursae Majoris. Even as they pulled dog-eared passports from their pockets and mumbled replies to his questions, what he saw in their eyes said more than words. Desperation, fear, loss, confusion . . . but more often than not, hope. Hope that the new world, so far away from everything familiar, would offer a fresh start.

So Hawk listened to them, and handed out the proper forms, and tagged their passports before sending them to the inspection tables or, in the cases of those who were obviously sick, to the health officials who'd make sure they weren't carrying any contagious diseases and quarantine them if they were. Although he was careful never to expose his emotions, nonetheless he secretly resented them. Because as shattered as their lives might be, at least they had the belief that the worst was behind them and that tomorrow would be a better day.

That was something he'd lost a long time ago.

Ten hours in the cube, then his shift ended and it was time for him to go home. Hawk took a few minutes to straighten his desk, then he pushed back his chair and left the kiosk, shutting the door behind him. He didn't say good night to the other inspectors—none were his friends, and in fact he didn't even know most of their names—and they'd long since stopped saying hello or good-bye to him. So there was nothing more for him to do than simply leave, with the knowledge that, tomorrow morning, he would be back there again.

The spaceport was located on the outskirts of New Brighton, on the northern coast of Albion, across the Great Equatorial River from New Florida. Although the colony had been established only a few years ago, it had grown faster than any other settlement on Coyote. Much of the expansion was because of the spaceport; the most immediate problem faced by most immigrants was finding a place to live, so a small city had quickly risen where there had once been only a seacoast fishing village.

Hawk unlocked his bicycle from where he'd parked it at an EMPLOYEES ONLY rack outside the main entrance. Mounting the saddle, he pedaled away from the terminal to join the stream of shag wagons, rickshaws, hoverbikes, and the occasional coupe moving down the gravel road leading into town. A loud clatter overhead, and he glanced up to see the arrival of the late-afternoon gyrobus from Liberty; if he remembered the launch schedule, it would be bringing in the crew of the *Robert E. Lee*, scheduled to depart from orbit tomorrow for its next biweekly flight to Earth. He'd heard that the gyros might soon be replaced with airships imported from Germany; he had little idea where Germany was, but if airships would help reduce the noise pollution over New Brighton, then he was all for it.

A two-mile ride, then he passed through the red Japanese gate marking the city limits. Immigrants from the Pacific Coalition had erected the *torii* a year earlier as their gift to the new world; traditionally found at the entrance to Shinto shrines, it was supposed to ward off demons, but so far as Hawk could tell, it hadn't done much good. Most of New Brighton consisted of tenement houses built of cheap parasol wood harvested from Albion hill country. They'd originally been meant to serve as temporary shelter for immigrants making their way to Coyote since the opening of the starbridge. In that, at least, the intent had been benign. No one wanted a repeat of what had happened many years ago during the Union occupation, when thousands of settlers from the Western Hemisphere Union had been forced to live in the tents and shacks of Shuttlefield.

Yet temporary solutions often become permanent; not only had the tenements become a lasting fixture, but more were being built. The gravel road came to an end shortly after he passed through the *torii*, and Hawk was soon pedaling through narrow, packed-dirt streets past three- and four-story buildings so close together that children sometimes dared each other to jump out their windows and into those of their neighbors across the alley. Clotheslines formed a dense web between buildings, while ground-floor shops, bodegas, and cafes crowded one another for room. The evening was unseasonably warm for late winter, so men and women who'd just come home from work took advantage of it by sitting out on front steps, gossiping with friends and family. From hundreds of brick chimneys, the smoke of kitchen fires rose into the air, adding to the miasma that seemed to perpetually hover above the rooftops.

A right turn on Freedom Avenue, then left on Fortune Street, and a couple of blocks later Hawk rolled to a stop in front of his building. A handful of neighborhood kids were playing soccer in the middle of the street, under the watchful eye of their mothers as they cooked dinner in their apartments. No one paid attention to him as he climbed off his bike; stepping onto the concrete sidewalk, Hawk picked it up by its frame and carried it on his shoulder up the steps to the front door. He added it to the row of bikes chained to a rack inside the foyer, then climbed the staircase, its smudged plaster walls scrawled with graffiti in several languages. The multicultural nature of the residents was reflected by the voices he heard as he walked down the third-floor hall; from behind closed doors, he heard Anglo, Spanish, Korean, and Russian— sometimes in calm conversation, more often arguing, occasionally punctuated by the cries of hungry or frustrated babies. When he'd first moved in, the noise had kept him awake at night. Now it was simply a background hum that he barely noticed anymore.

Hawk's apartment was a one-room flat in the southwest corner of the building, its windows overlooking both the street and the adjacent alley. Its furniture, sparse and utilitarian, had come with the place: a metal-frame bed with a cheap foam mattress; an unfinished faux-birch dresser; a small square table with a couple of chairs; a wood-pellet stove which supplied both heat and the means by which he cooked his meals, with a fire extinguisher clamped to the wall next to the chimney duct; a cabinet for food, cookware, and other belongings. The flat's only luxury was that it had its own private bath, although the toilet seat was broken and the shower leaked; whenever the people in the apartment above relieved themselves, Hawk knew about it from the gurgle of flushed water rushing down exposed pipes running across his ceiling.

Hawk took off his uniform, placing his shirt and trousers on the kitchen sink so that he could wash them later. The control bracelet stayed in place, though, as did the inhibitor patch affixed to his rib cage beneath his left arm. His parole officer was due to visit him tomorrow after work; he'd change the patch then, once he'd made sure that Hawk hadn't murdered anyone this week.

He changed into drawstring pants and a loose tunic, preferring to go barefoot unless it got cold. From the cabinet's refrigerator box, he pulled out a jar of leftover turkey chili. Unscrewing its top, he took a quick sniff to make sure it hadn't gone bad, then emptied the jar into an iron skillet. Dinner was eaten at his table as he watched the kids wind up their soccer game.

The last light of day was fading above the rooftops as Hawk sat at the table, plate and fork still in front of him, hands clasped together in his lap. His mind was a blank, filled only by the sounds that entered his range of hearing. Down in the alley, two men argued about which one of them had failed to close a Dumpster, thus allowing swampers to scatter garbage all over the place. Across the hall, the woman who was his closest neighbor opened her door, inviting a man who'd come to visit inside; Hawk hadn't met her, but he suspected that she was a prostitute. Farther down the hall, a little girl was having a tantrum; her mother yelled at the child to shut up. And down on the front steps, another one of his neighbors strummed at his guitar, the evening breeze carrying his words to Hawk's open window:

> *I am a man of constant sorrow,*
> *I've seen trouble all my days;*
> *I bid farewell to old Kentucky,*
> *The place where I was born and raised . . .*

Hawk didn't know where Kentucky was, either, but he did remember another night, not so long ago, when he'd watched the sun go down upon the Black Mountains. Back when he'd been a free man and his life, hard as it might have been, had more meaning than it did now.

> *For six long years I've been in trouble,*
> *No pleasure here on earth I found,*
> *For in this world I'm bound to ramble,*
> *I have no friends to help me now . . .*

Unable to laugh, unwilling to cry, he sat at the window and watched as darkness once again settled upon the town.

A few hours later, he'd washed his uniform and laid it out to dry, Hawk was in bed, reading *The Chronicles of Prince Rupurt* by Leslie Gillis. Like everyone else born and raised on Coyote, he had been brought up with the novel, written under strange circumstances by a crewman aboard the *Alabama*; unlike others, though, Hawk hadn't left it behind with adolescence, but often revisited the epic fantasy. Comfort food for the mind, yet—as many before him had noted—oddly resonant with the world in which he lived.

He'd just reached the scene where the exiled prince was bargaining with the merchant-king of Yawhana for the price of an enchanted sword when he heard a loud slam within the apartment across the hall, followed a moment later by the muffled sound of a woman crying out in pain.

Hawk looked up from his pad, listened more closely. His apartment was dark now that he'd turned off the ceiling panel, the only illumination coming from the pad's screen. Another thud, a little louder; he couldn't be sure, but it sounded as if someone had been thrown against the door. Then a man's voice, unintelligible yet angry; an instant later, the sharp crash of breaking glass, followed again by a woman's scream.

For a few seconds, he lay still in bed, not quite knowing what to do. Then the man yelled something obscene; another impact against the wall, and now he could hear the woman whimpering. He couldn't be sure, but it sounded as if she was begging for her assailant to stop, please stop . . .

Before he knew what he was doing, Hawk shoved aside the blanket and pushed himself out of bed. As usual, he wore only his briefs; he considered getting dressed, but when he heard something shatter as if it had been hurled across the room, he realized that there was no time for such niceties. Someone was being hurt. He could pretend to ignore what was going on and wait for it to stop on its own, or . . .

The woman screamed again, and there was such pain in her voice that he grabbed his shirt and pulled it on, then unlatched his door and threw it open. Down the hall, some of his neighbors stood in the doorways of their own apartments. They'd heard the fight, too, and a few had dared to peek outside to see what was happening. But he knew that that was as far as they'd go; in the crowded tenements of New Brighton, the first rule of survival was mind your own business.

Apparently the maxim didn't apply to him. Everyone looked his way, as if expecting him to do something. Hawk suddenly realized that he was wearing his uniform shirt. At this moment, he was the closest they had to a law-enforcement official. Even if someone had called the law—which was doubtful—the New Brighton proctors were notoriously slow about responding to domestic disturbances; it might be a while before someone showed up.

Another second or two of hesitation, then Hawk stepped across the hall. Raising a fist, he banged it against the door.

"Hey!" he yelled. "Is everyone . . . Are you okay in there?"

Silence, then a man's voice: "Get the hell outta . . . !"

"Help!" A woman's voice, shrill with terror. "Please, someone . . . !"

"Shut up!" The dull sound of flesh striking flesh, then something struck the door. The knob started to turn, and suddenly stopped. "Oh no, you don't, bitch! You're not getting away from . . ."

The woman shrieked, and Hawk grabbed the doorknob. The door was unlocked; he shoved it open and entered the one-room flat, which had been torn apart. The bed was disheveled, its sheets lying askew from a mattress that was half-off its frame; a chair lay on its side, and broken glass was scattered across the floor beneath the shelf from which it had fallen. An earthenware jug had been hurled against the wall, leaving a crater in the plaster; he caught the reek of the corn liquor it had once contained.

But the first thing that he saw was a naked man dragging a woman across the floor by a fistful of her long blond hair. She wore only a silk teddy; its front was ripped open, and what he first took to be a embroidered red rose was a smear of blood from where she'd been punched in the nose. She was reaching above her head, trying to pull her assailant's hands away. He was older than Hawk, but no larger; with a shaved head and ugly goatee, his potbelly attested to too many nights spent at the tavern.

He looked up at Hawk, his eyes dark with fury, and in that instant, his face seemed to disappear, and Hawk saw someone else: his father, the nights he'd come home from the lumber mill and take out his frustrations on Hawk's mother. A childhood memory he'd tried very hard to suppress, along with everything else he remembered about the old man. But in less than a second, the lessons learned during two and a half years of therapy were forgotten.

The bracelet beeped, announcing that its sensors had detected a sharp rise in the adrenaline and vasopressin levels of his bloodstream. A moment later, there was a sharp jab in the soft flesh beneath his left arm as the inhibitor patch, signaled by the bracelet, administered a dose of benzodiazepine. Hawk knew that it would be only seconds before the drug triggered the release of inhibitory neurotransmitters in his brain, slowing down his thoughts as well as his muscles. If he was going to act, it would have to be immediately.

"Get outta here!" Letting go of the woman, the man started toward him, right hand pulling back as a fist. "None of your goddamn . . . !"

The bearshine jug lay at his feet, unbroken despite being thrown against the wall. Hawk snatched it up and, curling his forefinger through its neck ring, swung it wildly at the stranger. To his amazement, the jug connected on the first try; it slammed into the side of the man's face, and he yelled in pain as he lost his balance and fell against the bed. His right foot caught the edge of the sheets; he tripped and toppled over, his left hand clutching at the welt that had appeared on his cheek.

He was still trying to get up when Hawk kicked him in the stomach. An angry jolt in his big toe, and he knew at once that he'd jammed it. Yet the pain was dull; the benzodiazepine had kicked in, and already he was beginning to feel sluggish. Meanwhile, the bracelet continued to beep madly, as if scolding him for becoming violent without permission.

But the man was down. Right arm wrapped around his stomach, he whimpered as he crawled across the floor. Hawk was still trying to fight the drug when the woman managed to get to her feet. Cursing beneath her breath, she staggered over to her assailant and kicked him herself, this time in the ribs; he gasped and rolled over, and she mercilessly rammed her foot into his balls.

Hawk barely noticed any of this. Unable to focus, he lurched through the door, back out into the hall. Someone caught him as he fell, but he wasn't fully aware of that either.

All he knew was that he'd failed.

He never really passed out, but lapsed into a lethargic stupor. Unable to stand on his own, he let one of his neighbors carry him back to his room, where he collapsed on the bed. Someone else came in to see if he was all right; he nodded, and the neighbor got him a glass of water, which he sipped before putting it on the floor. After a while they left him alone, closing the door behind them.

Across the hall, he could hear people moving about; his neighbors had turned their attention to the woman and were taking care of her as best they could while trying to figure out what to do with the injured man who'd attacked her. Their voices were soon joined by those of a couple of proctors who had finally showed up. Hawk listened as they questioned everyone they'd found at the scene; as to be expected, no one had actually seen anything, so the proctors had only one reliable witness, the victim herself. Although Hawk wanted to doze off, he knew what was going to happen next, so he forced himself to stay awake.

It wasn't long until he heard a familiar voice. It spoke for a few minutes, quietly asking questions of the proctors. Then there was a knock at his door. Before he could answer, the door opened and Joe Bairns walked in. One look at Hawk, then he sadly shook his head.

"I thought I told you to stay out of trouble," Bairns said.

"I tried . . . I did." The benzodiazepine had largely worn off, but his tongue still felt thick. "The lady over there . . ."

"I know. I got that part of the story already." Bairns shut the door, then walked over to the bed. "You okay? Sit up, let me take a look at you."

Hawk rolled his legs over the side of the bed and rose to a sitting position. He was still too weak to stand up, but Bairns was being easy with him. For the last six months since he'd moved to New Brighton, the parole officer had been the closest Hawk had to a friend. Grey-haired and thickset, a plainclothes proctor on the verge of retirement, Joe had been assigned to his case by the magistrates who'd approved Hawk's release from the farm. Although he'd never been unkind to Hawk, Bairns had made it clear that he was keeping him on a short leash.

That leash was the bracelet attached to Hawk's wrist, which would automatically alert Bairns if the inhibitor patch was ever activated. Until that night, the bracelet had remained mute. Judging from the disappointment in Bairns's eyes, Hawk realized that the parole officer had come to expect that he'd never hear it.

"I'm all right. Really." Hawk had a hard time meeting Bairns's gaze. "Joe, I'm sorry. But when I heard what was going on over there . . ."

"You just had to get involved." Bairns bent over to gently open the left side of Hawk's unbuttoned shirt. "You thought you were doing the right thing," he said as he inspected the patch, "and maybe you were . . . but I'm going to have to report this, y'know. Just hope the maggies are in a forgiving mood."

Hawk shook his head. "Joe, I'm telling you . . . if I hadn't been there, she might've been killed. That guy . . ." He stopped. "Who was he, anyway?"

"A disappointed customer, or at least so I've been told." Bairns touched a button on the patch, watched as a tiny diode flashed red. "I'm going to have to give you a new one." Hawk shrugged; the parole officer changed the patch during their weekly meetings, anyway, so its replacement would come only a day earlier than usual. "Actually, maybe we should thank you. Appears that she's an unlicensed sex worker. Once she gets out of the hospital, she's going to have to go to court."

Hawk wasn't surprised. It only confirmed what he'd already suspected.

"Hardly seems fair. I mean, considering the way he knocked her around . . ."

"Believe me, her boyfriend got the worst of it. Hold still." Bairns carefully peeled away the patch, and Hawk winced as it detached from the cannula that had been inserted into his brachial artery. "And once he's out of the ER, he's going to be charged with assault and battery, maybe attempted rape. So he's in trouble even more than she is."

"And what about me?"

Bairns didn't respond. Instead, he made himself busy with the procedure Hawk underwent every week during their meetings. After checking the bracelet to make sure that Hawk hadn't tampered with it, he pulled out his datapad and, after hardwiring it to the bracelet, entered the six-digit code that would reset it. Next came the replacement patch; the parole officer tore open its cellophane envelope, and after Hawk raised his left arm above his head, Bairns removed the adhesive backing and carefully put it in place just beneath the armpit. Once he was satisfied that it was securely fastened, Bairns located the activation tab and firmly pressed it with his forefinger. The diode blinked, signaling that the patch had been successfully mated with the cannula.

"I'm going to have to put this in my report," he said at last. "Sorry, but that's my job. But I'll also make sure to say that there were mitigating circumstances. One of your neighbors was being attacked, and when you stepped in to save her, the other guy came at you." He looked Hawk straight in the eye. "That is what happened, isn't it? He threw the first punch?"

"Yeah." The fact of the matter was that the other guy hadn't even gotten a chance to land a blow before Hawk picked up the jug. But Bairns didn't have to know this.

Bairns nodded. "I'll get a copy of the arrest report and send that along as well. The magistrates won't like it very much . . . the terms of your parole are that you stay out of trouble and don't commit any acts of violence . . . but you haven't been charged with anything, and I'm willing to bet that the maggies will take that into consideration."

"Sure. Okay." Hawk lowered his arm, flexed it a little. A new thought occurred to him. "Maybe they'll even . . . I mean, since I did something good back there, maybe they'll even think about reducing my sentence."

"Hawk . . ." The parole officer sighed. This was an old subject, something they'd discussed several times already. "You know better than that. You're on probation for seven years . . . six and a half, counting the time you've already served. You should count yourself lucky that you're not still in rehab. Even luckier that you're not doing time in the stockade. If it wasn't for your uncle . . ."

"I know, I know." This, too, was old news. If it hadn't been for the fact that Uncle Carlos—hero of the Revolution, former president of the Federation—had interceded on his behalf, Hawk's punishment would have been more severe. Indeed, it sort of continued a family tradition; long ago, his uncle had also arranged for Hawk's parents to be released from the Liberty stockade and sent into exile. Indeed, that had happened during the time that Hawk himself was conceived.

It might be said that getting into trouble with the law was congenital to the Thompson clan, except that his uncle Garth, his father's brother, had himself recently been elected Federation president, and Hawk's younger sister, Rain, was in training to join the Federation's merchant fleet. So Hawk was the black sheep of the family. His mother seldom spoke to him anymore, and he knew that he was a political embarrassment to both of his uncles. Only Rain came to visit him, when she was in New Brighton between flights, but even she carefully maintained a certain distance; it wouldn't do her career any good if it became generally known that her big brother was a convicted killer.

"Well . . . there it is." Which was Bairns's way of saying that their time was up. He slipped his pad back in his pocket, then stood up. "Unless there's anything else you want to talk about."

Once again, Hawk felt a surge of irritation. Bairns meant well, of course. In fact, Hawk was aware that the officer had a certain paternal fondness for him. But he wished that Joe would stop trying to play psychologist; he'd had enough of shrinks, and didn't want even one more person trying to find out what was in his head.

"No . . . no, nothing else." Hawk forced a smile. "Thanks, Joe. Sorry to get you up in the middle of the night."

"Think nothing of it. Just doing my job." Bairns stepped toward the door, started to open it. "Now get some sleep. See you again next week . . . usual time, okay?"

"Sure." As if Hawk had any say in the matter. Either next week, or for the next six and a half years. "See you later."

He went into work the next morning, and it was pretty much a normal day, aside from the arrival of a freighter carrying fifty head of cattle. Livestock had lately begun to be exported from Earth; with the eradication of boids just north of Liberty and in the Pioneer Valley of Midland, ranches were being established on vast tracts that had been cleared of native plants and replanted with grass more suitable for grazing. Children no longer had only goat's milk to drink, and already it was possible, in some of the more expensive restaurants in New Florida, to order a steak dinner.

Having grown up eating chicken, goat, pork, shag meat, and creek crab, Hawk often wondered what beef tasted like. A brief encounter with cows, though, was enough to make up his mind that he'd just as soon never have a hamburger for lunch. One of the health officials had picked that day to call in sick, so Hawk was drafted to help the others by herding cattle into a corral where they'd be checked for parasites and obvious signs of disease. He soon discovered that cows were more stupid than even the dumbest shag; they didn't understand even the most simple of verbal commands, and it wasn't long before his shoes were caked with manure. He stayed until the officials completed their task, then returned to the passenger terminal, where the other inspectors complained about the stench he'd brought back with him.

When Hawk got home that evening, he noticed that the apartment across the hall was quiet; for the first time since he'd been living there, his neighbor wasn't entertaining any male guests. The next day was Zamael, the beginning of the weekend; he had the day off, along with Orifiel, but although he went out only a few times—shopping for groceries at the farmer's market, buying a new pair of shoes at the boot maker, picking up a replacement cell for his pad—he didn't see the woman whom he'd rescued a couple of nights earlier.

Late Orifiel afternoon, he'd just begun to cut up celery, carrots, and potatoes for a pot of soup when there was a quiet knock at his door. Thinking that it might be Bairns coming to check on him, he laid down the knife and went to the door, and instead found his neighbor standing in the hall.

"Hello," she said. "Hope I'm not bothering you. May I come in?"

"Umm . . . sure." It took a moment for Hawk to recognize her. Purple bruises beneath her eyes, a thick bandage across the bridge of her nose, and a collarlike brace fastened around her neck; the hemp dress she wore was much less revealing than the teddy she'd had on the first time he'd seen her. Stepping aside to let her in, he cast a wary glance down the hall. To his relief, no one else was in sight; he didn't want to be observed inviting a prostitute into his apartment.

"Thank you." She waited until he closed the door, then looked around, her gaze falling on the counter next to the stove. "You making dinner? I could always come back later . . ."

"No, no . . . it's all right. I'm just . . ." At a loss for what to say or do, he gestured toward the nearest chair. "Have a seat, please. I'll . . . I mean, I can . . . Would you like some coffee?"

"No, thanks anyway." A sly smile as she glided across the room. "Actually, I brought something else instead." For the first time Hawk noticed the bottle of waterfruit wine in her left hand; she placed it on the table, then looked at him expectantly. "Got a couple of glasses? Or I could go over to my place and . . ."

"No, you don't have to do that. I'll get one for you." Turning to the cabinet, he found a glass he normally used for his breakfast apple juice. "I . . . Not to be rude, but I don't drink." The fact of the matter was that he *couldn't* drink; the bracelet would detect the subtle change in his metabolic rate, and since abstinence from alcohol was a condition of his parole, Bairns would have something to say about that during their next session. "But please, feel free."

"Maybe I'll just save it for later." She didn't uncork the bottle, but instead pushed it aside as she took a seat at the table. "Actually, I brought it for you. Sort of to . . . y'know, thank you for saving me the other night." Her smile faded. "That was very brave, coming to my rescue like that. If you hadn't . . ."

"Are you all right?" Hawk couldn't help but stare at her bandaged nose. "Looks like he beat you up pretty badly."

"Yeah, well . . . nothing that the doctors couldn't fix." The corner of her mouth ticked upward. "Seriously, if you hadn't shown up when you did, he might have killed me. That guy was completely psycho. I should've never . . ."

Her voice trailed off, and Hawk was surprised to see a blush appear on her face, nearly matching the bruises beneath her eyes. She glanced away for a moment, as if trying to find the right thing to say, then looked at him again. "Anyway, my name's Melissa Sanchez. And you're . . . ?"

"Hawk . . . Hawk Thompson." As always, he hesitated before saying his full name.

"Glad to meet you, Hawk-Hawk Thompson." A grin. "That is your real name, isn't it? In my line of work . . . former line of work, I mean . . . a girl hears a lot of fake names. John Doe, John Smith, John Cooper . . . There's a reason why we call them johns, y'know."

"Never occurred to me." Apparently she hadn't heard of him, for there was no sign of recognition. Something she'd said, though, took him by surprise. "You're no longer . . . um . . . ?"

"A prostitute?" Melissa shook her head. "Not anymore. Not since I got busted for operating without a license." She idly traced her finger across the label of the unopened wine bottle. "Truth is, I was ready to get out of the business anyway. Never really wanted to do it in the first place, and I didn't want to join the guild and have to pay a manager. But I couldn't get a job anywhere else, and we all need to pay the rent one way or another, so . . ."

Hawk nodded. Unemployment was a chronic problem in New Brighton; immigrants were coming in faster than jobs were being created for them. And Melissa didn't look much older than his own sister, nor did she appear to be particularly robust; it was hard to imagine her finding work in a timber crew or on a fishing boat, and impossible to picture her wearing a miner's helmet. After that, her options were limited at best.

"Maybe you could . . ."

"Don't worry. I'll find something else, eventually." A soft laugh. "Whatever it is, it can't be any more dangerous than what I was doing before now. At least I won't get beat up for refusing to . . . Well, never mind."

Hawk didn't know what to say. Melissa made him vaguely uncomfortable. There had been a couple of prostitutes in the timber camps where he'd spent most of his youth: fat, cynical whores his father frequently brought home and whom he'd tried to avoid as much as possible. She reminded him of them, yet he didn't want her to leave. It was the first time since he'd moved in that anyone had come to visit him; even Rain stayed away from his flat, preferring not to venture into the tenements.

He also realized that, if Melissa noticed the bracelet on his wrist, she wasn't saying anything about it. Perhaps she'd seen ones like it before; given her former occupation, it was all too likely that she had. Whatever the reason, the fact that he didn't have to explain or apologize for his past made him more willing to overlook her sins.

So he turned back to the counter and, picking up the knife, began to cut vegetables again. "I'm making dinner. Not much, really . . . just some vegetable soup . . . but you're welcome to join me. I always make more than I can eat."

Melissa didn't reply. When he looked back at her again, he saw that her face had gone pale, and she was staring fixedly at the knife in his hand. "Please put that away," she said, very quietly. "Knives . . . scare me."

He almost asked why, then thought better of it. None of his business, and he didn't want to say anything that might jeopardize their relationship. "Sorry," he murmured, and hastily put the blade back on the counter and dropped a dishrag over it. "Won't happen again."

"Thank you." But the damage was done; she'd already risen from the chair and was heading for the door. "I need to get going. Just wanted to drop by and thank you for . . ."

"Sure. I'm just glad I . . . well, that I was there when you needed me."

By then, Melissa had opened the door. She stopped, turned to look back at him. "Yeah," she said. "I'm glad you were, too." A pause. "Hey, if you ever need anything . . . anything at all . . . I'm right across the hall. All you need to do is ask."

Hawk didn't know how specific the invitation was meant to be; he decided to interpret it in a less-than-intimate way. "Thanks. I could always use a little company." Realizing that this could be misconstrued, he quickly added, "Perhaps we could do dinner some other time?"

"Yeah . . . okay, sure. I'd like that." She hesitated. "Y'know, maybe I don't need to go anywhere just now. I mean, if you'd still like for me to stay . . ."

He shrugged. "Like I said . . . I always make too much for one." Hawk figured he could finish cutting the vegetables while his back was turned to her; that way, she wouldn't have to see the knife. He waved a hand toward the table. "Please . . ."

Melissa closed the door. "Thank you. Yeah, I think I will." There was a twinkle in her bruise-shadowed eyes. "You know, Hawk-Hawk, I think we're going to get along just fine."

Spring came with the gradual warming of the days as winter reluctantly let go of its long, cold grip. The rainy season began in the fifth week of Asmodel; almost every afternoon, sudden downpours turned the streets of New Brighton into mud slides and caused leaks to spring in the tenement ceilings. Between arrivals of inbound shuttles, the skies above the spaceport were often filled by flocks of swoops, squawking as they made their return migration from nesting grounds in the Meridian Archipelago to the northern climes of Midland, New

Florida, and Great Dakota. Once again, Coyote was waking up; change came slowly to this world, but it came nonetheless.

Hawk discovered that his life was undergoing change as well. The fact that he had someone to go home to made all the difference. Melissa wasn't exactly a girlfriend—although she never gave him the impression that she'd reject sexual overtures on his part, he didn't find the idea of sleeping with her very appealing—but it wasn't long before she became more than just a neighbor across the hall. When he came home from work, he often found that she'd already made dinner for both of them; since she was currently unemployed, she had plenty of time to do the cooking. They began to go shopping together on the weekends, picking up the things they wanted to eat during the coming week. And if he had a little extra money on payday, they'd treat themselves by going out to dinner. Although Melissa avoided the taverns where she might be spotted by one of her former clients, Hawk soon learned that she knew which cafes were the best in town. One Zamael night, she even went so far as to insist that they both dress up so that they could get into a fancy restaurant in Riverside, the part of town near the docks that was the closest New Brighton had to a wealthy neighborhood. They dined on grilled redfish and roasted waterfruit stems as they watched fishing boats move along the Great Equatorial River, and pretended to be old friends of Morgan Goldstein, the billionaire entrepreneur whose manor stood near the lighthouse.

Hawk knew that her friendship didn't come without a few strings attached. Melissa hadn't been able to get a job, so part of his salary went toward helping her meet her rent. He'd also assumed the role of being her personal bodyguard; men often dropped by her apartment, still believing that she was "a working girl" (Melissa's term for her former occupation), so he'd learned to listen for a signal the two of them had worked out—three hard raps against her door—that was her way of asking him to come over and help evict any would-be john who didn't know how to take no for an answer. But Hawk had enough money to spare, and so long as he didn't have to use force, he didn't mind being her chaperone.

He decided not to let Bairns know about her; it wouldn't do any good to have his parole officer find out that a prostitute, even one who was retired, had become his companion. So Melissa made herself scarce when Bairns came over for their weekly meetings, and if she happened to see Hawk while Joe was around, she pretended not to know either of them. As it turned out, though, Bairns never seemed to see her; as Melissa explained, most men tend to notice prostitutes only from the neck down. And since Bairns had seen her only once—and that when her nose was broken and her eyes were blackened—chances were that he wouldn't recognize her unless she was nearly naked.

The two of them became close, but they still kept secrets from one another. Hawk never spoke to her about his father, and she never asked why he wore a bracelet and inhibitor patch. And although he learned that her fear of knives came from having been raped when she was a teenager, she never told him why she'd become a prostitute despite the trauma of that experience. Each had boundaries; so long as they knew where the lines were and didn't cross them, their friendship remained untroubled.

Hawk hadn't fully realized how lonely he'd been until he met Melissa. Having a friend, he discovered that his existence no longer seemed so bleak. His job was still boring, but as long as she was there to say good-bye when he left for work and hello when he got home, that was enough to get him through the day. And although immigrants continued to shuffle past his window in a seemingly endless procession, he no longer envied their desire to find new lives for themselves.

He'd almost come to enjoy his job when an incident occurred.

On schedule, the EASS *Magellan* returned to 47 Uma. Unlike the Western Hemisphere, whose relations with the Coyote Federation were still constrained by its refusal to sign the U.N. treaty acknowledging the Federation's sovereignty, the European Alliance enjoyed full diplomatic relations with the new world. Even so, the Alliance hadn't quite forgotten the showdown that occurred a few years ago when the *Magellan* had nearly opened fire on Starbridge Coyote during a short-lived rebellion by a handful of colonists. Few people remembered that Hawk had been involved in the affair, if only in a peripheral way, and it was one more thing that he didn't like to talk about.

So he was always nervous whenever the *Magellan*'s crew shuttled down to New Brighton. None of them had ever recognized him, nor was it likely that they would. Nonetheless, Hawk tried to keep his face down as they went through passport control. Unlike its former sister ship, the *Robert E. Lee*, the *Magellan* was primarily a military vessel; the fact that it also carried cargo and a handful of passengers was almost an afterthought. So it was a relief that the next person to approach Hawk's kiosk wasn't wearing a uniform.

A young man, only a year or two older than Hawk, dressed casually in trousers and a zipped-up Windbreaker. A nylon duffel bag was slung from a strap under his arm, and, despite having just arrived, he seemed already accustomed to Coyote's lighter gravity and thin atmosphere. From the corner of his eye, Hawk casually sized him up as he processed the passport of the ESA lieutenant who'd preceded him in line. Clearly not an immigrant—he wasn't carrying enough baggage—but apparently neither was he a tourist or a tradesman: his clothes weren't expensive, and indeed appeared to be a bit cheap. Hawk doubted that he was a diplomat or government official; nor did he look like any clergyman that he'd ever seen.

And he was nervous. It wasn't obvious, but Hawk had learned to pick up the subtle signs of someone who was anxious about being here: the stiff stance, the constantly roaming eyes, the hand that surreptitiously left the bag strap to wipe sweat on his trousers. A smuggler? Perhaps . . . but what could he possibly be carrying in such a small bag?

The ESA officer finished filling out the declaration form and slid it through the window. Hawk made sure that everything was properly entered, then placed it in the OUT box. "Welcome to Coyote," he murmured as he stamped the officer's passport, then looked at the young man waiting behind next in line. "Next, please."

The newly arrived passenger jerked slightly, almost as if trying to unlock his knees, then sauntered forward. "Good morning," he said as he approached Hawk's window; his voice had a faint British accent, and was much too cheerful to be entirely innocent. "How are you today?"

Hawk ignored the overture. "Name, please?"

"Desilitz. Peter Desilitz." He'd already produced his passport and placed it on the desk, open and ready to be tagged.

"Citizen of Coyote or nonresident?" Hawk took the passport and slipped it past the comp's eye. An instant later, all the pertinent data contained with its smartpaper appeared on the screen. The questions were little more than a formality, really; nonetheless, it was Hawk's job to ask them.

"Nonresident." Desilitz casually ran a hand through his sandy hair. "European Alliance . . . Great Britain, to be precise."

"Reason for visiting?" Hawk pretended to study the passport as he watched the biometric scanner's display. A real-time model of Desilitz's face was rapidly being traced upon the screen; in the upper-left corner, dozens of pictures of men, each of whom somewhat resembled him, flashed by in rapid succession, as the comp sought to match the images in its database against the individual standing on the other side of the desk.

"Pleasure." A grin meant to be easygoing trembled ever so slightly at the corners of his mouth. "Just here on holiday, really."

A red bar appeared at the top of the comp screen: DETAIN FOR QUESTIONING. And below it, a blue bar that he'd never seen before: SUSPECT MAY BE DANGEROUS.

There was more, but Hawk didn't have a chance to read it. Any hesitation might tip off Desilitz that he'd just been red-flagged. Instead, he casually shifted in his chair, as if making himself a little more comfortable, while letting his left hand drop beneath the desktop. "Expected length of stay?"

"Umm . . . two weeks." Desilitz's eyes missed nothing; his gaze followed Hawk's hand as it briefly disappeared from sight. "No, four, I think." A nervous smile. "I've got an open-ended ticket for return."

"Very good." Any other time, Hawk might have asked him to be more specific. Yet he'd just pressed the button that would alert the proctor stationed nearby; now it was his job to distract the suspect long enough for help to arrive. "Are you importing any items valued at more than one hundred colonials?"

"No. None." Desilitz patted the shoulder strap of his bag. "Just my clothes."

"I see." Stalling for time, Hawk pulled an immigration form from the stack and slid it across the counter. "Well, you'll need to fill this out, please."

Desilitz glanced at the form. "I think I already did that, while I was still aboard ship. I gave it to the steward just before we—"

"That was a different copy. This is the one you need to do for us." It was an old feint, but Hawk was unsure how much longer he could play the persnickety bureaucrat. If Desilitz wasn't already suspicious, he would be soon. Where was that proctor?

The passenger stared at Hawk through the window, as if trying to decide what sort of idiot he was dealing with. Hawk gazed back at him, his expression stoical; from the corner of his eye, he could see the proctor making his way past the passengers lined up at the inspection tables. Just another few moments . . .

"If you need a pen," Hawk said, "I've got—"

Someone in line snapped "Hey!" as the proctor bumped against him. The voice caught Desilitz's attention; looking around, he saw the proctor coming his way. His face went pale, and then his bag dropped to the floor as his right hand dived into his jacket pocket.

"Hold it!" The proctor had already unholstered his stunner; bringing it up in a two-handed grip, he pointed it straight at the young man. "Freeze!"

Desilitz hesitated, but only for a moment. Between him and the proctor were about a half dozen people, none of whom had the slightest idea what was going on, yet each a potential casualty. And Desilitz knew that the proctor didn't have a clear line of fire.

His hand emerged from his Windbreaker pocket. Hawk caught a glimpse of a fléchette pistol, a weapon far more lethal than the one the proctor carried. Desilitz was no longer paying attention to the inspector, yet he was beyond Hawk's reach, nor were there any heavy objects that he could throw through the window at him. Outside his kiosk, Hawk heard the frightened screams of other passengers; on the other side of the aisle, another inspector turned around to see what was going on. And in that instant of dilated time, Desilitz was leveling the pistol at the proctor . . .

"Hey!" Hawk yelled. "You forgot your form!"

Absurd, but it was the only thing he could think of to say or do. Yet it worked. Desilitz glanced at him, and when he did, he lost his aim. A moment of distraction was all the proctor needed; Hawk couldn't hear the soft *zing* of the stun gun being fired, but he knew that the high-voltage charge had struck its target when Desilitz yelped in pain.

The suspect collapsed, falling from sight on the other side of the counter. More screams throughout the terminal as the proctor rushed forward, knocking bewildered passengers out of the way. Hawk stood up and, leaning through the window, watched as the proctor, still keeping his stunner trained on Desilitz, kicked the fléchette pistol away. Not that Desilitz was in any condition to use it; barely conscious, he was curled up on the floor, whimpering in pain.

"Nice work, Thompson." The proctor, whom Hawk had spoken to only once or twice in the last six months, glanced up at him. "Thanks for the help."

"Yeah . . . sure." Hawk slowly let out his breath. It felt as if an hour had gone by since Desilitz first appeared at his window. Around them, other inspectors were doing their best to restore order. "Glad I could do something."

The proctor nodded, not looking away from the semiconscious figure at his feet. "Well, it worked, that's f' sure." He paused, then glanced up at Hawk again. "Who is this guy, anyway?"

Hawk shook his head. Everything happened so fast, he hadn't a chance to read the rest of the data on his screen. For the moment, that would have to wait; the first priorities were making sure the guy was under control and calming down the bystanders.

Just as Hawk stepped out of his kiosk, the crowd parted to allow a couple of Colonial Militia soldiers to get through; he'd later learn that they'd just arrived to board a suborbital shuttle to Hammerhead, where they were to join the garrison at Fort Lopez. He stood quietly to one side and watched as one of the blueshirts aimed her carbine at Desilitz while her partner knelt beside him and used a plastic strap to tie his hands behind his back. By then, the proctor had retrieved the fléchette pistol; he clicked its safety in place, shoved it in his belt, and reached down to pick up the duffel bag.

"Leave it alone," the female soldier said. "No telling what's in there."

The proctor hastily withdrew his hand. "Better clear these people out of here," he murmured to no one in particular. "If he's got a bomb in there . . ."

"No bomb." Facedown on the floor, his wrists lashed together, Desilitz turned his head to peer up at them. "Nothing in there but clothes. Swear."

The proctor and the soldiers glanced uncertainly at one another, then one of the militiamen turned toward the bystanders. "All right, everyone," he called out, raising his hands above his head, "we need you to back up. Those of you who've already had their passports tagged and bags inspected, please leave the building through the doors to your left. Everyone who was waiting to be processed, leave through the doors to the right. Don't rush, just . . ."

The other inspectors came forward to ease the crowd toward the appropriate exits. Hawk started to join them, but the proctor shook his head. "Stay here. I'm going to need to get a statement from you."

"Yeah, do that." The female soldier glanced at him. "And while you're at it, give him a medal or something. He just saved your ass."

Hawk shook his head. "But I didn't . . ."

His voice trailed off; they'd stopped paying attention to him, at least for the moment. At the urging of the customs officials, the passengers shuffled out of the terminal, murmuring to one another as they tried to make sense of what had just happened. The proctor planted his boots on either side of Desilitz's bag, making sure that no one touched it until it was checked for explosives. Somewhere in the distance, there was the high-pitched warble of a police coupe coming from town.

The soldiers waited until the terminal cleared out, then the two of them reached down to Desilitz. Taking hold of his arms from beneath the shoulders, they hauled him to his feet. Desilitz was still groggy, but he was able to stand on his own two feet; he looked around as if searching for a way to escape, but seemed to give up when he saw the rifle pointed in his chest. The warble grew louder, then stopped abruptly as the coupe glided to a halt outside the front entrance.

"Okay, let's go." The soldier who'd secured his wrists prodded him toward the door. "Take it easy, and we won't have any problems. Understand?"

"Sure. I understand." All the fight had gone out of him; it appeared as if he'd given up. But before the soldiers took him away, Desilitz turned his head to look straight at Hawk. In his eyes, Hawk saw pure hatred . . . and the stark, unblinking gaze of a fanatic.

"Consider yourself an enemy of the Living Earth," Desilitz said, just loud enough for only Hawk to hear him. And the soldiers led him to the door.

"Oh, God . . ." Melissa's face had gone white, her voice little more than a whisper. "Hawk-Hawk, do you know who those people are?"

"Not really." He picked up the mug of coffee he'd just poured for himself. "Never heard of them before today . . . Some kind of group, right?"

"Some kind of . . ." She shook her head, then leaned across the table to stare at him. "Don't pay much attention to current affairs, do you?"

Hawk shrugged. The pot of lamb stew she'd spent the afternoon preparing for their dinner simmered on her apartment stove, ignored for the time being. Hawk hadn't yet changed out of his uniform; he'd come home to find her waiting for him on the front steps of their building. Melissa had already heard about what happened at the spaceport; indeed, it seemed as if everyone on the street was watching him as he climbed off his bike and carried it inside. News traveled fast in New Brighton, especially when it came to crime.

"Not really." He saw the look of disbelief in her eyes, and shrugged again. "Look, if it's something that doesn't have anything to do with me, I just don't care very much about—"

"Yeah, well, now it does, okay?" Melissa wasn't about to let it go. "And Living Earth isn't a social club. They're a major terrorist organization . . ."

"So I've been told."

"Remember the bombing of the New Guinea space elevator? They claimed responsibility for that. Same for the blowout of the Descartes City dome." She saw the blank look on his face. "On the Moon, Hawk. Seventy-six people killed. You never heard about that?"

"Must have happened while I was . . ." *On the farm,* he was about to say, but stopped himself. He didn't hear a lot of news while he'd been in rehab, and events back on Earth had never interested him very much in the first place. "Okay, maybe I haven't been paying a lot of attention. So what's their problem?"

Melissa stood up from the table. "Ready to eat? Don't know about you, but I'm hungry." He nodded, and she took a soup ladle down off its hook. "Living Earth is a group opposed to off-world colonization," she went on as she scooped stew into a couple of wooden bowls. "They believe that the money spent to support colonies on the Moon and Mars would be better used to preserve what remains of Earth's environment."

"Little late for that, isn't it?" Hawk might not pay attention to the news, but he'd learned Earth history in school and knew that lunar colonies had been around for nearly three hundred years, with the first outpost built by the old United States before the Liberty Party took over the country and renamed it the United Republic of America.

"Yeah, well . . . old grudges die hard, I guess." Melissa carried the bowls over to the table, then went to the cabinet to fetch napkins and spoons. "They started as a legitimate environmental organization but went underground when their leaders opted for direct action instead of working through the system. Rumor has it that they're secretly bankrolled by the Union—can't be a coincidence that all their strikes have been directed at the European Alliance—but they deny that, of course."

She put a spoon in front of Hawk, then sat down across the table from him. "Until now, they've had nothing to do with us . . . Coyote, I mean. But if you caught one of them trying to get through customs . . ."

"He was pretty stupid about it." Hawk tried the stew. As usual, it was a little bland for his taste; he reached for the pepper mill. "Fake name, fake passport . . . nothing the biometrics couldn't sniff out. Should've known better than to think he could get through customs without someone catching on." He grinned. "I had him pegged the minute I spotted him."

"All right, so he was stupid. That's not the point. If there was one, then what's to say that there haven't been others before him?"

Hawk didn't say anything for a moment. Like it or not, Melissa was right. Peter Desilitz—or rather, David Laird, his real name—had been caught, but there was no telling how many other members of Living Earth might have slipped through customs. True, he could have been only the first person to try . . . or he could have been the fifth, or the fifteenth, or the fiftieth. Hawk knew better than anyone that customs inspectors didn't always pay as much attention as they should. On a busy day, they might process dozens of passports. And Laird might have been just the one guy unfortunate enough to have a face that was identifiable through biometric profiling.

"I don't know," he said at last, not looking up at her. "I'm just glad we managed to get him."

"Hawk-Hawk . . ." Melissa sighed, then put down her spoon and reached across the table to take his hand. "I'm scared. What you told me he said . . . If there are others like him, they may come for you."

That thought had occurred to him, although he'd tried to suppress it. Until now, he'd been safe in his anonymity: just another person living in the tenements, trying to get by as best he could. But he remembered the way everyone on the block had looked at him when he'd come home. If there were other members of Living Earth in New Brighton, and if they decided to take revenge upon him, he wouldn't be hard to find.

"So what do you want me to do?" Hawk looked back at her. "I can't just hide here all day, y'know. I've got a job to go to. And my uniform . . ."

"Leave." Her voice was low, almost a whisper. "Get out of town."

"I can't just leave. I . . ." His gaze fell to his left wrist, and the bracelet wrapped around it. "You know that's impossible."

"No. Not impossible." Melissa paused. "Hawk-Hawk, there's nothing here for you . . . for either one of us. I haven't wanted to tell you, but . . . I've been thinking about this for a while now, and I want to get out of here. New Brighton's a dead end. If I stay here, I'm just going to end up turning tricks again. I don't want to do that. And I've heard about places a long way from here where people can . . . y'know, disappear."

"Maybe you can." He held up his left hand. "But I can't."

"Yes, you can." A smile crept across her face. "If you want to bad enough."

Hawk was still thinking about what Melissa had said when there was a second incident at customs. It wasn't violent, but it changed his life. After that, nothing was ever the same again.

A few days after David Laird was arrested at the spaceport, a *hjadd* vessel came through the starbridge. Its arrival wasn't unexpected; once the aliens had an embassy on Coyote, ships from Hjarr had begun making occasional visits to 47 Uma. Before, their shuttles had landed at their compound in Liberty, touching down within the center of the odd doughnut-shaped structure that the *hjadd* had erected almost overnight from native materials. As a result, few people had ever met the denizens of Rho Coronae Borealis; their affairs were cloaked in secrecy, as mysterious as before.

Sometime in the last few months, someone at Government House had apparently decided that the *hjadd* should be subjected to the same immigration protocols as anyone arriving from Earth. Whether the *hjadd* objected to the new rules, no one in New Brighton knew; nonetheless, Hawk was surprised to learn that, for the first time, a new *hjadd* ambassador would be arriving at the spaceport.

That morning, the customs inspectors were convened in the break room, where a senior government official briefed them on what would happen later that day. In deference to hisher desire for privacy, no other vessels would be allowed to land at the same time, and the terminal was to be cleared of all nonessential personnel. In light of the arrest a few days earlier, strict security procedures would be enforced while heshe was on the premises. Once the shuttle was on the ground, the ambassador would be met by a Federation liaison who would then escort himher through customs. Otherwise, all the usual protocols would be observed, with one important exception: the ambassador's personal belongings would not be examined, but instead would be exempt from search under U.N. rules regarding diplomatic immunity.

For once, Hawk shared the same feelings as his fellow agents. Although they were intrigued by the prospect of seeing one of the aliens in the flesh, they also knew that it would be a major headache. A squad of Colonial Militia in full dress uniform had been flown in for the occasion; although they were little more than an honor guard, their presence was intimidating all the same. The arrest of a Living Earth terrorist was still fresh in everyone's mind. And since no other spacecraft would be allowed to land until the emissary left New Brighton, there would be a logjam later in the day. So while they looked forward to the break from the routine, they were also aware that the *hjadd* ambassador would pose a nuisance.

Yet Hawk was in for one more surprise: the unexpected arrival of Uncle Carlos.

In the years since Carlos Montero had left office, the former president of the Coyote Federation had become the official liaison to the *hjadd* embassy. Since this coincided with the period Hawk spent on the farm, he was barely aware of the role his uncle played in fostering relations between Coyote and Hjarr; Uncle Carlos had become a distant relative, as remote from him as he was from nearly everyone else. Only a couple of people in New Brighton knew that they were related, and Hawk was just as happy to keep it that way. So he was stunned when, little less than a half hour before the *hjadd* shuttle was scheduled to land, he heard a voice speak his name, and he turned around to find his uncle standing just outside his kiosk.

"Hawk?" Carlos gazed at him through the glass. "Good to see you again."

It took a second for Hawk to recognize his uncle. He'd grown older since the last time he'd seen him; his hair was almost completely grey, and sometime in the last few years he'd cultivated a trim white beard.

"Uncle Carlos?" he said at last. "Is that you?"

A smile appeared on Carlos's face. "Sorry I didn't let you know I was coming, but . . . well, I've been busy lately." A pause. "Think you can step out to see me?"

Hawk hesitated. With the terminal vacant of incoming passengers, the only other persons around were his fellow inspectors. They'd turned around in their kiosks to regard him with surprise; they weren't aware that one of their own knew President Montero. Behind Carlos, their supervisor quietly nodded.

"Sure . . . okay." Pushing back his chair, Hawk opened the door and stepped out of the booth. "Been a long time," he added, not knowing what else to say.

The smile faded. "Like I said, I've been busy lately." Carlos looked him over. "You're doing well. I hear you were responsible for a major arrest just recently."

Hawk shrugged. "Just doing my job."

"All the same, it was above and beyond the call of duty." Carlos looked over his shoulder at the supervisor. "I hope you've put my nephew in for a raise. He certainly deserves it."

The customs supervisor gave him a nod, although that was the first time a pay hike had been mentioned. Hawk felt his face grow warm. He'd never said anything to anyone about a relationship to a famous uncle; all of a sudden, he found himself wishing that Carlos had never shown up. "It's not necessary, really," he said hastily. "Like I said . . ."

"Just doing your job. Of course." The smile reappeared, but it seemed as if Carlos had sensed Hawk's discomfort. "Still, this sort of thing shouldn't go unrewarded." He paused, then lowered his voice. "I'm wondering if you could do me a favor . . . in an official capacity, of course."

Hawk said nothing but nodded. Putting his hand on his arm, his uncle pulled him aside. "I have a small problem," he went on, once he was out of earshot of the others. "This idea of having the *hjadd* go through customs . . . it's something I didn't want. They don't understand the concept of passports and visas, and although I've tried to explain it to them, they still consider it an insult. An indication that we don't trust them."

"Sure, but I can't . . ."

"I know. You don't make the rules, and there's nothing you can do about it." Carlos kept his voice down. "I'm trying to persuade the Colonial Council to change their minds and make an exception for the *hjadd* ambassadors, but until I do, I need to work out some sort of compromise."

Hawk followed his uncle's gaze through the terminal windows. A squad of Colonial Militia were lined up on either side of a red carpet that had been unrolled along the concrete apron; at parade rest, they awaited the arrival of the *hjadd* shuttle. "What I'd like to do," Carlos continued, "is have you meet the new ambassador out there instead of making himher come through the terminal. That way, you can process himher in a way that's a bit less . . . well, conspicuous."

Hawk was hesitant. "I don't know if I can do that." He glanced over his shoulder at his supervisor, who was watching them from beside the kiosk. "My boss . . ."

"I've already spoken to him, and he says that, so long as you do everything you'd normally do, he has no problem with it. We're not breaking any rules, only bending them a little. With luck, this may be the last time we'll have to go through this foolishness. But until we revise the procedures, it's the best I can negotiate at the last minute." Carlos smiled. "And besides, you'll get an opportunity very few people have had so far . . . you'll meet a *hjadd* face-to-face. Interested?"

Although Hawk had no particular fondness for Carlos, the fact remained that he owed him a favor; after all, if he hadn't arranged for his parole, Hawk would still be on the farm. And, he had to admit, the prospect of meeting a *hjadd* intrigued him. It also occurred to him that, if he played his cards right, he might be tapped for permanent duty in that particular area. Much more interesting than dealing with tourists all day.

"All right," he replied. "Sure. I can do that."

"Great. I was hoping you'd say so." Carlos briefly put his arm around Hawk's shoulder, then turned toward his supervisor and gave him a quick nod, which the other man accepted with a stoical frown. "Very well. Get whatever you need, then come with me."

The *hjadd* shuttle was unlike any spacecraft Hawk had ever seen. Resembling a manta ray, its aquamarine hull lacking any obvious seams, it descended upon the spaceport with little more than a high-pitched whine, the pods of its reactionless drive emitting a deep blue glow that faded the moment its landing gear touched the ground.

So accustomed had he become to hearing the blast of descent engines, Hawk found himself vaguely unsettled by the nearly silent arrival of the alien craft. Here was technology so advanced that it made anything made by his own race seem primitive by comparison. No wonder his uncle was concerned about not wanting to offend their visitors.

They stood together at the end of the red carpet, the Colonial Militia on either side of them. At an order from their commanding officer, the soldiers snapped to attention, backs straight, hands to their sides. Someone had apparently instructed the militiamen not to present arms, because their carbines remained strapped to their shoulders; Hawk noticed, though, that the straps were loose enough that the soldiers could easily unlimber their weapons. He was also aware that, just out of sight, other soldiers were carefully watching the landing field. It had apparently occurred to others that David Laird might not have been the first member of Living Earth to visit Coyote.

For a minute or so, there was no motion or sound from the *hjadd* shuttle. Then there was a faint hiss of escaping pressure as a hatch on the craft's underside slid open, and a moment later a ramp slowly lowered to the ground. Another minute went by, then the *hjadd* ambassador walked down the ramp.

Although Uncle Carlos had already told him what to expect, Hawk felt a shiver. The emissary wore an environment suit that completely concealed hisher body, yet it was obvious that heshe was an extraterrestrial. Shorter than a human, with a broad torso carried upon two short, thick legs, hisher face was hidden behind the reflective faceplate of a helmet that rose from hisher elongated neck. A brown satchel hung by a narrow strap from hisher right shoulder; Hawk noticed that hisher hand never left it.

Apparently heshe would be the only one of hisher kind to disembark, because no one followed himher down the ramp. The ambassador stopped just an inch or two before setting foot on the ground; heshe silently waited, ignoring the soldiers on either side of the carpet.

"Let's go," Uncle Carlos murmured, then began to march down the aisle. Hawk took a deep breath and fell in behind him.

Carlos came to a halt in front of the *hjadd*. "Greetings," he said, raising his left hand palm-outward. "I am Carlos Montero, former president and official liaison for the Coyote Federation. Welcome to Coyote."

"Thank you, President Montero." The voice that came from the grille beneath the helmet faceplate was pleasant yet androgynous; although Hawk knew that *hjadd* environment suits contained translation devices, nevertheless it seemed odd to hear Anglo being spoken. Heshe raised hisher left hand, six-fingered within its glove. "I am Jasahajahd Taf Sa-Fhadda, Cultural Ambassador for Hjarr. May I have permission to visit your world?"

"Yes, Taf Sa-Fhadda, please do." Carlos moved back a little. "May your stay be comfortable and in peace."

"Thank you." The *hjadd* stepped off the ramp, hisher feet coming to rest upon the carpet. "May relations between our races continue to prosper."

"So say we all." Carlos nodded and lowered his hand. "I hope that your journey was without incident."

"It was." Taf's head moved back and forth on hisher neck. "The courtesy you've shown us has been appreciated, although the recent change in landing site has been"—the slightest of pauses—"noted."

"Profound apologies for the inconvenience." Carlos lowered his head in supplication. "My government has decided that all spacecraft are to land here, regardless of origin. I'm currently negotiating for a more private location at this spaceport for future arrivals by your vessels."

Looking up again, Carlos gestured toward the honor guard on either side of the carpet. "In the meantime, we will try to extend every possible courtesy to you and your kind. Once we are done here, these soldiers will escort you to an aircraft waiting nearby, which will transport you directly to your embassy. First, though"—a meaningful pause—"we have a small ritual that we are obliged to perform."

Hawk tried not to smile. He'd never thought of his job as conducting a ritual; apparently this was how the former president had presented it to the *hjadd*. But he managed to keep a straight face as Carlos turned toward him. "Allow me to introduce Hawk Thompson, an officer of our government's Bureau of Customs and Immigration. He is the son of my sister, and he has been given this duty today."

Uncle Carlos moved aside, giving him a brief nod. Feeling his heart thudding in his chest, Hawk stepped forward. His left hand trembled as he raised it. "Greetings . . . uh, Taj Fhadda . . ."

"Taf Sa-Fhadda." Carlos cast an urgent glance at the *hjadd*. "My apologies, Ambassador. No insult was intended."

Taf said nothing, but once again hisher head swung back and forth on hisher neck. Hawk took the gesture to be an affirmative. "Pardon me," he said quickly. "I . . . Sorry, but I didn't . . ."

"You are pardoned," Taf replied. "Please continue."

Hawk took a deep breath, tried to remain calm. Raising his datapad, he switched to vox mode so that he wouldn't have to write on the screen. "Yes . . . umm . . . name, please?"

Too late, he realized that he'd committed another gaffe. From the corner of his eye, he saw his uncle stiffen; behind them, one of the soldiers stifled unkind laughter. Yet the emissary didn't seem to mind. "I am Jasahajahd Taf Sa-Fhadda," heshe said, repeating what heshe had said only seconds ago. "Cultural Ambassador to the Coyote Federation from Hjarr."

"Uhh . . . yes, thank you." Hawk had the presence of mind to skip the next two questions; his uncle had already told him that passports and visas were meaningless to the *hjadd*, and the ambassador had already told him where he was from. "Reason for visiting?"

"I have come to facilitate the exchange of cultural information regarding our respective races," Taf said, his words coming effortlessly from the grille. "In particular, matters of history, art, social customs, and spirituality." Heshe paused. "I hope that this visit will be to our mutual benefit, Hawk Thompson."

Any other time, and from anyone else, that would have been more than Hawk needed to know. Yet he couldn't help but smile. "So do I . . . ah, Taf Sa-Fhadda," he replied, feeling a little more at ease. "Expected length of stay?"

A long pause. "I do not understand."

Hawk didn't need to look at Carlos to know that his uncle was glaring at him. "Umm . . . how long do you expect to be here? On Coyote, I mean."

"For as long as it takes for me to fulfill my mission," Taf said. "Unless my people decide that my work here is inadequate and decide to replace me, it will be indefinite."

"Yes, right . . . of course." Again, Hawk realized how unsuitable his questions were. Yet all he could do was carry on as best he could. "Are you carrying any items valued at more than one hundred colonials?"

"Ambassador . . ." Carlos moved forward. "Forgive us, please. My nephew didn't mean any . . ."

"No need to apologize." Taf's head swung toward him. "He is only performing a ritual as dictated by the customs of your people." The *hjadd* looked at Hawk again. "I do not understand your question. I carry items, yes. Are you asking me if any of them are valuable to you?"

Before Hawk could respond, Taf opened the flap of hisher satchel. Hisher hand disappeared for a moment; when it emerged again, heshe held a small black box, six inches on a side. "This may be worth something to you," Taf said. "Is that what you mean to ask?"

"No, I . . ."

"I'm sorry, Taf Sa-Fhadda." Carlos came to the rescue. "My nephew has made a mistake. As ambassador, by our laws you are exempt from having to declare . . . that is, to formally state . . . the value of any items you may be carrying."

"Yes. I understand now." But Taf didn't put away the box; instead, hisher head cocked slightly to one side. "You seem to be uncertain of yourself," heshe said quietly. "I do not think you know what you are doing."

"I . . ." Hawk sighed, shook his head. "No. You're right, Ambassador. I don't know what I'm doing." He saw the scowl on his uncle's face, and added, "I'm not even sure why I'm here."

Taf didn't respond for a moment, yet heshe took a step closer, as if to study the customs agent a little more closely. Hawk saw his face reflected in the faceplate of the *hjadd's* helmet: nervous, unsure of himself. Little more than a functionary, and an inept one at that.

"Yes," heshe said at last. "I see that now. You search for something, but you do not know what it is, nor will you ever be happy until you find it."

Hawk didn't know what to say, but it was as if the *hjadd* had found a window to his soul and opened it. Everything Taf said was true; he'd just never admitted it to himself. He nodded, then went quiet, looking down at the ground in humiliation.

"I believe that you need this," Taf said, hisher voice so low that only Hawk and his uncle could hear it. Hawk looked up to see that the emissary was offering the box to him. "Take it. Consider it a gift."

"I . . ." Hawk stared at the small box. "I'm sorry, but I can't. Rules say that I'm prohibited from accepting any . . ."

"Hawk . . ." Carlos began, and Hawk caught the expression on his uncle's face. He suddenly realized that if he didn't accept a gift from the cultural ambassador, Jasahajahd Taf Sa-Fhadda would doubtless consider it an insult.

"Thank you, Taf Sa-Fhadda." Hawk took the small box from the *hjadd*. Now that it was in his hand, he noticed that it was a little heavier than it seemed; a narrow crack ran down its center, revealing the location of two hinged flaps. The box rattled faintly in his grasp, as if it contained something inside. He started to open it, but the *hjadd* quickly laid hisher hand across his own.

"No," heshe said quietly. "Not here. Later, when you are alone and your mind is at peace. Do you understand?"

"Yes." Hawk hesitated. "What is it?"

"It is *Sa'Tong-tas* . . . the Book of *Sa'Tong*." Taf paused. "Speak to it, and it will speak to you."

"Thank you." Hawk didn't know what else to say.

"*Sa'Tong qo*, Hawk Thompson." The ambassador turned away from him. "If we are finished with this ritual," heshe said to Carlos, "I would like to leave now."

"Yes . . . sure, of course." For once, Carlos appeared to be flustered; he was obviously shocked that his nephew, whom he'd ignored for so long, would be the recipient of an alien artifact. One last glance at Hawk, then he extended a hand toward the carpet. "If you will follow me, please . . ."

Without another word, Jasahajahd Taf Sa-Fhadda allowed himherself to be led away. Hawk watched as his uncle escorted the ambassador past the double row of soldiers; not far away, the twin props of a gyrobus were already beginning to turn, its pilot preparing for immediate takeoff.

Not once did the *hjadd* look back at him. Hawk waited until the emissary, accompanied by his uncle, boarded the aircraft. Its passenger door slammed shut, and a few seconds later the gyro rose from the ground, heading northwest to New Florida.

By then, the *Sa'Tong-tas* had disappeared within his trouser pocket. No one except Carlos had seen Hawk take it; no one had to know that the ambassador had given him a present. Perhaps it was only a trivial item. Nevertheless, he had a feeling that it was important.

Hawk left work early. He told his supervisor that he was feeling a little ill; something he'd eaten for breakfast, along with the stress of greeting the ambassador, had upset his stomach. His boss was a bit miffed—they were expecting a larger than usual number of passengers later that afternoon—but Hawk almost never called in sick, and he had an extra day off coming to him. So he grudgingly let Hawk go and assigned another inspector to take his place.

As he expected, his building was quiet when he got home; everyone else was still at work, and even Melissa was nowhere to be seen. That suited him well; he needed some time to himself.

He locked the door and closed the windows, then took the *Sa'Tong-tas* from his pocket and placed it on the table. His first impulse was to open it at once, yet he stopped himself. Taf had told him not to do so unless his mind was at peace. So he took off his uniform, then went into the bathroom and gave himself the luxury of a midday shower. Once he toweled off, he found an old robe that he seldom wore and pulled it on. All the while, he tried to empty his mind, deliberately avoiding thinking about anything in particular. He didn't know exactly why he did all these things, only that it seemed natural.

When he was ready, Hawk sat down at the table. The black box rested where he'd placed it, inert and mysterious. He found the crack at its center and, ever so gently, pulled open the flaps.

Inside the box was an object little more than five inches in height. Carefully removing it from the box, he found what appeared to be a small, delicate sculpture: two gold rods, supporting a translucent cylinder capped by a small glass orb, anchored to a pedestal inscribed with script that somewhat resembled Farsi. Some sort of fluid, golden brown and viscous, was suspended within the cylinder. Tiny jewels sparkled from the support rods, and sunlight entered the sphere as if it were a prism, breaking into multicolored rays that fell across the table. The *hjadd* script on the pedestal seemed to glow with a luminescence of its own.

At first glance, the *Sa'Tong-tas* appeared to be little more than an objet d'art, beautiful but nothing else. Resting it on the table, Hawk cautiously probed it with his fingers. Taf had said that it was a book, but it certainly didn't look like any book he'd ever seen. Unless it was, in fact, only a decorative piece, something which didn't have any purpose except to look pretty.

Speak to it, and it will speak to you. That was what Taf had said. Feeling just a bit silly, Hawk cleared his throat. "Hello? Are you listening? Can you hear me?"

A moment passed, then the jewels flashed in a random pattern, and the orb took on a soft internal glow.

"Hello," a voice said, coming from some source near the sculpture's base. *"Yes, I am listening. Yes, I can hear you."*

Startled, Hawk withdrew his hand from the object. The voice was neither male nor female, yet it was quiet and kind. The fact that it spoke Anglo, though, somehow didn't seem strange at all. If it was *hjadd* in origin, then it only made sense that it might know a human language.

"Hello," he said again. The *Sa'Tong-tas* didn't respond but instead seemed to wait for him to go on. "Umm . . . my name is Hawk Thompson. What are you?"

Again, the jewels flashed. *"Greetings, Hawk Thompson. I am your* Sa'Tong-tas. *Are you ready to begin?"*

Hawk blinked, not quite understanding. "Begin? Begin what?"

"To learn those things that you should know." It sounded like a patient teacher addressing a student for the first time. *"Are you ready to begin?"*

At a loss for what else to say, Hawk nodded. "Yeah . . . uhh, yes, I think so."

The orb grew a little brighter, then the *Sa'Tong-tas* spoke again. *"You are God . . ."*

The sun had long since set, with night coming upon the town, by the time Hawk put the *Sa'Tong-tas* back in its case. He carefully closed the box, then sat at the table for a little while longer, his hands at his sides. Many hours had passed since the *Sa'Tong-tas* began to speak to him, yet he'd been only barely conscious of the passage of time. From all around him, he heard the usual sounds of the tenement—the voices of his neighbors, the occasional flush of the upstairs commode, the lonesome notes of a guitar—yet they were little more than a slight distraction. All he knew for certain was that he'd learned things that he'd never known, yet which were so obvious that he marveled at the fact that they hadn't ever occurred to him.

He now knew that the *Sa'Tong-tas* was an artificial intelligence created by a miniature quantum computer, yet it was more than that. It was the voice of a system of spiritual beliefs older than human history, a way of knowledge that went far beyond religion. And even after the long session he had just finished—listening, asking questions, listening some more—he was all too aware that he'd barely scratched the surface. There was more, much more, that he still needed to learn.

Hawk looked around the room, and it was as if he was seeing it for the first time. Something had changed within him; he knew that he'd never be the same again. His job, his way of life, everything that had happened to him until today . . . unimportant, almost meaningless.

So much more to learn. So many questions, and so few answers. He wouldn't find them here, nor did he want to search for them alone.

Hawk took a deep breath, then stood up from the table. His back ached from the hours he'd spent sitting there; he took a moment to stretch, then turned and walked to the door.

As he expected, Melissa was in her apartment. Her eyes widened when she opened her door. "Hey, what's going on? I thought I heard you talking to someone, but when I knocked . . ."

"You did?" Hawk shook his head. "Sorry. Didn't hear you."

She peered at him. "You okay? You look . . . I dunno. Weird."

"I'm fine. Really, I am. It's just that . . ." He stopped. If he tried to explain what had just happened to him, she wouldn't understand. No. That would have to come later. Best to start with the most immediate problem. "I've been thinking about what you said the other day, and I think you're right. We need to leave. New Brighton, that is."

A smile stole across her face. "Y'know, I kinda thought you might come around. Yeah, sure . . . we gotta get out of this place." A pause. "So when do you . . . ?"

"Now." He hesitated. "Tonight."

Melissa stared at him, her mouth falling open in shock. "Tonight? But . . . Hawk, how . . . I mean, why . . . ?"

"I'll tell you later. It's . . . Look, it's complicated, but . . ." He let out his breath. "Now. Tonight."

For a few seconds, she didn't say anything. Then she slowly nodded. "All right . . . but we can't go right this minute. We'll have to wait until dawn." He started to say something, but she shook her head. "I know a way out of here, but I can't do anything about it until early tomorrow morning. Can you wait until then?"

"Sure, all right." Hawk was reluctant to put off leaving for so long, when every impulse told him to depart at once, but he wanted Melissa to go with him. Besides, she'd said that she knew a way to get out of town that wouldn't attract any attention. Which led to another question. "What am I going to do about . . . ?"

He held up his left hand. "That thing?" Melissa finished, and he nodded. Taking his wrist, she carefully inspected the control bracelet. "Shouldn't be too much hassle getting this off," she said at last. "I know a guy downstairs who works as a handyman. He owes me a favor"—a salacious wink—"so maybe I can borrow some tools from him. A pair of bolt cutters should do the trick."

"We'll have to wait until the last minute. If I take it off now, it'll send a signal to my parole officer. Same for the patch." That was the first time he'd thought of Joe Bairns. He didn't like the idea of betraying the one person who'd been on his side since he was released, but it went without saying that he couldn't tell Joe what he intended to do.

"Sure." Melissa didn't let go of him, though, but instead clasped his hands within her own. "What is it, Hawk-Hawk?" she asked quietly, gazing into his eyes. "What's made you change your mind?"

"I've . . . discovered something. Something very important." He caught a flash of fear in her eyes, and he quickly shook his head. "No reason to be frightened. It's just . . . something that I've got to do, and I don't want to do it alone." He paused. "Will you trust me? Please?"

"All right." Melissa nodded. "Sure. I'll trust you."

The early morning sun rose above the Great Equatorial River, dappling its dark blue waters with streaks of orange and silver. To the west, Bear was beginning to sink below the horizon, its rings touching the last fading stars. The low clouds that shrouded the night sky had begun to disappear; once they were gone, the new day promised to be bright and clear.

The fishing boat tied up at the dock gently bobbed on the morning tide, its ropes creaking against its moorings. Hawk stood quietly nearby, watching as Melissa completed her negotiations with the captain. A handful of colonials made a swift transition from her pocket to his; the older man nodded, then gestured toward his boat. Melissa looked over at Hawk and gave him a furtive nod, then reached down to pick up the hempcloth duffel bag at her feet.

Hoisting his own bag by its strap, Hawk walked down the dock to join her. "They'll get us as far as Bridgeton," she whispered as they watched the crew load their nets aboard the aft deck. "After that, we're on our own."

"Did he ask any questions?"

"Sure, he had questions." A sly smile. "A hundred colonials gave him all the answers he needed to have . . . and fifty more made sure that he's never seen us."

Hawk nodded. He knew that it wouldn't be long before Joe discovered that he was gone. Indeed, the parole officer was probably already on his way to Hawk's apartment; once he used his badge to get the landlord to unlock his door, Bairns would find the flat just as he'd last seen it, except for the severed bracelet and discarded patch lying on the table. But the dresser would be empty and a bag would be missing, and the only other evidence that Hawk had once lived there would be his customs uniform, neatly folded on his bed.

Joe was a smart guy. He'd eventually figure out how Hawk managed to leave New Brighton. But he and Melissa would have something of a head start, or at least if the captain kept his word. And even if he didn't, by the time Joe tracked them across the river to Bridgeton, the two of them would've long since left New Florida. Heading for some place where they would never be found.

The captain walked across the gangplank onto his boat. He looked around, making sure that everything was where it should be, then he turned and gave Melissa a quiet nod. "It's time," she murmured, taking Hawk's hand again. "Ready?"

"Yes," he said, and let her lead him across the plank. Finding a place to sit on the hatch cover above the live hold, they watched as ropes were untied and sails unfurled. The wind caught the sheets, billowed them outward; without any fuss, the boat slipped away from the dock.

As the fishing boat sailed out into the harbor, Hawk took a moment to gaze back at New Brighton. One last look, then he deliberately turned away from its tenements and smoke. Sitting beside him, Melissa rested her head against his shoulder.

"So," she whispered, "where are we going?"

"I don't know." Taking her hand, he gazed at the distant horizon. "We'll find out when we get there."

Part 2

WALKING STAR

(from the memoirs of Sawyer Lee)

We grow up believing that our minds are citadels, unassailable fortresses behind whose walls our thoughts are protected, unknowable to all save when we choose to open the gates of our mouths, our eyes, our hearts. Certain that ours is a separate reality, we spend our lives creating inner worlds, ones whose relationship to the true nature of things is tangential at best. We see the same things, but we perceive them differently; all we have in common, really, is a universe that we've agreed upon by consensus.

At least, this is what I once thought. Then I met Joseph Walking Star Cassidy, and nothing was ever the same again.

By the time I returned to Leeport on the last day of the seventh week of Asmodel, the springtime rainy season had begun. I'd spent the last few days in the southern half of New Florida, in the savannas of the Alabama River; three wealthy German businessmen had come to Coyote to hunt boid, and they'd hired me to be their guide. It hadn't been an easy trip; my clients had more money than sense, and none of them had ever fired a gun at anything more threatening than a hologram on a Berlin rifle range. So when I wasn't trying to keep them from tipping over our canoes or showing them how and where to set up their tents, I was worrying whether a boid would kill them instead of vice versa.

Yet we got along well enough, and on the morning of the fifth day, I'd managed to track down a boid just northwest of Miller Creek, in the equatorial grasslands where boids were known to migrate for the winter. It was only a young male, no taller than my head, nonetheless ferocious enough to give my clients their money's worth. The Germans opened fire as soon as the creature charged us from the high grass; although most of their shots went wild, enough struck home to bring it down; once I was sure that the boid was mortally wounded, I allowed Herr Heinz, the group's leader, to approach the giant avian close enough to deliver a coup de grâce to the narrow skull behind its enormous beak. After we dragged the carcass to the nearest blackwood and strung it up from a lower branch, I took the pictures that would give them bragging rights once they returned home, then we cut the boid down and everyone got feathers as souvenirs before I butchered it. Boid meat is actually rather gamey—those of us who live here eat it only when we're desperate—but it was all part of their vacation, and once I broke out another jug of bearshine, they didn't mind the taste so much.

The other two Germans wanted to stay longer, perhaps hoping they'd bag a creek cat, but I knew we were pushing our luck; where there's one boid, there are bound to be more, and the last thing I wanted was to be surrounded by a pack with tourists at my back. So I used my satphone to call for a gyro pickup—another C500 fee, not including my own surcharge—and by early evening we'd been airlifted northeast to Liberty. I settled the bill with my clients at the upscale B&B where I'd first met them, then let them take me to Lew's Cantina for some serious drinking. Truth to be told, by then I was sick and tired of their company, but experience had taught me that a little indulgence goes a long way; once they'd put away a few pints of ale, the three of them emptied their wallets and put another C300 on the table. And they even paid the bar tab.

The next morning, after I returned the canoes to the outfitter from whom I'd rented them, I hitched a ride home on a shag-team wagon hauling a load of Midland iron from Liberty to Leeport. I was exhausted by the time we rolled into town late that afternoon, but with C5,000 deposited to my account at the Bank of Coyote—minus expenses, it came to C3,000 that I could call my own—and another C300 in my pocket that the Ministry of Revenue didn't have to know about, I was solvent for another month or so. Not rich, by any means, but with luck I wouldn't have to get a real job anytime soon, so long as I didn't do something stupid like blowing a wad at the poker table.

My place was a two-room flat on Wharf Street, above a ceramics shop where in winter I had the benefit of hot air carried up through vents from their kiln. Once I put away my gear, I pumped some water into the tub and lit the heating coil. While the bath warmed up, I hid my cash within a knothole in the wall behind the dresser, then peeled off my filthy clothes. A long soak in the tub with a glass of waterfruit wine, then I dried off, pulled on a robe, and went to bed. I was asleep before I remembered to check my comp for messages.

I woke up later that evening, hungry and restless. So I trimmed my mustache and ran a pick through my hair, put on some clean clothes, and hit the town in search of a decent meal. Leeport was still a small settlement in those days—a dozen or so wood-frame-and-adobe buildings on either side of three muddy streets, a waterfront with tugboats and barges lined up at the piers—so that time of night there was little question where I was going to find dinner and a pint of ale.

Not surprisingly, the Captain's Lady was only half-empty. It was Orifiel night, after all, and Leeport was a workingman's town. Tomorrow morning, the barges would be back on the channel, the wharf lined with wagons. A handful of boatmen sitting around the hearth, warming their feet by the fire; a few more locals gathered around a nearby table, cards in hand and a modest pile of chips between them. The usual faces; a few of them looked up as I shut the door behind me, and I nodded as I hung up my jacket, then sauntered to the other side of the room. The bartender saw me coming; Hurricane Dave had already pushed a mug beneath the ale spigot by the time I reached the roughbark bar where he spent his evenings.

"Welcome back," he said, favoring me with a seldom-seen smile. "How was the trip?"

"Good 'nuff. Where's the chief?"

"Off for the night. Town business." He topped off the mug, passed it to me. "On the house. Good hunting?"

"Okay." I lifted a hand, waved it back and forth. "A little one. Made the tourists happy." The porter was black as coal, bitter as a lie; the Lady's ale came straight from the brewpots down in the cellar, which Dave tended as lovingly as if they were his own children. "Thanks, I've been waiting for this. What's on the menu tonight . . . the usual?"

"Got a fresh batch in the kitchen. Want some?"

"Only if I have to pay for it." I dug a couple of wooden dollars out of my vest pocket and dropped them on the counter. "Corn bread, too, if you've got it."

"Sure. We've got some left, I think." Yet Dave didn't leave the bar. Instead, he picked up a rag and, making a pretense of wiping down the counter, moved a little closer. "Expecting trouble?" he murmured.

Dave was a big guy, a giant even in a town full of men with a lot of muscle. His boss didn't tolerate troublemakers in her establishment, and neither did he; firearms were surrendered at the bar, and anyone caught with a knife larger than those used to clean fish were evicted at once. So if Hurricane Dave sensed a problem, it was worth taking seriously. "Not really," I said quietly. "Why do you ask?"

"Two guys, at the table behind you to your left." Dave kept his voice low, didn't look in their direction. "Came in a couple of days ago. Took a room upstairs, paid for it a week in advance. Been asking questions about you."

"Uh-huh." I felt the hair on the back of my neck begin to rise. There wasn't a mirror behind the bar; otherwise, I might have been able to sneak a peek at them. "What sort of questions?"

"Where you've been, mainly . . . also if you're reliable." Dave continued to swab the deck. "Dana's done most of the talking. She told them that you're a good guide, if that's what they're asking, and that you're out of town and she didn't know when you were getting back. Didn't let 'em know where you live, just that you drop in now and then."

"I see." Good old Dana: always watching my back. "Anything else?"

"Sure. Two more things. They wanted to know if you and her were . . . y'know. Related."

An old question, yet one I still hadn't become used to, even after all these years. There weren't very many people of African-American descent on Coyote, and sometimes I wondered if people thought we all came from the same family. "I hope she set 'em straight," I muttered, and when Dave raised an eyebrow I knew she hadn't. "Aw, hell . . . so what's the other?"

"One of them's coming over now." Dave backed away from the counter. "White chili and corn bread," he said aloud, scooping up the money I'd just put down. "Anything else, sir?"

I might have asked for the stunner he kept under the bar, just so I could have it in case this was someone's jealous boyfriend, yet that was out of the question. Dana Monroe wasn't only the proprietor of the

Captain's Lady, but also Leeport's mayor, not to mention one its found-ers. So while she and I were close friends, a brawl was the last thing she wanted in her place of business. Not good for either commerce or politics.

"No," I said, "thanks anyway." Dave nodded and headed for the kitchen. I picked up my mug and took another sip of ale while I waited for someone to ask my name.

"Pardon me, sir," a deep voice said a moment later, "are you Sawyer Lee?" And that was how it all began.

The guy who'd come up behind me was only slightly smaller than Hurricane Dave, with long blond hair pulled back in a ponytail and a thick beard. I wondered how I could have missed seeing him; perhaps I was more tired than I thought.

"You've found him," I said. "May I help you?"

"Yes, sir, you can." His voice was surprisingly mild; despite his size, there was nothing menacing about him. "I have someone with me who'd like to speak to you, if you don't mind."

"Sure." I nodded toward the beaded curtain through which Dave had just disappeared. "I just ordered dinner. If your friend wants to come over here . . ."

"He'd like to speak to you alone, please. At our table." He paused. "If that's inconvenient just now, we'll gladly wait until you've finished your meal."

Jealous beaus are never so polite, and this bloke could have easily wrenched my arm behind my back and frog-marched me wherever he pleased. Instead, he was giving me the option of eating in peace before attending to whatever business his friend had in mind. Not only that, but apparently the guys had been patiently waiting for me to reappear in Leeport, to the point of renting an upstairs room and staking out the tavern for the last two nights. And Dana's accommodations don't come cheap; she provides soap with a bath and even changes the bedsheets three times a week.

I decided to take a chance. "No, no . . . I can have dinner over there just as well as over here, Mr. . . . um?"

"Kennedy." A dour nod. "If you'll follow me, please . . . ?"

As he led me across the room to his table, a few people I knew in the place gave me curious looks. One of them was George Waite, a tugboat operator who'd carried me and my clients as passengers on more than one occasion. He was having a drink with his nephew, Donny; the boy ignored us, yet I couldn't help but notice the cautious expression on George's face. I gave him a brief nod, and he reciprocated with one of his own, and in this way a silent understanding was reached: if there was trouble, he'd back me up. That's the way things are out on the frontier; friends look out for each other, particularly when strangers are involved.

The other man seated at the table had his back turned to the room. Despite the warmth of the nearby fireplace, he wore a dark blue travel cloak, its hood pulled up over his head. Clearly, he didn't want his face to be seen. He stood up as we approached, and I saw that he was a small man, no taller than my shoulder, middle-aged and thickset. Yet it wasn't until he pushed back his hood that I recognized him.

"Mr. Lee?" he said quietly, holding out his hand. "Good evening. I'm Morgan Goldstein."

If St. Nicholas had suddenly appeared in the Captain's Lady, I wouldn't have been more surprised.

There was no one on Coyote who didn't know his name. The founder and CEO of Janus Ltd., Morgan Goldstein had been one of the richest men on Earth even before his company managed to negotiate a near monopoly on hyperspace shipping rights to 47 Ursae Majoris; since then, he'd become even more wealthy, if that was possible. Over the last couple of years, he'd relocated his business from North America to Coyote, where he'd established a sizable estate just outside New Brighton.

Yet Goldstein hadn't been content with merely having more money than anyone else; two years ago, he'd run for president of the Coyote Federation. His defeat by the incumbent, Wendy Gunther, in a second-term bid for office, apparently settled his political ambitions. Since then, he'd retreated to his manor; according to the *Liberty Post*, he was underwriting a major expedition to the unexplored regions, and rumor had it that he was trying to negotiate a trade deal with the *hjadd*. Although he occasionally emerged for one public event or another, lately he'd become something of a recluse. We heard a lot about him, but no one ever saw his face.

And now, here he was, nursing a pint of ale in a beat-up cantina halfway between somewhere and nowhere. It took me a moment to unglue my tongue. "Pleased to meet you, Mr. . . . ."

"Roth" He lowered his voice as I grasped his hand. "So far as anyone here knows, my name's Irving Roth." He grinned as he sat down again. "I like this town. Everyone minds their own business."

"It's a nice place." I took a chair across the table from him. Kennedy moved behind me to take the chair between us. "I understand you've been looking for me."

Goldstein raised an eyebrow. "How did you . . . ?"

"Pardon me." Unnoticed until that moment, Hurricane Dave placed a bowl of white chili and a plate of corn bread on the table in front of me. "That it? Want another drink?"

"No, thanks." I pointed to Goldstein, then Kennedy. "You? How about you?" Goldstein had already raised his hood again, and Kennedy silently shook his head. "We're fine, Dave. Thanks."

"What is that stuff?" Goldstein peered at my meal. "I saw it on the chalkboard, but I didn't ask . . ."

"White chili. Made from chicken, not beef." I picked up a spoon, stirred the grated onions and goat cheese on top. "Try it. House specialty. So what brings you here, Mr. Roth?"

"A job." Goldstein settled back in his chair, clasped his hands together in his lap. "But first things first. I understand you're a professional wilderness guide, Mr. Lee . . ."

"Uh-huh. Best in the business." Not to mention almost the only one in the business. True, Susan Gunther and Jonathan Parson had their

Coyote Expeditions outfit in Liberty, as a sideline to Susan's teaching job at the university, but they specialized in camera safaris and refused to take hunters. I liked them well enough; nonetheless, we had a certain difference of opinion. They saw boids as an endangered species, while I saw any creature that could disembowel me with one swipe of its claws as a danger only to me and my clients. So if you wanted to take pictures of a boid from the safety of an armored skimmer, you hired Sue and Jon; if you wanted to take home its head, I was the man you went to see.

"So I've heard." Goldstein watched while I dipped my spoon into the chili. "I've also heard that you've gone north . . . across the Highland Channel, up to Medsylvania."

"A couple of years ago." The chili was hot and spicy, just the way I liked it. I reached for my ale. "I once led a group from the university up there. We spent a week or so mapping the southern peninsula."

"Find anything interesting?"

"Not really. Mainly forest. The trees are a bit taller . . . different species of roughbark, with faux birch as the understory. Other than that . . ." I shrugged. "Swamp. Ball plants. Creek cats and swampers. Seen one, seen 'em all."

"Uh-huh." Goldstein smiled. "You don't sound very impressed, considering . . ."

"Considering what?"

"From what you've told me, you've visited a part of this world few people have seen, yet it seems to have made no more of an impression on you than . . . well, the compost heap out back."

"It's my business. After a while, it all begins to look the same." It wasn't quite true; there were places, like the view of Mt. Bonestell from the Gillis Range, that still took my breath away. But the people who usually hired me as a guide were never interested in seeing these beauties; more often than not, I found myself babysitting rich tourists who just wanted to shoot a boid or a creek cat. For them, it was a rich man's thrill. For me, it was something that paid the bills and kept me in ale without demanding that I find honest work.

"Uh-uh. Of course." Goldstein sipped his beer. He remained quiet for a minute or so, giving me a chance to eat. I welcomed the silence; no one made chili like Dave. I was working my way to the bottom of the bowl when Goldstein spoke up again. "I understand you may be related to Captain Lee . . . Are you?"

I hated it whenever someone mentioned this. Captain Robert E. Lee—himself a descendant of the Confederate Army general of the American Civil War—was nearly as famous as his namesake, for being the commanding officer of the URSS *Alabama*, the first starship to reach the 47 Uma. There's a life-size statue of him in front of Government House in Liberty, but you'd have to look hard to detect any family resemblance. Quite a few generations separate him from me, but I rather doubt any of my ancestors married into his family. My kin left the United Republic of America just after the Liberty Party took over, and watched the old country go to hell from the safety of Switzerland.

"I don't think so." I put down my spoon and reached for a napkin. "There's a lot of people who claim they're related to Captain Lee . . . or General Lee, for that matter . . . but I've never made that assertion." Not deliberately, at least.

"Aren't you curious?" Goldstein raised an eyebrow. "If you're a descendant, I mean."

"Not really." I wiped my mouth, tossed the napkin on top of the bowl. "He was before my time. So far as I know, we've got nothing in common."

Not entirely true. Once I migrated to Coyote aboard one of the first ESA ships to carry passengers through the starbridge, it wasn't long before I made my way to Leeport. My first night here, I met Dana Monroe; I was trying to gamble my way to passage aboard a boat bound for Great Dakota and made the mistake of trying to hide an ace of spades up my sleeve. Another guy at the table caught me, and that was when I learned that card cheats weren't tolerated in Leeport. Dana saved my skin; using her authority as mayor, she hauled me into the kitchen and put me to work washing dishes until I earned enough money to cover my civil fine.

That was when I discovered why the place was called the Captain's Lady. Dana Monroe had been the chief engineer aboard the *Alabama*; indeed, there was a torn piece of metal mounted above the fireplace that had once belonged to the ship, recovered from its wreckage on Hammerhead. But it went further than that; Chief Monroe was Captain Lee's partner in the last years of his life, and although they'd never been formally married, she still carried a torch for her man.

So there I was, some guy from Earth so down on his luck that he'd try to cheat at poker just to buy his way aboard a tugboat to a place where he might get a job at a sawmill, only to have his fortune change when he met a woman who was the former lover of a legend. A legend with whom I shared a last name. One of the great regrets of Dana's life was that she and Captain Lee never had any children; although she never came right out and said so, I became the son she didn't have. I was almost the right age, after all, and since there weren't too many other dark-skinned people on Coyote, that only tended to strengthen our bond.

So this was how I came to live in Leeport, and why the Captain's Lady was a second home to me. I never called Dana my mother, and she never called me her son, but the relationship was nearly the same. And once I became a safari guide, willing to escort visitors into the wilderness for a fee, I discovered that having the surname of Coyote's most famous figure worked to my advantage. It helped attract clients, and I couldn't fool myself by believing that the reason why I had an extra $C300$ in my cubbyhole wasn't because three guys could go home to Germany and claim that they'd gone boid-hunting with a possible descendant of Captain Lee.

But that sort of secondhand fame can also be a curse. As I looked across the table at Morgan Goldstein, I saw from the look in his eyes that he was expecting more than I could deliver. Although I didn't yet know what he wanted from me, Goldstein wasn't some rube looking for a stuffed boid head to hang above his fireplace.

"Perhaps. Perhaps not. Mike . . . ?" He pointed to my half-empty mug, then made a gesture to Kennedy. Without a word, his aide—or maybe he was Goldstein's bodyguard—left us, marching across the room to the bar. "Regardless, I have great need of an experienced guide. Someone who can take me to Medsylvania."

"Hunting?"

"Yes . . . but not for animals. For a person." A pause. "A friend, to be exact. His name's Joe Cassidy . . . Joseph Walking Star Cassidy."

Kennedy returned to the table with two fresh mugs of porter. Goldstein took a drink, smiled. "One nice thing about coming all the way out here . . . best ale on Coyote." I nodded, hoping that he didn't like it so much that he got it in his mind to buy the place. Noting my impatience, he put down his mug. "Joe came with me from Earth, where he'd worked for me for many years as my equerry." I raised an eyebrow, and he added, "Stable master. Someone who takes care of horses."

"Gotcha." One of the first things that brought Goldstein to the attention of everyone on Coyote was his gift to the colonies of his private collection of horses. Forty-eight in all, everything from Arabians and Percherons to quarter horses and donkeys: breeding stock, possibly the last herd of its size left in existence. He'd given most of the horses to the different settlements, with the stipulation that they would be treated well and allowed to have offspring. Horses had become nearly extinct on Earth, and it was Morgan's intent that, by introducing them to Coyote, they'd have a chance to survive; yet he'd reserved a half dozen or so for himself, which he continued to raise on his estate. "Go on," I said.

"Joe was. . . . is . . . an employee, but . . ." Morgan hesitated. "Well, over the years I've come to consider him a friend. He's something of the last of the breed himself. Full-blooded Navajo, and a shaman at that. His people were scattered when climate change caused the reservation to become uninhabitable, and Joe made his way up to New England. I was looking for someone to take care of my horses, and . . ."

He shrugged. "I suppose we were meant to find each other. Neither of us ever had much in the way of a family, and Joe always made it clear to me that he didn't give a damn how much money I had, it was the fact that I cared so much about horses that mattered. So I took crap from him that I would have fired anyone else for saying, and he let me know when he thought I was wrong about something, and . . . well, I guess you can figure out the rest."

And indeed I did. In my line of work, I'd seen my share of rich and powerful men, enough to know that extreme wealth bears a curse of its own: you never know for certain who's really your friend, and who's just kissing your butt so that they can keep their seat on the gravy train. If Cassidy was as sincere as Morgan Goldstein made him out to be, then he was as rare as the horses he tended.

"And you say he's missing," I said. "Why do you think he went to . . . ?"

"Let me finish." Goldstein lifted one finger from the handle of his mug, a subtle-yet-imperious gesture that had probably intimidated entire boardrooms. "As I said, Joe has a mystical streak in him. Now, I don't know for sure if what he told me about himself is true . . . that he comes from a long line of Navajo medicine men, that he talks to the spirits and they talk back to him . . . and I've never had much use for religion of any kind, but he believes it, and that's been fine with me. When we had the estate in Massachusetts, he built a sweat lodge on the property, and from time to time he'd go there to commune with the gods, that sort of thing. I tried to talk to him about it, but that was one part of himself that he always kept closed to me. And I let him, because . . ."

"Because it was none of your business."

"Exactly." Morgan picked up his mug again, took another sip. "I even knew that he'd cultivated peyote, in flowerpots in a corner of the greenhouse where my gardener raised roses. Duncan was rather upset when he found them, and wanted to rip them up, but I forbid him to do so, because I knew that they belonged to Joe and that he used them for . . . y'know, spiritual reasons."

"That's interesting, but I don't know why . . ."

"Let me continue, please." Again, a cold stare. Goldstein was someone who didn't tolerate interruptions. "When we relocated my estate to New Brighton, I let Joe build another hogan so that he could continue his practices. I think he might have brought some peyote seeds with him . . . in fact, I'm sure he did . . . but something happened, and he was unable to cultivate any plants."

I wasn't surprised. Although most of the crops humankind had attempted to introduce to this world had been successful, there had also been notable failures. Coyote's long seasons had much to do with it; although our springs and summers collectively lasted for a year and a half by Earth reckoning, so did our autumns and winters. Corn and bamboo did well, for instance, but tubers like carrots and potatoes were notoriously finicky. The hardier strains of apples and peaches were able to withstand cold snaps, but citrus fruits like oranges and grapefruit were nearly impossible to grow even in the equatorial regions. Native predators and plant diseases also took their toll; grasshoarders loved turnips and soybeans, it was very difficult to keep strawberries clean of fungus, and apiarists had to find and import bees aggressive enough not to be massacred by pseudowasps.

"But Joe needed something to assist him in his meditation," Goldstein continued, "so he began to look around." He sighed, started to pick up his mug again, then put it down without taking a drink. "He found . . ."

"Sting." For the first time since he'd approached me at the bar, Mike Kennedy spoke up. I'd almost forgotten he was there; he sat between me and Goldstein, and although his expression was as stoical as before, his eyes were glacial. "He started using sting."

Goldstein glared at him. "Mike . . ."

"C'mon, boss. I knew about it before you did." The bodyguard reached for a piece of corn bread on my plate. "So did everyone else. He got into that stuff like there was no—"

"I know that," Goldstein said angrily. "But what I still don't understand is why you didn't tell me."

Kennedy shrugged and said nothing, looking away as if it were some minor detail he'd neglected to mention to his employer. Yet I knew exactly where he was coming from. He and Joe Cassidy had one thing in common; they both drew their paychecks from the same source. And only a fink rats out the other guy to the head man, particularly when it comes to drugs.

And sting was pretty powerful stuff. I mentioned pseudowasps: large flying insects that nested within ball plants, the large spherical plant that grew in abundance in grasslands and marshes across most of Coyote's western hemisphere. Indeed, ball plants and pseudowasps formed part of an interesting symbiosis. Swampers, the ferretlike creatures that inhabited those same areas, hibernated within the ball plants during the winter; the weak and old perished during that period and decomposed within the plant's hollow core, thus supplying nutrients. Pseudowasps built their nests within the plant's tough outer shell; they protected the swampers by attacking potential predators who might try to get an easy meal by ripping open the inner cell, and also the insects pollinated the plants. That was why pseudowasps went after bee colonies; they saw them as natural competitors.

Sting was derived from pseudowasp venom. Containing a natural hallucinogen similar to mescaline, it wasn't fatal, but instead made animals like creek cats and boids so confused that they simply forgot what they were doing and wandered off, while lower forms of insects were so paralyzed that the pseudowasps were able to feed upon them while they were still alive. For humans, though, the effect was more pronounced; the original *Alabama* colonists stung by pseudowasps staggered around like happy drunks, with some having hallucinations. After that, they learned to avoid ball plants, particularly during the autumn and spring seasons, when the pseudowasps tended to be most active.

Yet once more settlers arrived on Coyote aboard the Western Hemisphere Union ships that followed the *Alabama*, someone discovered how to trap pseudowasps by dropping a sticky-net, like those used by Union Guard troops, over the ball plants. Once the insects exhausted themselves and died, it was possible to extract them from the nets and, with careful use of a pair of surgical forceps, crush their bodies until the venom seeped from their sacs. It was a slow and painstaking process, to be sure, but it yielded a quarter centimeter or two of fluid that, once diluted with sugar water, gave everyone who put it on his tongue a cheap high that would last for hours.

That was sting, as it was commonly called. It had been made illegal long before I came to Coyote, but that never stopped it from being sold or bartered on the black market. I'd tried it once, for the bloody hell of it, but didn't like it very much; when an old girlfriend stuck her head up from the ground and asked if I wanted to come down for a quick screw, that was enough fun for one night. There were stingheads all over Coyote; the stuff wasn't supposed to be addictive, but you can't tell me that people didn't become psychologically dependent upon it . . . and there was nothing worse than seeing some poor fool clawing at the walls and screaming that he'd seen his mother coming for him with a knife between her teeth.

"Never mind." Goldstein looked away from his bodyguard, turned his attention back to me. "Fact is, Joe started using sting. I don't think he meant to use it as . . . as dope, I mean . . . but rather as a substitute for peyote. All the same, though . . ."

"He got whacked on the stuff." Kennedy didn't try to hide his contempt. "He dropped it whenever he could . . ."

"Mike . . ." Again, there was a note of warning in Goldstein's voice. Kennedy shut up, and his boss went on. "I didn't know what was happening at first, but when I did . . ."

He absently ran a hand across his hairless head. "I told him that I couldn't have someone on my staff who was abusing drugs. He argued, of course, that his reasons for using it were spiritual, that he wasn't doing it just to get high, but I couldn't accept that. There was too much evidence that he was taking sting whenever possible . . ."

"Such as?"

"I first realized that he was using it when people started coming to the estate that I'd never met before. Friends of his, whom he'd met in New Brighton. One or two of them were suppliers, others were just . . ." He sighed. "Lowlifes. Scum. Immigrants who'd come here without any plans, just trying to get by however they could."

I bristled a bit when he said that, for he was describing guys like me. One thing that frequently ticks me off about the wealthy is that they often don't realize that not everyone has a burning ambition to acquire money and material possessions. Ever since the starbridge opened, more people were arriving every month; most were simply trying to flee their ruined homelands on Earth and didn't have any plans other than getting by as best as they could, one day at a time. The rich don't understand this; unless someone has made it his or her mission in life to die with more toys than anyone else, then he or she is a deadbeat.

Goldstein didn't notice that he'd just insulted me, but Kennedy did. His face remained stolid, yet his eyes briefly rolled upward. "Anyway," Goldstein went on, "Joe and I had a long talk, and we eventually agreed that he needed to take some time off. I knew that the university medical school had recently started a drug-treatment program, so I told him that

I'd put money in his account to pay for him to travel to Shuttlefield and get help. Joe said he'd do it, and a few days later he caught a gyro to New Florida."

He ran a fingertip around the rim of his mug. "When a few weeks went by, and I hadn't heard anything from him, I called the university, and that's when I discovered that Joe had never checked in. So I called the bank, and found out that he'd dissolved his account at the branch in Liberty, taking out all the money I'd put in, plus his own earnings."

"I imagine you were rather upset."

"To put it mildly, yes." The lines around his mouth tightened. "But more than that, I was concerned about what he was doing to himself. Understand, I like Joe. As I said before, I've always regarded him as being more of a friend than an employee . . . and from what I could tell, he was in trouble."

"When did all this happen?"

"Last Barchiel . . . a little more than two months ago." Like everyone else born and bred on Earth, I mentally made the conversion from Gregorian to LeMarean calendars. Approximately 190 days, give or take a couple of weeks: the middle of winter. "To make a long story short, I put some people I knew on Joe's trail and found that he met up with several people in Liberty . . . some of whom were the same guys he'd met earlier in New Brighton . . . and together they'd hired a boat to take them to New Boston."

"All the way up there?" That surprised me. Aside from Fort Lopez, New Boston was the most remote colony of the Federation, located on the northern coast of Midland. No one went there in wintertime unless they absolutely had to do so. "Why?"

"From what I've learned, Joe and his friends stayed just long enough to buy food and supplies, then they hired a boat to carry them across the Medsylvania Channel." Goldstein picked up his mug again, took another sip without any of his previous pleasure. "After that, the trail goes cold."

"So I take it that you want me to go up there and find him."

"No. I want you to take me up there, so I can find him." He gave a sidelong glance at Kennedy. "My associate will only be going part of the way, assuming that our first stop will be New Boston. Apparently he has no desire to assure himself that his colleague is alive and well."

"Sorry, boss," Kennedy rumbled. "My job description doesn't cover chasing junkies."

Not very sympathetic, although I wasn't sure that I blamed him. People like Joe Cassidy made disappearing acts like that all the time on Coyote. Most were would-be frontiersmen, harboring ill-conceived fantasies of going into the wilderness with little more than a backpack, a tent, and a hand ax; sometimes they succeeded at homesteading, but more often than not they simply vanished, never to be seen again. Others were holy fools, believing that Coyote had some mystical powers that would bring enlightenment. A gravesite just below the summit of Mt. Shaw on Midland held the bones of the members of the Church of Universal Transformation, who went cannibal when they were trapped on the mountain during a winter storm.

I didn't know if either fate had befallen Joe Cassidy and his friends, nor was I eager to find out. In fact, I was still getting over my latest trip. But clients like Morgan Goldstein don't fall from the sky; if I played my cards right, I could stand to make enough money to last me until summer.

"Five grand up front," I said, "and another three grand for expenses . . . not including a gyro ride to New Boston."

Goldstein didn't even blink. "Fair enough . . . but no gyro. I want to go by boat, all the way." He caught the puzzled look on my face. "Not many gyros fly to New Boston, I'm told . . . and if Joe's just across the channel, he'd see one coming. I don't want him to be expecting me."

"If you say so." I turned my head to look at George Waite. As I expected, he'd leaned back in his chair, pretending not to eavesdrop but doing so nonetheless. George caught my eye, gave me a sly grin; he knew a lucrative deal when he saw it coming. I turned back to Goldstein. "I think that can be arranged."

"I thought so." He hadn't missed the silent exchange between me and George. Goldstein polished off his drink, then pushed back his chair. "See you here tomorrow morning, Mr. Lee," he said, reaching into his pocket to toss a handful of colonials on the table. "I hope your reputation for reliability is well earned."

I hoped it was, too.

We left Leeport early the next morning, as passengers aboard the *Helen Waite.*

Before I met Goldstein and Kennedy again, I went down to the wharf and negotiated passage with her captain. George was a buddy, so I held nothing back from him; I told him that my client was none other than Morgan Goldstein, and that although we were heading for New Boston, our destination would be somewhere in Medsylvania. As it turned out, George had already intended to go to New Boston; three barges of coal were waiting for him up there, for shipment to Clarksburg farther south. I wasn't surprised when he told me that he'd recognized Goldstein, nor was I particularly shocked when he hit me up for a larger fee than usual. C1,000 for the three of us was steep, but George knew the money wasn't coming from my pocket; in return, he agreed to wait a few days for us in New Boston and continue to pretend that one of his passengers was named Irving Roth.

I'd packed equipment for both of us, but once I rendezvoused with Goldstein at the Captain's Lady, I discovered Goldstein had brought his own gear. Although I was pleased that he'd come prepared, some of his stuff was unnecessary; the brand-new solar tents and particle-beam rifles were fine, but I made him leave behind the portable hydrogen-cell stove, the infrared motion-detection system, and the seven-day supply of freeze-dried rations, telling him that, unless he wanted to carry all that junk on his back, he'd do just as well living off the land. He argued with me, of course, but I put my foot down, and he reluctantly agreed to put the extra equipment in storage at the Captain's Lady until we returned.

Just before we left, I linked my pad with his and downloaded C5,000 into my private account. George did the same, taking C1,000 for passage to New Boston. Goldstein performed the transactions with scarcely a blink: more evidence that the rich have different lives than mere mortals. Kennedy and I shared another glance—he was accustomed to this sort of free spending and was quietly amused that I wasn't—then I shepherded him and Goldstein aboard the *Helen Waite*. Donny untied us from the pier. George yanked twice on the cord of the steam whistle, and the tugboat chugged out of the Leeport harbor.

The journey to New Boston took two days. The first leg of the trip was spent traveling upstream along the West Channel to the northern tip of New Florida; we dropped anchor overnight at Red Point, the mouth of North Creek where, ten Coyote years ago, Carlos Montero had led his team from Midland on the morning of Liberation Day. All had gone well until then, but the *Helen Waite* was meant more for hauling barges than passengers; its cabin had only three racks, and those were occupied by George, Donny, and Jose, the retarded man whose job it was to shovel coal into the tugboat's steam engines. It took a lot of talking for me to get it through to Goldstein that, as passengers, our accommodations were little more than a tarp stretched across the aft deck, and his money didn't cover anything more than this.

Goldstein grumbled about the arrangements, going so far as to try to bribe Jose into giving up his bunk. George put a stop to that, though, and he finally had to resign himself to sleeping out in the open. I did my best not to smile; it was time that Morgan Goldstein got used to the absence of luxury. Once we had dinner in the pilothouse, he retired to his sleeping bag, complaining to the moment that he finally fell asleep, while the rest of us stayed up for a while to share a bottle of wine and watch Bear rise to the east, its silver rings reflecting upon the cold, black waters of the delta.

The following day we crossed the confluence of the West and East Channels and entered the Medsylvania Channel. To our right lay the northern coast of Midland, the lower steppes of the Gillis Range just visible on the southeastern horizon; to our left, on the far side of the broad channel, lay Medsylvania, its rocky shores and dense forests dark and forbidding. That far north, winter still lingered, yet with spring approaching, the snow was beginning to melt. Boulder-sized chunks of ice, carried downstream from the North Circumpolar River, bobbed

along the channel like miniature icebergs, making the passage treacher-
ous. George hugged the Midland coast as much as possible, keeping the
engines at one-third throttle; Donny stood at the bow, calling out to his
uncle whenever the boat came too close to some ice, yet even so there
were occasional bumps and scrapes as the hull collided with something
that came up too fast for George to dodge.

It was slow going, and so we didn't reach New Boston until almost
twilight. I'd been there only a few times in the past, and never by choice.
The most northern of Coyote's settlements, it was also the most remote;
its closest neighbor on Midland was Defiance, nearly fifteen hundred
miles away on the other side of the Gillis Range. Like Leeport, New Boston was a river town, a shipping port for the coal, nickel, and iron mines
located farther inland, yet even Leeport was a bustling metropolis com-
pared to this lonely place. As the *Helen Waite* chugged into the shallow
harbor, I saw lights gleaming within the windows of log houses and
wood-frame buildings and heard the low gong of the lighthouse bell as
the watchman signaled our arrival.

"Hope you have a place to stay." George twisted the wheel to follow
the harbormaster's lamp to the nearest available slot in the pier. "Me
and the boys are sleeping aboard."

"Uh-huh. I've always had good luck with the Revolution . . ."

"Why are you staying aboard?" Goldstein stood next to us in the pilothouse, leaning against the railing. "You said you were going to pick
up coal . . . Why not sleep in a decent bed while you're here?"

"No, thanks. We'll stay on the boat."

"I insist." Reaching into his jacket pocket, Goldstein produced a money
clip stuffed with enough colonials to plug a leak in the hull. "You've done
well by us. Let me make it up to you."

Once again, George and I exchanged a glance. "Put that away, Mr.
Roth," the captain said. "First, we're going ashore tonight just long
enough to get a bite to eat. So far as accommodations are concerned . . .
I appreciate the offer, but there's nothing in town much better than
what we have here. Second, this isn't . . . shall we say, the safest place to
be." He nodded toward Kennedy, who stood silently beside his boss. "If
I were you," he added, "I'd keep your friends close and your money even
closer, if y'know what I mean."

"I . . ."

"Do what he says." I gave Goldstein a hard look. "You hired me to be your guide. So let me do my job, all right?"

"Of course. Certainly." The wad disappeared as quickly as it had appeared. Kennedy handed him his cloak; he pulled it on, tugging the hood over his head. Once again, Morgan Goldstein became Irving Roth, an anonymous traveler. Or so I hoped.

Once we tied up at the pier and George paid the harbormaster, we went into town, leaving Jose behind to watch the boat. Fish-oil lamps illuminated our way along the muddy main street; potholes covered by thin skeins of ice crunched softly beneath our boots. The evening air was cool, warmed by the aroma of fish and herbs, boiled meat and tobacco. Kiosks lined both sides of the street, their tables offering skins, handmade jewelry, liniments, secondhand electronics. Prostitutes and hard-eyed men lingered in doorways, watching us as we passed by.

The Revolution Inn was located a couple of blocks from the waterfront, a ramshackle two-story building that looked as if it had been hammered together by a crew of drunk carpenters. Which probably wasn't far from the truth; despite the patriotic name, the Revolution was little more than a beat-up tavern, with sawdust on the floor and benches in front of a fireplace half-filled with ash and soot. There were a few guest rooms upstairs, and although they were most commonly used by the local hookers, they'd do for the night.

Once I paid the barkeep for two rooms, we parked ourselves at a vacant table in the corner. Dinner was creek-crab stew, watery and undercooked; one bite, and Morgan pushed aside his plate, muttering that he'd rather go hungry. I distracted myself by studying the crowd. It was early evening, and already the place was full: fishermen, farmers, a handful of loggers and miners who'd come down from the mountains for a night on the town. I polished off my stew—it was wretched, but since it was probably the last hot meal I'd have for a few days, I made myself eat it—then left the table and wandered over to the bar, ostensibly to buy a drink but really to ferret out some information.

It didn't take long for me to find out what I needed to know. The barkeep remembered Joe Cassidy, all right; he'd come through town about two months ago, along with seven other people: four men and three women. They'd stayed in New Boston just long enough to buy supplies, then they hired a local boatman to ferry them across the channel to Medsylvania. As luck would have it, the same boatman was at a table on the other side of the room; at first he pretended not to recall who I was talking about, but the jug of bearshine I bought for him and his cronies helped restore his memory. Sure, he remembered those people . . . and for a modest fee of *C*200, he'd be happy to give me and my friend Mr. Roth a ride to the exact place where he'd dropped them off.

Something about me must have smelled like money. Either that, or I'd spent too much time lately with rich people. We dickered for a bit, and finally agreed that he'd get fifty colonials up front, and the rest once our feet touched dry land on the other side of the channel. I went back to our table and reported what I'd learned.

Goldstein wasn't happy with the arrangement. "Two hundred for a lift across the channel?" he muttered, glaring at me from across the table. "Hell, we could buy our own canoe for that kind of money."

"Sure, we can . . . but what would we do with it?" I took a drink of ale. "This guy knows exactly where he put off Joe and his pals. Chances are, they're not far from that spot. Without knowing that, though, we could wander up and down the coast for weeks and not find them."

Goldstein considered this for a moment, then turned to George. "Mr. Waite, if you knew where to go . . . that is, if we were to get directions from this fellow Sawyer just met . . . ?"

"Not a chance." George shook his head. "Sorry, but I'm not about to risk my boat trying to make landfall on a shore that doesn't have a deep harbor. *Helen* draws too much water for that sort of thing."

"I'll pay you . . ."

"Uh-uh." He picked up his mug. "Nice to make your acquaintance, Mr. Roth, but this is as far as I go." George looked at me again. "I'll wait until Camael"—by this he meant four days from now—"for you to do your business, but if I haven't heard from you by then, we're going to have to cut you loose. My people in Clarksburg are waiting for their coal, and every day I hang around here means that I lose money."

"I understand. Thanks for being willing to wait." I looked at Goldstein again. "So there it is, Morgan . . . Mr. Roth, I mean." He blanched when I said his real name; George and Donny pretended not to notice.

"Either we take our chances with that guy over there, or George carries us back home. Your call."

Goldstein scowled, then slowly let out his breath. "You know I don't have a choice," he said quietly. "Mike . . . ?"

"I'll stay here." Kennedy was the only one at the table who seemed to like creek-crab stew; he was working on his second helping. Meeting Goldstein's gaze, he went on. "Look, chief, Joe and I never got along. That's a fact. If I go with you, he'll just get pissed off when he sees me. You've got a satphone. If you run into any trouble, you call me and I'll come to the rescue."

Goldstein seemed so hesitant that, for a moment, I thought he was going to abort the rest of the trip. The place had clearly given him the willies—not that I blamed him—and for the first time, I think, he'd come to realize exactly what it meant to leave behind even a rough excuse for civilization and venture into the wilderness. The temptation must have been great: abandon Cassidy to whatever uncertain fate had befallen him, pay George for return passage to Leeport, then retreat to the comforts of his estate, where he could play with his horses and spend his free time making even more money.

Yet there was something within him that simply wouldn't let this go. For better or worse, he had to see this through. Joseph Walking Star Cassidy was his friend . . . perhaps his only friend. Like it or not, he couldn't give up.

"We'll do it," he murmured. "Dammit, we'll do it."

Without another word, he pushed back his chair, stood up, and marched across the room to the stairs. He left so suddenly that it took Kennedy a moment to remember his duty; he quickly left the table, following his boss upstairs. I wondered if his job included tucking in the boss's bedsheets and singing him a lullaby.

George watched them go, then quietly shook his head. "Sawyer, I appreciate the work, and you won't hear me complain about the money . . . but if you ever bring aboard someone like that again . . ."

"I hear you, man." And indeed, I was beginning to have second thoughts about the entire business.

The boatman's name was Merle—no last name, or at least none that he was willing to give me; "Just call me Merle," he said—and his craft was a single-masted pirogue that he used to inspect the trotlines he'd rigged along the Midland side of the channel. Once Goldstein and I loaded our gear aboard, we cast off from the dock, with the boatman and me using the oars until we were clear of the harbor, at which point he unfurled the sail and set out across the channel.

It had rained during the night; a dense fog lay low and thick upon the water, making it difficult to see more than a few dozen yards ahead. Yet the boatman knew the channel well; he steered between the ice floes, tacking against the cool morning breeze that drifted up the river. At first he said little to us, but after a while he began to ask questions: who were we and why were we so interested in finding the guys he'd carried over to Medsylvania last Barchiel. I told Just-Call-Me-Merle that my name was Just-Call-Me-Sawyer and my friend was Just-Call-Me-Irving, and the rest was none of his business. He got the message and shut up after that.

It took a little more than an hour to cross the channel, but much longer than that to reach the place where he'd dropped off Walking Star and his companions. It turned out to be the mouth of a narrow creek, about sixty miles southwest of New Boston; the *Helen Waite* had cruised by it only yesterday. Yet George wouldn't have been able to take his craft safely that way even if we'd known of its existence; as we glided closer, I caught sight of jagged rocks just beneath the pirogue's flat keel. The tugboat would have run aground.

Merle lowered the sail and unshipped the oars once more, and we paddled the rest of the way to shore. We beached the pirogue just above the creek; Merle remained in his boat, not lifting a finger to help us as Goldstein and I unloaded our packs, waded through the ice-cold water, and hauled them to the rocky shore.

"You sure this is the right place?" I asked.

"Yessir. Right on this very spot, that's where I left 'em." Merle had produced a tobacco pouch from his jacket; as he spoke, he pulled out a chaw and tucked it into his right cheek. "Last time I saw 'em," he said, pointing to the tree line a few yards away, "they were headed . . ." He hesitated, then grinned. "Y'know, I think I done forgot."

I glanced at Goldstein. He reached into his jacket, pulled out his money clip, and counted out C150. I coughed; he scowled and added another C50. "Yeah, I think I remember now," Merle said as he took the money. "Right thataway, through those trees." He pointed to the thicket of faux birch that formed the tree line just a few yards from the riverbank. "That's as much as I know."

"Thanks." Wading ashore, I picked up my pack. "You got a satphone code in case we need a pickup?"

"Yup." Merle spit brown fluid into the river. "Nancy Oscar two-two-three-niner. If my ol' lady picks up, ask for me. Just call me . . ."

"Merle. Got it. Thanks for the ride."

"Think nothing of it." Merle thrust an oar into the water and shoved off. "Good luck," he called back, then he sidestroked until the prow of his boat was pointed back the way we'd come.

"Think he was being honest with us?" Goldstein was seated on a nearby boulder; he'd taken off his boots and opened his pack, and was in the process of exchanging his waterlogged socks for a dry pair. "He could have dropped us off anywhere, you know."

"He could, but what's the point?" I didn't mind hiking in wet socks—they'd dry out soon enough—so I hoisted my pack and settled its straps upon my shoulders. "He knows better than to lie to us."

"Why . . . ?"

"Because people out here in the boonies play it straight, Mr. Goldstein. Word gets around that you're a liar, then no one trusts you anymore . . . and when the chips are down, that kind of trust is more precious than all the money you've got in the bank." As I spoke, I was scanning the tall grass between us and the tree line. "Of course, you already know that, don't you?"

He said nothing, only grunted as he relaced his boots. Once again, I doubted that Morgan Goldstein had seen much more of Coyote than what he'd viewed from the windows of a gyro. After fifty Earth-years of human colonization, almost two-thirds of the planet was unexplored; even Medsylvania barely felt the human presence. The population was growing, but the world itself was still untamed. With any luck, it would remain that way for a long time to come.

"So which way do we go?" he asked.

"That way." By then, I'd spotted what I was looking for: a place where it looked as if the frozen grass had been trampled and pushed down, creating a narrow trail that led into the trees. Even though months had gone by, the grass was only beginning to thaw; the trail still remained. Not by coincidence, it ran parallel to the creek. Made sense: follow the creek, find the people.

Goldstein peered in the direction I indicated, yet he didn't see the clues I'd spotted. "Whatever you say," he said, standing up and hoisting his own pack. "You're the guide. Lead on." A moment of hesitation. "How far do you think . . . ?"

"No idea." I picked up my rifle, checked its charge. "As far as it took for your friend to find wherever he was looking for."

Goldstein gave me a sharp look. "You think he was looking for something? What?"

"Don't know." Pulling the rifle strap across my left shoulder, I led the way toward the trail. "Reckon we'll find out when we get there."

We followed the trail into the forest. It hadn't been used in quite a while, yet there was still enough snow on the ground, sheltered from the sun by the faux birch that rose around us, that I was able to discern the occasional footprint. As I had figured, the trail ran parallel to the creek; if Cassidy and his people set up camp somewhere nearby, then it made sense for them to be near a source of fresh water.

The terrain was flat, but that didn't make the going any easier. Faux birch soon gave way to Medsylvania roughbark so tall that we couldn't see the treetops. The trail had vanished by then, forcing us to rely upon the creek as our only guide; now and then I stopped to pull nylon ribbons from my pack and tie them around lower branches, a precaution I'd learned to take against getting lost. Before long we found ourselves entering a low swamp. Trudging through ankle-deep pools of brackish water, we used our machetes to hack through thickets of clingberry and spider bush.

We were halfway through the swamp when my nose caught an out-of-place odor: woodsmoke, wafting through the woods from a nearby campfire. Goldstein smelled it, too. Looking around, he pointed toward a bright place between the trees where it seemed as if the sun had penetrated. "Over there, maybe?"

I stopped, peered more closely. Yes, it looked like a clearing. "Worth a try," I said as I tied another ribbon around a branch. "Let's go."

Morgan's guess turned out to be correct. We left the swamp behind and went up a low rise, and suddenly came upon a broad natural clearing, a place where a lightning storm had long ago caused that part of the forest to burn, leaving behind only bushes, rotting stumps, and tall grass. And it was there that we found the camp.

A half dozen dome tents, like blue-and-red-striped pimples, were arranged in a semicircle around a stone-ringed fire pit from which brown
smoke tapered upward. The grass had been cleared away, but not recently; tufts of green rose here and there among untidy stacks of firewood and under sagging clotheslines strung from one tent to another.
On the far side of the camp was a low, six-sided wooden structure, its
windowless walls fashioned from crudely cut roughbark logs, its roof a
thatchwork of tree limbs stuffed with lichen. At first glance, I took it to
be a Navajo-style sweat lodge. As we came closer, we passed a small,
tarp-covered shelter that reeked of urine and feces: a latrine, probably
little more than a hole in the ground, with tarpaulins rigged around it
for a modicum of privacy.

The camp was run-down and ill kept, as if the people who lived there
no longer cared about maintaining it. If, indeed, anyone was still there.
There was no one in sight; were it not for the smoke rising from the pit
and the damp clothes hanging from the lines, I could have sworn the
place was deserted. Frost-covered grass crunched beneath the soles of
our boots as we ventured closer; looking down, I realized that I'd unconsciously pulled my rifle off my shoulder and was holding it in my
hands, my right forefinger an inch away from the safety.

"Oh, my god." Goldstein's eyes were wide. "What happened here?"

"I don't know. I . . ." Then I glanced his way, and felt my heart skip a
beat. "Morgan . . . freeze. Don't move a muscle."

"What are you . . . ?" Then he saw what I'd spotted, and stopped dead
in his tracks. "Aw, crap."

No more than three yards to his right, half-hidden among the brush,
lay a ball plant. It wasn't very large, yet its shell was still closed; the immature flower rising from its top showed that it was in early bloom. A
bad time to be close to one of these things; the pseudowasps would be
coming out of winter dormancy, ready to protect the plant while they
pollinated it.

That wasn't the worst of it. I looked around, saw another ball plant to
my left, a little farther away and yet just as menacing. Glancing to my
right again, I spotted yet another, only a few feet past the one near
Goldstein.

A chill went down my spine. The field was practically evil with ball plants. Which only made sense, in ecological terms. Marshland nearby, affording shelter for hibernating swampers, yet with enough sunlight to allow for photosynthesis. And although these specimens were a little smaller than the ones closer to the equator, they weren't so close to the subarctic region farther north that they couldn't survive. I was no botanist, but if they could make it through winter here . . .

"Don't worry, Morgan," a voice called out. "Just back away, and everything will be fine."

A tall, muscular man stood at the edge the campsite, arms folded across his broad chest, long black hair gathered in a braid behind his neck. Tough as a slab of Arizona sandstone; one look at him, and you knew that nothing could ever scratch him.

"Joe!" Goldstein looked around. "Thank God, I thought we'd never . . ." He stopped, remembering where he was. "What do you think you're doing, camping so close to these things?"

An amused expression appeared on Cassidy's face. "They're not so dangerous, once you know how to approach them. You'll only get swarmed if you come within six feet of them. Just back away, and you won't be harmed."

Goldstein was less than confident, yet he took Joe at his word. He carefully walked backward, picking his way across the field until he'd joined Cassidy. I followed him, keeping a wary eye on the plants. Under different circumstances, I would've retreated to the safety of the woods . . . yet this was the person we'd come to find, so that wasn't an option.

"Good to see you again." Once Morgan was away from the ball plants, he visibly relaxed. "You don't know how worried I've been about you. I mean, you just . . ."

"Disappeared, yes." Cassidy shook his head. "Sorry I didn't leave word where I was going, but this was something I just had to . . ."

"Don't give me that." Once again, the imperious tone crept into Goldstein's voice. "If there's something wrong, if there's something bothering you, you can come to me. We'll work it out."

"There's nothing wrong, really." An elusive smile crossed Cassidy's face. "I don't expect you to understand, but . . . everything's fine. You didn't have to hire a guide to find me."

How did he know who I was? Sure, it was probably a safe assumption, but . . .

"The name's Sawyer," I said. "Like your boss . . . like Mr. Goldstein says, he's been worried about you."

"Of course." Cassidy's eyes barely flickered in my direction. "I appreciate your concern, but you shouldn't be here. This place isn't for you."

As he spoke, I gazed past him. People were crawling out of their tents, like nocturnal animals cautiously emerging into the light of day. Men and women, their hair unwashed and matted, their clothes threadbare and soiled. Shielding their eyes from the midday sun, they regarded us with silent curiosity, as if Morgan and I were mirages that would vanish as suddenly as we'd appeared.

"Maybe, but . . ." Goldstein's puzzlement gave way to stubborn resolve. "Joe, I've come a long way to find you. I'm not leaving until I get some answers."

"Mr. Goldstein . . ."

"Don't 'Mr. Goldstein' me." Morgan stepped closer. "That's all there is to it. Come clean, or so help me . . ."

"Look"—Cassidy sighed—"I'll make you a deal. If I let you know what I'm doing . . ."

All of a sudden, he stopped. An absent look appeared on his face. At first I thought that he'd simply lost his train of thought, yet there was a moment, when his head cocked slightly to one side and his eyes shifted to the ground, that he seemed more like someone who was listening to a comment whispered in his ear. He could have been wearing a comlink implant, but . . .

"If I let you spend the night," Cassidy went on, looking straight at Goldstein once more, "and I show you that we're fine, will you leave? Leave and promise to never come back?"

"Joe, you know I can't . . ."

"Please. It's the best I can do." Cassidy's voice became insistent, almost pleading. "If you'd only understand what I'm . . . what we're doing here . . ."

"What *are* you doing here?" Until then, I'd kept my mouth shut. "I'd like to know myself, if you don't mind."

Cassidy scowled at me. "I *do* mind, Mr. Lee . . . but you're here, so there's no avoiding that, is there?" He let out his breath, as if resigning himself to the inevitable. "All right, c'mon. Least I can do is offer lunch."

Already I was feeling uncomfortable about being there. There was something that wasn't right about the place. Yet it would have been rude to turn down our host's offer, however reluctantly it might have been made. I fell in behind Goldstein as Cassidy led us through the clearing to his camp . . .

And it didn't occur to me, at least just then, that he'd called me "Mr. Lee," even though I'd told him only my first name.

Lunch was rice and red beans, congealed and unappetizing, left over from dinner the night before. Cassidy told us that his group had been getting by on this ever since they'd made camp here; now and then, someone would go down to the creek, chop a hole in the ice, drop in a fishing line, and manage to pull out a brownhead or two. Otherwise, their diet pretty much consisted of what they'd bought in twenty-pound bags in New Boston.

We ate sitting on logs beside the fire pit. After a while, other residents of the camp wandered over to join us. It was obvious that they'd lost weight; their faces were gaunt, their clothes hanging off their slumped shoulders. There were open sores on their faces and hands, and one or two of them looked as if they'd recently lost teeth; one of the men walked with a makeshift crutch, in a bowlegged gait that was an early sign of scurvy. They smelled bad; when a woman bent over me to offer another helping from the rusty pot, I had to hold my breath to keep from gagging. Cassidy was the healthiest of the bunch, yet even he looked malnourished.

No one spoke. That was the weirdest part. On occasion, they'd exchange a word or two, perhaps a gesture, but otherwise they remained silent. Yet despite their hunger and obvious ill health, their eyes remained lively; they constantly looked at one another, exchanging glances that might have been furtive except that they didn't bother to hide them from us. And between those glances were all the usual expressions—indifference, amusement, dissatisfaction, curiosity—that normally accompanied a conversation, except they came in the absence of speech.

Goldstein noticed none of that. He regarded the camp with disgust, his gaze roving across the dilapidated tents, the unwashed plates and skillets piled beneath the tarp that served as a communal kitchen, the rubbish carelessly discarded here and there. He did his best to be polite, making small talk with Cassidy about how the horses were doing at his estate, yet when a young woman ambled over to a nearby patch of grass to lift her skirt, squat, and pee, he lost his patience.

"For God's sake, man," he muttered. "How can you live like this?"

"Like how?" Cassidy shrugged. "You've got a problem?"

"Do I have a . . . ?" Goldstein stared at him. "Look at yourselves. You're living like animals."

Cassidy studied him for a moment, not saying anything. A smirk inched its way across his mouth. "You'd rather see me back at the manor. Sitting around the fireplace, feet propped up, glass of cognac in hand . . ."

Goldstein's face went red. "I didn't . . ."

"You know, you're right." Closing his eyes, Cassidy arched his back, his hands resting lightly upon his knees. "I can almost taste it now. And there's music . . . classic jazz, twentieth century. Herbie Hancock . . . no, wait, John Coltrane . . ."

"Don't make fun of me."

"I'm not." Opening his eyes again, Cassidy calmly gazed at his employer. "I miss those evenings, believe me. I wouldn't mind having more like them. But out here . . ." He let out his breath, gave an indifferent shrug. "That all seems so superficial, so . . . limited, really. A rich man at home with his toys, lonely now because no one will share them . . ."

"Pet." Standing nearby, a wild-haired man intently stared at Goldstein. "Nice doggy. Ruff-ruff . . ."

Goldstein's face went pale; there was shock in his eyes. Seeing this, Cassidy became angry. "Ash . . . out!" he snapped, glancing over his shoulder at him. "Go away!"

The other man winced, recoiling as if he'd been slapped, then he turned his back to us and shuffled away. Cassidy watched him go. "Sorry. That was uncalled for."

Morgan looked shaken. "Thanks . . . thank you," he stuttered. "I . . . I . . ."

"Ash knows who you are. He assumes too much." Yet there was a cool tone to his voice that had been absent before.

"Ash . . ." There was something about what Cassidy had called him that got my attention. "Is that really his name?"

Again, the others gathered around the fire pit cast knowing looks at one another. Yet no one spoke until Cassidy did. "His last name," he replied. "No one ever calls him Gordon, though. Ash has become his tribal name, just as my original tribe gave me the name Walking Star. He's called Ash because . . . well, because it fits him."

"Your tribe. I see." I glanced at the others; some glowered at me, others were defiant. "And the rest of these people . . . ?"

"They'll tell you if they wish to do so." Ignoring me again, Walking Star picked up a stick, snapped it in half, and fed it into the smoldering fire. "You shouldn't have come here, Mr. Goldstein . . ."

"Morgan." Goldstein put down his plate, inched a little closer. "I told you, Joe. We know each other better than that."

"I know we do." Cassidy stared at the fire intently, as if closely examining every smoking ember. "Believe me, I do. But this is not the place for you, trust me . . ."

"How can I trust you?" Goldstein became insistent. "I gave you money, sent you to a doctor . . ."

"A doctor is the last person I want to see. What I want . . . what *we* want is be left alone. I appreciate your concern, but there's a reason we've come out here."

Goldstein looked away, gazing toward the edge of the field where we'd encountered the ball plants. "I think I can guess what it is. You and your . . . your tribe . . . have gotten hooked on sting. So much that you've decided to go straight to the source. Why buy it on the street in Liberty when you can . . . ?"

His words trailed off as he became aware of the reaction of the people around us. For the first time since we'd entered the camp, they displayed some sort of emotion. A few concealed grins behind their hands, while others quietly giggled; some snorted back derisive laughter. Cassidy tried to remain respectful, but there was no hiding the smirk on his face.

"We're just a bunch of junkies. Is that it?" His voice was seasoned with contempt. "Sting may be many things, Morgan, but even a doctor would tell you that it's not addictive."

"Not physically, at least," I added.

Cassidy looked at me. "You're right. It can be habit-forming, at least in the psychological sense. But so is cannabis, and that's cultivated in the colonies. If getting high was all this was about, we would've just as soon stayed home and taken jobs on hemp plantations." He turned back to Goldstein. "But you're half-right. Yes, we came here because of the ball plants. We needed to find a wild stand that hadn't been discovered, and the privacy in which to . . ." Again, he paused. "Shall we say, experiment."

"Experiment. Right." It was Goldstein's turn to show contempt. Standing up, he raised a hand to encompass the run-down camp. "Look at this place. You're so far gone, you don't even realize how . . . how sick you've become."

"No." Cassidy pushed himself to his feet. "Not sick. In fact, we've become something you can't possibly imagine . . ."

"Don't say." This from the gap-toothed woman who'd served me earlier. Cassidy looked around, stared at her. A moment passed, then she seemed to wither, visibly recoiling from his dark brown eyes. Indeed, it seemed as if the others did the same, all at the same moment. Almost as if . . .

"Perhaps they should know," Cassidy said. "It's unfortunate, because I think we need more time to study this." Then he looked at Morgan again. "But I know you all too well, boss. You're tenacious. Once you learn about something, you don't give up easy. And I can't allow you to go home with misconceptions about what we're doing here."

Goldstein smiled with the confidence of a man so accustomed to winning that losing was no longer a possibility. "That's all I want. Just straight answers."

"Then you'll get them. Not now, though. This evening . . ."

"Joe . . ."

Cassidy nodded toward a vacant spot within the campsite. "Pitch your tents over there," he said. "Rest. Take a nap. Don't eat, and drink as little water as you can. Around sundown, go over there . . ." He pointed to the log hogan at the periphery of the camp. "We'll be waiting for you."

Goldstein studied the shack with suspicion. "Why can't you just tell me . . . ?"

"Because you'd never believe me. This is one of those things you have to experience yourself." Then he looked at me. "I don't expect you to attend. You can sit this out, if you wish."

"I'll . . . think it over." I was already considering the possibility of something going wrong. What, I didn't know. But it was comforting to know that I had a satphone in my pocket. If worse came to worst, I could always call Mike Kennedy, get him to bring in the cavalry.

"I'll leave it to your discretion, then. But . . ." Cassidy held out his hand. "One condition. I'll need your satphone, please."

I felt a touch of suspicion. "Why?"

"You'll get it back. Promise." A wry smile. "I just want to make sure that we're not interrupted."

Again, subdued laughter from those around us, as if Walking Star's tribe had caught a whispered joke I hadn't heard. I traded a glance with Morgan; he didn't know what was going on, either, yet he reluctantly nodded. I dug the satphone out of my jacket and handed it to Cassidy.

"Thank you, Mr. Lee . . . Sawyer, I mean." Then he turned away from us. "Tonight at bear-rise. See you then."

The last rays of sunset were filtering through the trees when Goldstein and I left our tents and walked across camp to the hogan. The evening was chilly; we could see our breath before our faces. To the east, the leading edge of Bear's ring plane was already rising above the forest, its silver bow bright against the twilight sky. Tall, slender torches had been lit on either side of the hogan, their flickering light illuminating the faces of the men and women waiting for us outside its open door.

"You don't have to do this, you know," Goldstein murmured, as we approached them. I noticed his pensive expression. We'd spoken little that afternoon; once we'd erected our tents, we'd spent our time taking catnaps and . . . well, just waiting. I regretted having surrendered my satphone; I at least could have called Kennedy with it, told him that we'd located Cassidy.

"Goes with the service," I replied, keeping my voice low. "Besides, I'm just as curious about this as you are."

He looked as if he was about to say something, but then Cassidy stepped forward. "You've accepted my invitation," he said. "I hope you've taken my advice not to eat anything." Goldstein nodded, and so did I. "Very well, then. Before we go in, though, you're going to need to do one more thing. If you'll please remove your jackets . . ."

"Joe, it's freezing out here." Goldstein stared at him in disbelief. "I can't see why . . ."

"I wouldn't ask you to do so if it wasn't important." Even as Cassidy spoke, the others were pulling off their jackets and serapes, neatly placing them on the ground just outside the hogan before entering one at a time, ducking their heads to pass through the low doorway. "Trust me, it'll be warm inside. But you've got to do it."

Goldstein hesitated, then reluctantly unzipped his fleece-lined, Earth-made parka and placed it outside the door, just a little apart from the others. The evening wind bit at me as I did the same; I wore a light sweater beneath my cat-skin jacket, and Cassidy paused to look me over. "Take that off, too," he said. "Loosen your collar and roll up your sleeves. It's important."

"Yeah, sure." I removed my sweater, noticing that he hadn't yet taken off his jacket. "Any reason why you're not . . . ?"

"No. Just waiting for you." Cassidy unbuttoned his jacket, carelessly tossed it aside. "After you, gentlemen."

One last, uncertain glance at each other, as if trying to decide who'd go first, then Goldstein lowered his head and, crouching almost double, entered the lodge. I was about to follow him when Cassidy stepped in front of me. He said nothing, yet it was plain that he wanted to be with his old boss. I waited until they disappeared through the door, then I followed them inside.

The hogan's interior was dark, almost pitch-black; torchlight seeped through narrow cracks between the log walls, the only source of illumination. I smelled the dank odor of dirt, mildew, and roots, heard the faint scuffling sounds of a lot of people crowded into a small space. When I tried to stand erect, the back of my head connected with the ceiling; I snarled an obscenity, then someone grabbed the back of my shirt, roughly hauled me down to a sitting position.

"Hush," Cassidy hissed at me. "Be quiet."

My eyes soon adjusted to the gloom. Ten men and women, Goldstein and me included, seated in a circle within the hogan, so close to one another that our elbows and shoulders nearly touched. To my left was Cassidy; to his left was Morgan. Almost directly behind me was the door; a woman to my right leaned over to pull it shut, and we were all together in the suffocating darkness.

There was something in the middle of the lodge. A tall, rotund object, only half-seen yet so close that, if I'd leaned forward, I could have touched it with my fingertips. My nose caught a faint vegetable fragrance, the smell of something alive and growing. Suddenly I began to suspect what was in the room . . .

"See," Cassidy whispered. "See and know."

He broke open a lightstick and tossed it on the floor, and in the wan chemical glow we saw what grew from the center of the lodge. A ball plant, perhaps the largest I'd ever seen; nearly five feet in diameter, it rose from the ground like a giant tumor, malignant and obscene.

My immediate reaction was to shrink back in horror. Yet even as I did, I noticed that, despite its size, the planet was somehow retarded. By that time of the season, leaves should have sprouted from its upper shell, with the first flower stalks beginning to blossom. Deprived of sunlight, though, it did neither; only the most smallest, vestigial leaves had begun to appear, and those were withered and stunted.

That was when it occurred to me what Cassidy and his people had done. They'd found the largest ball plant in this field and built the hogan around it. I glanced up at the ceiling, spotted a circular crack of light. A ceiling hatch, like a removable skylight; once a day, I surmised, they'd open the hatch, allowing in just enough sun and rain for the plant to remain alive, but not enough for pollination. In that way, they managed to keep the ball plant a captive specimen, contained within its own miniature greenhouse.

"Oh, for the love of . . ." Goldstein was just as horrified as I was. "Joe, what are you . . . ?"

"You'll see." Then Cassidy raised his left foot and slammed his heel down on the packed-earth floor.

The others did the same, stamping on the floor, causing the plant to shake. When I realized what they were trying to do, my first thought was to get out of there as fast as I could. Yet by then it was too late; the door was shut, and there was no escape.

I couldn't see the pseudowasps when they emerged from their nests within the shell; there wasn't enough light. Yet I heard an angry buzz from the plant, and for an instant the immature leaves parted just slightly.

Something small purred past my face, and I felt insect wings against my cheek. I reached up to swat it away, and a white-hot needle lanced into the back of my hand.

I yelped, and instinctively started to clamber to my knees. Cassidy grabbed my shoulder, forced me to sit down. "Just be calm," he said quietly. "It'll all be over in . . . *ah!*"

"Joe, for God's sake . . . *dammit!*" I heard Goldstein slap at something, then he cried out again in pain. "Holy . . . Get 'em off! They're all over me!"

By then the air was alive with pseudowasps. They swarmed the small room, buzzing all around us, stinging everyone with whom they came in contact. I tried to bat them away, but there were too many; I was stung again on my face, and when I leaned forward to put my head between my knees and cover the back of my neck with my arms, they attacked my wrists and shoulders.

Glancing up from my folded arms, I caught a glimpse of Cassidy. It was as if he was in meditation; seated beside me in lotus position, his eyes were shut, his body relaxed. Others had done the same; although they occasionally gasped in pain, they weren't bothering to fight off the insects. Goldstein was curled up on the floor, rolling this way and that, screaming in terror as he tried to ward off the insects. Then a pseudowasp alighted upon my face, just below my right eye. I managed to swat it away before it stung me, then I buried my head within my arms again.

It seemed to go on forever. Then I heard a wooden creak from somewhere above, felt a cool breeze. Hesitantly, I raised my head again. Someone had used a rope to move aside the ceiling hatch; bearlight streamed down through the opening, and I saw a thin cloud of insects fly upward, their wings appearing as tiny silver halos.

For a moment it seemed to me that they were miniature angels, vengeful yet innocent, spiraling upward into the night. Despite the pain, I found myself entranced by their beauty; I laughed out loud and watched their ascent with fascination. Others chuckled, as if understanding what I'd seen.

"There, see? The way has been prepared." Cassidy handed me a catskin flask. "Drink. Relax."

The water in his flask was tepid, yet it tasted like wine. I drank a little, then passed it to the woman sitting beside me. A certain numbness was rapidly spreading through my body; the places where I'd seen stung no longer burned; the wounds itched for a few minutes, but even that sensation gradually passed away. Goldstein was on his hands on knees, violently retching, yet he was no longer my concern. All I knew was that the hogan wasn't as menacing as it'd once been; indeed, it was as comfortable as my favorite table at the Captain's Lady, and all the people in it had become my friends.

Time lost meaning. I watched Bear slowly come into view through the skylight, its silver-blue radiance painting the log walls with colors I'd never seen before. Ash stared up at the stars, humming beneath his breath; the gap-toothed woman rocked gently back and forth on her haunches, muttering to herself as if carrying on a conversation with some invisible person. Across the room, a man and a woman pulled off each other's clothes and, oblivious to everyone else, started to have sex; I observed their fornication with disinterest, neither aroused nor offended. A skeeter, wandering in from the nearby marshes, flittered above the ball plant, performing a delicate ballet in the bearlight just for me. It was as if a universe I'd never known to exist had opened before my eyes, and I was an astronomer seeing its hidden wonders for the very first time.

—Do you see . . . ?

At first, I thought Cassidy had spoken to me. When I looked at him, though, he was staring straight ahead.

"What?" I said. "Do I see what?"

—Do you see? . . . do you hear? . . . do you feel?

His lips never moved, and he didn't look my way. Yet I could hear his voice—no, more than that; I could sense his presence—as clearly as if he'd spoken in my ear.

"I . . . I can . . ."

His eyes shifted in my direction.*—No . . . don't speak . . . don't need to . . . open your mind . . . hear me with your thoughts . . .*

I stared at him. At first, it seemed as if there was a barrier between us, translucent as rice paper, solid as iron . . .

—Concentrate!

I squeezed my eyes shut, fought against the barrier. A sharp pain within my temples, almost like a migraine headache. Then, suddenly, an audible snap, as if someone had broken a twig within my head . . .

(The smell of horse manure, sour-sweet and ripe. A flash-image of a hand holding a brush, gently stroking a coarse brown mane. The horse raises its head, looks at me, love within its dark brown eyes . . .)

I snapped out of the trance. What the hell . . . ?

—You saw the horse, didn't you?

Again, I looked at Cassidy. A quiet smile played at the corners of his mouth, yet he continued to gaze straight ahead. "Yeah," I mumbled. "Yeah, I saw the . . ."

Then the shock of what had just happened swept through me, and with it an uncommon clarity. Looking away from Cassidy, I stared at the couple screwing on the other side of the hogan . . .

(Flesh moving across flesh, rough hands gripping smooth thighs, soft hands stroking back muscles. The odor of sweat, warm and close. Loins straining for release. The rapture of sex . . .)

I glanced away from them, saw Cassidy staring at me.

—Do you feel them?

Confused, I hastily looked away, only to find myself gazing at the woman with the missing teeth. All at once, I knew that her name was Alice Curnow, although she now preferred to be known as First Light of Day . . .

—Donald I'm so sorry so sorry I never meant to hurt you but you asked too much of me, and I couldn't Donald I'm sorry so sorry please forgive me I'm sorry so sorry . . .

Too much. Far too much. Within the hogan were places where I was never meant to be, secrets I was never meant to share. Sick at the pit of my stomach, feeling an overwhelming urge to vomit, I frantically crawled toward the door. A hard shove, and it fell away before me.

On hands and knees, I crawled out of the lodge. Cold air blasted me like an arctic wind; at once I was chilled to the bone. I managed to get a few feet from the hogan before my guts betrayed me. I vomited across grass that looked like a plain of emerald stone.

Then I passed out. Yet not before Cassidy's voice came to me one last time . . .

—You're not ready yet.

I awoke in the same place where I'd lost consciousness. It was early morning, the sun just beginning to rise above the trees at the edge of the clearing. Someone had thrown my jacket over me, yet my clothes were damp with dew, my arms and legs stiff from sleeping on bare ground. My head throbbed with the worst headache I'd ever had.

For a long time I simply lay there, feeling every ache and pain in my body. If I could have, I would've gone back to sleep again, but I was kept awake by the sore places on my neck, arms, and hands where I'd been stung. I finally rolled over and sat up, and found Joe Cassidy staring at me.

He sat cross-legged upon the ground, a blanket wrapped around his shoulders. Behind him, burned-out torches smoldered; a cool breeze caught their acrid black smoke, caused it to drift past the hogan. Its door was shut once more. No one else was in sight.

Walking Star and I regarded each other for several long moments, neither of us saying anything. After a while, he closed his eyes, lowered his head slightly. A few seconds passed, then he raised his head again, opened his eyes.

"You didn't hear that, did you?" he asked. I started to shake my head, but it hurt too much, so I simply looked at him. "Didn't think you would," he added, a smile touching the corners of his lips. "If I concentrate really hard, I can send an image to someone who's gone through this only once, but it usually takes several sessions for"—a pause, as if he was groping for the right words—"the change to become permanent."

"Permanent?" There was a copper taste in my mouth. I spit, saw that my saliva was tinged with blood. Apparently I'd bit my tongue sometime during the night and not even realized it. "What change?"

"You really have to ask?" He squinted at me, as if searching for something. "You know what happened. You just won't admit it to yourself."

All I knew for certain was that I was thirsty, although my stomach roiled at the very thought of food. Without my asking, Cassidy picked up a cat-skin flask from the ground beside him. "You probably won't want to eat for a while," he said, tossing the flask to me. "No one ever does."

A shiver ran down my back as I picked up the waterskin. "You can read minds, can't you?"

Cassidy gazed at the camp, motionless within the early morning haze, the silence disturbed only by the songs of grasshoarders stirring within the field. "We all do, now," he said after a time. "Telepathy, you might call it, although I prefer to think of it as a form of mental gestalt . . . a joining of minds. After a while, you don't even need the pseudowasp venom. It just . . . happens, y'know?"

The water rinsed away the blood in my mouth. I spit out the first mouthful, swallowed the next. "I don't believe it. I think we were all just . . ."

"Hallucinating?" A wry smile. "Just a weird experience we all shared at the same time. That's what we thought, too, back when we first started using sting. I thought it was nothing more than peyote dreams. But then . . ."

He held out his hand, and I passed the flask back to him. "Well, it became obvious this wasn't just a drug thing, that we might actually be onto something. It would take a neuroscientist to explain it to you, but there's a theory that a small part of the brain . . . just a few dormant neurons, really . . . contains a certain potential for psychic ability. Sort of a throwback to primitive times, when our forebearers had to rely on their senses for survival. No one's ever been able to explain it, or at least test it to any reliable degree, but . . . well, it's there."

"And you think sting has something to do with this?"

"No." He took a drink of water. "Sting only gave us a hint. The stuff we found in the colonies was always diluted. Usually with sugar water, but more often with other drugs to make it more potent for guys who just wanted to get high." He shook his head. "That's not what we were after. We were . . . we *are* . . . searching for a more transcendental experience. A way to open the doorways of the mind."

Cassidy was persuasive, to be sure, yet there was something within me that remained unconvinced. "So you came all the way up here just to camp out in a field full of ball plants, when there's plenty in New Florida and Midland . . ."

"Being wiped out as fast as they're found. And this far north, their pollination season occurs later in the year. Besides, we needed isolation for our experiments."

"Experiments. Yeah, right . . ." Tents on the verge of collapse, trash scattered here and there, a group of men and women suffering from malnutrition. "You're making a lot of progress."

Cassidy was quiet for a moment. "One of the drawbacks," he said after a moment. "You get to the point where you can easily read another person's thoughts or emotions, it's hard to be around them. Everyone here has their secrets, their hidden pain. We're still learning how to cope with that."

"Sure. Okay." I sat up a little straighter, pulling the blanket around me. What I wouldn't have given for a bottle of aspirin just then. "So you decided to come straight to the source. Build a shack around the biggest ball plant you could find, and crawl inside every night to get a mighty fix of . . ."

"Your full name is Sawyer Robert Edward Lee," Cassidy said, looking straight at me. "Your parents . . . Carl and Jessica . . . named you after your father's older brother, and added your middle names because the family likes to believe they're related to Captain Lee. Although you have personal doubts about your ancestry, you didn't have many qualms about using your name to your advantage once you immigrated to Coyote."

I felt my face go warm. "How did you . . . ?"

"You've got a lifelong fear of reptiles," he went on, "which is lucky for you because there are none on this world. You prefer dark-haired women to blondes, unless they wear glasses, in which case you feel yourself drawn to them because the first girl who let you kiss her was a blond-haired girl who wore glasses . . . That was when you were about nine or ten, right? You're good at poker, but you like to cheat sometimes just because you know how to. You drink, but when you get drunk, you feel guilty about it because your father—"

"Shut up!" I hastily pulled on my jacket, yet I couldn't keep myself from trembling. "Just . . . shut up."

"Sorry. There was no other way. If there was any other way to make you believe . . ."

"Okay. All right. Just . . . no more, okay?" I shuddered, not willing to meet his eyes. "So . . . what is it that you want from me? Why are you telling me this?"

Walking Star slowly let out his breath. "From you, very little. So far as I can tell, you're just some guy caught up in all this." Then he rose to his feet, offering a hand to help me up. "But Morgan Goldstein . . . that's another issue entirely."

We found Morgan in his tent, in no better condition than I was. His face was haggard, and he slumped on his sleeping bag, clutching at the waterskin Ash had brought him. The other man quietly nodded as Cassidy and I came in, then left the tent without a word, leaving the three of us alone.

Or at least so it seemed. I noticed that several of Cassidy's friends were beginning to gather near the fire pit. They said nothing, only quietly observed us. I wondered if there was a limit to the distance for their newfound abilities. Did it even matter? If they now shared a mental gestalt, then there were no secrets among them . . . or, indeed, with anyone with whom they came in contact.

"So it's true, isn't it?" Goldstein stared at Cassidy with haunted eyes as he gently touched the side of his head. "I heard your voice in here last night, Joe. Goddamn it, I felt you in my *mind* . . ."

"It's telepathy, Mr. Goldstein." Although he hadn't spoken to me, I felt as if he needed an explanation. "The pseudowasp venom, it's—"

"He knows." Cassidy folded his arms together, regarded him with implacable stoicism. "In fact, he's known all along. Just one more thing I found out about him last night."

Not believing this, I looked down at Goldstein. Unwilling to meet my gaze, he hastily averted his eyes. "I didn't, no," he murmured. "At least not for sure . . ."

"Yet you suspected." Cassidy's gaze didn't waver from him.

Goldstein sharply looked away. "One of my people in New Florida reported to me that you were trying to . . . to do this. I didn't think it was possible, but . . ."

"But you had to find out for yourself, didn't you?" Cassidy squatted down to sit at the toe of Goldstein's sleeping bag. "Don't feel so abused, Sawyer. What he told you was true . . . somewhat, at least. He really was concerned for my well-being." A sardonic smile played upon his face. "And for that, at least, I'm grateful. So glad to know that I have a true friend."

"Go to hell, Joe." There was murder in Goldstein's eyes. "I meant it when I said I'm your friend."

"Morgan . . ." Cassidy shut his eyes, shook his head. "I know how you feel about me. More than you realize. But Ash was right . . . it's the affection one might have for a favorite dog." A wan smile. "Or one of your horses, to be more precise. I know that, and if you were honest with yourself, you'd know it, too. And when I dared to slip the reins and run away, you came after me to take me back to the stable."

"You've no right to . . ."

"Just as you had no right to intrude on our privacy." As with me, Cassidy was perpetually one step ahead of the conversation. "You should've left us alone. Yet you decided to seek us out, because you thought that, if your suspicions were true, just perhaps . . ."

"You could take advantage of this." Things were beginning to come clear to me; I didn't need to be a telepath to figure out the rest. "It'd be a real asset to have a mind reader on your payroll, wouldn't it? Awfully handy to have one for your next business deal . . ."

"Get out of here." Goldstein angrily gestured to the open flap of the tent. "Make yourself useful and find your satphone. Call Mike, tell him I want a gyro pickup in—"

"Find it yourself. I want to see how this plays out." I looked at Cassidy. "Go ahead. Sorry for the interruption."

"No problem." Cassidy picked up the flask at Goldstein's feet, treated himself to a sip of water. "Let's get to the end of this, all right? Then we'll get you a ride out of here. First, I quit . . ."

"You can't . . . !" Goldstein stopped himself, then shrugged. "All right, go ahead. Sort of figured that was coming anyway." He hesitated. "I'm going to miss you, Joe. Despite what you say, you've been a good friend . . ."

"I'm not your friend." Joe re-capped the flask, dropped it on the ground. "But it doesn't mean we won't see each other again. Because now that you know what we're doing here, you're going to help us."

Goldstein's expression became puzzled. "What? I don't . . ."

"Understand? Let me make it clear." Cassidy rested his elbows upon his knees, clasped his hands together. "You've already remarked upon the sorry condition of this camp. Well, you're going to make it better. Soon as you get home, you're going to hire a construction crew to come up here and build a permanent settlement for us. A few cabins, to start . . . just to get us out of these tents . . . but we'll need something better than that. A large building where we can all live together. Solar electrical system, wind turbine, toilets, artesian wells, and water-filtration systems . . ."

"Like hell!"

"More like a monastery really . . . or a perhaps a sanctuary." A sly grin appeared on Cassidy's face. "Come to think of it, I sort of like the sound of that. The Sanctuary." He chuckled quietly. "The people you hire, of course, won't be told the purpose of this place, and you yourself will say nothing about it to anyone. Is that clear?"

"And you expect me to pay for it?" Goldstein was incredulous. When Cassidy nodded, he shook his head. "Forget it. There's no way you can expect me to . . ."

"You don't understand. This isn't a request." Cassidy stared straight at him. "I found out a lot of things about you last night, Morgan. Here's what I learned . . ."

Once again, he closed his eyes, lowered his head. His brow furrowed, and he gritted his teeth for a few moments. Morgan was about to say something just then, yet then his jaw went slack. Only a few seconds went by, yet in that brief time, I saw his eyes go wide, the color drain from his face.

What Cassidy revealed to him, I'd never learn. Perhaps it was just as well that I didn't. All the same, when the moment passed and Walking Star opened his eyes again, Morgan Goldstein looked as if someone had just told him the worst thing anyone could ever imagine. Which was what you might expect, if someone revealed your darkest and innermost secrets to you.

"You . . . you'll have it," he said, very quietly.

"Thank you. I thought you'd see things our way." Cassidy pushed himself to his feet, then turned to me. "You can call Mike now," he said, reaching into his jacket pocket to produce the satphone. "He can have Merle pick you up same place he left you yesterday"

He started to leave the tent, then he stopped, looked back at Morgan. "See you around. Not too soon, I hope, but . . . see you around."

Goldstein said nothing. I left him in the tent, still staring at the ground, as I followed Cassidy outside. The others were still hovering near the fire pit. Cassidy started toward them, but stopped when I touched his shoulder.

"Just one more thing . . ." I began.

"You've got nothing to worry about." Walking Star didn't look back at me. "I'm not interested in your secrets. Only your intentions." He paused. "You're a good man. Just never come here again."

I let go of Cassidy's arm, slowly backed away. I didn't need to say anything, and he didn't need to ask. And meanwhile, his tribe silently regarded me with eyes capable of unlocking the doorways of my mind.

A few hours later, Morgan Goldstein and I had returned to the rocky coast of Medsylvania. It was early afternoon, the sunny warmth of an early-spring day slowly baking away the cold memory of the night before. Across the waters lay the Midland coast; not far away, we could see a small white sail. Merle's pirogue, slowly making its way across the channel toward us. We'd found a large boulder upon which to sit while we waited for him; our backpacks lay next to us, our sleeping bags and tents rolled up and lashed to their frames.

Neither of us had spoken much since we'd left the camp. No one said farewell; we were guests who'd overstayed our welcome, and our hosts were only too happy to see us leave. There'd been little conversation between Morgan and me as we followed the creek back through the forest, avoiding the marshes.

The ribbons I'd tied around trees on the way in helped make it easier to find our way back to the trail. On the way out, though, whenever I found one of them, I used my knife to carefully cut it loose and shove it in my pocket. Morgan noticed me doing this, but didn't say anything about it. Not until then at least.

"Think you're ever coming back here?" he abruptly asked.

I looked around at him. He was idly picking up pebbles and tossing them into the shallows. I didn't know if he was genuinely curious, or just making small talk.

I found a small, flat stone. A flick of the wrist made it skip across the still blue waters. "I doubt it," I said, then decided to be honest. "No. If anyone ever tries to hire me as a guide again . . . up here, I mean . . . I'll say no. At least not as far as this place is concerned."

"Can't say I blame you." He picked up a piece of loose shale, tried the same trick. It sank as soon as it hit the water. "What would you tell 'em?"

"I'll tell them there are dangerous creatures in these woods." Realizing what I'd just said, I smiled. "Not too far from the truth, really."

"No . . . no, it's not." Morgan tried again with another rock; this time he managed to make it skip twice. He learned fast. "What if I asked you?"

I looked at him again. He continued to peer at the channel; no expression on his face, and his thoughts were unreadable. By me, at least.

"I'd still say no," I replied. "Why? You think you're coming back?"

He glanced over his shoulder at the woods behind us. Almost as if he were expecting to see someone standing there, studying us from the shadows of the tall roughbark that lined the shore.

"No . . . no, I don't think so," he said at last, looking back at the channel again. "You're right. There are too many dangerous creatures here."

The pirogue was closer, near enough that we could see Merle sitting in its stern. Mike Kennedy was with him; he raised a hand in greeting, and I raised mine in return. "That's probably wise," I said quietly.

"Uh-huh." Morgan skipped another rock, then hoisted himself to his feet. "Not that it matters."

"Come again?"

Morgan was quiet for a moment as he leaned down to pick up his pack. "Joe's not going to stay here forever," he said at last. "We're going to see him again . . . him and the rest of his tribe. Oh, they'll stay here as long as it takes for them to learn how to control what they've learned to do. But when they're ready . . ."

He fell silent. He didn't need to finish his thoughts. Nonetheless, I felt a chill despite the warmth of the midday sun. He was right. Sooner or later, we'd see Walking Star and his people among us.

And when we did, our thoughts would never be our own again.

Part 3

TRUE RELIGION

The Church of the Holy Dominion was a modest two-story building on College Street in Liberty. Modeled after the Spanish missions of old California, it was built of adobe brick, with twin bell towers rising above its tiled mansard roof. The first Dominionist missionaries to Coyote were fortunate enough to acquire land near the Colonial University, so the church was established in an ideal location, directly across the street from the college library; it was hoped that students seeking respite from their secular pursuits would discover the nearby church and, God willing, find enlightenment in the word of the Lord.

A cold spring rain was falling when the Reverend Alberto Cosenza climbed out of the shag wagon that had carried him into town. The driver who'd picked him up at the gyroport in Shuttlefield waited patiently while Cosenza pulled a few colonials from his overcoat pocket; the deacon noticed the frown on the man's face when he saw that the amount he received was no more than the stated fare, and Cosenza grudgingly added another colonial as a tip. Perhaps it was still not enough, but the driver would have to be satisfied; the Church was on hard times, and Cosenza was keenly aware of how much it had cost for him to travel to 47 Ursae Majoris. The driver didn't say anything, though—the fact that his passenger was a holy man, and an older one at that, might have kept him from complaining—but instead shook the reins and clucked his tongue. The shag farted loudly, and Cosenza barely had enough time to retrieve his suitcase before the hairy beast trudged away, its immense feet stamping through the mud.

Cosenza turned toward the church, pulling the brim of his fedora down against the rain. He'd just walked up the steps when the front door opened and another man dressed in the black suit and red shawl of a Dominionist clergyman appeared within the arch.

"Reverend Cosenza," he began. "I'm so sorry, I hadn't realized that you . . ."

"Arrived, yes. Late, no." Cosenza scowled as the pastor moved to take his suitcase from him. "The least you could have done was send someone to pick me up."

The minister blanched at the admonishment, and Cosenza immediately regretted the harshness of his tone. Tall and thin, with a sparse beard and long brown hair pulled back in a ponytail, the Reverend Grey Rice had the monastic look of a young pastor only a few years out of divinity school. "My apologies," he added, more quietly now. "I'm sure you meant no disrespect. It's just that I could have done without the means by which I got here."

Rice forced a rueful smile. "You've just met your first shag, I take it." Cosenza nodded, and the pastor shook his head. "It would've made no difference. If I'd hired a cab to pick you up, it would've been the same thing."

"You couldn't have sent a coupe instead?"

"Coupes are rather expensive, I'm afraid, and . . ." Rice's voice trailed off, the rest of what he meant to say left unspoken. *Sorry to make you ride in a wagon, but the Church doesn't have enough money in its coffers to provide you with modern transportation.* "At least you didn't have to walk," he finished, a lame excuse if Cosenza had ever heard one.

The deacon grunted as he removed his hat. "Well, at any rate, I'm here," he murmured, shaking rainwater from the fedora and tucking it under his arm. "Perhaps you can show me to my quarters."

"Of course. Right this way." Rice turned toward the open door, then hesitated for a moment. "Midday services are scheduled to begin in about five minutes, but . . ."

"Then perhaps you should hurry. You don't want to keep your congregation waiting."

It seemed as if Rice wanted to add something else, but decided instead to keep his mouth shut. He quickly ushered Cosenza through the foyer, giving the deacon just enough time to notice certain details—the sign-in book that no one had signed, the stacks of untouched tracts on the front table, the bulletin board which bore only a two-week-old notice for an Easter dinner—until they reached the double doors leading into the sanctuary.

"The guest room is upstairs," Rice said as he opened the door. "We can cut through the chancel to—"

"Just a moment." Cosenza came to a halt just inside the door, let his eyes sweep the room. The sanctuary was little larger than the wedding chapel of his own church in Milan, but it had obviously been built with loving hands. Dim sunlight slanted down through mullioned windows upon polished faux-birch pews arranged on either side of the center aisle. On the raised nave at the far end of the room, a felt-covered altar stood beneath the helix-backed Dominionist crucifix; to the left stood the choir stall, its high-backed chairs facing the elevated pulpit box. Cast-iron chandeliers suspended from blackwood rafters illuminated the cherubs and seraphim that gazed down from the limestone but-tresses holding up the barrel ceiling.

The church was beautiful. It was also empty. Although only a few minutes remained before commencement of midday services—indeed, the tower bells were already beginning to toll—no one was seated in the pews. Even those parishioners who habitually showed up early were absent, and when Cosenza turned his head to gaze through the open door, he saw no one waiting in the foyer.

The deacon looked at the young pastor, who lowered his eyes in em-barrassment, acknowledging the unasked question. "No," Rice said qui-etly, "there's no one here. They didn't come yesterday, and I don't think they'll come today."

Cosenza stared at him. "And Sunday . . . Orifiel, I mean. What about then?"

"Sometimes I get a few. Two, three . . . no more than five or six, and then only on holidays. Of course, the Gregorian calendar isn't observed here, so it doesn't make much sense to hold Christmas or Easter mass three times a year. But . . ."

His voice faltered, his humiliation complete. "No," Rice went on, "that's not really an excuse, is it? There are other churches in town . . . Catholic, Episcopal, Presbyterian . . . and we also have a synagogue and a mosque. I've checked with them, and they've told me that they always draw worshippers."

"And you don't."

Rice let out his breath as a quiet sigh as he placed the deacon's bag on the floor. "Let me show you something," he said as he reached into the inside pocket of his jacket to pull out a folded sheaf of paper. "This is my sermon. I've memorized it, of course, but I always bring a copy in case I forget something. I wrote it two weeks ago . . . you may read it if you'd like." He offered it to Cosenza, but when the deacon didn't take it from him, he self-consciously lowered his hand. "I haven't uttered a word of it in public."

"Why?"

"Because . . ." Again, Rice hesitated, and it seemed as if the younger man was mustering his courage. "Because no one wants to hear what I have to say. Plain and simple."

"No." Cosenza shook his head. "I can see no wants to hear you. That's not what I'm asking. What I want to know is *why* they don't . . ."

"That's the reason why I contacted the elders." Rice abruptly became impatient, as if he were trying to explain the obvious to an obstinate old fool. "They've sent you to talk to me, and I appreciate that, but the fact of the matter is that I don't . . . I can't do this any longer."

"What are you trying to say?" Cosenza peered closely at the pastor. "Are you having a spiritual crisis?"

Rice was quiet for a moment. "Yes," he said at last. "Yes, I am. I feel that this church no longer has any relevance, and I wish to resign from my post."

"But . . ." Cosenza stopped, then went on. "I don't understand. Tell me, please, what leads you to the conclusion that this church is no longer relevant. I don't . . ."

"No. Of course you don't." Rice gazed back at him, and for the first time, Cosenza saw the sadness in his eyes. "That's because you've never met a *hjadd*."

At Cosenza's insistence, they waited another fifteen minutes, just in case someone might happen to show up. As Rice predicted, though, no one came; the pews remained vacant, the hymnals untouched, the offering plates empty. Cosenza passed the time by taking a seat in the chancel behind the choir stall and reading the pastor's sermon. Titled "God's Plan for Coyote," it wasn't anything he hadn't heard before—the Almighty had sent humans to this world as the first step toward fulfillment of His holy plan to propagate the race throughout the universe. Standard Church doctrine, but neither was it the sort of hellfire-and-damnation rant in which young ministers occasionally indulged themselves, often at the expense of their congregations. Whatever Rice was, he wasn't a radical . . . which, indeed, was what Cosenza had been told when the Council of Elders asked him to go to Coyote.

After a while, Rice stood up from his seat in the choir. Cosenza watched as he snuffed out the altar candles and collected the offering plates, then he followed the pastor as he stepped behind the chancel and went to the sacristy. There were a couple of chairs in the small antechamber; Rice gestured to them, then went about putting away the plates and hanging up his shawl.

"So . . . where should I begin?" Rice asked as he sat down across from Cosenza.

"At the beginning."

"That would only make sense, I suppose." Rice sighed. "You know, of course, that our first missionaries came here a little less than three Coyote years ago . . . eight by the Gregorian calendar . . . right after the starbridge was opened. Since then, our people have dispersed throughout the colonies. We now have smaller missions in Clarksburg, Leeport, Defiance, New Brighton . . ."

"I'm aware of all that." Cosenza was trying not to lose patience, but it seemed as if Rice was stalling. "Tell me about the *hjadd*. What do they have to do with . . . ?"

"I'm getting there." Rice held up a hand. "At first, we were welcomed . . . or at least I was, when I arrived to take over this ministry. My predecessor, who'd established this mission before deciding to return to Earth, left me with a congregation of nearly a hundred. Most were recent immigrants, but we also had a few who were second- or third-generation descendants of the original colonists. Not all that many, relatively speaking, but they were open to our message all the same. And then . . ."

He paused. "Well, I'm sure you know about that, too. The *hjadd* arrived, and that changed everything."

"I think you overstate the situation," Cosenza said. "Not everything changed."

"On Earth, perhaps not . . . but no one back home has seen an alien, have they? Not in the flesh, at least." Rice shook his head. "It's different here. Most people here haven't laid eyes on them, either . . . they're quite reclusive . . . nevertheless, their presence is as obvious as the embassy they've built."

He nodded in the general direction of the university. "It's not far from here, if you'd like to see it. Just on the other side of the campus. Amazing how quickly it went up . . . only a couple of days." A shallow grin. "In fact, you could almost call it a miracle . . . but then again, isn't it true that only God can perform miracles?"

Cosenza's mouth tightened at the remark; coming from a clergyman, it was dangerously close to apostasy. Yet he couldn't deny the fact that the unexpected return of a long-lost European spacecraft bearing a representative of an extraterrestrial race had thrown the Dominionists into an ecumenical crisis. The Church of the Holy Dominion was founded on the belief that, since no intelligent races had been found beyond Earth, God had created Man in His own image, and therefore it was incumbent upon humankind to spread itself throughout the galaxy in order to fulfill His plan. Knowledge of the existence of alien civilizations—not just the *hjadd*, but apparently many others as well—was a refutation of this fundamental principle.

"We've had . . . some loss of support back home, too." Cosenza picked his words carefully. "But the Council of Elders has studied the matter and come to the conclusion that, since the *hjadd* are clearly not human, they cannot have been created by the Almighty." He smiled. "Come now, Grey. You know this already. When the first colonists discovered a native species . . . sandthieves, I believe they're called . . . ?"

"*Chirreep*. 'Sandthieves' is the old word for them. We don't use it anymore." Rice shook his head. "That's different. The *chirreep* are hominids, little more than simians. Even the most advanced tribes are barely capable of using tools. The *hjadd* are different."

"Certainly they're different. That's why they're the exception." The deacon confidently raised a finger. "Have they heard the word of the Lord? No? Then they're not part of His plan, any more than . . ."

"But that's just it. They . . ." Rice stopped. "Look, I'm getting ahead of myself, and I'm afraid you won't understand me unless I take this one step at a time. If I may . . ."

"Of course. Sorry." Cosenza was feeling his stomach begin to growl. It had been many hours since he'd had breakfast in New Brighton, and he'd been expecting to be off to lunch by then. But Rice was determined to explain himself, and as a senior clergyman, Cosenza was obliged to hear him out. "Please continue."

"Thank you." Rice clasped his hands together in his lap. "I tried to make that argument in my sermons, but it didn't help. We started to lose parishioners . . . only one or two at first, but then I began to notice, every Orifiel, the pews were gradually becoming more empty with each passing week. I'd run into my former parishioners on the street and ask why they were no longer attending services, and they'd all tell me the same thing . . . it was no longer possible for them to have faith in a religion based upon a belief that they knew to be untrue."

"They've all lost faith in God?" Cosenza raised a skeptical eyebrow.

"No, no." Rice shook his head. "They still believe in the Lord. It's our interpretation of Him that they no longer accept. The very presence of the *hjadd* was evidence of . . ."

He let out his breath as an expansive sigh. "Forgive me, Deacon, but I began to play down certain aspects of our faith. Instead of insisting that Man is alone in the universe, I emphasized that we are the Lord's chosen people and, as such, it is our duty to populate the galaxy. My sermon . . ."

"Yes, I've read it. A satisfactory interpretation of the Church's reformed doctrine. And you say you still continued to lose attendance?" Rice nodded. "But, of course, the Church has a social role as well. Have you tried . . . ?"

"Family nights. Charity drives. Bingo games. Pork roasts." The minister shrugged. "We do all these things, with what few resources we still have, and sometimes they're successful. About a dozen or so showed up for Easter dinner a couple of weeks ago. But none of this has brought in new members, or at least not permanently." Rice hesitated. "I should add that I use the word 'we' only because I'm so used to saying so. Truth is, I'm now on my own. My associate minister resigned four weeks ago. He renounced Dominionism, has converted to the Presbyterian faith, and now belongs to that church."

Cosenza glared at him. "You didn't tell the elders this in your communiqué."

"I prayed that he'd change his mind before you arrived, but I assumed it was the Lord's will that I carry on alone. Now"—Rice looked down at the floor—"I'm not even sure of that anymore."

"What do you mean?" Despite his rising anger, Cosenza reached out to grasp the minister's hand. "Grey, there are worse things than losing one's congregation. If you still have your faith . . ."

"Deacon, please . . ." Rice raised his eyes. "It's not that simple. Something else has happened." Before Cosenza could ask, he went on. "A few days before I sent word to the elders, I had a visitor . . . a young man whom I'd never seen before. He wouldn't tell me who he was but allowed that, until recently, he'd been living in New Brighton, where he'd worked in some official capacity."

"That's rather secretive, don't you think?"

"Yes, it is. In fact, I had the impression that he was in trouble with the law. A woman about his own age was with him, but she was reluctant to set foot in the church, so I let her remain outside while he and I went in to speak."

"If he was a criminal, you should have . . ."

"Notified a proctor, yes, I know. But what he had to tell me was so incredible that I decided to give him sanctuary." Rice paused. "He told me that he'd met a *hjadd*, and that it . . . heshe, rather . . . had given him a device of some sort that was, in essence, a recording of their spiritual doctrine."

For an instant, Cosenza felt as if his heart had stopped. "Dear God, man," he whispered, staring at the young pastor in astonishment. "Did he let you see it?"

Rice shook his head. "I asked, but he refused. Said that he left it elsewhere, in a place where he knew it would be safe until he returned for it. He didn't say as much, but I think he was reluctant to show it to anyone of any established religion, lest it be confiscated and destroyed."

"But . . . I don't understand. Why would . . . ?"

"My visitor told me a little of what he'd learned from his . . . well, examination . . . of this object, and it contradicted everything we believe to be true." Cosenza opened his mouth to speak, but Rice quickly went on. "Not just Dominionism . . . virtually every major religion as well. Christianity, Judaism, Islam, Hindu . . ."

"Heresy."

"That was what I thought, too. And I told him so." Rice shook his head. "In hindsight, I know now that doing so was a mistake. He became upset, told me that he'd come seeking spiritual guidance, not recrimination. Then he and his companion left. When I realized that I'd said the wrong thing, I went out to search for them. But apparently they've left town, and I haven't seen them since."

Cosenza's hands were shaking. He clasped them together in his lap to keep them still. "Perhaps it's a hoax," he said quietly. "Or maybe he was delusional . . ."

"That possibility occurred to me, too. But I had to find out for myself." Abruptly, Rice stood up from his chair and, head lowered, began to pace the small room. "What I did next may have been . . . well, questionable . . . yet it was the only recourse I felt was open to me."

He stopped, gazed at the deacon. "I went to see the *hjadd*."

The door to the alien embassy bore an uncomfortable resemblance to a sphincter, and when it silently swirled shut behind him, Rice had the eerie feeling that he'd entered a womb. The chamber in which he found himself was dark, save for abstract patterns etched into the rock walls that emitted a sanguine glow, and unnaturally warm. Whatever he'd been expecting to find in the *hjadd* habitat, that wasn't it.

His eyes had barely adjusted to the gloom when a beam of light came down from the concave ceiling, revealing a couchlike recamier in the center of the room. Once again, Rice heard the disembodied voice that had addressed him outside the building. *"Welcome, Reverend. Please make yourself comfortable. One of our people will be with you soon."*

Rice swallowed, even though his throat was dry. The voice spoke perfect Anglo. It lacked a human accent; nevertheless, he'd been surprised to hear his own language. "Thank you," he said, then he approached the recamier, his footsteps echoing faintly from the stone floor. Another surprise: resting upon a small table beside the couch was a small copper pitcher, with a matching cup next to it. The water in the pitcher was lukewarm, but at least he was able to quench his thirst; he poured some into the cup and, taking a drink, sat down on the couch.

Rice tried to remain calm, yet he was amazed how easy it had been to gain admission to the embassy. It had taken a couple of days for him to get in touch with Carlos Montero, and when the Federation liaison to the *hjadd* finally returned his call, he'd warned Rice not to expect much. "I'll pass along your request, Reverend," Carlos had said, "but you should know that a lot of folks have tried to meet them. So far, they've only let in two people . . . myself and Morgan Goldstein. With all due respect, I doubt that they'll want to talk to you."

So Rice was shocked when, later that same day, the former president called back to inform him that the *hjadd* had agreed to a meeting. Indeed, Carlos seemed surprised; perhaps he'd believed that the aliens had better things to do than have a conversation with a Dominionist minister. Yet he kept his opinion to himself, and instead instructed Rice to go to the north wall of the *hjadd* compound, where the public entrance was located.

"Any time will do," Carlos added. "Right now, if you'd like. The *hjadd* . . . well, they're rather quixotic when it comes to schedules. Either they'll let you in, or they'll tell you to go away and come back later."

So Rice had put on his shawl and hurried out of the church, making his way on foot across the university campus until he reached the embassy. It wasn't until he'd almost reached the stone torus that he realized, in his haste, he'd neglected to bring along his Bible. Not that it mattered much—he knew the Holy Scriptures by heart—but nonetheless, if he was going to discuss religion with the *hjadd*, it might have helped if he'd brought the gospels.

So here he was, sitting in what he took to be a reception room, drinking warm water and wondering how long the aliens would keep him waiting. Not long, as it turned out. He'd barely become accustomed to his surroundings when a new voice spoke to him—*"Good afternoon, Reverend Rice"*—and he looked around to discover a *hjadd* standing behind him.

Startled, Rice almost dropped his cup. The *hjadd* wasn't wearing an environment suit, but instead was dressed in a togalike outfit made of some iridescent fabric, its folds and bell sleeves embroidered with intricate, almost arabesque designs. He'd seen pictures of the aliens, of course, yet he found himself unprepared for the sight of one up close. Slightly shorter than the average human, heshe looked somewhat like a bipedal tortoise, only lacking a shell. A short, ribbed fin rose from the top of hisher hairless skull, while two slitted eyes protruded above a beaklike snout, its lipless mouth perpetually frozen in a solemn frown.

"Again, good afternoon." The *hjadd* raised hisher left hand in a gesture of greeting. *"You are the Reverend Grey Rice, or am I mistaken?"*

"Yes . . . yes, I'm Reverend Rice." He fumbled to put the cup back on the table, then hastily stood up and turned to face the alien. "Sorry, I . . . You just startled me a bit, that's all."

The fin rose a little higher as the *hjadd* made a sputtering hiss that Rice hoped was laughter. *"Quite understandable. Our projector"*—hisher six-fingered hand motioned toward the ceiling—*"has a somewhat limited range, I am afraid. We are not always able to appear in exactly the proper place to greet our guests without alarming them."*

It was only then that Rice realized that the *hjadd* wasn't actually in the chamber with him. Yet the hologram was so realistic that the only evidence of intangibility was the lack of shadow. He also noticed that, when heshe spoke, hisher voice didn't match the movements of hisher mouth, but instead came from some indirect source. Apparently a translation device was being used.

"No reason to apologize," he said, stepping around the recamier to approach the holo. "I . . ."

"My name is Jasahajahd Taf Sa-Fhadda," the *hjadd* continued, as if Rice hadn't spoken. *"You may address me as Taf. I am the Cultural Ambassador to the Coyote Federation from Hjarr. Our Prime Emissary, Mahamatasja Jas Sa-Fhadda, has given me the privilege of meeting with you."* A brief

pause. *"I understand you wish to discuss a matter regarding our spiritual beliefs."*

"Um, yes . . . yes, I do." Nervously straightening his shawl, Rice tried to collect himself. "A few days ago, I had a visitor at my church . . ." Realizing that the alien might not understand such human terms, he stopped and tried again. "Among my kind, a church is a place of worship. We believe in the existence of a divine creator. The Church of the Holy Dominion—"

"Forgive me, Reverend, but I should let you know that our knowledge of your race isn't limited to your languages." Taf's eyes twitched independently of one another, a mannerism Rice found disconcerting. *"We know what a church is, as well as the Church of the Holy Dominion . . . a denomination of Christianity, which in turn is one of the major monotheistic religions of your world."* Hisher head weaved back and forth on hisher neck. *"A curious belief, particularly for a starfaring species . . . but please, continue."*

"Yes, of course." The last comment roused Rice's curiosity, but he decided to let it pass, at least for the moment. "As I was saying, a young man recently visited my church, stating that he'd met one of your kind. Our meeting was brief, and he didn't tell me his name, but he informed me that he'd been given some sort of information retrieval device that was apparently . . . well, a holy book, much like our own Bible, which described your own religion."

"I believe I know this person." Taf's fin rose slightly. *"In fact, if it is the same individual whom I met shortly after I arrived on this world, it was I myself who gave him the object of which you speak."*

"You did?" Rice tried to hide his astonishment. "What's his name? As I said, our meeting was very brief, and I'd like to know who he is. Perhaps . . ."

"If this individual chose not to identify himself, then he must have had a reason to do so. If that is the case, then perhaps it's best for me to observe diplomatic jurisprudence." Hisher head cocked to the left. *"However, I will tell you that I believed him to be someone who was in need of spiritual guidance, which is why I decided to give him a gift."*

Taf held out hisher left hand. A moment later, a small object materialized in hisher palm: a tiny jar suspended within a pedestal-mounted gold frame. *"This is a* Sa'Tong-tas *. . . literally, the Book of the* Sa'Tong. *It is* *an interactive teaching device, containing the wisdom and knowledge of* Sa'Tong *as passed to the races of the Talus by its Great Teacher, the* chaaz'braan."

Rice stepped a little closer to examine the *Sa'Tong-tas*. It didn't look like any sort of book he'd ever seen; indeed, if he hadn't been told what it was, he might have mistaken it for little more than an interesting curio. "So this thing"—a short, angry hiss from the *hjadd* as hisher throat sacs inflated slightly—"pardon me, the *Sa'Tong-tas* . . . it's about your religion?"

"Yes, except that your choice of words is in error." Taf seemed to relax, because hisher throat resumed its former appearance. *"Sa'Tong is not a religion, or at least not as you define it, but rather a system of spiritual beliefs. More akin to a philosophy, although even that is not an accurate description."* A pause. *"Call it a higher form of ethics, if you will."*

"Then"—Rice hesitated—"if *Sa'Tong* is not a religion, then I take it that you do not believe in God?"

"Do you mean to ask if I believe in the existence of God?" Again, the sputtering hiss that Rice had come to recognize as *hjadd* laughter. *"Then, yes, I believe in God. How can I fail to do so? After all, I am God."*

Rice stared at himher. "What?"

"I am God." The *Sa'tong-tas* faded from hisher palm, and Taf pointed a finger at him. *"And so are you."*

"What?"

"I am God. You are God. So is everyone in this embassy and outside these walls. Indeed, every sentient creature in the known universe, and even those we have yet to discover, is God." The *hjadd's* heavy-lidded eyes slowly blinked. *"This truth is self-evident. As I said earlier, it is rather surprising that an advanced species such as your own has not already determined this."*

"No, we haven't!" Rice felt his face grow warm. Unable to conceal his disgust, he took a step back. "In fact, I'd have to say that it's blasphemy! How dare you . . . ?"

"My apologies, Reverend." Taf held up a placating hand. *"It was not my intent to offend you. I forgot that your race still adheres to deistic beliefs."* Heshe paused. *"It is only that the notion that the universe is the creation of a divine entity is . . . shall we say, immature."*

Rice's first impulse was to stalk angrily from the room. Leave the place behind and return to his church, there to pray for God's mercy and forgiveness. Yet he remembered that his role as a missionary was to bring the word of the Lord to those who'd never heard it. Surely that would include extraterrestrials as well as humans. So he took a deep breath and tried again.

"No need to apologize, Ambassador," he said. "It's just that what you say doesn't make sense. If you and I are both God . . . or gods, rather . . . then who created us?"

"I use the word God in the singular sense, as a term for a collective presence." Taf's head bobbed slightly. *"Furthermore, your question is based on the assumption that God created you, when the fact of the matter is that you created God."*

"Not an assumption at all. It's clearly stated in the first chapter of Genesis, the first book of our Bible . . . 'So God created man in his own image, in the image of the God he created him; male and female he created them.'"

"Interesting." Taf seemed to reflect upon this for a moment. *"Obviously, I do not look like you. Also, I'm not strictly male or female, but instead periodically change genders for purposes of mating and reproduction. Therefore, according to your scriptures, God did not create me. Is that correct?"*

Rice had no immediate answer, or at least none that was not potentially embarrassing. "My Church has recently decided that God may have created other beings that were not in His own image," he said carefully. "However, this does not necessarily mean that the *hjadd* aren't part of His Holy Dominion."

"Yes. Of course." Taf's eyes moved apart from each other. *"It may surprise you that this is a typical assumption, usually made by primitive races that haven't yet progressed to the point where they become aware that their existence is not unique. Allow me to demonstrate . . ."*

Hisher mouth silently moved. Whatever Taf said wasn't translated, but a moment later, heshe vanished, to be replaced by another hologram: an enormous *hjadd*, twice life-size and completely naked, exposing the ridged external spine that ran down hisher back. The *hjadd* was surrounded by a nimbus of soft light, and Rice noticed an expression in hisher eyes that could only be described as maternal.

The creature abruptly bent over and spread hisher thick legs apart. The fin on hisher head extended to its full height as hisher throat sacs rapidly puffed and deflated; the *hjadd* opened hisher mouth and emitted a strangled cry, and a second later a large egg, speckled blue and white, emerged from an orifice between hisher legs. The egg fell to the ground beneath the *hjadd*, and as heshe turned to gaze at it, the egg cracked at its center and burst open. From within its shell, stars, planets, entire galaxies rushed forth, spewing outward to fill the entire chamber.

The hologram faded, and Taf reappeared. *"That was a representation of the creation myth of my own culture. Many centuries ago, before my race developed the means to leave our homeworld, our dominant religion stated that this was the way the universe was born . . . as a giant egg, conceived and hatched by a god that, not coincidentally, looked exactly like us."* Heshe peered at Rice. *"Are you saying that this is inherently wrong, because it contradicts what is stated in your own scriptures?"*

"Well, I . . ."

"No need to be polite. Of course it is wrong. We now acknowledge it to be nothing more than a myth, concocted by an infant culture trying to make sense of its place in the universe. Much the same goes for every race we have encountered. There are variations, naturally . . . the primitive soranta *had a creation myth that was wonderfully complex . . . but the pattern almost always remains the same, with everything else predicated upon that essential belief."*

Hisher head moved up and down. *"Yet as our race matured, gradually developing the scientific means to study and understand the nature of the universe, the truth became obvious. Our god did not create us . . . we created our god. In time, we discarded our old beliefs, simply because we no longer needed to have a religion to comfort us with the notion that we were unique. The* hjadd *are unique, as are humans . . . but the truth remains that we are not alone in the universe."*

"So you have no religion." Although he was discomfited by what he'd just seen, Rice nonetheless felt a certain pity for the *hjadd*. "I'm sorry to hear that."

Taf's fin rose slightly. *"You should not be sorry. For my part, I am amazed to learn that your race continues to believe in the existence of an omniscient entity which, in turn, created you in its own image."* Heshe paused. *"It is . . . amusing, if you'll forgive me for saying so."*

Rice's face felt warm. "No. I'm sorry for you. Without religion, you have no belief in a higher power . . . something that gives meaning or purpose to your life."

"Another fallacy." Hisher fin lowered again. *"Sa'Tong teaches us that, once you accept the fact that God is your own creation instead of the opposite, then you yourself are God, and so is everyone else you may encounter, regardless of their race or origin. That is to say, you are responsible for your own actions, and therefore your own destiny."*

Rice raised an eyebrow. "Then you don't pray?"

"Certainly we pray. All spiritual beings pray."

He smiled. "Then you do believe in a higher power."

"Of course. We believe that our better nature . . . that is, our ability to choose a benign course for our actions . . . is by definition a higher power. Yet such decisions are our own responsibility, not the result of supernatural influence."

"But . . . then all you're doing is praying to yourselves."

"No. We pray to one another, in hopes that those around us will make the correct decisions." Taf's eyes twitched. *"We have found that we are more likely to get a response that way."*

Rice was no longer smiling. Feeling an urge to sit down, he rested upon the recamier behind him. "But without religion, you have no . . . no moral center. No means by which to determine the difference between right and wrong."

"Yet another fallacy." Taf folded hisher hands together within the sleeves of hisher robe. *"Through the teachings of the* chaaz'braan, *we have learned that* Sa'Tong *has five Codicils. The First Codicil, you have already heard . . . you are God, for God is the creation of the self. The Second Codicil states that, if you accept this principle, you must also accept the fact that everyone else is God, and therefore must be treated as such, with the same amount of reverence and respect. The Third Codicil states that, in order to obey the Second Codicil, you must never take any action that will harm others or yourself. Likewise, the Fourth Codicil forbids any inaction that will lead to others being harmed, or which in turn will do harm to yourself. And the Fifth Codicil states that wrongful acts must be atoned for with righteous acts of equal or greater proportion."*

The *hjadd* paused. *"This may sound simple. Indeed, many religions have complex social codes and commandments. Nevertheless, the Codicils provide a guide to moral behavior. Accept yourself as your own higher being, respect others as if they are higher beings themselves, do no harm to anyone or to yourself, or tolerate lack of actions which, in turn, will result in harm to yourself or oth-*

ers around you, and make amends for your failures. As I said, this a philosophical stance more than it is a religious belief, but you cannot say that it is immoral."

"I'm sorry, but I disagree." The reverend shook his head, "Without faith in the Lord, there can be no morality."

Taf cocked his head sideways, a gesture that seemed to echo Rice's. *"Do you really believe this? If so, then ask yourself . . . how many wars have been waged in the name of your god? How many nonbelievers have perished because they have refused to submit to a dominant religion? I confess that we are unfamiliar with the details of human history, but if it is similar to those of other races that once worshipped a supreme deity . . . my own race included . . . then I have little doubt that much blood has been shed. And is not murder the most immoral of all acts, and war an evil that must be avoided?"*

Rice knew that there was no honest answer that would disprove what Taf had just said. Instead, he decided to change the subject. "You say that your race used to worship . . . well, a divine creator. What made you change? How did you come up with . . . um, *Sa'Tong*, as you call it?"

The *hjadd's* hands reappeared from the sleeves of hisher robe. *"Sa'Tong is not our invention, if that is what you are asking. It was brought to us, as it was brought to most of the other starfaring races of the known galaxy, by the one we know as the* chaaz'braan."

Taf made a small motion with hisher left hand. A moment later, another alien materialized to hisher right. To Rice's eye, it looked very much like a large and incredibly old frog standing upright on its hind legs. *"The* chaaz'braan *is the sole survivor of a race known as the* askanta. *Their world was destroyed by a force we call Kasimasta, or the Annihilator. The* askanta *had barely developed the means to travel beyond their planet when they were made extinct, but before this occurred, they were able to send away the one individual whom they valued the most."*

Rice stared at the holo. "And this *chaaz'braan* . . . he was a prophet? A messiah?"

"Not as such, no. A teacher, really, although the askanta *regarded him as a holy figure. As do we all."* Taf's head rose upon hisher neck as heshe regarded the image with what appeared to be reverence. *"I might add that it is incorrect to refer to him in the past tense. He still lives, and resides in* Talus qua'spah, *in orbit above Hjarr."* Heshe paused. *"Although my world has the*

honor of being his host, the chaaz'braan *belongs to all worlds, for he has brought* Sa'Tong *to all races who have learned of its wisdom."*

"So . . ." Rice hesitated. "Am I to understand that *Sa'Tong* is the dominant religion . . . or belief, or whatever you call it . . . of most of the galaxy?"

"This is correct." The *chaaz'braan* disappeared, and Taf turned to face Rice again. *"Beginning with the* hjadd, *the starfaring races of the Talus received its teachings, one after another, over the course of many years. Sometimes directly from the* chaaz'braan, *but more often by passing it along to one another."* Heshe made an open-handed gesture to the reverend. *"There is nothing to fear. It is possible to remain faithful to one's own religion and also adhere to the Codicils. To be truthful, though, I should tell you that most races tend to abandon their former beliefs, particularly when it comes to contradictory notions that God is omniscient, infallible, and the sole creator of the universe."*

"I doubt humankind will accept this quite as readily as you think," Rice said, more defensively than he intended.

"Perhaps. Perhaps not." The *hjadd's* head swung back and forth. *"However, that will not be for you to decide. A Sa'Tong-tas has already been given to one of your own kind . . . the young man who came to you a few days earlier. If you had listened to him . . ."*

"I didn't know." Something cold clutched at Rice's stomach as he realized what he'd done. "God forgive me . . . I didn't know."

Taf said nothing for a moment, yet it seemed to Rice as if the *hjadd* ambassador was regarding him with pity. *"God has nothing to do with this, Reverend . . . or at least not as you now perceive the meaning of your own existence. When you come to realize that the hand of God is felt in the actions of each and every person around you, perhaps then you will see things differently."*

Then, without so much as a farewell, Jasahajahd Taf Sa-Fhadda disappeared, leaving Rice alone in a dark room which offered no further answers, but only questions.

"And that was it?" Cosenza stared at the young minister. "That was all the alien told you?"

While Rice had been telling his story, he'd gradually bent over into a weary slouch, his elbows resting on his knees as he gazed down at the sacristy floor. When the deacon spoke, though, he looked up again, and for the first time Cosenza saw the haunted look in his eyes.

"'That was all'?" Rice echoed. "That wasn't enough? Didn't you hear a thing I just said?"

"Enough to recognize it as utter blasphemy." Cosenza's voice was cold. "I'm surprised . . . appalled, really . . . that you listened for as long as you did. If it had been me, I would've walked straight out of there, and told my congregation—"

"What congregation?" Rice's lips twitched into a humorless smile. "Yours, back in Milan? Mine was gone even before I set foot in that room. What am I supposed to do . . . stand on a crate in front of Government House and denounce the *hjadd* as being in league with the Devil?"

"That's a possibility. If you don't have a congregation . . ."

"'Then you find one.' Yes, I've heard that pearl of wisdom before." Rice shook his head. "Let me tell you what I did instead. I came back here and spent the rest of the day thinking about everything Taf told me. And that night, I sat down and wrote that sermon."

He nodded toward the papers in Cosenza's lap. "You said that it was a correct interpretation of Church doctrine. I agree . . . But the truth is, I didn't write it for my parishioners so much as for myself. I wanted to put down on paper, with my own hand and in my own words, what we Dominionists hold as being our articles of faith. That God created Man in His own image, that we are His chosen people, and that it is His will that we extend His dominion across the galaxy."

Rice looked away from Cosenza, his gaze coming to rest upon the Dominionist crucifix on the wall above the deacon's head. "I suppose you're right. I could have stood on a box and issued this sermon in a public place. At the very least, I could've delivered it from the pulpit on Orifiel morning, to the handful of parishioners who still show up for services. But I didn't . . . and now that I've told you everything that happened, I know why."

He took the sermon back from Cosenza. "And that's because I no longer believe it myself," he said, then he tore it in half. "It makes no sense. Not a word of it."

Cosenza stared at Rice, not quite knowing what to say. "Reverend . . . Grey . . . you can't honestly think that . . ."

"Yes, I can." Rice let the papers fall to the floor, where they lay like dead leaves scattered at their feet. "In fact, if honesty is the issue, then I have to . . . because what good is religion if it isn't about truth? Faith alone is not enough. There must also be . . ."

"Grey . . ." Cosenza reached forward to take Rice's hands in his own. "Reverend, pray with me. Please." Before Rice could respond, the deacon lowered his head, closed his eyes. "Lord, we ask that you be with us now, as we beg your forgiveness for . . ."

"No." Rice pulled his hands from Cosenza's grasp. "I'm sorry, but I can't . . . I can't do this anymore." He stood up from his chair. "The next time I pray, it will be . . . well, I think it'll be to a God that you don't understand."

As Cosenza watched in horror, Rice reached behind his neck and un- clasped the gold chain that held his crucifix. Cupping the cross and chain in his hands, he carefully placed them on the chair. "I must be leaving now," he said quietly. "I trust you'll be able to find someone to take my place."

And then he turned and walked out of the sacristy, leaving Cosenza with the symbols of his lost religion.

Grey Rice left the church that same day. He returned to the par- sonage and packed up his personal belongings, and by late afternoon a shag wagon pulled up in front of the cottage. Cosenza silently watched from a church window as the driver helped the former minister load his bags and boxes onto the back of the wagon. Just before he climbed aboard, Rice looked back at the church. Spotting Cosenza, he raised his hand in farewell, but the deacon refused to acknowledge him; instead, he deliberately turned his back to the window. A few moments later, he heard the rain-muffled creak of wagon wheels as they moved away from the parsonage.

Cosenza went upstairs to the second floor of the church, where the pastor's private study was located. Apparently there was nothing there that Rice had wanted to take with him, because the office remained just as he'd left it. Sitting down at the desk, the deacon spent a few minutes composing a brief hyperlink letter to the elders, informing them that

Rice had decided to resign from the ministry and that Cosenza himself would stay on Coyote indefinitely, or at least until the matter was resolved and a permanent replacement for Rice had been found.

Cosenza sent the message, then he put on his hat and coat and left the church. Following the vague directions Rice had given him, the deacon made his way across the university campus. The rain had stopped by then, but the sky remained overcast, the last light of day cold upon the soggy ground. Climbing a small hill behind a baseball field, Cosenza found a place where he could see the *hjadd* embassy, a grey edifice that squatted among the trees just a short distance beyond the university.

The deacon stared at the compound for a long time, trying to find the words for the thoughts that moved through his mind. When he finally spoke, his voice was little more than a whisper, yet it wasn't that of compassion but of complete and utter hate.

"Damn you," he murmured. "Damn you to Hell."

Part 4

THE ORDER OF THE EYE

The wanderer crossed the river, seeking enlightenment.

From the passenger windows of the gyrobus, the forests of Medsylvania appeared as a dense green carpet, flat and unbroken by hills, that extended as far as the eye could see. It was only after the aircraft flew across the Highland Channel, and the pilot dropped altitude, that Hawk saw the first sign of habitation: a broad meadow, like a bare spot in an otherwise unblemished rug, which appeared to have been cleared of brush. Even so, the settlement was almost undetectable from the air; there weren't any boat docks on the channel, and its few dwellings were close to the tree line. He doubted that even satellites would have detected a human presence.

A faint bump from beneath the floorboards as the landing gear was lowered, then the rotors tilted upward and the gyrobus began its final descent. In the seat next to him, Melissa quietly took his hand. Hawk gave her a reassuring squeeze; she forced a smile, but there was no mistaking the uncertainty in her eyes. She'd agreed to follow him on this journey into parts unknown, and that was more than he could have reasonably expected; Hawk just hoped that her loyalty hadn't been misplaced.

Looking around the passenger compartment, he could tell that Melissa wasn't the only one having second thoughts. Of the dozen men and women who'd boarded the aircraft in New Boston, few remained unruffled. Most of them gazed nervously through the windows, getting their first look at their new surroundings as their hands gripped their duffel bags and backpacks. No one had been told exactly where they were going or how long they would be there, only that a fat paycheck awaited each of them in the end. And even though jobs were at a premium these days, not many had been willing to sign up for employment under such mysterious circumstances.

There was an abrupt jolt as the gyrobus touched down. Hawk expected to hear the rotors wind down, but apparently the pilot wasn't planning to stop for very long. Instead, he twisted around in his seat to look back at his passengers. "All right, you're here!" he yelled above the engine noise. "Make sure you've got all your stuff and that you haven't left anything behind!"

As if to emphasize the point, he reached up to an overhead console to snap a toggle switch. A faint *pop* as the passenger hatch was unsealed, followed a few seconds later by a sudden rush of air as someone outside pushed it the rest of the way open. Seat belts clicked as the new arrivals pried themselves from their seats, everyone checking to see whether they'd forgotten any belongings. In the rear, a couple of master carpenters reached beneath their seats to retrieve the toolboxes they'd brought with them. Then, one by one, everyone stood up to shuffle out of the aircraft. Hawk instinctively ducked his head against the prop wash as he and Melissa walked down the steps and followed the others out from beneath the starboard nacelle.

The gyrobus had landed on the northwest side of the clearing, where the grass had been burned away to form an airstrip. A few yards away, a couple of men wearing identical red field jackets stood nearby. One of them raised a hand above his head, gesturing for the workers to come together. They waited until everyone had disembarked, but it wasn't until the aircraft had lifted off again that one of them spoke.

"Okay, then . . . let's make sure everyone is here who's supposed to be here." He consulted the datapad in his hand. "Sound off when your name is called. Arnold, Juliet . . ."

Melissa tentatively lifted her hand. "Here."

Hawk tried not to smile. She hadn't forgotten her alias; if anyone happened to ask, she had a phony ID to go with it, picked up on the black market in Liberty. Yet the foreman barely glanced at her; a quick nod, then he continued the role call. "Bronson, Mike . . . Everly, Tim . . . Kastner, Ann . . ."

As the foreman went down the list, Hawk took a moment to look around. Now that the gyrobus had departed, he could see the northern side of the clearing. A large, round structure, sixty feet tall but still little more than a half-finished wooden frame surrounded by scaffolds, stood near the tree line; scattered around it were stacks of lumber, bagged sand, and flagstone, and not far away was the tilted drum of a cement mixer. In the stillness of the late-spring morning, he heard hammers pounding at nails, the occasional whine of a power drill, the steady mechanical *thump* of a posthole digger.

"Lewis, Henry." Not receiving an immediate answer, the foreman raised his head. "Henry Lewis! Speak up if you're here!"

Distracted as he was, Hawk almost forgot to respond. "Here," he said, quickly raising his hand. The foreman frowned at him, then went back to calling out names. Hawk continued to look around. A curlicue of smoke rose from a cluster of large canvas tents: obviously the workers' camp. Yet, although he spotted a portable electrical generator, nowhere did he see any satellite dishes, nor any vehicles besides a dozer and a couple of small traks used to carry material from one side of the building site to another. It was as if a deliberate attempt were being made to isolate the place as much as possible.

The foreman finished reading the list. "All right," he said as he lowered the pad, "now that everyone is present and accounted for, we can get down to business. I'm Jerry, the project supervisor, and this is Bill"— a brief nod toward the man beside him—"and he's the payroll manager. We're pretty much on a first-name basis here, so all you have to do is ask for us at the office shack. If you have any questions or problems, that's where we'll be."

A few nods, but for the most part, the group remained quiet. "I'd like to welcome you to this place, but since it doesn't have a name yet, I don't know what to call it either." That earned a couple of laughs, which Jerry accepted with a faint smile. "In fact, I can't even tell you where you are, other than what you already know . . . somewhere in Medsylvania, just north of the channel. As you were told when you signed up, one of the conditions of your employment is that you do not know its exact location. That's why all satphones, pads, or other sat-enabled devices were confiscated before you left New Boston . . . and if you're still holding out, it's a good idea to fork 'em over now, because if we find them on you, your employment will be immediately terminated, along with forfeiture of all payment owed to you. Have I made myself clear?"

He waited to see if anyone said or did anything. After a moment, one of the workmen sheepishly stepped forward to surrender the satphone he'd taken from his jacket pocket. "Thanks," Jerry said. "You'll get this back when you leave." He handed the phone to Bill, who used a pen to mark it with the workman's name. "Which brings us to the next item of business. You're here until the project is finished, or at least until you've completed your particular job and we don't have any reason to keep you around any longer. We have very good first-aid facilities, so if you're injured, we'll be able to take care of you on-site, but anything severe enough to warrant you being airlifted to a hospital will mean that you'll be terminated as well." A few grumbles, and Jerry raised a hand. "Sorry, but that's the way it is . . . although if you are severely injured, you can rest assured that your bills will be paid and you'll receive full compensation. But as our people explained to you before you signed the contract, there will be no days off and no vacations while you're here. We work nine days a week, twelve hours a day, until this place is finished. Period."

Again, Jerry paused. When no one said anything, he went on. "You'll be paid every week, and payday is Raphael morning. If you'd like to have your paychecks automatically deposited at the Bank of Coyote, you can see Bill about it. Otherwise, you'll each be issued a voucher, tagged to your thumbprint, that you'll be able to redeem for cash once you leave. If you really want, you can take it in colonials, although I wouldn't recommend it . . . there aren't any places where you'll be able to hide 'em where someone else couldn't find 'em. Besides, there's nothing here you need to buy."

Hawk made a mental note to talk to the payroll manager sometime later and make sure that Melissa did the same. Since neither of them had bank accounts, they'd need to take their pay in cash and do the best they could to keep it from being discovered. Jerry went on. "Food, clothing, hard hats, tools, whatever . . . they'll all be supplied to you. Except for the stuff you're not supposed to have, of course, and that brings us to the next order of business."

The project supervisor became more serious. "This is a clean site. That means no liquor and no dope. Booze, weed, sting . . . if we catch you with any of that, you're outta here on the next gyro, and forget about getting paid. Don't even think about trying to get cute with us. A couple of weeks ago, we found a bearshine still out in the woods. We caught the guys who built it, and . . . well, four of you have your jobs because they no longer have theirs. So don't push your luck."

A few murmurs at this, and Hawk wondered how many of the workmen had marijuana or whiskey flasks stashed away in their bags. If they were smart, they'd get rid of them as soon as possible.

"Finally, one more thing . . . and this may be the most important rule of all, because it has to do with what we're building here." Jerry cocked a thumb at the unfinished structure behind him. "This is going to be a monastery, to be used by a group of monks who don't want to have anything to do with the rest of the world. They call themselves the Order of the Eye, and that's as much as I can tell you about them other than that they're the reason for all the secrecy. Once the place is finished and these guys move in, they don't want visitors. A certain anonymous benefactor has generously agreed to foot the bill for the construction costs. Since he's also the nice man who's meeting the payroll, all you need to know about him is that his name is Mr. Mind Your Own Business . . . and that goes for the monks, too."

Jerry turned to point toward the southern end of the clearing; for the first time, Hawk noticed a small collection of cabins built near the forest's edge about a half mile away. On the other side of a chicken-wire fence with a small gate at its center, a field of tall grass separated the settlement from the construction site.

"That's where the Order is staying while we're building their new home," the supervisor continued. "You may see them from time to time . . . they wear brown robes, sometimes with their hoods pulled up . . . but that doesn't mean they want to talk to you, or even have anything to do with you. So a major stipulation is that you ignore them as much as possible. If they happen to drop by, just leave 'em alone. Don't try to visit them, either"—a wry grin—"because, believe me, you don't want to. That field is practically crawling with ball plants, and I shouldn't have to warn you about those."

Some of the workmen shook their heads. No one in their right mind wanted to be swarmed by pseudowasps. "Okay, that pretty much covers everything. If you have any questions about payroll, come over and see Bill. Otherwise, you can pick a tent wherever there's a vacant bunk . . . Ladies, your quarters are in the two to the far left. Once you're settled in, check the duty roster to find out which team you're on. It's posted on the bulletin board outside the office shack. Your first shift begins right after lunch. And that's it."

The workers picked up their bags and began to leave the airstrip, a few heading over to the payroll manager. Hawk shouldered his bag and began to saunter toward the camp. Melissa fell in beside him, but neither of them spoke until they were sure that no one was close enough to overhear them; even then, they were careful to keep their voices low.

"Looks like we won't be sharing a bed after all," Hawk murmured. He gave Melissa a sly smile. "Think you can handle that?"

"Oh, well . . . it was fun while it lasted." She and Hawk had started sleeping together a few weeks earlier, not long after they'd reached New Florida. At first, it had been out of necessity—since they'd been posing as a newly arrived immigrant couple, it was part of their pretense to occupy the same room at the boardinghouse where they'd stayed—but soon their relationship had become more intimate, and Hawk had discovered that there was something to be said for having a former prostitute as a lover. "Maybe I can sneak over, when no one is . . ."

"Better not risk it." Hawk shook his head. "We're not married anymore, remember? And I don't want to do anything that might put us at risk."

"Yeah, okay." Melissa pouted, but she knew Hawk was right. When they had heard about the job, one of the things they'd learned was that the project was specifically looking for unmarried individuals. That was when they'd changed their names again, for what they both hoped would be the last time. "But at least I can slide you an extra biscuit when you come in for breakfast."

That gave Hawk another reason to smile. She'd been hired as a cook, while his job was as a carpenter. Before he could reply, though, Melissa moved a little closer. "Are you sure we've got the right place?" she whispered, gazing past him at the distant cabins. "I mean . . . do you think . . . ?"

"He's over there?" Hawk didn't say anything for a moment. "If he isn't, then I don't know what else to do." He shrugged. "At least we won't be bothered. I grew up in a camp like this. It's not likely that we'll see any proctors way out here."

"That's not what I'm asking."

"I know what you said." They were getting close to the camp, with more people around to hear them. To buy themselves a little more time, Hawk dropped his bag, then knelt to lace up his work boots. "If he and his people are who we've heard they are, then it makes sense that they'd want to pretend to be monks. Maybe they *are* monks. In any case, though, they'd probably want to keep to themselves. That's what I'm thinking."

Melissa didn't respond. When he glanced up at her again, he saw she was still gazing at the settlement, a pensive look on her face. "Going to be hard for us to talk to them," Hawk went on, "but it's not like we're in any hurry. As I said, this place probably doesn't get visited by proctors. So let's just . . . y'know, be patient. Do our jobs, keep our heads low, and wait to see what comes up."

"Sure. Whatever you say." Melissa rubbed her arms against the morning cool. "But you . . . no talking about *Sa'Tong* with anyone, all right? That business back in Liberty . . ."

"That was a mistake. Won't do it again." The *Sa'Tong-tas* was at the bottom of his bag, a small box concealed within a rolled-up shirt. After the debacle with the Reverend Rice, Hawk had vowed not to discuss what he'd learned until he found someone who wasn't committed to any established religion.

Which was why they were here.

Hauling the bag over his shoulder, he stood up again. "C'mon . . . let's make ourselves at home. And in the meantime, keep an eye out for someone called Walking Star."

It was a long time before they finally met Joseph Walking Star Cassidy. Even so, they didn't find him; instead, it was he who found them.

Hawk was assigned to the team tasked with building the monastery's interior walls. Erected on a concrete foundation, the structure was comprised of three floors, with a small cupola rising from a circular roof that was still unfinished. Hawk worked with nine other men and women to install the partitions that would separate one room from another, beginning with the ground floor.

He'd learned carpentry during the years he'd spent in Black Mountains timber camps, He wasn't master-class, but he knew enough to be able to follow directions given by the team leader, who in turn consulted blueprints drawn up by an architect hired by their mysterious employer. The rest of his crew were experienced as well, and he got along with everyone. As Jerry had said, the people working on the project were pretty much on a first-name basis; although they knew that this was only a temporary job, they'd also been informed that, if they did their work well, a generous bonus awaited each and every one of them if the monastery was completed by Verchiel, the first month of summer.

So Hawk spent his days fitting wall boards against support beams, hammering them into place with three-and-a-half-inch nails he carried in a tool belt around his waist. He shared a tent with nine other men, and although they had little privacy—just a couple of hempcloth curtains that they could pull around their bunks when they slept—they spent the evening playing gin rummy or five-card stud while sitting around the potbelly stove that supplied heat to their quarters. They woke with the sun and knocked off work when it went down again. There were few arguments, and fights were practically nonexistent; the absence of liquor was something everyone complained about, but the fact of the matter was that sobriety contributed greatly to camp morale.

Hawk saw little of Melissa. Her job as assistant chef kept her in the mess tent's kitchen nearly around the clock; as a result, he'd usually see her only at mealtimes. Although her tent was only fifty yards away, it was generally understood by all the men that the women's quarters were off-limits. There were on-the-job flirtations, of course, along with a couple of serious affairs—one member of Hawk's team was known to sneak off to the woods every now and then after dark—but he and Melissa agreed to refrain from that. As lonely as they were for each other, it was crucial that they kept a low profile. No one in camp must learn that Henry Lewis and Juliet Arnold had a previous relationship under different names.

After a while, though, they worked out a system through which they could have secret meetings. Melissa worked the chow line during breakfast. If she wanted to see him that evening after dinner, she'd ladle an extra helping of grits on his plate as he passed by. Likewise, if Hawk wanted to see her, he'd drop a spoon on the counter in front of her station. A quick glance, a furtive nod, and the meeting was set, with the lumberyard near the construction site as the rendezvous point.

But even though Melissa was in a good position to hear and see much of what was going on in the camp, never once was Cassidy's name mentioned in her presence. And although Hawk occasionally caught a brief glimpse of the so-called monks—every now and then, one or two of them would come across the field to check on the progress of their monastery—none matched the description he'd been given of their leader: a tall man, of American Indian descent, with long black hair tied back in a braid. Of course, since the Order usually wore dark brown robes with their hoods pulled up around their heads, it was very difficult to tell one from another; any of them could have been Cassidy, and Hawk wouldn't have known it.

The weeks went by, the days gradually becoming warmer as Ambriel faded into Muriel. As the monastery's interior was being completed, work continued on the windows and roof. Gyros from Midland and New Florida began to arrive, carrying pallets of mountain-briar shingles and crated plates of glass. As before, none of the building materials came from Medsylvania itself; the monks had stipulated that the surrounding woodlands were to remain untouched. The very same day Hawk's team was reassigned to work on the cupola, three electricians showed up to begin laying the interior wiring that would carry power through the building from the solar farm and wind turbine being erected nearby.

Hawk realized that it was only a matter of time before the monastery was finished. Indeed, a few nights later, Jerry stood up during dinner to announce that the new completion date would be Muriel 92, the last day of spring. Although the supervisor praised everyone for keeping ahead of schedule, Hawk couldn't help but feel anxious. In only a month—perhaps even less—their work here would come to an end; when that happened, he and Melissa would have no choice but to leave.

They would receive their final pay, then board a gyrobus and, along with the others, be transported back to Midland, never again to return to this place or even to have more than a vague idea of where it was located.

He couldn't wait any longer. He had to act.

The following morning, he dropped a spoon in front of Melissa. She caught his eye and nodded: same time, same place. He went off to work as usual, yet even as he loaded shingles onto a wheelbarrow and pushed them over to the pulley rope that would hoist them up to the roof, his thoughts were on other matters. How could he get across the field to the monks' settlement without being noticed? And once he got there, what would he tell them? It wasn't them who he really wanted to see, but rather their leader, yet would Walking Star even listen to him, or would he simply dismiss Hawk as some sort of . . . ?

Something itched at his mind. At first, he thought it was only a low-level headache, perhaps brought on by a pulled muscle in his neck. But it became more persistent: not actually painful, but noticeable all the same. If he'd had to describe the sensation, Hawk might have said that it felt as if a skeeter had somehow entered his cerebral cortex.

He set down the wheelbarrow, carefully making sure that it wouldn't tip over, then took off his hard hat. He'd just begun to rub the tendons at the back of his neck when it occurred to him that he was being watched. He didn't know how he knew this, but nonetheless . . .

He looked around, and saw a monk only a few yards away. A tall figure, hood pulled up over his head to shade his face against the morning sun; he'd apparently come over to visit the construction site. By then, everyone had become accustomed to seeing the Order, even though no one but Jerry was allowed to speak to them. Indeed, the project supervisor stood beside this one, back turned toward Hawk as he pointed out something on his pad. Yet the monk was paying little attention to Jerry but instead stared past him at Hawk.

For a few moments, the two men silently regarded each other. Despite all reason, Hawk had the distinct feeling that the monk had somehow overheard his thoughts, just as clearly as if he'd been talking to himself. A cold chill crept down his spine; putting on his hat again, he hastily turned away. His hands trembled as he bent down to pick up the wheelbarrow; the moment he touched its handles, the cerebral itch stopped. He glanced back at the monk, only to see the figure suddenly walk away, leaving Jerry with a perplexed look on his face.

The incident haunted Hawk for the rest of the day. Distracted, his work became sloppy; twice he hit his own thumb with a hammer, causing him to yelp and drop the roofing nail he'd been trying to drive home, and at one point he discovered that the shingles he'd been placing beneath the cupola were misaligned with one another, forcing him to tear them up and start over again. Fortunately, no one made an issue of his mistakes—everyone on the crew had bad days—but Hawk knew that there was a reason for his lousy performance. So it came as a relief when, an hour before sunset, Jerry blew the evening whistle.

Hawk joined the others as they climbed down from the scaffolds. A quick trip to his quarters to drop off his hat, gloves, and tool belt, then he went over to the mess tent. He lingered over dinner, giving Melissa a chance to finish up in the kitchen; everyone else had finished eating and returned to their tents by the time he stood up from the bench and, under the cover of darkness, wandered over to the lumberyard.

He didn't have to wait long for Melissa to show up. As always, they looked around to make sure they weren't being observed before giving each other a quick hug and a kiss. Before he could speak, though, Melissa gently placed a finger across his lips.

"Don't say anything," she whispered. "Just listen. I've got a message for you . . . from Walking Star."

"From . . . ?" He stared at her in astonishment. "You've met him? How . . . I mean, when did you . . . ?"

"This afternoon, just after lunch. I'd gone out back to fetch some firewood when he came up to me. I didn't know who he was . . . thought he was just another monk, even though they've come around the mess tent before . . . but then he told me who he was, and how he'd just seen you."

Hawk felt his heart skip a beat. "There was someone at the site today, a monk, but I didn't . . ."

"I know. He told me." She moved closer, wrapping her arms around him, and he realized that she was shaking. "Hawk-Hawk, it was scary . . . I mean, really spooky. Like everything I was about to say, he knew it already." She took a deep breath, trying to calm herself. "He stayed just long enough to give me a message to pass along to you."

"What's that?"

Melissa looked up at him again. "He told me to tell you that he knows who you are and why you're here . . . and for you to come see him to-night. Alone."

As luck would have it, the sky was overcast that night, the bear-light dim enough for Hawk to leave camp without being observed. Avoiding the tents and office shack, he quietly went to the fence sepa-rating the construction site from the field. It didn't take long for him to reach the gate, and he'd just unlatched it and swung it open when a cloaked figure emerged from the darkness on the other side of the fence.

"Hawk Thompson." It wasn't a question so much as it was a state-ment; nor was there any pretense of addressing him as Henry Lewis. Hawk started to reply, but the monk had already turned away. "Please follow me. I'm to take you to Walking Star."

A narrow dirt path led through the center of the field, with high grass rising on either side of it. The night was dark enough that, if it hadn't been for the figure walking before him, Hawk probably would have lost his way. He was relieved when, once they were about thirty yards from the gate, the monk paused to light a battery-powered lamp. "You may want this," he said softly, handing it to Hawk. "I can do without it, but you might be more comfortable if you can see where you're going."

"Thanks." Hawk took the lamp from him. In its wan glow, he was able to make out the shadowed face within the hood: an older man, probably in his middle years, with a sparse beard outlining a thin-lipped mouth. "Who are you, anyway . . . I mean, if you don't mind me asking?"

The monk said nothing for a moment, as if trying to decide whether to answer that question. "I'm called Swamper," he replied before turn-ing away. "Come. He's waiting for you."

Swamper? Odd for someone to be called by the name of one of Coy-ote's native creatures. To be sure, Hawk's parents had christened him after an Earth bird that he'd never seen except in pictures. But why would anyone want to be identified with a rodentlike animal that raided garbage . . . ?

Then Hawk got a better look at where he was, and forgot all about Swamper. Through the grass to his left, he saw a ball plant; nearly half his own height, it was larger than any he'd seen before. Behind it was another one, and past it, yet another. He glanced at the other side of the path, and froze in midstep. More ball plants to his right, each nearly as big as the others.

"Don't worry." Just ahead, Swamper had come to a halt; he didn't turn around, but instead looked back at Hawk over his shoulder. "Pseudowasps are dormant at night. So long as you don't disturb the plants . . ."

"Right. Sure." Careful not to get too close to the edge of the path, Hawk hurried to catch up with him. "I don't . . . y'know, why haven't you . . . ?"

"Cleared them out? We have our reasons." A low chuckle. "Besides, they're great for scaring away pests."

Like the people building your monastery, Hawk thought, and for an instant it seemed as if Swamper was about to stop again to say something more. Yet he kept on walking, and Hawk decided that it might not be wise to ask any more questions.

They reached the end of the path; just past another fence lay the settlement. Now that they were closer, Hawk could see that the cabins were nothing more than faux-birch prefabs much like the office shack, obviously meant to serve as temporary shelter until the monastery was finished. If they were recent, though, he wondered where the Order had been living before the prefabs were airlifted in. Their windows glowed with the mellow luminescence of fish-oil lamps, yet their curtains had been drawn and there was no one outside. Indeed, the settlement was so quiet—no voices, no laughter, no human movement of any kind—that, if it weren't for the lighted windows and the faint aroma of woodsmoke, he could have sworn that the place was deserted.

Swamper brought him to a cabin near the center of the settlement, stopping at the steps leading up to its side door. Hawk expected him to knock, but instead the monk stood quietly for a few seconds, as if waiting for their presence to be noticed. Then, even though Hawk hadn't heard anything, Swamper walked up the steps and opened the door.

"Come on in," he murmured. "He's expecting you."

Hawk followed him into the cabin. It had only one room, with a hemp blanket hanging from a ceiling rafter separating one side from the other. An oil lamp on a low table fashioned from a tree stump cast a dim radiance, and once Hawk's eyes adjusted to the light, he saw someone sitting in a bamboo armchair beside the table.

"Welcome, Mr. Thompson," he said. "I'm Walking Star . . . Joseph Walking Star Cassidy." A pause. "You've come a long way to find me. I'd like to know why."

Cassidy's hood was pulled back, revealing black eyes that regarded Hawk with curiosity. Now that he knew the identity of the monk whom he'd seen earlier that day, Hawk suddenly found himself reluctant to speak; there was a sublime sense of power to the man that was intimidating. Yet Walking Star was right; Hawk had sacrificed much to be here, and there was even more at stake in this meeting.

"I . . . I thought you knew that already," he replied. "That's what you told Juliet . . . Melissa, I mean." Something else occurred to him. "Come to think of it, how did you . . . ?"

"Discover your true names?" A sly smile. "The same way I discovered that you were looking for me . . . and I'm sorry, but that's my secret. At least for the time being."

Hawk was confused. "Then . . . if you know who we are, and that we've been looking for you, then you must also know the reason why."

"Not exactly." Walking Star shook his head. "Your names, yes. That you made your way here in order to find me, yes. The rest . . ."

He leaned forward a bit, peering closely at his visitor. "You're in search of something, I believe. Answers . . ." Again, a slight pause. "No, more than that. Knowledge. You've discovered something, and you're trying to find a way to make sense of it. And you believe that I can help you."

Hawk wondered how he could possibly know these things. Were his motives so transparent, or was there something else going on? Before he could reply, Walking Star looked past him at Swamper. "Would you be so kind as to bring us some coffee? It's a cold night, and I think

Mr. Thompson . . . Hawk . . . could use a little refreshment." Swamper left without a word, closing the door behind him, and Walking Star nodded toward another chair on the other side of the table. "Sit, please. You can begin by telling me how you and your companion learned about me."

"Back in Liberty . . . we were there for a little while, trying to . . ." Hawk let out his breath as he sat down across from Walking Star. "Look, the whole thing is complicated."

"I think I can guess most of it already." Sitting back in his chair, Cassidy folded his hands together. "While you were in Liberty, you heard rumors about me and my people. A bunch of guys, led by some crazy Indian, who'd up and vanished into the wilderness in search of spiritual enlightenment."

"That's pretty much it, yeah." Now that he was seated, Hawk found himself a little more at ease. "We asked around and finally learned that you'd gone north. So we caught a boat to New Boston, and once we got there, we found out that people were being hired for some sort of construction project on Medsylvania. I wasn't sure until we got here, but when we were told that we were going to be building a monastery . . ."

"You knew that you'd come to the right place." Walking Star sighed, looked away for a moment. "You're not the first to track us down. We've taken precautions to guard our privacy, but I hadn't realized just how effective word of mouth can be."

"Sorry. Didn't mean to intrude." Hawk hesitated. "I also heard that you were . . . well, a cult of sting addicts. The ball plants I saw . . ."

"Sting isn't addictive, or at least not in the physiological sense. Yes, we used it for a time, as a means of . . . shall we say, unlocking the doors of the mind . . . but since then we found a more effective way to achieve that." Walking Star looked back at him. "As for the notion that we're a cult of some sort . . . no. In fact, we tell outsiders that we're monks because that's easier for them to understand. Safer for us, too."

They were interrupted by the door opening again. Swamper walked in, carrying a tin pot of coffee and a couple of ceramic mugs. He placed them on the table, then quietly turned and left once more. Walking Star picked up the pot and poured coffee into one of the mugs. "The truth of the matter," he continued, "is that we're more like a commune." He paused to offer the mug to Hawk. "If you want to call us anything, you can use the name we've chosen for ourselves."

"The Order of the Eye?" Hawk couldn't help but smile. He'd been wondering about that. "Which one? The left or right?"

"The third, actually." Walking Star didn't seem to take offense; there was a wry grin as he poured coffee for himself. "The one that looks inside the mind itself, perceiving one's own soul. Which is what we've endeavored to do here, and which is why we've decided to isolate ourselves as much as possible from everyone else."

"I see."

"If that's a joke . . ." Walking Star started to smile, then he shook his head. "No, it isn't, is it? But, no, you're wrong. You *don't* see . . . nor will you ever, unless you answer my question. You've told me how you and your friend came here, but I still haven't learned the reason why." He stopped. "If you're trying to find God, or the meaning of life, or anything like that . . ."

"That's not why I'm here." Again, Hawk found himself hesitating. He covered his reticence by taking a sip of coffee; it was hot and strong, and somehow gave him the courage to go on. Putting the mug down on the table, he took a deep breath. "Until a couple of months ago, I was a customs inspector in New Brighton. Lonesome, depressed, and pretty much waiting to die. And then . . . well, something happened."

Shortly before sunrise, Hawk returned to camp. Although he went across the field by himself, he no longer dreaded the ball plants as much as he had earlier. He'd spent the night in conversation with Walking Star, and he'd learned from him of their significance to the Order. There was nothing there that could harm him.

The camp was just beginning to wake up when he closed the gate behind him. The other men in his tent had already noticed that he hadn't slept there that night; a couple of them asked where he'd been, but he ignored them as he began to gather his belongings, shoving everything into his bag. His money was where he'd concealed it, a rolled-up bundle of colonials in the bottom of an old sock; he wouldn't need it, but neither was there any point in giving it away. After a few minutes, the others realized that Henry was up to something; one of them hurried out of the tent, and Hawk knew that he was probably on his way to the office shack.

It didn't matter, though. His time with the construction crew had come to an end. Pulling his bag across his shoulder by its strap, Hawk sauntered over to the mess tent. As he expected, he found Melissa in the kitchen, stirring the vat of oatmeal that she was about to carry out to the chow line. Her eyes widened when she saw him enter, and she was even more surprised when he told her, openly and without any subterfuge, to drop what she was doing and pack her bag.

"We're leaving?" Melissa's voice was little more than a whisper; she glanced warily at the two other cooks, who stared at them in astonishment. "What . . . you mean, now?"

"Yes. Right now." Hawk gently took the ladle from her hand, placed it on the counter next to the stove. "We're done here. No reason to stay any longer." He smiled at her. "Don't worry. Everything's going to be fine. But it's time for us to leave."

"But . . ." Bewildered, she glanced at the vat. "What about breakfast? I was just about to . . ."

Her voice trailed off, and Hawk had to keep from grinning. He hadn't appreciated just how important the job had become for her; over the course of the last month she'd found an occupation that didn't require lying on her back. It might not be much, but at least it had given her a measure of self-respect that she didn't have before.

"If you don't want to go," he said quietly, "you don't have to. You can stay here, if you really want. But I've talked to Walking Star and he . . ." Realizing that the others were listening, he shook his head. "Look, I think he's got the answer . . . or actually, a way for me to find the answer. So I've got to go." He paused. "I'd like for you to come with me, but if you don't . . . I mean, if you want to stay behind . . ."

"No. I'm with you." Melissa turned toward the chief cook. "Sorry, Deb," she said, reaching back to untie her apron, "you're going to have to finish up without me. I quit."

Melissa had even less to take with her than Hawk did. She was in and out of her tent in only a few minutes, carrying her bag under her arm. By then, a small crowd of workers had gathered nearby, watching the two of them as they prepared to depart. Melissa had just joined him again when Jerry appeared. Apparently the project supervisor had been caught taking a morning shower in the bathhouse, because his hair was wet and he was still buttoning up his shirt.

"Henry, what do you think you're doing?" Despite his irritation, it was clear that Jerry was confused more than anything else. "Who said you could leave?"

Again, it took a lot of self-control to keep from laughing out loud. "Didn't know I had to ask permission," Hawk replied. "Sorry, boss, but I quit. Thanks for the job, but . . . well, I've got something else to do."

The supervisor stared at him, speechless for a moment. Hawk realized that this was probably the first time anyone had walked off the project of their own accord. "Your contract . . ."

"Says I can terminate my employment anytime I wish, so long as I notify you." Hawk shrugged. "Sorry for the short notice."

"You know, of course, you'll be forfeiting your bonus . . ."

"I can live with that," Hawk said. Melissa remained quiet, but reluctantly nodded. "Like I said, thanks for the work, but it's time for us to go."

Hawk started to turn away, but Jerry still wasn't satisfied. The supervisor planted himself in front of him and Melissa. "I don't know where you think you're going, but if you think I'm going to call in a gyro . . ."

"Don't need a ride. Just our own two feet." Hawk nodded toward the fence. "We're headed that way. Got an invitation from the—"

"You spoke with them?" Jerry became angry. "I thought I told you . . ."

"Yes, you did. Right after we got here." Hawk grinned. "Guess that means we're fired. Same difference. Excuse me . . ."

He moved to walk past the supervisor. Jerry started to raise his hands to stop them. He seemed to realize that further argument was pointless, though, because he lowered his arms and reluctantly stepped aside.

"All right, go on," he muttered. "Do what you want. But if this is some kind of joke . . ."

"Believe me," Hawk said, "I've never been more serious about anything in my life." And then, with Melissa at his side, he continued toward the gate, and the destiny that awaited him.

Hawk sat on the front step of Walking Star's cabin, idly watching as the members of the Order went about their afternoon chores. Once again, he was struck by how uncommonly quiet the place was. Although everyone was busy with one task or another—washing clothes, gathering and stacking firewood, planting vegetable gardens, making minor repairs to the cabins—they seldom spoke to one another, instead working in silent unison, as if they shared the same consciousness.

Which, indeed, they did. If what Cassidy had told him was true, then the Order had discovered a way to become telepathic. Hawk didn't know which was more unsettling: the idea that someone could read another person's mind, or the notion of someone deliberately allowing himself to be stung, again and again, by swarms of pseudowasps. But even that thought, in itself, was enough to convince him; a passing acolyte paused to glance sharply in his direction. Hawk stared back at him, and received a faint nod from within a raised hood. Yes, he'd been heard . . .

Unnerved, Hawk stood up from the steps. When he'd last seen Melissa, she was unpacking their belongings in the vacant shack that had been set aside as their temporary quarters; perhaps she might like some help. But he'd just begun to walk away when the door opened, and he looked back to see Cassidy step outside.

"Going somewhere?" There was a knowing smile on Walking Star's face, as if he'd just shared a private joke with someone else. Perhaps he had. "Not having any second thoughts, are you?"

"Even if I was . . ."

"There's not much you can do about it now. Jerry wouldn't take you back even if you asked him." A pause. "Not that you really intend to do so," he added, "but it did cross your mind. About five minutes ago, in fact."

Hawk felt his face grow warm. "Do you really have to do that? I mean, couldn't you give me at least a little privacy?"

"Sorry. Can't help it." The smile faded, replaced by Cassidy's usual stoicism. "None of us can. To us, it's as if you're some poor guy with

Tourette's syndrome, unable to control himself from saying out loud everything that comes into his head. That's why I had you sit out here while I was studying this thing you brought me . . . even then, I could hear your thoughts."

Hawk nodded. This was why the Order deliberately avoided the construction site. Too many people over there; too many stray thoughts. "How do you guys stay sane? If this happened to me . . ."

"You'd go crazy? We were about to, before we learned how to discipline ourselves." Walking Star nodded toward the others. "You can't tell from watching, but everyone here has their own method of blocking out the thoughts of those nearby. Little songs. Memorized poems. Focusing on the tactile sensations of every passing moment." His expression darkened. "Some are better at it than others. Ash, for instance . . . you haven't met him yet, but he's one of our strongest mind readers. Probably a latent telepath even before he joined us. But since then, he's become a drunk, able to get along only by putting away a jug of bearshine every day. We've had to build a still just for him."

"I couldn't imagine . . ."

"Doing this yourself?" Seeing the annoyed look on his face, Cassidy shook his head. "Just guessing. Believe it or not, I wasn't reading your mind just then. I was doing this instead." He raised his left hand from within the folds of his robe, and Hawk saw that the tips of his thumb and forefinger were constantly rubbing against each other, making soft snaps. "Doesn't take much concentration, but it lets me think about other things."

"Like *Sa'Tong*."

"Uh-huh. Like *Sa'Tong*." Cassidy let out his breath, then turned to step back into the cabin. "Come on in. We've got a lot to talk about."

The *Sa'Tong-tas* was where Hawk had left it, resting on the tree-stump table next to Walking Star's chair, its case beside it. The small orb that topped the gold frame was dark, but he had little doubt that, only a few minutes ago, it had glowed brightly, its voice extolling its wisdom. For the last couple of hours, he'd left Walking Star alone with it: a calculated risk, leaving the precious artifact with someone whom he'd just met, but he intuitively knew that the *Sa'Tong-tas* was something that had to be experienced rather than explained.

"You're right. This really is . . . something new." Walking Star moved about the cabin, opening curtains that he'd drawn shut against the afternoon sun. "And while it's not unlike the sort of thing we've been exploring ourselves, it's very different than conventional religion . . . conventional human religion, that is."

"What do you mean, 'the sort of thing we've been exploring ourselves'?"

"The Five Codicils." Walking Star motioned to the other chair, then sat down himself. "One of the things that happens when you become telepathic is an acute awareness of other people's emotions. Every day, each and every one of us has these little moments . . . unintentional insults, casual snubs, envy, lust, hatred, even brief thoughts of homicide . . . that we carefully hide from each other. So long as your mind is your own, you're able to do that . . . unless you're a 'path, in which case nothing is hidden. And if everyone around you is a 'path, too, then there are no secrets, unless you constantly recite 'Annabelle Lee' in the back of your mind at all times."

He gazed at the *Sa'Tong-tas*. "So the Second and Third Codicils . . . 'do no harm to others, or to yourself' and 'the only sin is any action that leads to others being hurt, or harm to one's own self' . . . are much like our own code of conduct. It's how we've been able to survive as a community, and more than once we've wondered how much better off the rest of the human race would be if they adhered to the same general principles."

"I've had the same thought myself."

"Have you?" Walking Star raised an eyebrow. "I wonder if the *hjadd* who gave this to you had that very idea in mind. After all, *Sa'Tong* is the spiritual practice . . . 'religion' really isn't an appropriate term for it, is it? . . . to which the rest of the galaxy adheres. So this gift may have been hisher way of introducing *Sa'Tong* to humankind. Find one person, give them a *Sa'Tong-tas*, then stand back and let nature take its course." He paused. "Did you get to the part where it talks about *chaaz'mahas*?"

"*Chaaz'mahas*?" Hawk shook his head. "Sorry, no. Haven't gotten much further from where I left off after my session. Since we left New Brighton, there hasn't been a chance for me to continue my studies. When we were in Liberty and New Boston . . ."

"You didn't want to pull this out, for fear of being exposed. I understand." Catching the irate look on Hawk's face, Walking Star shook his head. "Apologies. Couldn't help myself. At any rate, a *chaaz'maha* is a spiritual teacher . . . much like the Great Teacher himself, the *chaaz'braan* . . . who takes it upon himself to spread the word of *Sa'Tong* to the members of his race. Historically, this is how *Sa'Tong* has been propagated. One person, tasked with the job of enlightening others of his own kind."

Walking Star paused, then looked straight at Hawk. "I believe that person may be you."

Hawk stared at him. "Me? You've got to be joking. Do I look like some sort of . . . ?"

Reluctant to say the rest, his voice trailed off. "Messiah?" Walking Star finished. "Didn't need to read your mind to know what you're thinking. 'Teacher' is a more apt term, really, but . . . yeah, 'messiah' would probably be what they'd call you if you were successful." He paused. "Of course, there's a lot of risk involved with being a messiah. They tend to come to rather messy ends."

"Not for me, thanks." Hawk started to reach for the *Sa'Tong-tas*. "Look, sorry to bother you with this, but maybe it's time for me to go . . ."

"Go where?" Walking Star bent forward to clasp the back of his wrist. "What else do you intend to do with your life? You can't go back to where you were before the *hjadd* found you. You can't even get back your job as a carpenter. And someone needs to be the *chaaz'maha* for the human race . . ."

"Then you do it!" Hawk wrenched his hand free, then stood up. "You're already a spiritual leader! I'm just . . . I'm just . . ."

"Yes. You're just you. An outcast." A solemn nod, followed by a smile. "But you've learned something that no one else knows, and that makes you perfectly suited to teach others what you know. It'll probably take a long time for you to discover the way to do this. After all, you still don't know for yourself all there is about *Sa'Tong*. But if you'll let me, I may be able to show you how."

Hawk's first impulse was to head for the door. Find Melissa and grab their stuff, then hurry back to the camp and beg Jerry to rehire him for the construction crew. Or at least ask for a return trip to New Boston.

Yet he knew that Cassidy was right. There was nowhere left for him to go . . . not if his life was to have any meaning.

"What do you have in mind?"

Walking Star rose from his chair. Hands clasped behind his back, he strolled over to the window. The sun hung low upon the horizon, casting long shadows from the forest upon the nearby field. "When night comes," he said at last, "I'll take you to a sacred place . . . a hogan we've built out there. That's when we'll begin."

"Begin?" A chill ran down Hawk's spine. "Begin what?"

Walking Star turned to gaze at him. "I think you might call it a baptism."

Book 2

Two Journeys

Arthur Clarke has said that Christian orthodoxy is too narrow and timid for what is likely to be found in the search for extraterrestrial intelligence. He has said that the doctrine of man made in the image of God is ticking like a time bomb at Christianity's base, set to explode if other intelligent creatures are discovered. I don't in the least agree. I think that the only sense that can be put on the phrase "made in God's image" is that there is a sense of intellectual affinity between us and higher organisms, if such there be.

—**CARL SAGAN,**
The Varieties of Scientific Experience

Part 5

BEYOND THE MERIDIAN SEA
(from the memoirs of Sawyer Lee)

The first time I laid eyes on the CSS *Ted LeMare*, it was Hamaliel 1, c.y. 17, the day the Exploratory Expedition set sail for the far side of the world. Considering that I was an expedition member, you'd have thought that I would've familiarized myself with the ship before I set foot aboard it. But my invitation to join the ExEx was something of an afterthought, and although I jumped at the chance to visit territories beyond the Meridian Sea, I'd soon have reasons to regret my decision.

As it was, my first sight of the *LeMare* came as I was walking down the New Bridgeton pier, knapsack over my shoulder and carbine beneath my right arm. No one noticed my arrival; the pier was crowded with crew members, while dockworkers labored to unload the last few dozen crates and barrels of supplies from wagons parked alongside the ship. I knew that I was supposed to see the captain, but since I didn't know where he was, I stopped for a moment to put down my pack and give the ship a quick once-over.

Of course, I'd known that the *LeMare* was under construction and that it was intended to make the first circumnavigation of the Great Equatorial River. No one on Coyote was unaware of these things, or at least not if they read the *Liberty Post*. Yet I'd enjoyed steady work as a guide throughout the spring of c.y. 17, so I kept up with the news only when I was back in Leeport, which hadn't been very often. Although I wasn't surprised to learn that the ship was finally finished, my recent travels hadn't taken me to Bridgeton. As a result, I hadn't realized just how big the vessel really was.

And it *was* big: 210 feet from stern to bow and 43 feet abeam, its twin masts topping out over 110 feet above its waterline, the *LeMare* dwarfed everything else in the harbor, taking up one entire side of the pier. Even the tugboats tied up beside it were little more than bath toys by comparison. Nor did it look like any other ship in Bridgeton . . . or anywhere else on Coyote, for that matter. Its long, sleek hull, constructed of whitewashed blackwood, lay close to the water, while sunlight reflected brightly from the glass panes of the greenhouse nestled amidships between the fo'c'sle and aft cabin. Even its masts, oval and constructed of carbon fiber, were unusual, with five yardarms apiece supporting square-rigged mainsails that were still retracted into the yards themselves. Satellite and radar antennae rose from the wheelhouse roof, while two small tenders rested beneath davits on the poop deck, one on each side of the aft cabin.

Overall, the *LeMare* vaguely resembled a Chinese junk as reimagined by an architect who'd previously designed racing yachts. I had no doubt that it was seaworthy—the best shipwrights on Coyote had worked on it, and Morgan Goldstein had opened his pocketbook wide for its construction—even so, I had a bit of last-minute reluctance. For the next month or two, the *LeMare* would be my second home. We were going places in the world where no one else had ever gone; if it sprang a leak because Morgan had decided to trim the budget here or there, then . . .

Well. Too late for second thoughts. I'd just bent over to pick up my knapsack when I heard a familiar voice behind me.

"You're not bringing that, are you?"

As soon as I heard this, I knew I was in trouble. But I forced a grin as I turned to see Susan Gunther walking toward me. I didn't have to ask what she meant. "Of course," I said, laying my rifle barrel across my shoulder. "You're not suggesting that I leave it behind, are you?"

There was a scowl on her face as she stared at my gun. "This is a scientific expedition, Sawyer, not one of your big-game hunts. If you think you're going to be bringing home any trophies . . ."

"Nope. Only for protection . . . which is why Morgan Goldstein hired me. A little extra insurance for his investment." I hoped that would trump her objections. "If it makes you feel any better, though, I'll keep it unloaded. Until we go ashore, that is."

Susan opened her mouth as if to argue when I heard another voice call down from the ship. "Any problems, dear?"

Jonathan Parson was standing on the poop deck, leaning forward against the bulwark rail. The ship's captain had become a tad thick around the middle since the last time I'd seen him; married life had apparently domesticated him a bit. I'd never thought of Susan as being the wifely type, and once again I wondered what Jon saw in her. Perhaps their mutual fascination with the natural sciences was enough; I shared the same interests, too, although I had a different way of collecting specimens.

Susan, Jon, and I had known each other for a while now, ever since I began hiring myself out as a wilderness guide. By then, she'd taken a leave of absence from the Colonial University to start up Coyote Expeditions with Jon, who'd met her not long after he'd jumped ship as second officer of the *Columbus*, the first European Alliance starship to reach 47 Uma. As I said, we had a certain difference of opinion when it came to the native fauna. Not that I minded the fact that they wanted to preserve endangered species; I had no interest in bagging *chirreep* or creek cats. But boids were another matter entirely, and until the day came that they succeeded in persuading the Colonial Council to pass laws protecting them from people like me—fat chance; they'd tried already—I reserved the right to show my clients the proper way to add boid skulls to their living-room walls.

"He's brought a gun, Jon." Susan raised a hand against the morning sun as she peered up at her husband. "I've told him that this is a . . ."

"Scientific expedition, right. I understood that soon as Goldstein gave me a call." Lowering my carbine, I reached down to pick up my knapsack again. "Look, I'm not going to waste time with this. Tell me my gun goes, and I'll go with it . . . then you'll have to explain things to Morgan." I shrugged. "Either way is fine with me. I've already been paid. But I don't think he's going to be very pleased, if y'know what I mean."

By then, we'd begun to attract an audience. Around us, dockhands stopped hauling cargo up the gangway to listen in, while aboard the *LeMare* itself, several people quietly murmured to one another. Truth was, I'd told a little white lie; Goldstein had only paid me a retainer, with most of my fee held in escrow until the ExEx returned home. If I walked away, I'd be giving up enough money to pay rent for the rest of the year. But they didn't have to know that, and I was counting on the fact that they were too beholden to the expedition's principal backer to risk his ire.

Jon was still mulling this over—I had to feel sorry for him, being forced to choose between his wife and his patron—when someone came up from behind to tap him on the shoulder. I couldn't see who it was, but Jon turned his head to listen to him. He frowned, nodded, and looked back at us.

"All right, Sawyer," he said, his voice almost too low for me to hear. "C'mon aboard . . . and bring your gun with you."

Susan's expression alone was worth the hassle. She'd not only lost the argument, but it was her own husband who'd settled it in my favor. Yet it wasn't until I stepped away from her that I saw that it wasn't Jon who'd had the final say, but someone else. And when I saw who that was, I damn near dropped my gun in the water.

Morgan Goldstein might be the wealthiest man on Coyote, but ask anyone who they thought was the most famous person in the world, and chances were that they'd name Susan's father. I'd been told that Carlos Montero would be leading the ExEx, of course, but until that moment it had been little more than an abstraction, no more or less important than the dimensions of the ship.

In recent years, the former president had become a remote figure, seldom seen except when he came into Liberty on official business. He and his wife, Wendy—another pivotal person in Coyote history, not to mention being Susan's mother—had retreated to a manor built on top of the Eastern Divide; if I turned my head, I would've been able to make it out, an eyrie overlooking the East Channel from atop the granite bluffs. I'd spotted President Montero only two or three times since I'd been living here, but always from a distance. Certainly never so close.

For a second, he regarded me with aloof appraisal, much as if I was a bum who'd managed to hitch a ride aboard his fine new ship. I nodded back at him, silently thanking him for interceding on my behalf. He didn't appear to notice, though, but instead turned toward Jon. I couldn't hear what they were discussing, but it probably wasn't me; so far as they were concerned, I was little more than a minor distraction.

Susan, on the other hand, was still sore about being overruled; that much was obvious from the look in her eyes. I didn't want to make an enemy of her, so I sought to appease her. "Look," I said quietly, "I meant it when I said I'm bringing this along only for protection. I've worked for Morgan before . . . I was his guide on a trip up to Medsylvania last year . . . and he knows I'm handy with this thing." I paused. "If it makes you feel any better, you can keep it in your cabin. That way you'll know I won't go charging off into the woods first chance I get, shooting everything in sight."

Susan's expression softened. "No . . . no, that won't be necessary. If Papa's willing to trust you, I guess I should, too." She let out a sigh. "Although if Morgan were here, I'd have words with him."

I could imagine what they'd be, but I didn't say anything. Besides, she was probably relieved that Goldstein wasn't joining the expedition. Last summer, while the ExEx was still in its planning stages, he'd accompanied the first expedition to Rho Coronae Borealis, where he'd reached a trade agreement with the *hjadd*. Since then, he'd been working to establish commerce with the other races of the Talus; he was probably there again, doing his best to get his hands on more alien goodies. Just as well. From my own experience with him, I knew that Goldstein could be a handful.

"You can trust me." I offered my hand. "Promise . . . no hunting, no trophies. Fair enough?"

Susan hesitated, then nodded. "Fair enough," she said, and briefly grasped my hand before turning to walk away. "Now, if you'll excuse me, I'm needed aboard ship."

"All right . . . but just one more thing." She stopped to look back at me. "Not to be a pest, but where should I go? I mean, where am I staying?"

She raised an eyebrow. "You didn't know? You're sleeping on deck, beneath one of the boats." When I gaped at her, her mouth spread into a broad grin. "Gotcha. No, you've got a cabin, same as everyone else . . . although you may not be crazy about whom you're sharing it with."

"Who's that?"

"C'mon. I'll introduce you. It's on my way." Without another word, she started toward the gangway. I slung my knapsack across my shoulder and followed her up the ramp. And that was how I came aboard the *LeMare*.

The crew cabins were located belowdecks in the bow, but when Susan and I approached the companionway behind the wheelhouse, we found our way blocked by several dockworkers who'd formed a brigade line to carry crates down to the forward storeroom. It didn't look like they were going anywhere soon, so Susan changed her mind and instead led me back the way we'd come, along the portside deck past the greenhouse, until we reached the poop. I was glad that she'd been kidding about having me sleep there—the two sixteen-foot skiffs were adequate as ship-to-shore transport, but not as quarters—but I didn't have a chance to inspect them before she went down one of two companionways on either side of the aft centerboard trunk. I'd later learn that the *LeMare* had two retractable centerboards, located beneath both bow and stern, that could be lowered to help stabilize the vessel when it was in deep water, then raised to allow the ship to enter shallow coastal areas.

Despite its size, the *LeMare* was no luxury yacht. Every inch of available space had been carefully apportioned to make room for crew accommodations and laboratories. I caught only a glimpse of the galley and lounge before Susan escorted me to a narrow passage leading amidships.

She was about to open a hatch, when she paused to look back at me. "We're going to take a shortcut through the greenhouse, but you need to know that this isn't something you can do all the time. Once we're under way, we'll keep this place closed off as much as possible in order to preserve ambient temperature and humidity. So when you're going from one end of the ship to the other . . ."

"Use the topside walkways. Got it."

Satisfied that I understood, she opened the hatch . . . and I stopped, my mouth falling open in awe. Until then, I'd seen the greenhouse only from the outside. I knew that it took up nearly half of the ship's interior space, but even so, I wasn't prepared for the cavernous room before us. Beneath a vaulted ceiling of louvered glass panels were two long rows of hydroponics bays, arranged along aisles, one on each side of the greenhouse, with feed tubes dangling from nutrient sacks above them. Beneath the bays were metal racks containing empty trays; above those were slender pipes leading to small showerheads. Potting tables and lab benches were positioned here and there, with pegboards above them holding gardening tools.

Dominating the center of the greenhouse was an enormous fiberglass tank—or rather, upon closer inspection, four different tanks in tandem, with removable partitions separating one from another. One was filled with water, while the others were still empty. As Susan led me down the starboard aisle, she noticed that they had caught my attention.

"Live holds," she said, tapping one of the tanks with her fingertip. "For collecting aquatic specimens. We can open them from hatches along the bottom of the hull, or simply put fish in from the top, then fill the tanks with either salt water or freshwater as need be." I paused to look at one of the partitions, and she nodded. "And, yes, they're expandable, too. Just in case we capture something that's . . . well, a little bigger than usual."

"What? A catwhale?"

She smiled. "Maybe not that big, but who knows?" Susan pointed to the bays and racks. "Same thing for our gardens. We can transplant plants here and keep them alive in either water or native soil, and study them along the way. Nothing here now, but I expect this place will be filled up by the time we get home."

"I wouldn't be surprised." Our route was to take us all the way around Coyote, following the Great Equatorial River eastward until we returned to New Florida from the west. Once we passed the Meridian Archipelago, we'd be exploring parts of the world where no one had ever gone. "Hope we find something edible."

Her smile faded. "If we do, you'll be the last to know. Another reason why we'd prefer not to have visitors . . . no filching allowed."

By then we'd reached the forward hatch. Susan closed it behind us, then took me around the forward companionway, where the men were still bringing down cargo, to a central passage leading toward the bow. After the spaciousness of the greenhouse, the crew quarters felt cramped; the passageway was divided in half by the forward centerboard trunk, with a ceiling low enough that I automatically ducked my head. On both sides of the centerboard were the wood-paneled pocket doors of individual cabins. I thought she'd stop at one near the companionway. Instead she led me all the way down to the far end of the portside corridor, passing one of the heads, until we halted outside a door just aft of the bow.

"Here we are." Susan stopped to look me straight in the eye. "All right, one more time," she murmured, her voice nearly a whisper. "Swear to me that you'll keep that gun of yours unloaded and put the shells where they can't be found."

I was tempted to say something sarcastic, but her face told me that she was dead serious. "Word of honor," I responded, holding up my right hand. "I promise."

She still seemed dubious, but nodded in acknowledgment. "Very well, then. I'll hold you to that. Now let me introduce you to your room-mate."

She slid back the door, revealing a cabin not much larger than a walk-in closet. Two bunks, one above the other, with a round porthole above the top bunk and a couple of lockers recessed into the bulkheads on either side of the room. And sitting cross-legged on the top bunk, a picture book spread open in his lap, was a small boy.

"Jorge?" Susan said, and the boy looked up from his reading. "Here's your new roommate. His name's Mr. Lee . . . Sawyer Lee." Then she turned to me. "Mr. Lee, allow me to introduce you to Jorge Montero . . . my son."

Jorge and I stared at each other for a moment. For the life of me, I couldn't tell which one of us was more surprised. Neither of us seemed to know what to say. The boy was the first to break the silence.

"I get the top bunk!" he chirped.

I glanced at his mother. The smile on her face was fatuous, and I knew at once that any argument would be futile. Either I'd share a cabin with a two-year-old—six by the Gregorian calendar—or I'd be sleeping in one of the boats.

"All yours," I replied.

I remained in my cabin for only a few minutes after Susan left, just long enough to unpack my knapsack. While I put away my belongings, I did my best to strike up a conversation with Jorge. The boy remained as laconic as only a child could be, with mumbled replies—*yes*, *no*, or the occasional *I dunno*—to most of my questions, but after a while I managed to get a few things out of him. As I'd guessed, he was two years old, with his birthday only a week earlier. He was going with us because his folks didn't want to leave him behind for so long; because he'd be out of school for the rest of summer, his mother would be his tutor, with classes in the mornings and afternoons when nothing else was going on. And he had a job aboard the *LeMare* as well: cabin boy, running errands for his parents and any other adult who might need an extra set of hands at any particular time.

Other than that, Jorge didn't have much to say. He'd won the argument about who would get the precious top bunk and the porthole view, but it was obvious that he didn't like having to share quarters with someone who didn't belong to his family. I wondered why he hadn't been assigned to his grandfather's cabin. Perhaps I'd ask Jon or Susan about that later. Besides, I figured that, if things didn't work out between us, I could always talk another crew member into swapping berths with me.

The kid was a mixture of shyness and curiosity. Whenever I looked at Jorge, he was staring fixedly at the pages of his book, a children's version of *The Chronicles of Prince Rupurt*. But as soon as I'd turn away, I could feel his eyes on my back, carefully observing everything that I did . . . and when I placed my rifle in my locker, I heard a sharp intake of breath, as if he'd seen something that fascinated him. Just as I hadn't let him see the liquor flask I'd brought with me, I took a moment to make sure that the gun was unloaded; as an added precaution, I also removed the ammo magazines from my knapsack and put them in my trouser pockets. Unfortunately, there was no way to lock my cabinet.

When he wasn't around, I'd have to find a place to hide my bullets; if I couldn't, then I'd need to get someone else aboard to keep them for me. No sense in tempting small hands.

Once I was done, I told him that I was heading topside to see what was going on. A muttered "g'bye" was his only response; that would have to do. So I exited the cabin and went back down the corridor to the forward companionway. The last few crates were being carried aboard when I returned to the top deck; there didn't seem to be anything for me to do, though, so I leaned against the port rail and watched crew members say farewell to family and friends they were leaving behind. Most were younger than I: university students, mainly, recruited to the ExEx in exchange for academic credit, along with a handful of seasoned sailors who'd been hired by Goldstein. I didn't know any of them, nor did they know me, although I caught the occasional wary glance in my direction. I was the mercenary big-game hunter who'd been brought along as their unwanted protector. I could only hope that they'd warm up to me as time went on.

The sails were still furled, and when I turned to gaze up at the wheelhouse, I could see Jon conferring with an older gentleman who I took to be our pilot. It didn't look as if the *LeMare* was quite ready to depart, and I was getting hungry. Time to visit the galley and see what passed for chow aboard this tub. So I went aft again, passing the greenhouse—through the glass frames, I spotted Susan stowing away crates—until I reached the stairs we'd earlier used to go below.

The lounge was larger than I expected. Paneled with stained mountain briar, its walls were lined with caged bookshelves holding what appeared to be mainly scientific references and natural-history texts. Apparently no one was counting on comps having all the information we'd need, although an inlaid wall screen displayed a global map, our present position depicted as a tiny red dot on the East Channel. Fauxbirch armchairs and side tables were placed here and there, while a blackwood dining table long enough to seat the entire crew dominated the other side of the room. The adjacent galley was separated from the lounge by a serving counter; through its window I could see pots and pans hanging from hooks above stove tops.

Aside from a half-empty coffee carafe on a counter hot plate, there was no food to be found. The place was vacant except for a young woman sitting at the mess table, datapad open on the table before her. She'd hooked up a flexboard to the pad; her fingers tapped at its keys as I searched for something to eat, but I was just about to open the half door leading to the galley when she glanced up from the screen.

"Wouldn't do that if I were you," she said quietly. "The cook gets mad when someone raids the pantry."

I looked back at her. "That so?" I asked, and she nodded. "How would you know?"

"Because I've tried it already." She owlishly peered at me from above the pad screen. " 'Breakfast at seven, lunch at noon, dinner at six' . . . that's what I've been told. And no snacking in between." A shrug. "Guess they're concerned about us eating up the rations."

Until then, I'd assumed that she was another scientist; she was about the right age to be a university postgrad. But the way she spoke led me to believe that she was an outsider like myself. "Umm . . . so what's the penalty for mutiny? Do we get keelhauled? Or is it twenty lashes at the mast?"

"No. You've got to sit and let Susan Montero lecture you on the social structure of *chirreep* tribes. After an hour of that, you'll wish you'd taken twenty lashes."

She kept a straight face as she said that, but as soon as I broke up, she couldn't help but do the same. Just as well that I didn't have a cup of coffee in my hands, or otherwise it would have been all over the floor. For a minute or so we laughed our heads off until I finally managed to catch my breath.

"Sounds"—still snickering, I collapsed on the bench across the table from her—"sounds like you have some experience with this sort of thing."

"Uh-huh." She pointed at her pad. "It's all in here, every last word of it." She shook her head. "I've been trying all morning to get something useful out of the interview I did with her, but the woman doesn't talk . . . she pontificates."

"Interview?" That raised my curiosity. "I take it you're a journalist?"

"Uh-huh. On long-term assignment for Pan News Service, doing a series about life in the colonies." She extended a hand across the table. "Lynn Hu. And you are . . . ?"

"Sawyer Lee." I shook her hand. "Wilderness guide and part-time babysitter."

Lynn raised an eyebrow. "Sounds like an interesting mix of professions."

"Believe me, the second isn't by choice." Given the unkind joke we'd just shared about Jorge's mother, I decided to change the subject. "So your series is going to include a story about the Exploratory Expedition."

"More than one. My editors want me to file every week, no matter what they find out there." She sighed. "Serves me right for being so specific in my earlier stories. If I hadn't mentioned the ExEx in an interview I did with President Gunther . . . well, you don't want to hear about that."

"Try me." I cupped my chin in the palm of my hand. "It's either this or go back topside and watch everyone else say good-bye."

"Didn't know my job was that interesting." She shrugged. "Anyway, the short version is that my syndicate sent me here to spend a year writing this series. Sort of a first-person view of life on Coyote, for people back home . . . Earth, I mean . . . who want to know what it's like out here. Anyway, one of the first pieces I did was an interview with Wendy Gunther. Didn't amount to much, really . . . I don't think she wanted to talk to me, to tell the truth . . . but when she told me that her husband, Carlos, was going on the expedition, I made mention of it in my story. And when my editors saw this, they not only insisted that I stay longer so that I could cover the expedition, but also pulled some strings to make sure that I was included."

"I can guess how. They got in touch with Janus . . ."

Lynn nodded. "Uh-huh. You figured it out. Since Morgan Goldstein's bankrolling this whole thing, he gets to decide who comes along for the ride. Guess he saw it as good PR." A wan smile. "And . . . well, here I am. Not that I wanted to do this. To tell the truth, I'd just as soon have gone home. I'm beginning to feel sort of like a fifth wheel." She winced. "Now there's a lousy metaphor. Ships don't have wheels."

"Hey, if you're a fifth wheel, then I'm a spare oar." She looked at me askance and I went on. "Goldstein put me on at the last minute, too. Once we get past the meridian, I have no more idea of what's out there than anyone else on board. But Morgan wants someone to ride shotgun, so . . ."

"So here you are." Another smile, less cynical this time. I was beginning to realize that, if there was going to be another reluctant passenger aboard, we could do worse than to have one who was so attractive. Her smile faded as she glanced at her pad again. "Well, I hope your job is more appreciated than mine. The rest of my series will probably get pushed to the back of the blotter . . . if they're published at all."

"You don't think you'll find anything worth reporting?"

"Oh, I'm sure I will. It's just that . . . well, who's going to want to read my stuff, what with everything else that's going on just now?" Seeing the look on my face, she peered at me. "You mean you haven't heard? The Western Hemisphere Union is about to collapse."

"What?" I stared at her. "No, I haven't heard. What do you mean, it's collapsing?"

"Just what I said. The whole thing is falling apart." She nodded at her pad. "News came over the hyperlink early this morning. A mob stormed the Proletariat last night, led by a renegade Union Guard regiment. About sixty people were killed in Havana before they took over the capitol building."

"Holy . . . What about the government?"

"What government? The Matriarchs and Patriarchs were forced to evacuate Cuba. No one seems to know where they've gone, but quite a few were killed before they managed to escape. Now there are reports of riots in major cities throughout the Union, with other Guard units either under siege or joining the uprising." Lynn shook her head. "A lot of chickens coming home to roost."

I tried to absorb the news and found that I couldn't. Like everyone else on Coyote, I'd heard rumors that things were getting bad back on Earth. But even though the Western Hemisphere Union hadn't been immune to the long-term effects of global climate change, I'd assumed—like everyone else, really—that the WHU would ride out the storm, if only because the Union Guard had clamped down on previous insurrections. But if the Guard itself had turned on the Proletariat and its leaders were on the lam, then . . .

The sharp clang of a ship's bell interrupted my thoughts. Lynn looked up. "Sounds like we're ready to leave," she said as she folded up her flex-board and closed her pad. "Want to go topside, wave good-bye?"

I stood up from the bench. "Wouldn't miss it for the world." I hesitated, then gallantly offered my arm. "Care for an escort?"

She hesitated, then grinned at me. "Sure. So long as it's not a date or anything."

"No. For that, I'll bring you roses."

She laughed as she stepped around the end of the table. "Skip the flowers," she said, taking my arm. "I'll settle for a jug of bearshine."

Remembering what else I had stashed in my locker, I led her toward the companionway. "Perhaps that can be arranged."

The crew had gathered on deck by the time we got there, and it appeared that the rest of our supplies had finally been loaded aboard. Shags had hauled the empty wagons back to the wharf, and a small crowd stood upon the pier, waiting for the *LeMare* to depart.

Yet not everyone was on board. I was wondering what was keeping us from leaving—the crew was obviously impatient, and a pair of tugboats floated at the bow and stern, ready to take us out into the channel—but it wasn't until I looked toward the gangway that I saw the reason for our delay. Carlos Montero wasn't on the ship; instead, he was still on the pier, involved in a quiet conversation with a plump, middle-aged man whose straw hat didn't quite conceal his balding head. He seemed vaguely familiar, but I couldn't quite place him.

"Well, now . . . that's interesting." Standing beside me at the bow mast, Lynn followed my gaze. "Know who that is?" I shook my head, and she went on. "Dieter Vogel. The European Alliance ambassador. Didn't expect to see him here."

"Maybe he came to see us off."

"Hmm . . . no, I don't think so." Now that she mentioned it, I could see that the ambassador wasn't very happy; nor was the president. Their shoulders hunched, their faces close together, the two men appeared to be making an effort not to be overheard by those around them. "What do you want to bet that he's telling Carlos what I just told you?"

That seemed likely. Although it had been nearly four years since Carlos Montero was president, his most significant act while in office had been the negotiation of the United Nations treaty that had officially recognized the Coyote Federation as an independent entity. The Western Hemisphere Union had steadfastly refused to ratify the treaty, though, and so the WHU remained a major concern to our government. After all, the Union had once laid claim to Coyote, and no one here doubted that they hadn't yet given up hope of doing so again.

Of course the president would be informed of the insurrection, even as he was about to lead a major expedition into parts unknown. For a moment, I wondered whether he'd back out at the last minute, perhaps putting his daughter in charge. Glancing up at the wheelhouse, I spotted Susan and Jon; worried expressions on their faces told me that the same thought had occurred to them.

But instead, Montero patted Vogel on the shoulder, then stepped away. Vogel seemed reluctant, but he nodded. A grim smile as the president shook the ambassador's hand; a few parting words—*keep in touch, let me know what's going on*—then Montero marched up the gangway. When I looked up at the bridge again, I no longer saw Susan. A few moments later, she emerged from the deck hatch but said nothing to anyone as she made her way to her father's side. Pulling her close, he whispered something in her ear; whatever he said, it gave her reason for a relieved smile. Then, with his arm still around her shoulders, he turned to give his son-in-law a quick thumbs-up.

The ship's bell rang four times, announcing to all that we were leaving. A cheer rose from the crowd as, at both ends of the ship, dockhands unfastened the thick ropes that held the *LeMare* against the pier. The tugboat nestled against the stern bellowed its foghorn, and was answered a moment later by its companion idling near the bow; working together, they began to gently push and pull the *LeMare* away from the pier.

As the crowd continued its applause, a sailor on the poop deck raised the Coyote flag upon its mast. Hearing what sounded like an echo of the crowd noise, I glanced up the nearby Garcia Narrows Bridge, and saw for the first time the railing lined with onlookers. That brought a smile to my face; along with everyone else on board, I raised my hand to wave farewell.

As soon as the ship had cleared the harbor, the tugboat at the bow bellowed again, then released its line, while the one pushing the stern answered its call before reversing prop to fall back. The *LeMare* was floating free. I half expected to hear Carlos shout a command—*set sail* or somesuch—but apparently he felt no need for dramatics; Jon was the captain, and he knew what to do. A few seconds later, white polymer sails descended upon their rigging from within the yardarms, gracefully coming down like giant window shades, while the masts themselves rotated, each section tacking at a slightly different angle to catch the westerly wind blowing through the narrows.

The sails caught the offshore breeze and billowed outward, and it was our turn to let out a cheer as the *LeMare* moved forward. Salt spray kicked up by the bow licked at our faces as the ship emerged from beneath the shadow of the Eastern Divide. From the harbor behind us, we could hear the boat horns of other vessels, but they were already growing faint; off to the starboard side, a small schooner sought to escort us, but it, too, was quickly left behind.

Ahead was the East Channel, already growing wider as it flowed southwest toward the Montero Delta. Beyond that lay the Great Equatorial River, and the rest of the world.

We were on our way.

It took the *LeMare* the better part of the day to reach the delta. By then, everyone had assumed their assigned roles, even if the science team had little to do but reinspect the nets and bait boxes with which they hoped to capture live specimens once the ship was in unexplored waters. I lingered on deck for a while, watching the channel gradually grow wider, with sea-swoops circling the ragged cliffs of the Midland Rise on the eastern shore, before going below again to see about lunch.

In the lounge, I found that a smorgasbord of cold cuts, bread, pickles, and onion soup had been laid out on the galley counter. I made myself a sandwich, then sat down at the dining table next to a couple of university botanists. Their conversation was mainly devoted to speculating on possible floral habitats east of the Meridian Sea. It was interesting until it digressed into the effects of cross-species pollination on hybridization, at which point I was unable to keep up. They barely noticed when I excused myself from the table; indeed, I don't think they even noticed I'd been there at all.

With nothing else to do, I went back to my cabin. Much to my relief, Jorge was gone. I hadn't seen him on deck during the launch, but it would have been easy for a small boy to be lost among adults; I assumed that he was tagging along with his mother or father. His absence gave me a chance to put away my ammo. There weren't many hiding places in our quarters, so I had to settle on tucking it beneath my mattress. My rifle appeared to be untouched; this gave me hope that he'd respect my property. Satisfied that I'd done my best to keep my weapon safe for him, I lay down for an afternoon nap.

I must have been more tired than I thought, because when I finally woke up, it was to the sound of the anchor chain rattling down the other side of the forward bulkhead. Standing up, I saw Jorge curled up in his own bunk; the kid must have come in while I was asleep. Through the porthole above his bunk, I saw mellow twilight touching upon densely wooded shoreline a few hundred yards away. Careful not to disturb the sleeping boy, I pulled on my boots and went topside.

While I'd slept, the *LeMare* had sailed past the Montero Delta and turned east to enter the Great Equatorial River. We'd left New Florida behind, and were now just off the coast of Midland. With night beginning to fall, Jon had ordered the anchor lowered and the sails furled. One of the sailors told me our present position: fifty degrees west by two degrees south, just a few miles from the fishing village of Carlos's Pizza. An ironic place for us to stop for the night: it was where President

Montero had made camp during his first attempt to explore the river, many years ago when he'd been a teenager. I watched while the crew stowed away everything on deck, and shortly after the formation lights came to life atop the masts, the bell was rung, signaling everyone to come below for dinner.

To commemorate the end of the first day of the expedition, the cooks laid out a lavish spread: roast pork, grilled potatoes, asparagus with Hollandaise sauce, mixed greens, apple pie. Apparently I wasn't the only one who'd thought to bring liquor aboard, because several bottles of waterfruit wine were placed on the table. This time, I didn't have to dine with strangers; Lynn took a seat beside me, so we were able to keep each other company. She said little, though, but instead paid close attention to everything going on around us. A journalist at work.

We were having dessert, with a few people indulging in a second or third glass of wine, when Jon tapped a bread knife against his glass and stood up from his seat at the head of the table. After thanking us for being there this evening and expressing his appreciation for a successful start to our voyage, he asked everyone to introduce themselves, just so that we'd know each other if we weren't already acquainted. One by one, we all rose from our seats to state our names and reasons for being here. There were eighteen people aboard—eleven men, six women, and one boy—and most were scientists, with eight members of our company serving as crew. The majority were about my own age, more or less, yet the first mate and pilot was a grey-haired older gent who sat with the Montero family. Although he didn't say so at the time, I'd later discover that Barry Dreyfus was another one of the original *Alabama* colonists, and had been with President Montero during their ill-fated attempt to explore the Great Equatorial River.

When it came my turn to speak, I said little except my name and my profession as wilderness guide. Not much response to that, although I couldn't help but notice a few dark looks from some of the scientists. Lynn was a little more forthcoming, telling everyone that she was a journalist covering the ExEx for her news service on Earth. Again, the same cool reception; clearly the thought had occurred to many of these people that our berths could have been used to pack a couple more researchers aboard.

Once we were through with introductions, President Montero took the floor. He kept his remarks brief: how this was a historic opportunity, the first major effort to explore parts of Coyote as yet untouched by humankind, and how we'd soon visit places that, until now, had only been seen from orbit. He added his expectation that our findings would greatly increase our knowledge of this world, and hoped that no harm would come to any of us during the weeks ahead.

And that was pretty much it. A few more announcements from Jon—duty rosters to be posted in the crew quarters in the morning, lectures to commence next evening—and then we were dismissed. A few people lingered over coffee, but I decided that I needed a little fresh air.

I returned my plate to the counter, then went topside, wine stem in hand. The night was warm, but the humidity was kept down by a soft, steady breeze that wafted along the river. Off to the port side, a few miles away, were the lights of Carlos's Pizza, the beam of its lighthouse whisking by every couple of minutes. I carried my drink over to the starboard side and leaned against the bulwark rail near one of the tenders. Bear had fully risen by then, its ring plane completely in view; the giant planet cast a bright blue luminescence across the still waters, giving the river the appearance of a tarnished platter upon which the ship rested. I sipped my drink and watched Coyote's closest neighbor, Eagle, as it slowly moved into sight, a tiny reddish brown orb against the vast superjovian.

The creak of footsteps on the deck behind me. Thinking that Lynn had come up to join me, I didn't look around. "Romantic, isn't it?" I murmured, half-hoping that one thing would lead to another.

A low chuckle, then the soft sound of a match being struck. "If you say so, Mr. Lee. My wife often says the same thing, but then she usually has something on her mind."

Startled, I turned my head to see, in the glow of match light against his face, Carlos Montero lighting a cigar. I nearly dropped my glass. "Uhp . . . um, sorry, Mr. President," I stammered. "Thought you were someone else."

"I should hope so." He shook out the match and puffed at his cigar, coaxing it to burn a little higher. "Would that be Ms. Hu, your dinner companion?"

I had to give it to the old man: he didn't miss very much. I was still trying to decide whether I should stay or go when he stepped to the railing to stand beside me. "Do you mind?" he asked, holding up his cigar. I shook my head. "Thanks. Habit I've picked up lately, courtesy of a mutual acquaintance."

"Mr. Goldstein?"

"Uh-huh. Has them shipped to him from Earth. Every now and then he gives me a box." He blew smoke at Bear, briefly framing its rings with one of his own. "My daughter disapproves, and I suppose she's right. I'm only able to indulge myself when she's not around."

I didn't know what to say to that. Indeed, I was still getting over the fact that I was sharing a private moment with a former president of the colonies, and a legendary one at that. But he spared me the effort of trying to muster a response. "I just wanted to thank you for sharing quarters with my grandson. I would've done so myself, but I'm bunking with Barry in the wheelhouse cabin. We're old friends, and since he's recently lost his partner . . . well, I think he needs company at this time in his life."

"Not at all, Mr. President . . . I mean, only too happy to do so." I hesitated. "He's a nice kid. A little shy, but . . ."

"Please . . . knock off the 'Mr. President' bit, will you? Call me Carlos." A pensive frown. "Yeah, Jorge is a good boy, but . . . well, a bit sheltered, I'm afraid. Susan protects him far too much for his own good. She would've left him with my sister if she'd had her way."

"Why didn't she?"

"Jon wanted him to see the world, and so did I." He glanced over his shoulder to make sure that we weren't being overheard, then went on. "Also, I'd rather he didn't spend the summer with his aunt. Marie is a good woman, but her parenting skills . . . um, shall we say, leave something to be desired? Her son, Hawk . . ." He stopped himself, perhaps realizing that he was confiding too much in a stranger. "Anyway, I appreciate your looking after him. Perhaps it's good for him to spend time with someone who doesn't belong to his own family. If he gives you any trouble . . ."

"I'm sure he won't, Mr. . . . . Carlos, I mean." My throat was dry, and I took a sip of wine. "We're getting along just fine."

"Good. Glad to hear it." Leaning against the railing, Carlos tapped an ash over the side. "Since we're alone, let me ask you about something else. When Morgan told me that he'd wanted to have you join the expedition, he said that he'd hired you before . . . just last year, in fact . . . to take him north to Medsylvania. Is that correct?"

"Yes, sir," I replied, and he gave me a sidelong look, as if to remind me not to address him with unwanted formality. That would be a difficult habit to break. "He was looking for an old friend of his . . ."

"Joe Cassidy . . . Walking Star." He nodded. "I know him, though not as well as Morgan. Go on. Did you find him?"

My turn to become reticent. I'd kept my experiences in Medsylvania to myself, not telling anyone about what Morgan and I had discovered up there. The last thing I wanted anyone else to know was that Cassidy and his followers had learned how to read minds; I had little doubt that Walking Star could find ways of making my life miserable if I disclosed that little secret. "He's up there, yeah. With a few friends. Sort of a . . . a spiritual retreat, I guess you could call it."

"I see." Carlos was quiet for a moment. "And have you been back there since? Or heard anything from Walking Star?"

I shook my head. "No. Not a word. I have the impression that he . . . um, would rather be left alone."

"Hmm." Carlos gazed out at the river, puffing at his cigar. "Too bad. I'd rather hoped you'd found reason to visit him again. See what he's up to."

"I thought you said you didn't know him well. Why are you . . . ?"

"Hawk, my nephew, he's . . ." Another pause. "It's a long story, but he's been in a lot of trouble in the past, and last year he went missing altogether. I put out feelers, trying to find out where he went, but I didn't hear anything until just a couple of days ago when I received word that someone who looked a lot like him had been seen in Walking Star's camp. It was a while back . . . over a year, in fact . . . but apparently he'd managed to get a job as a carpenter on some sort of construction project up there . . . a monastery of some sort . . . only to walk away from it to join Cassidy's group. My source suspected that the building project was bankrolled by Morgan, but when I asked Morgan himself about it, he denied all knowledge."

Carlos paused, looked at me again. "You wouldn't know anything about this, would you?"

I felt a chill. "I . . . No, I don't. No idea."

Carlos quietly regarded me for a second or two. He knew I was lying, and for an instant I was afraid that he'd say so. But instead he slowly nodded, as if disappointed by my untruthfulness. "Of course," he said, standing erect and pushing himself away from the railing. "Just thought I'd ask."

One last drag from his cigar, then he flung it out into the water. "Well, then . . . perhaps I should go below. See if Jorge would like Grandpa to tell him a bedtime story." He patted me on the shoulder, then turned to walk away. "Good to meet you, Mr. Lee . . . Sawyer, I mean."

"Good to meet you, too." I was still unable to call him by his first name.

I waited until he vanished from sight, his footsteps taking him down the aft ladder, before I let out my breath. There was only a sip of wine left in my glass. Too bad; just then, I could have used a stiff drink.

In the autumn of c.y. 16, while plans were still being made for the Exploratory Expedition, a blue-ribbon commission comprised of representatives of the Colonial Council, various governmental ministries, and the Colonial University faculty convened on the university campus to discuss an unresolved issue: the map of Coyote.

One of the peculiarities of history was that, for the first sixteen years of human presence on the new world, most of Coyote had not only gone unexplored but unnamed as well. The reason for the first was easily explained; the Union occupation had stalled exploration of much of the planet, and even after the Revolution had succeeded in expelling the Union Guard, the ongoing struggle for survival had prevented any effort to find out what lay west of Great Dakota or east of the Meridian Archipelago. As a result, nearly three-quarters of Coyote remained unsurveyed except from orbit.

The reason for the second, though, was largely due to tradition. Since the time of the original *Alabama* colonists, it had been a long-standing practice not to name a place until someone actually set foot there. There were exceptions, of course: the subcontinents of Great Dakota, Medsylvania, Hammerhead, Highland, and Vulcan were christened before anyone visited them, but that was because of their proximity to New Florida and Midland. Likewise, the four major volcanoes—Mt. Bonestell, Mt. Pesek, Mt. Hardy, and Mt. Eggleton—had been named after astronomical artists of the twentieth century, although it had been forgotten who had done this. For the most part, though, the rest of Coyote was a blank slate in terms of nomenclature; the only means of identifying most of the world's surface features was a system of alphanumeric codes based on their map location. SW2, for example, designated a landmass somewhere southwest of the meridian.

Now that preparations were being made for the first circumnavigation of the Great Equatorial River, though, it was decided that the global map needed to be updated, with the remaining territories finally given proper names. One proposal was to continue the practice of honoring the original colonists or their benefactors by naming places after them. That was immediately rejected by the commission; while no one argued that people like Robert Lee or Tom Shapiro shouldn't have been memorialized, how many more places should be christened after Coyote's first human inhabitants before it became absurd? By much the same token, nor did the commission wish to allow expedition members the opportunity to bestow their own names upon newly discovered subcontinents or islands; as a compromise, they'd be given the right to name rivers or channels, so long as it wasn't after themselves. Likewise—although it went unsaid except in private meetings—no one wanted to give the ExEx's major benefactor the privilege of having Morganland or Janus

Island added to the map; Morgan Goldstein might be underwriting the expedition, but his ego didn't need to be assuaged in such a crass way.

After considerable debate, the group eventually decided that the most appropriate course of action would be to follow the pattern established by the original discoverers of the 47 Ursae Majoris system, way back in the twenty-first century, and use names derived from Native American culture. Just as Uma's planets and satellites had been given the names of Southwest Indian deities, the remaining major continents and subcontinents of Coyote would be christened after tribes and nations of both North and South America, with individual islands and major channels given the names of prominent historical figures.

And so, on Gabriel 1, c.y. 17, a revised map of Coyote was unveiled. East of Vulcan lay major landmasses with names like Cherokee, Pequot, Mohawk, and Huron, along with smaller islands such as Massasoit, Pocahontas, and Squanto, while to the west of Great Dakota were places such as Navajo, Apache, Sioux, and Comanche, with islands bearing names like Narabo, Geronimo, and Sacagawea. In the northernmost regions were lands like Aleut, Inuit, and Snohomish; south of the equator lay places such as Aztec, Maya, and Pueblo, with the south polar cap located on the massive continent of Inca. There were a few objections, of course—many European immigrants argued that English, French, and Spanish explorers of the Americas should have been honored as well—but most of Coyote's inhabitants accepted the new map without complaint.

This is a roundabout way of explaining why, as the *LeMare* sailed eastward along the Great Equatorial River, many of us aboard became fond of saying that we were heading into Indian country. For the first week of the journey, we saw only the southern coast of Midland and, just past the Midland Channel, Barren Isle. Both places had already been explored, though, so few specimens were collected; we went ashore only to replenish our freshwater supplies from streams and rivers. Yet as we entered the Meridian Sea, we came to realize that we were getting close to the real beginning of our expedition; once past the Archipelago, the *LeMare* would be entering uncharted waters.

The Meridian Sea is the broadest part of the Great Equatorial River, so wide that its nearest southern shore, on Iroquois, is over a hundred miles from Barren Isle. As we approached the archipelago, we saw cat-whales breathing the surface, mammoth creatures that could have rammed and even capsized the *LeMare* if they'd had a mind to do so. Yet they kept their distance, and everyone breathed a little easier when we couldn't see them any longer.

The *LeMare* anchored off the southeast coast of Barren Isle as, over the course of the next two days, Carlos led a couple of zoologists to the archipelago, where they studied the migrational nesting grounds of sea-swoops. I joined them on the first of the sorties as a boat pilot; from the back of the tender, I carefully steered between the enormous, pillar-like massifs that make up the string of islets, ready to pick up the rifle resting between my knees to ward off the birds in case they decided to defend their nests. But Carlos had been there before, many years ago when he was a young man, and he knew better than to get too close to any of the massifs. He asked me to throttle down the engine and told everyone to keep their voices low. Thus we remained unmolested as we observed great flocks of broad-winged birds pinwheeling around the massifs in endless gyrations, their ragged cries echoing among the stone columns.

On the second day in the Meridian Sea, a bird of a different feather came to visit us: a gyro from Ft. Lopez, carrying in last-minute supplies. The Colonial Militia base on Hammerhead, just northeast of Barren Isle, was the Federation's most remote outpost. Established on the site of a Union Guard fortress that had been destroyed during the Revolution, it served the settlements along the northern coast of Midland.

The gyro touched down on Barren Isle, careful to land on the beach, where it wouldn't disturb the *chirreep* colonies farther inland. Once it landed, we lowered a tender and sent it over to collect the crates of food that had been sent earlier from New Boston. It was only a brief rendez-vous, but everyone was all too aware that it would be our last contact with civilization for some time to come. Still, if the ExEx ran into any serious trouble, it was comforting to know that Ft. Lopez would be able to dispatch a rescue mission . . . or at least until we reached Pocahontas, at which point we would be beyond range of their aircraft.

The following morning, Jon ordered the sails to be set, and by mid-day, the *LeMare* was sailing north of the Archipelago, a steady ten-knot wind taking us toward the confluence of Short River and the Highland Channel. It wasn't long before we began to make out, rising above the horizon, the immense cone of Mt. Pesek, the vast shield volcano that comprised the continent of Vulcan. By the time we dropped anchor off the southern tip of Hammerhead, the volcano was towering before us, its snowcapped summit so high above sea level that it was hidden by low clouds; if anyone ever dared to climb it, they'd have to bring their own oxygen.

Nonetheless, something lived up there. As we approached Vulcan, we occasionally spotted birds circling the volcano just below the tree line. The zoologists attempted to study them through binoculars, yet except for only fleeting glimpses of an avian much larger than a swoop, they remained mysterious, vanishing almost as soon as they were seen. Someone called them thunderbirds, after a creature from Native American mythology, and the name stuck.

The *LeMare* spent the next two days traveling along Vulcan's rocky southern coast until we reached the Squanto River, a short channel separating the continent from the nearby island of Squanto. Sonar soundings from the bridge indicated that the river had a maximum depth of only four to six fathoms, and there was the hazard of shoals just beneath the surface. But the science team had reasons to investigate this part of the world—the geologists wanted to collect samples of igneous rock formations on Vulcan's river bluffs, while the botanists and zoologists were anxious to see whether Squanto harbored any unique habitats—so the centerboards were raised and, for the first time since our departure from New Florida, the *LeMare* left the Great Equatorial River.

Since the current was against us, we had to lower the tenders to tow the *LeMare* upstream. Although the Squanto River turned a little deeper than expected, Vulcan's southeast coast was largely inaccessible, its inland guarded by sheer cliffs. The geologists eventually found a small cove shallow enough for them to collect rock samples, but exploration of anything past that was prevented by the overhanging bluffs. However, the western side of Squanto was a low, sandy shoreline, giving the life-science guys plenty of opportunity to visit the dense rain forest beyond. At the northern tip of Squanto was a small sound where the Vulcan Channel forked west and east to form the Squanto and Pequot rivers, and it was here that Carlos and Jon decided to make anchorage.

We remained there for the next several days while the scientists took turns exploring Squanto and nearby Pequot. As the naturalists had predicted, Squanto's ecosystem was unique. Much of the island was covered by dense rain forest, its canopy principally comprised of parasol trees much taller than those found on Midland, within which nested species of birds unlike any yet seen elsewhere on Coyote. Scarlet grak, so-called because of their harsh cries, flitted from branch to branch, following us as we hiked into the jungle. Earsplitters, small birds whose high-pitched song could give you a headache if you got too close. And near the beach, a ground-nesting bird that came to be called the tufted crabbreaker, for its ability to pluck crustaceans from the shallows and bash them against rocks until their shells broke open.

But they were clearly not the dominant species. More than once, while walking through the forest, we noticed that all the birds suddenly went silent. Moments later, a shadow would swiftly travel past above the treetops, as if something menacing was gliding overhead. No one ever got a good look at it, but we had little doubt of what it was. A thunderbird, stalking the lesser creatures of the lowlands.

It was on Pequot that the scientists found the most interesting plants and animals. Like Squanto, the subcontinent was largely covered by rain forest; a medium-size tree was found within its understory that, at first glimpse, appeared to resemble a mountain briar, except that its broad, spadelike leaves were coated with some gummy substance. The naturalists who discovered it were still puzzling over it when they spotted a small arboreal mammal—later called glidemunks, because of their ability to soar from tree to tree upon thin membranes stretched between their limbs—alight upon one of the leaves. The tiny animal quickly found itself unable to struggle free before the leaf slowly closed around it, gradually suffocating the hapless creature. When one of the scientists used a knife to prize open a closed leaf, they discovered the desiccated remains of a glidemunk, its small body apparently dissolved by organic acids.

Judas trees weren't the only carnivorous plants they found. Both Squanto and Pequot also contained tall bushes whose six-leaved flower tops bore an uncomfortable resemblance to claws. And for good reason; like Judas trees, they attracted flying insects by the sickly sweet scent from their petals, only to trap them. Yet earsplitters were able to safely land upon the petals, where they'd insert their narrow bills within the stamens to drink the nectar. Further investigation showed that the nectar contained tiny seeds that, presumably, the earsplitters would later excrete, thus allowing the red snatchers to propagate elsewhere.

Even the waters of the Pequot Channel turned out to harbor aquatic species that hadn't been seen before. One afternoon, as I followed a group of naturalists I'd just escorted back from Squanto down to the greenhouse with their latest plant specimens, I found Susan and a couple of her students gathered in front of one of the tanks. At first, I couldn't see what they were looking at; it appeared as if the tank was empty. Then the fish they'd just captured turned sideways to us, and I saw then it was nearly as large as a redfish, but so thin that, in the water, it practically vanished from sight. The razorfish was superbly adapted to its environment; it possessed the ability to become nearly invisible to predators.

Yet the most intriguing discovery was on Pequot itself, where a zoologist found, in a freshwater pool fed by one of the streams that meandered through the forest, what appeared at first to be a salamander. Until then, no reptiles or amphibians had been discovered on Coyote; it was assumed that the world's long winters prohibited the existence of cold-blooded land animals. Once the creature was brought back to the *LeMare*, though, Susan and her team realized that it was, indeed, a fish . . . but one that was growing legs, and which could breathe fresh air through its mouth as well as use its gills. Clear evidence that life on Coyote was evolving in unexpected ways, with some species making the transition from living in the water to existing on land, despite the limitations imposed by the climate.

In only a few days, we learned that, in this small part of Coyote, lay an environment unlike any on the other side of the world. If the scientists could've had their way, the ExEx would have stayed there for the rest of the summer. But Jon and Carlos eventually decided that we needed to push on. There was more that still needed to be seen, and besides, another expedition could always return to Pequot. So on the morning of the sixth day, the anchors were raised, the sails set, and the *LeMare* turned in the direction of the Great Equatorial River. No one knew it then, but that would be a fateful decision.

After the *LeMare* left the sound and sailed down the Pequot River, we stopped for the night just off Pequot's southwest coast. The crew gathered in the lounge after dinner, where Susan led a review of the data they'd collected from our stay in the delta. I decided to skip it, though. I'd been run ragged over the last week, sometimes making up to three sorties a day; although I'd never had occasion to use my gun, having to shepherd the science teams had become exhausting. All I really wished to do just then was have a drink and watch Bear as it rose above the horizon.

Nonetheless, as I made my way along the bulwark rail to the bow, I reflected that the trip wasn't so bad after all. Once the scientists figured out that I wasn't some bloodthirsty maniac looking for something to kill, they'd stopped being so standoffish, and I'd even made friends with a few of them. Although Jorge was almost always with either Jon or Susan, they'd allowed him to go ashore with me a few times, once I'd ascertained that there was nothing on Pequot or Squanto that could harm him. I still wished that I could have an adult as my cabinmate, but the fact of the matter was that I had come to like the kid; once he was out of his shell, Jorge had a curiosity nearly as intense as the scientists'. And although Lynn and I hadn't much of a chance to pursue our relationship—there was little privacy aboard ship, and besides, she was always writing stories for her readers back on Earth—we were still able to see each other now and then, usually at night after everyone else had gone to bed, when we'd curl up together in one of the tenders and share a drink. There was an unspoken agreement between us that, once the expedition was over, we owed ourselves a romp in bed.

Indeed, I expected to meet Lynn on the forward deck that evening. I'd brought my flask with me when I left my cabin, and given her a hint during dinner that, just for a change, perhaps we could watch Bear come up from the bow instead. She'd told me that she would come along after a while, but first she wanted to sit in on the review session, to see if something came up that she needed to put in her next dispatch.

As I walked out on the bow, though, I saw that it was unlikely that I'd find a place where we might be alone. Lights were on in the wheelhouse, and through its half-open windows I could hear voices: Carlos, Jon, and Barry, engaged in conversation. I was about to turn and leave when Carlos said something that caught my attention:

"Turning back is out of the question. You're going to need to find some place to ride this thing out."

My first thought was that what they were discussing was none of my business. On the other hand, I was the expedition guide. If there was going to be any talk of turning back, for whatever reason, I should be in on it. So I found the hatch leading to the wheelhouse and climbed up the ladder to the bridge, politely knocking on the door just before I walked in.

The *LeMare*'s bridge was a narrow, semicircular compartment, with wood-paneled consoles arranged beneath the windows and a couple of swivel-mounted armchairs anchored to the deck. Although an old-fashioned captain's wheel was mounted below the center window, most of the ship was comp-controlled, its masts and stays manipulated by a touch-screen system that automatically rotated the sails to catch the wind. The ship had a full complement of experienced sailors, but I'd been told that, in a pinch, one person could operate the entire vessel.

The three men were gathered around the communications console, apparently studying something on its main screen. They looked up as I entered the bridge, and for a moment I thought they'd tell me to go away. But then Carlos waved me over. "Come on in, Sawyer," he said. "Maybe you ought to take a look at this. We could use another opinion."

Jon stepped aside to make room for me. As I came closer, I saw that the screen displayed a real-time satellite image of the western hemisphere. Or at least that was what I presumed; although it was still daytime on the other side of the world, most of the terrain was lost beneath a dense swirl of clouds. It appeared to be the southern half of Midland, but I had to look hard to recognize it.

"Oh, hell," I muttered. "Is that what I think it is?"

"Afraid so," Jon said. "Tropical depression, becoming a major storm. Coming out of the west, with wind speeds already up to forty knots." He hesitated, then added, "And before you ask . . . yes, it's developing into a hurricane."

Hurricanes are rare upon Coyote, but they *do* occur, with midsummer as their most likely season. Although Coyote doesn't have any major oceans, the Great Equatorial River becomes wide enough off the coast of Midland that, under certain conditions, a low-pressure system can produce a tropical cyclone that starts moving down the river, picking up moisture as it rolls along. Yet Coyote hurricanes are different from those on Earth. Because Coyote has a lower atmospheric density, the storms are generally less severe, and Bear's gravitational influence, combined with the close proximity of the westerly and easterly trade winds near the equator, causes them to follow an eastward track instead of westward.

The last is fortunate for most of the colonies, since the worst effects are usually felt east of Midland, where the hurricanes would pick up most of their force as they traveled across the Meridian Sea before dying out when they hit the narrow part of the river south of Narragansett. In this case, though, it also meant that this particular storm was barreling straight toward us.

"If you want my opinion," I said, "I think it's pretty obvious. If we try to turn back, we'll only be sailing straight into that thing. Our only option is"—I let out my breath—"well, find some place to drop anchor and ride it out."

My advice was only an echo of what I'd heard Carlos himself say while I was out on deck, but it seemed like the proper course of action. Barry cleared his throat. "The situation is a little more complicated than that," he said, glancing at Carlos. "There's something else you should know."

For a moment, Carlos seemed reluctant to answer. "I've been asked . . . well, more than asked, really . . . to return home at once. We received word just before dinner that I'm needed at Government House. The sooner the better, storm or no storm."

"Now? Lousy timing, don't you think?"

"Actually, my timing hasn't been so good either." He sat down in one of the deck chairs. "Sorry, gentlemen. I should have never come along on this trip . . . or at least I should've dropped out when I heard about what was happening on Earth."

I remembered something that had occurred just before the ExEx left Bridgeton. "Is that why the EA ambassador came to see you off? To ask you to stay behind?" Apparently surprised that I'd recall the incident, Carlos raised a eyebrow, then slowly nodded. "I don't get it. What difference does it make whether you're there or here with us? Can't President Thompson handle this on his own?"

"Our current president is . . ." Carlos sighed, rubbed the bridge of his nose between thumb and forefinger. "Garth's a capable administrator, so far as the day-to-day job of running the government goes, but when it comes to something like this, he's out of his depth. Right now, he needs someone who has firsthand experience in negotiating with the Western Hemisphere Union. And before you ask . . . no, Wendy can't handle this by herself. I'm the one who worked out the details of the U.N. treaty, not her."

I still didn't comprehend what he was saying, but it wasn't the time for me to get a crash course in political science. "At any rate," Jon went on, "the Council sent word that he needs to return to Liberty at once. They're preparing to send a gyro from Ft. Lopez to pick him up and fly him back to Hammerhead, where he'll transfer to another gyro that will take him to New Florida once the storm passes through. All well and good . . . except for two problems."

"The hurricane . . ."

"The hurricane, yes, that's one. The gyro is going to have to fly out here, pick him up, and return to base within the next . . ." Jon paused to gaze at the satellite image of the approaching storm. "Forty hours, I'd say. Call it a day and a half, at best, before that thing reaches us. But that's just the first problem."

"There's no place around here where an aircraft can land safely." Barry shook his head. "Believe me, I've been keeping that in mind while we were in the sound, just in case we needed an emergency rescue. The terrain is either too steep or too wooded, and the ship's masts would prevent a rope ladder from being lowered from a gyro. Not even a suborbital shuttle could do this. Besides, we've got to move away from here as soon as possible."

"Oh, I agree." Jon absently gnawed at a fingernail. "The last place we should be two days from now is on the river. The *LeMare* is built to weather a storm, but a hurricane is out of the question. So wherever we go, it has to be where we can ride it out, but also within range of the gyro . . . and it's got to be soon. Very, very soon."

"You mean, hoist anchor right now?" I couldn't quite believe what the captain was suggesting.

Jon didn't say anything for a moment, but instead quietly gazed at Barry. The pilot's mouth tightened into a thin line as he contemplated the question. "I think we can do it," he said at last. "It's a clear night, so we'll have plenty of bearlight, and we've got the radar to warn us of any floating debris." A grim smile. "At least we won't have to worry about colliding with any fishing boats. We're all alone out here."

"So the question is, where do we go?" Jon walked over to the navigation console, where he pulled up an orbital map of Coyote on its main screen. As the rest of us followed him, he zoomed in on our present position. "Farther downriver, there's this channel here, between Pequot and Pocahontas," he went on, pointing at the screen. "If we travel far enough up it, we may be able to find safe anchorage."

"True . . . but that still puts us square within the storm's track." Carlos seemed apprehensive. "Also, that's the limit of the gyro's range. The pilot would be able to get there, but I'm not sure he'd be able to get back."

"A shuttle from Albion . . ." I began.

"New Brighton's shut down. All spacecraft grounded. We thought of that already." Carlos paused. "I have another idea, but I'm not sure anyone here is going to like it."

Reaching past Jon, he manipulated the trackball with his fingertips, moving the cursor in a southerly direction. "Here," he said, pointing to the image. "South of the equator, off the coast of Cherokee."

I felt something catch in my throat. Due south of Pequot, on the opposite side of the Great Equatorial River, lay the continent of Cherokee. And within its northern coast, we could see a broad crescent bay, with small barrier islands on each side. "If we move the ship here," Carlos went on, pointing to the southernmost end of the bay, "we should have enough protection, provided we anchor far enough away from the beach that we're not hit with storm surges. Not only that, but it also puts us on the hurricane's lee side, where the winds will be a bit less violent. With luck, we might catch just a glancing blow, instead of being smack in the path of its eye."

He was right. While Coyote's trade winds in the northern hemisphere predominantly blew from the west, the opposite occurred south of the equator, where they came in from the east. Cherokee was a little farther away from us than Pocahontas, but if the *LeMare* were to sail across the Great Equatorial River and make anchorage in its northern bay, that would put the ship far enough south of the equator that it might avoid the worst effects of the hurricane.

"And the gyro?" Barry asked. "Do you think it's going to be able to get there? Or even land?"

"By air, it's closer to Hammerhead than Pocahontas. As for whether it can land"—Carlos studied the satellite imagery for a few moments—"looks like coastal savanna, for the most part. Might be a little muddy once you're past the beach, but I don't mind getting my boots wet." He hesitated. "If the gyro lifts off first thing tomorrow morning, it should be able to rendezvous with the *LeMare* sometime later in the day . . . provided, of course, that we leave here within the next hour or two."

He looked at Jon. "Your call, Captain. I'll abide by whatever decision you make . . . including telling Government House that they'll just have to get along without me. But I think this is feasible."

No one said anything for a few moments. Hearing a floorboard creak behind me, I glanced over my shoulder to see Lynn standing in the doorway. How long she'd been there, I couldn't know, but the look on her face told me that she'd heard much of our conversation. No time to snuggle tonight.

Jon finally let out his breath. "All right, then," he said, his voice low yet decisive. "We'll make for Cherokee." He laid a hand on Barry's shoulder. "Start plotting a course. We hoist anchor within the hour. And Carlos"—he glanced at his father-in-law—"put in a call to Liberty, tell them to send the gyro. I'll go below and inform the rest of the crew."

And that was it. Barry turned to begin making preparations to set sail, while Carlos took a seat at the communications panel. I followed

Jon as he headed for the door; he ignored Lynn as she stepped aside to let him pass, but her eyes were wide when I paused to talk to her.

"Break out your pad," I murmured. "You're about to get the story of your life."

Night crossings of the Great Equatorial River were uncommon. Although lighthouses had been erected in the Bridgeton, New Brighton, and Carlos's Pizza harbors, they were mainly there to help vessels find their way home if they stayed out too long. A fishing boat or freighter still on the river after sundown usually dropped anchor off the nearest coast, where its crew would spend the night sleeping, drinking, and playing cards. After all these years, the Great Equatorial was still considered dangerous, its depths hiding mysteries as yet unrevealed. In the wharf-side taverns, sailors told stories of friends whom they no longer counted among the living after their boats had vanished, never to be seen again.

So it was no small thing for the *LeMare* to attempt crossing the river in the middle of the night, particularly in an unexplored part of the world. A little more than 120 miles of water separated Pequot from Cherokee; tacking against a fifteen-knot wind meant that the ship would have to trace a shallow southwest arc until its sails caught the easterly trades below the equator. That would put us in the bay somewhere between twelve and fifteen hours after leaving Pequot; if the *LeMare* waited until morning to depart, the delay would increase the chances of being caught by the storm while we were still on open water. A few of the crew might have argued with Jon, but not for very long.

Even with the approaching hurricane, though, there was an almost uncanny silence upon the river as the *LeMare* slipped away from shore. With the exception of a few high clouds illuminated by bearlight, the night sky was clear, the stars gleaming like thousands of distant candles. Bear was nearly at zenith, its rings fully exposed; standing at the bow, one could see the giant planet reflected upon the waters; it might have been easy to pretend that the ship was gliding across a mirror, if not for the waves gently lapping against the prow and the slow rocking of the deck,

Indeed, the nocturnal peace lulled many of the crew. By midnight, most of the scientists had gone to bed, while the sailors took turns standing watch on deck. Jon, Barry, and Carlos decided to stay awake through the night; someone stoked up the wheelhouse coffeemaker, and once the automatic pilot was set, the three of them hunkered down for the graveyard shift.

I could have sacked out, but I didn't. Call it a premonition, or perhaps the result of having heard those stories about vanished ships, but I felt an obligation to do my job. So I went below to fetch the carbine from my cabin. I thought Jorge was asleep, yet as I sat on the edge of my bunk to load my weapon, I heard him stir, and looked up to find him peering down at me. Over the past couple of weeks, I'd been careful never to let him see me handling my rifle, lest he discover where I'd hidden the ammo. I quietly told him to go back to sleep—*nothing here you need to see, Jorge*—and his face disappeared again. I wondered how long he'd been watching me, though, and hoped that he hadn't spotted me removing the magazines from beneath the mattress.

There were a couple of sailors in the peak when I came up to the fo'c'sle again, using the windlass cover as a poker table. They noticed my rifle, of course, but didn't say anything about it. I pulled up a barrel and joined them for a few hands, using a couple of colonials I happened to have in my pocket as my stakes. I was good, but they were better. I won the pot, only to lose it again, and once it got to the point where I'd have had to start writing IOUs, I surrendered and wandered up to the bridge to see what the other guys were doing.

As it turned out, the conversation up there was rather interesting. Carlos had begun to reminisce about his younger days when he'd assumed the identity of Rigil Kent to wage guerrilla war against the Union Guard. Pouring myself a mug of coffee, I parked myself against a bulkhead and quietly listened in. Like everyone else on Coyote, I already knew about his years as a resistance leader during the Revolution. Yet it's one thing to read his wife's memoirs, and quite another to hear it from the man himself. Like anyone who'd lived a long and adventurous life, Carlos was prone to exaggeration; whenever his tales began to get too tall, though, Barry would playfully correct the record, and it became fun to watch the two of them argue about who did what when.

Carlos was telling us about how the Matriarch Hernandez had set up an ambush for him and his troops at Goat Kill Creek, when he was interrupted by a shrill *beep* from the navigation console. Still cradling his coffee mug in his lap, Jon twisted around in his seat to check the radar. A frown appeared on his face as he peered more closely at the screen.

"Something coming up off the port bow," he murmured. "Ninety-eight degrees east, about a half mile away."

"Driftwood?" Next to him, Barry bent a little closer. "Could be a log . . ."

"No. It's in motion." Jon paused, then sucked in his breath. "Uh-oh. Signal's split . . . now there's two of them."

Carlos immediately forgot about the story he'd been telling. "Still coming toward us?" he asked, and Jon nodded. "Might just be catwhales, but . . ." His voice trailed off, then he looked over at me. "Sawyer . . . ?"

"Right." Pushing myself off the floor, I picked up my rifle from where I'd rested it against the bulkhead. Barry was already on his feet; he switched off the autopilot and resumed manual control of the wheel. "Better turn off the formation lights, too," I added. "And kill the floods while you're at it."

Jon was about to put down his coffee mug. He nearly dropped it when he heard that. "All the lights?" he asked, giving me an uncertain look. "Are you sure?"

"Do what he says." Carlos's face had gone pale; he had risen from his chair and was heading for the door leading to the captain's cabin, located behind the bridge. "If that's what I think it is, we need to get those lights out."

Jon didn't argue; he'd suddenly realized what we were talking about.

I didn't wait any longer, but left the bridge as fast as I could, not bothering to use the ladder, instead jumping straight down to the deck hatch.

The formation lights on top of the masts and at the bow and stern had been extinguished by the time I made it to the fo'c'sle. The sailors with whom I'd been playing cards were still sitting at the windlass; they looked up in puzzlement as the floodlights that had illuminated the bow abruptly went out, then they turned to see me trotting toward them.

"Clear the deck," I said. "Get below and stay there." One of them started to gather up the cards until I pulled him away from the windlass. "Don't worry about that. Just get out of here."

With the floodlights off, the fo'c'sle was plunged into darkness. I glanced back at the wheelhouse in time to see the ceiling lamps go out as well; against the back-glow from the consoles, I could just make out Jon and Barry standing at the windows. But there was still light coming from the belowdecks portholes, little bright ovals that reflected off the surface of the river just above the waterline. I swore beneath my breath; even though Barry was turning the ship to the west, the porthole lights resembled the sort of bioluminescence that would attract the things coming for us.

Too late to do anything about that, though. Bracing my rump against the windlass, I shut my eyes, counted to ten, then opened them again. My pupils had become a little more dark-adapted; I avoided looking up at Bear, but peered straight out at the dark waters off the port bow. I couldn't see anything, though, and I prayed that the creatures out there had lost interest in the *LeMare*.

But I wasn't counting on it.

I flipped off the rifle's safety, switched to full-auto, then raised it to firing position, bracing the stock against my left shoulder. Activating the infrared night-vision scope, I squinted through it with my right eye. Within the eyepiece was a clear view of the river for a range of about fifty yards, a greenish grey surface that rippled beneath the bearlight. Still nothing. Maybe they had gone away . . .

"Sonar contact!" Jon had opened one of the wheelhouse windows to yell down to me. "Bearing one-seven-eight, twenty yards off port bow!"

Damn it! They'd gone under! Still watching the river through my scope, I took a deep breath, trying hard to keep my hands from trembling. If those goddamn things went under the ship, they could pop up just about anywhere . . .

"Easy, son." Carlos's voice, from just behind me. "I've got your back."

I was so startled to hear him, I nearly looked away from the scope. "Mr. President, you shouldn't be out . . ."

That's when they attacked.

The first few years after humans arrived on Coyote, it was be-lieved that boids were the most dangerous animals on the planet. And for good reason; they had killed Carlos's parents, Jorge and Rita Montero, only a few days after the *Alabama* party set foot on New Florida, and over time they'd brought death to many more colonists.

But we were wrong. There were creatures on the new world far more menacing than boids. It just took a while for humans to find them . . . or rather, for them to find us.

The first time anyone encountered a river horse was in c.y. 06, when a group of fishermen from New Boston who'd wandered up the Great Equatorial River ran into a pack near a small island just off the coast of Great Dakota. According to an account written by Carlos's sister Marie, who'd led the rescue effort from the nearby camp that would later be named Clarksburg, only two men survived the attack, with one of them dying on the way back to Great Dakota. Indeed, a member of Marie's party was killed while they were getting the men off the island. In both instances, the river horses had come in fast and hard, and struck with neither warning nor mercy.

Even though river horses had rarely been seen since then, those who made their living on the Great Equatorial were all too aware of their existence. Every so often the half-eaten carcass of a catwhale would wash ashore, and once the crew of a schooner spotted a pack ganging up on one just north of Albion, circling the giant fish like hungry wolves. And, of course, there was the occasional disappearance of a fishing boat unwary enough to be caught out on the river after dark.

The river horses that attacked the *LeMare* probably mistook us for a cat-whale. Or perhaps they knew exactly what we were and just didn't care; they'd seen our lights, and decided that we were easy prey. Whatever the reason, it mattered little what had drawn them to us; I barely had time to prepare myself before the first one threw itself at the ship.

Within the pale glow of my scope, I saw a giant, serpentine head, vaguely resembling that of a sea horse back on Earth except many times larger, breach the surface just a dozen yards off the port bow. Like something from a nightmare, the river horse rose before me, its narrow eyes glistening within a bony skull. For a second, it seemed to hesitate, as if surprised that the *LeMare* wasn't quite what it expected to find. Then its jaws opened, exposing a row of jagged teeth . . .

That was enough for me. I opened fire, keeping my forefinger locked down against the trigger. A loud *braaap!* as the rifle jolted against my shoulder and spent shells cascaded upon the deck next to my feet, but I wasn't paying attention to anything except the river horse. I wanted that monster dead.

My first few bullets missed, then dark blood spurted from just above its chest. The river horse recoiled, and from its mouth came a sound like a lizard being strangled. Then its head went down again, disappearing beneath the surface so close to the *LeMare* that a spray of water hit me in the face.

Salt stung my eyes, blinding me for a moment. Wiping my hand across my face, I was about to head for the railing when I heard gunshots from behind me. Glancing over my shoulder, I saw Carlos using a rifle to fire upon another river horse that had appeared on the other side of the ship.

I don't know which surprised me more—that the second creature was canny enough to attack from a different direction, or that Carlos was armed as well—but his aim was better than mine. A rasping scream, and I caught a brief glimpse of blood and pulpy tissue spewing from the creature's right eye. Then it reared back, momentarily revealing one of the spadelike flippers of its forequarters, before it toppled sideways into the water.

From somewhere behind me, people began to cheer, and I glanced to my right. Despite my warnings, the sailors I'd told to go below were standing near the forward companionway . . . and right behind them, several other crew members. And damn it, one of them was Jorge. The kid had come up from below, and was clinging to a float ring hanging from the bulkhead beneath the wheelhouse windows, watching everything with fascination.

"Get back!" I yelled. "It's not over yet!"

I didn't wait to see whether they paid attention, but instead vaulted over the windlass to join Carlos at the starboard railing. He was still firing at the river horse he'd just hit, but if it wasn't already dead, at least it was mortally wounded. Lying on its side, the creature angrily thrashed at the water with its tail as we continued to pump bullets into its chest and stomach . . . then, just as I thought we'd have the satisfaction of seeing it die, the monster suddenly vanished from sight, as if something below it had reached up to seize its wounded body and drag it beneath the waves.

"My god." Carlos whispered. "They eat their own."

Better them than us, I wanted to say, but I couldn't. My heart was pounding against my chest, my breath coming in gasps. How many shots had I fired in those last few seconds? I didn't know until I raised my rifle again and, aiming it toward the last place we'd seen the second horse, experimentally squeezed the trigger. One shot, then a hollow click. I'd run through an entire magazine in less than a minute . . . Then I knew that, if Carlos hadn't been there, I wouldn't have had a chance to reload.

So I said the only thing I could: "Thank you."

"You're welcome." He let out his breath, then gave me a wry grin. "Nice shooting there. Remind me to thank Morgan for hiring you."

I nodded. I got a closer look at the weapon in his hands: an old Union Guard carbine, its stock pitted and well-worn. "Picked this up during the Revolution," Carlos murmured, holding it up for me to see. "Thought I'd bring it along just in case."

I wondered if Susan knew about it, but decided not to ask. "Glad you did," I said as I studied the river again. Both river horses had disappeared, the live one dragging away its dead companion. The crew who'd witnessed the battle were starting to come over to us, but I wasn't quite ready to believe that the danger had passed. "Hold on, folks," I said, raising a hand to stop them. "Let's make sure they're gone."

Carlos nodded, then turned toward the wheelhouse. "Jon?" he called out. "Anything on the scope?"

Through the windows, I saw both Jon and Barry bend over the radar and sonar screens. A moment passed, then Jon looked back at us. "All clear!" he shouted back. "They're gone!"

I sagged against the rail, both exhausted and relieved, as the crewmen let out another cheer. Carlos clapped me on the back, then Jon turned on the floodlights again and everyone came over to congratulate us. I have to admit, I took some small pleasure at being the hero of the hour, but what I really wanted was a drink.

"I've got some bearshine down in my cabin," I told Carlos, whispering in his ear. "Care to join me for a nightcap?"

He thought about it for a moment. "I'm going to stay up for a while longer," he said quietly, "but I could use a drink, yeah. Meet me on the bridge?"

"Sure thing." Tucking my rifle beneath my arm, I made my way through the crowd. Just before I reached the forward companionway, though, I found Jorge waiting for me, Susan right behind him. The boy's eyes were round with awe, and I realized just then that, so far as he was concerned, I was ten feet tall and fought monsters with my bare hands.

"Can I . . . ?" He stared at the rifle beneath my arm. "Can I see that?"

For a moment, I was tempted to let him hold my weapon. With the chamber empty and its magazine spent, it was harmless. But one look at his mother's face told me this might not be a good idea. Regardless of what her father and I had just done, she clearly didn't approve of her son being exposed to firearms.

"Maybe another time," I said. Jorge was disappointed, but gave me a sheepish grin as I ruffled his hair. Then I eased past the two of them and went belowdecks.

Once I was alone, I put the rifle back in my locker, then removed the spare magazines from my pocket and returned them to their hiding place beneath the mattress. Then I grabbed my flask and went topside again. Now that the excitement was over, everyone was going back to bed; I passed Jorge on the companionway and gave him a playful swat on the arm as I went by. Susan was behind him, and I figured that she'd tuck him in bed. The kid would probably be asleep by the time I returned to our cabin.

Carlos was waiting for me on the bridge, and Jon and Barry were ready for a drink, too. My flask was nearly empty, but I figured that it was as good a time as any to kill the rest of my bearshine, so I poured a shot into everyone's coffee mug. The night was calm again, yet when I happened to glance at the chronometer, I was surprised to see that no more than fifteen minutes had gone by since the radar had alerted us of the river horses. As always, it was astonishing how slowly time passes when you're in danger.

We'd just toasted each other's good health, and Carlos was saying something about how shocked he'd been to see a river horse willing to cannibalize its wounded companion, when there was a muffled bang from somewhere belowdecks. My first thought was that someone had dropped a heavy object down in the crew quarters . . . but then Susan screamed, and I suddenly realized what had just happened.

I wasn't the only one who did. Jon, Carlos, and I stared at each other for a moment . . . and then we were out of the wheelhouse, practically falling over ourselves as we scrambled down the ladder. By the time we reached the crew quarters, we found the passageway crowded with people emerging from their cabins to see what was going on. Jon impatiently shoved them aside as Carlos and I followed him, and I felt a cold chill run down my back when my worst suspicions were confirmed. The noise had come from my cabin.

We found Susan crouched on the floor, holding Jorge in her arms. For an instant, I thought the boy had been harmed, but then I saw that he was unhurt. He was clearly terrified by what had happened, though, for his face was buried against his mother's chest, his small body quaking with fear.

My rifle lay on the floor, its spare magazine attached, its muzzle still smoking. And within the ceiling was a small, splintered hole, showing the entry point of the bullet Jorge had fired.

Susan's arms were still wrapped around her son when she gazed up at us. When she saw me, the look in her eyes was as murderous as that of a river horse.

No question about it: the accident was all my fault.

If I hadn't been so intent on having a drink with Jon and Carlos, I would've made sure that the rifle's safety was on and that the extra magazines were stowed away some place where Jorge couldn't find them. At the very least, I should have realized that the boy had become curious about my weapon after seeing me use it to fight off the river horses and that he might take advantage of my absence to reload it. He'd later claim that he hadn't intended to fire it, that his finger had slipped when he'd inserted it within the trigger guard, but that didn't make things any better. Indeed, the fact that he hadn't actually been aiming at the ceiling only made matters worse; the faint powder burns on his cheeks were proof that the barrel had been less than a foot away from his face when the gun had gone off.

The only thing that stopped Susan from tearing me limb from limb was Carlos. Stepping between his daughter and me, he finally managed to calm her down, reminding her that it was an accident and no one had been hurt; at her insistence, he removed the rifle from my quarters, taking it up to his cabin. I didn't protest. I was all too aware my negligence had almost caused her son to be killed.

Susan was still angry, though, and I couldn't blame her. Jorge spent the rest of the night in her cabin, sleeping in his father's bed while Jon remained on watch. I presume the kid slept well, but I certainly didn't. It was a long time before I finally dozed off, and when I awoke a few hours later, the first thing I saw was the bullet hole in the ceiling, mute testimony to my negligence.

Almost everyone was still asleep when I went topside again. The morning was cold and bleak, with low clouds to the west masking Bear as it dipped below the horizon. Cherokee still couldn't be seen, but I knew that the *LeMare* was only a few hours away from reaching its northern coast. A couple of sailors were standing watch on the bow; neither of them wanted to talk to me, though, but instead turned their backs when I came up the companionway. Gazing up at the wheelhouse, I spotted Jon through the windows. He caught my eye for a second, then deliberately looked away. He'd already heard my apologies; forgiveness would have to come later, if ever.

With nothing else to do, I went aft to go belowdecks again to the lounge. The cook was still working on breakfast, but coffee had already been made. A couple of scientists had risen early, but they clearly didn't want to have anything to do with me either. Whatever status I'd briefly enjoyed last night had already been negated by the near tragedy that had occurred afterward. So I poured myself a mug of coffee and, deciding that I didn't want harsh eyes staring at my back, took it back upstairs.

I was leaning against the starboard rail, sipping my coffee and watching sea-swoops catching breakfast from the wake of the ship, when I heard someone come up behind me. Looking around, I saw Lynn. She didn't say anything for a moment, and I braced myself for another round of recrimination, but after a second or two she came over to slip her hand within the crook of my elbow.

"It's okay," she whispered, giving me a brief hug. "It wasn't your fault."

"Thanks for saying so . . . but you're wrong. If I hadn't . . ."

"I know, I know. But you'd told Jorge not to touch your gun, and he deliberately disobeyed you. That's what everyone's forgetting." She paused. "They've also forgotten that, just a few minutes earlier, you'd used that same gun to save lives. I was there, remember?"

"Sure, but . . ." I shook my head. "Look, maybe you're right about both those things, but it doesn't matter, does it? I should've never left that gun in my cabin. Not after Jorge saw me loading it, and when he could see where I was hiding the ammo. He's a two-year-old, for God's sake . . ."

"Six in Earth-years. Which makes him old enough to know that when an adult tells him not to do something, he'd better pay attention." Lynn released my arm to lean against the railing beside me. "Not that

Susan is going to recognize that. Every mother believes her child to be the center of the universe and that everyone and everything must revolve around him."

I gave her a sidelong glance. "Sounds like you have experience."

Her face reddened, and for a second I wondered if I'd said the wrong thing. "Not personally, no," she murmured, "but after watching my sister spoil her own children rotten . . ." Lynn shook her head. "No. Kids aren't something I plan to have. At least not anytime soon."

Lynn didn't strike me as being the motherly type, but I let it pass. "Well, anyway . . ." I shrugged, took a sip of lukewarm coffee. "I imagine there's going to be some changes. Carlos has my gun now, and unless Susan insists on throwing it overboard, it'll probably stay in his cabin for the rest of the trip. I guess she'll make sure Jorge is removed from my cabin, too, which means I'll soon be getting a new roommate." I smiled at her. "Interested? I don't think I have any other friends on board just now."

She didn't return my smile. "I'd like to, but . . ." She hesitated, then stepped a little closer. "Maybe I shouldn't be telling you this, but I don't think you're going to be here very much longer."

I stared at her. "What are you saying?"

"After everyone went back to bed, I stayed awake awhile. Couldn't sleep after what happened." She peered at me. "From the circles under your eyes, I don't think you did either . . ."

"Never mind that. What did you mean by . . . ?"

Hearing footsteps, we looked behind us. The sailors I'd seen earlier walked across the deck, apparently relieved from duty and heading below to get breakfast. She waited until they disappeared down the companionway, then went on, keeping her voice low. "So I went aft to see if I could steal a snack from the galley, and that's when I heard Susan and Jon in their cabin." She paused. "She wants you off the ship, Sawyer. I mean, right now . . . or at least as soon as the gyro arrives to pick up her father."

I felt my face grow warm. "Oh, for the love of . . . She can't be serious."

" 'Fraid so, love." Her expression was grim. "If she had her way, she'd probably just as soon have you marooned on Cherokee. She's that angry. As luck would have it, we've got that gyro coming in, so . . ." She shrugged. "I think they're going to be taking on another passenger. And that's you."

I didn't quite know what to say. What had happened was my fault, no matter how much Lynn might try to mitigate it . . . but, damn it, it had been an accident. I might have been guilty of carelessness, even stupidity, but certainly not reckless disregard for the safety of everyone aboard. Susan couldn't honestly believe that I'd allow something like that to happen again; she was ousting me out of spite, plain and simple.

My coffee had gone cold. I poured the rest of it over the side, resisting the angry temptation to hurl the mug into the river. "Well, hell . . . and just when things were getting interesting."

"Yeah. Sorry you won't be along for . . ." Lynn stopped herself, and for a moment it appeared that she was gnawing her lower lip. "All right, I'll let you in on another little secret. I'm thinking about leaving, too."

I gave her a sharp look. "Not because of me, I hope."

A wry smile. "Don't flatter yourself. No, it's because I think I'm covering the wrong story." Another glance over her shoulder to make sure that we weren't being overheard, then she went on. "Look, I managed to catch a bit of what you guys were talking about last night . . . on the bridge, I mean. Carlos didn't come right out and say it, sure, but there has to be a reason for the government going to the trouble of sending a gyro all the way out here. Something that they need a former president . . . no, scratch that, this particular former president . . . to handle."

The same thought had occurred to me as well, but I hadn't had time to ask. Not that Carlos seemed willing to discuss it. "So you want to follow him back, see what's going on?" She nodded. "Think they'll let you do it?"

Lynn shrugged. "How can they stop me? I'm not an expedition member, just a reporter who happened to tag along. Besides"—a confidential wink—"I think these guys would be just as relieved to get rid of me as they are you."

I was about to respond when we heard someone else walking around the bulwark railing. Looking over my shoulder, I saw Susan heading for the companionway, leading Jorge by the hand. When the boy saw me, his face became bright red, then his eyes turned shamefully toward his feet. Susan glared at me, and she pulled her son a little closer as they marched downstairs to the lounge.

"So much for breakfast," I muttered after they'd disappeared.

"I'll bring you a muffin." Lynn gently patted my wrist as she backed away from the railing. "Try to act surprised when they break the news."

As it turned out, none of the expedition leaders said anything to me until the *LeMare* reached Cherokee. I like to think that they were still mulling it over, weighing the benefits against the costs of losing their wilderness guide, but it's more likely that no one wanted to tell me that I was being thrown off the ExEx until they were sure the gyro was on the way. Or maybe they were afraid I'd make a public stink if I found out too soon.

I was angry. No sense in denying it. By the time I returned to my cabin, I'd already decided to insist upon Morgan paying me the balance of my retainer once I was back in New Florida; I'd done my job as best as I could, and I couldn't be held accountable for the rash decisions of the expedition's lead scientist. I was also thinking about relocating my business from Leeport to Liberty while starting to offer camera safaris, just to give Susan and Jon the unfriendly competition I'd avoided up until then. Hell, I might even consult a lawyer about taking Susan to court if Goldstein refused to cough up.

I spent the rest of the morning in my cabin, lying on my bunk and staring at the walls, determined not to pack up my stuff until someone came by to give me the news. True to her word, Lynn brought me a muffin and some dried fruit; she seemed to see that I was nursing a rage, because she left again without saying much else. Not a long time after that, Jorge dropped by. Apparently he hadn't expected to find me there, because he hesitated just outside the door, uncertain whether to enter. I told him that it was okay, I wasn't mad at him, and the kid shuffled into the room, still unable to look at me. The fact that he stayed just long enough to retrieve his toothbrush, and not the rest of his belongings, confirmed my suspicions: one of us would soon get the cabin all to himself, and it wouldn't be me.

Before he left, though, Jorge stopped at the edge of my bunk. "I'm . . .

I'm sorry 'bout what I did last night," he murmured. "That was bad of me."

"Yes, it was. You should have listened to me. I . . ." Then I saw the tears welling in the corners of his eyes, and realized that the boy was carrying a man-sized burden of guilt. No point in loading on him even more. "But I forgive you," I finished. "I'm in trouble, not you."

Jorge nodded. He was probably aware of something he believed I didn't know, but had been forbidden to tell me. For a second it seemed as if he wanted to say something else, then Susan called for him from the other end of the passageway. She obviously didn't want him to spend time with that bad ol' Mr. Lee.

"G'bye," he said, then he hurried from the room, not bothering to close the door behind him.

Cherokee had just appeared off the starboard bow when a sailor came below to tell me that I was wanted on the bridge. When I got there, I found everyone who mattered waiting for me: Jon, Carlos, Barry . . . even Susan, who stood off to the side, arms folded across her chest.

As captain, it fell to Jon to break the news. I didn't bother pretending to be surprised, but neither did I let my temper get the best of me. No sense in letting Susan have the satisfaction of seeing me make accusations I couldn't defend. Besides, I didn't want to say anything that might come back to haunt me in a courtroom. But the hypocrisy of the situation still irked me. No one made mention of the fact that Carlos had carried a rifle aboard as well . . . but then, Carlos was Susan's father, wasn't he?

So I took the news as best I could, and went below to pack up my stuff. And that was it. I was no longer a member of the Exploratory Expedition.

Cherokee's northern coastline was a long expanse of white-sand beach littered with driftwood and the decaying remains of dead fish. Just beyond the beach lay tidal marshes leading to equatorial savanna; it could well have been New Florida, were it not for the low mountains farther inland. Here and there, we made out groves of tall, broad-branched trees that appeared to be second cousins to blackwoods. Sea-swoops circled overhead, protesting our intrusion upon land that they'd become used to calling their own.

The *LeMare* dropped anchor at the southernmost extent of the bay, about five hundred yards offshore, where Barry and Jon were fairly confident the ship would be able to ride out the storm. It appeared that we hadn't arrived too soon. To the west, the sky above the Great Equatorial River was already darkened by an ominous wall of cumulus clouds, their purple masses tinted yellowish orange by the midday sun. The hurricane had entered the Meridian Sea and was lashing the archipelago; it wouldn't be long before its leading edge touched the southern coast of Vulcan.

Once the sails were furled, Jon ordered one of the tenders to be lowered over the side to take Carlos, Lynn, and me ashore. A couple of naturalists wanted to come along, saying that their best chance to study the coastal wildlife would be before the storm hit, but the captain refused; he didn't want anyone on the beach when the hurricane arrived. On the starboard poop deck, Susan and Jorge said good-bye to Carlos while Lynn and I stood quietly nearby, then Jon climbed down the accommodation ladder to the tender and helped his father-in-law disembark. The crew waved farewell as we headed for the beach, but I knew that it wasn't me they were going to miss.

The gyro arrived less than a half hour after we made landfall; leave it to the Colonial Militia to have such good timing. The aircraft came in low over the bay, its twin rotors causing small curlicues of spindrift to rise from the water, and we shielded our eyes against windblown sand as it touched down a few dozen yards from where we'd beached the tender. The pilot was obviously in a hurry, because he kept the engines going while he opened the side passenger hatch. There was no time for long speeches, but I couldn't help but notice the apologetic look in Jon's eyes when he shook my hand. If he'd wanted to say anything to me, though, he'd already had his chance, so I gave him a polite smile before I shouldered my knapsack and rifle and followed the others to the waiting gyro.

Until then, I'd been tough about the whole situation, telling myself that it was probably just as well; I was no longer welcome on the ExEx and probably never had been. But when the gyro lifted off from the beach, and I gazed down from the portside passenger window to see the *LeMare* floating in the bay, I couldn't help but feel something catch in my throat. Until only a day ago, I'd thought I'd be aboard her all the way around the world, helping to make history. Instead, I was destined to become little more than a footnote.

The gyro was a small, five-seat version meant for long-range sorties. The pilot was a young guy by the name of Charlie Banks; he assured us that his craft had more than enough hydrogen in its cells to get back to Hammerhead. Almost as soon as we left the bay and turned northeast to cross the river, though, he received a text message from Ft. Lopez over the wireless. The hurricane had just sideswiped the outpost, causing significant damage, and the commandant had grounded all air traffic in and out of Hammerhead for the next few hours. To make matters worse, the eye of the storm was presently above the Meridian Archipelago; if we attempted to fly straight to Ft. Lopez, there was no question that we'd run smack into the hurricane.

The gyro was already being buffeted by headwinds, its stubby winglets rocking back and forth as the engines at their ends growled menacingly. The aircraft hit an air pocket and dropped a dozen feet or so; Lynn grabbed my hand so hard that I nearly yelped, and when I looked at her, I saw that her jaw was clenched. Praying that she wasn't about to become airsick, I put my arm around her and hoped our pilot wasn't prone to displays of machismo.

Fortunately, he was smarter than that. A quick look at his nav screen, then he glanced over his shoulder at us. "Gonna take a little detour, folks," Charlie said, raising his voice above the engines. "I'm going to fly north to Vulcan and fly around Mt. Pesek. If I'm right, that'll get us around the bad weather, and the volcano should shield us from the worst of the wind."

I nodded, but Carlos seemed skeptical. "That's a pretty long distance, especially if you aim to go around the mountain," he said, leaning forward to peer at the screen. "Isn't that going to drain your fuel reserves?"

"Yes, sir, it'll be a stretch . . . but it's either this or try to fly through that thing." Charlie gave Carlos a sidelong stare. "Of course, if you're in a hurry, Mr. President . . ."

"No, no. You're the driver. You know what you're doing." Carlos settled back in his seat, then looked at me. He didn't say it aloud, but I knew what he was thinking: *Better* hope *he knows what he's doing.*

That pretty much settled the issue. The pilot turned the yoke, and the gyro peeled off to the right, putting us on a new course that would take us almost due north, straight across the river toward Vulcan. Now that the aircraft was broadside to the wind, the turbulence became more violent. The gyro bucked like a young shag that had been saddled for the first time, and I pulled Lynn closer to me, putting her head against my chest as I clutched an armrest with my free hand.

The gyro made it across the river in a fraction of the time it had taken the *LeMare* to make the same trip. A little more than an hour after we left Cherokee, we were past the equator and approaching land again. Charlie shed altitude as we came upon Squanto; through my porthole, I caught a glimpse of its dense rain forest, and briefly wondered if the island's birds and animals were aware that a hurricane was bearing down on them. The sun had disappeared behind swollen clouds, and raindrops were already beginning to spatter the cockpit windows and drool across the portholes.

We passed over the Vulcan Channel, and suddenly Mt. Pesek loomed directly before us, its broad flanks completely filling the windshield. There was no way the gyro could fly over the summit—it was too high for unpressurized aircraft—so Charlie decreased altitude again until we were flying parallel to its lower slopes, then made the northwest turn that would begin our orbit of the volcano. Once we had the mountain between us and the hurricane, the ride became less choppy; the gyro settled down, and gradually Lynn raised her head from my chest to peer cautiously through the porthole.

Seen from above, Mt. Pesek was astonishing. Although only its steppes were visible, what lay below us was a vast forest, with trees clinging precariously to granite bluffs hundreds of feet tall. As the gyro circled the northwest side, we caught sight of an enormous waterfall, higher than even Johnson Falls on Midland, spilling water from a glacial plateau into a deep gorge. Here and there were clearings where wildfires, spawned by lightning storms, had burned away woodlands to expose the rocky ground beneath, yet even these bare places showed evidence of regrowth; the volcanic topsoil, rich in nutrients, was responsible for the lushness of the forest.

"This is amazing." From his seat on the other side of the gyro, Carlos stared down at the volcano's northern slopes. "We have got to come back here again. There's a whole world down there we haven't seen before."

"Maybe . . . but not by boat." It had been a while since I'd lost sight of water; the Vulcan Channel lay many miles behind us. "And I sure wouldn't want to bushwhack my way through all that."

"Why not? Where's your sense of . . . ?"

"Holy crap!" Charlie yelled. "What the hell is . . . ?"

I looked up just in time to see a mammoth winged shape directly before us. I barely had time to realize that it was a thunderbird before the creature slammed straight into the gyro, colliding with the cockpit so hard that it was as if the windshield had been hit by a giant hammer. Lynn yelped as both Carlos and I instinctively threw up our arms to cover our faces; the windshield remained intact, but as the thunderbird tumbled away, it left behind a spiderweb of shattered glass.

A half second later, there was a sudden jolt from the left side of the aircraft. For a moment, I thought another thunderbird had hit us. Then the master alarm began to shriek and the gyro pitched to the left.

"Dammit to hell!" Charlie shouted. "That goddamn thing just took out the port engine!"

My porthole was streaked with gore, but nonetheless I could see smoke billowing from the nacelle. In an instant, I knew what had happened. The thunderbird had been chopped to pieces by the rotors, but nonetheless it was large enough that most of its carcass had entered the air intake and jammed the turbine.

"We're gonna crash!" Lynn screamed.

"Shut up!" Charlie clenched the yoke with both hands, fighting for control of his craft. "We're not going to crash!" He reached forward to flip a switch on his dashboard, and the grinding clatter of the stricken engine abruptly died. "We're not going to crash," he repeated, a little more calmly now. "So long as we've still got one engine, we can make it to the ground."

Over his shoulder, I could see the altimeter. Its needle was rapidly moving from the right side to the left. "But we're not going to make it to Hammerhead either, are we?"

"Nope." He stole a hand away from the yoke to reach for the wireless. "Mayday, mayday. All stations, this is Mary Zulu Foxtrot five-two, reporting a flight emergency. Midair collision with unknown object, going down on Vulcan. Please respond. Mayday, mayday, calling all stations, this is Mary Zulu Foxtrot five-two . . ."

As he spoke, Charlie pulled back the lever that rotated the nacelles to vertical landing position. The gyro shuddered, its fuselage creaking against the strain, and I looked out my porthole again. The port rotors had gone still, but oily black smoke continued to pour from beneath the cowling, with the nacelle itself still frozen in horizontal cruise mode. Absurdly, part of one of the thunderbird's wings remained stuck to the air intake, its dark brown feathers fluttering in the slipstream, almost if the creature was trying to help keep the gyro aloft.

Lynn was almost hysterical. She was certain that it was the last minute of her life. I kept an arm around her, telling her again and again that everything was going to be all right, even as the gyro spiraled toward the ground, the pilot continuing to radio for help even as he struggled with the yoke. Through the shattered windshield, I could see treetops racing toward us. If we went down in all that . . .

"You know," Carlos said all of a sudden, his voice weirdly calm, "perhaps we should reconsider how we explore this planet."

I stared at him, my jaw sagging open in amazement . . . and then I broke out laughing. He gazed back at me, a wry grin on his face. "You might have something there," I managed to say. "Maybe next time . . ."

"Get your heads down!" Charlie yelled. "We're going in!"

I barely had time to catch a glimpse of the small clearing that had miraculously appeared below us. Then I bent double in my seat, pulling Lynn down with me. My head was between my knees when the gyro hit the ground. The windshield broke apart, spraying glass across my back and neck. Charlie cried out in pain, and Lynn screamed, and then it was all over.

It was a good landing. We walked away from it.

Charlie Banks got the worst of it. His forehead was lacerated by flying glass, and his neck was badly sprained from being whiplashed against the back of his seat, but otherwise he was okay. When Lynn raised her head, I saw blood on her lips, and thought for a moment she'd suffered internal injuries, but all she'd done was bite her tongue. Both Carlos and I were unhurt, although my hands trembled for a long time.

The gyro was totaled. Carlos managed to pry open the side hatch, and we climbed out, with Charlie using our point of exit since his own hatch was staved in. We saw then that, although the landing gear had buckled, at least it had absorbed most of the impact. We hastened to get away from the aircraft, but there was no danger of explosion; Charlie later told us that he'd voided the hydrogen cells in the last few seconds we were still airborne, a precaution that probably prevented the aircraft from blowing up when we crashed. But one look at the ruined nacelle, with its twisted rotors and burned-out engine, and I knew that the gyro had just become a permanent human landmark on this little part of Coyote.

I had to hand it to Charlie. In the couple of minutes between the thunderbird colliding with us and the gyro hitting the ground, he'd located what was probably the only clear and relatively level place within a couple of square miles. The clearing was about a third of the way up the mountain, a few thousand vertical feet below the tree line, one of those places we'd noticed earlier where the vegetation had been burned away by a wildfire and hadn't yet regrown, leaving a bare, rock-strewn patch just large enough for a gyro to make an emergency landing.

A hard rain was coming down on us; the hurricane may have missed Vulcan, but nonetheless Mt. Pesek was receiving squalls from its blow-off. We still had seven hours of daylight left, but there was no telling how long it would be before we were rescued. Charlie had radioed our position on the way down, yet no one had responded before we crashed; with the wireless out of commission, we didn't have any way of getting in touch with Fort Lopez. However, once Carlos found a survival pack beneath one of the passenger seats, we discovered that it contained a satellite transponder. Although we couldn't use it to send or receive verbal messages, the instrument was able to transmit a repeating signal, including our coordinates. I carried it to the center of the clearing and unfolded its dish, using my watch's electronic compass to align the dish along the proper azimuth for its signal to be received by one of Coyote's geostationary comsats. I held my breath when I turned it on, but a red diode on its panel showed me that the instrument was still in good working order.

That done, we went about setting up camp. While Carlos used the first-aid kit to tend to Charlie, Lynn and I unfolded a tarp from the survival pack and lashed it between some trees on the uphill side of the clearing. Once we had shelter from the rain, she and I gathered fallen branches and twigs, digging beneath leaves to locate ones that hadn't been soaked. A few feet from the shelter, I carefully arranged the wood as a small teepee and surrounded it with loose stones, then used a fire-starter from the pack; a few minutes later, we had a campfire. The pack also contained a small supply of ration bars, but I hoped that we wouldn't be there long enough to have to rely on them.

Carlos cut up a seat cushion to fashion a neck brace for Charlie; as soon as Lynn and I set up the tarp, he moved the pilot beneath it and made him lie down, propping his head up on the empty pack. Charlie soon went to sleep, and although Lynn volunteered to watch over him, it wasn't long before she'd dozed off herself, her head cradled between her knees. I was content to let her; the crash had scared her out of her wits, and she needed rest just as much as Charlie did.

That left Carlos and me to stand watch. The rain had let up by then, so we sat on the ground next to the fire, where we could keep an eye out for a rescue gyro. Although we hadn't spotted any animals other than the occasional glidemunk, just to be on the safe side I reloaded my rifle and kept it by my side. After that, there wasn't much left for us to do but hope that we wouldn't have to spend the night on Mt. Pesek.

As it turned out, we had a good view of the mountainside. Beyond the edge of the clearing, the northern slope stretched away as a vast, unexplored forest, a thin mist hanging above the treetops. Just beyond the visible horizon lay the North Sea, the widest point of the North Circumpolar River. Every so often, we caught sight of thunderbirds soaring overhead; now that we could see them a little better, it was evident that they had a wingspan of nearly eight feet, and their circling patterns indicated that they were raptors, possibly related to swoops. Despite our circumstances, Carlos was fascinated by the vista. If we hadn't been awaiting rescue, I think he might've packed up his gear and wandered down the mountain, just to see what he could see.

"I'm going to have come back here sometime," he murmured, his arms crossed together upon his knees as he warmed his boots by the fire. "I just think I'd like to do it differently, though."

I recalled that he'd said much the same thing just before we crashed. "Uh-huh. Next time, we gotta watch out for high-flying birds. Especially the big ones."

"Well, yeah . . . but that's not what I mean." He paused. "I've been thinking about the ExEx, especially about what happened to you. I couldn't say so while we were still aboard ship, but that shouldn't have happened. You were careless . . ."

"I know, I know." Using a branch to stir the fire, I shook my head. "I'm really sorry about that. If I hadn't . . ."

"Let me finish." He raised a hand to shush me. "Yes, you were negligent . . . but, hell, my grandson shouldn't have even been on board in the first place. An expedition like this is no place for a kid his age. In fact, I'm not even sure if half of the scientists on the *LeMare* should be there. They're book-smart, sure . . . but how many of them would know how to handle a situation like this?"

"You've got a point." I remembered the number of times I'd had to stop naturalists from blindly charging off into rain forests without first considering what might be lurking out there. Scientific interest is no excuse for lack of common sense, but that seldom occurred to a lot of the university students aboard the *LeMare*. "Maybe survival training . . ."

"No. Not just that. Something more . . . knowledge of how to live in the wild, without having to rely on a guide to keep them out of harm's way. Without even having a ship as home base. Just the clothes on your back, and being able to use a rifle as well as a microscope. That's what we're going to need if we're going to explore the rest of this world."

I glanced over my shoulder at Charlie. "Kind of like the Militia, you mean, only with a different set of skills."

"No. Same skills . . . just different priorities." Carlos seemed to think about it for a moment. "Sort of an exploration corps," he added, then he grinned. "In fact, that'd be a good name for them . . . the Corps of Exploration."

"The Corps of Exploration." I liked the way it rolled off my tongue. "Catchy. Of course, you'd have to get Goldstein to fund something like that . . ."

"The hell with Morgan." Carlos scowled as he picked up a twig, snapped it in half, and flung it into the fire. "You know the real reason why he bankrolled the ExEx? He isn't interested in exploration for its own sake . . . just finding locations for new settlements, so he can corner the market on the real-estate business."

It hadn't occurred to me that Goldstein might have a hidden agenda. When I thought about it, though, it made perfect sense . . . or at least it did if you knew Morgan. "You certain about this?"

"Oh, yes. He told me so himself. After all, I'm one of his major investors." Carlos let out his breath. "And the hell of it is, he may be right. A long time ago, a friend of mine said to me that, even if a thousand ships arrived over the next hundred years, they still wouldn't bring in more than a million people. He was generalizing, of course . . . but that was during the Occupation, when Union ships took nearly fifty years to get here. Now that we have the starbridge, we've got shuttles landing at New Brighton on a daily basis. And before long . . ."

He stopped himself, and instead quietly gazed off into the distance. It seemed as if he was trying to decide whether to confide in me, so I said nothing. After a few moments, he looked back at the fire again. "You know why I dropped out of the ExEx to head home?"

"The Union is collapsing, and Government House needs to have you there to negotiate with their leaders. That's what you said . . ."

"Yes, yes, that's what I told you and the others last night. But I didn't tell you *why* I'm needed there." He picked up another twig, absently played with it in his hands. "Remember, the Union never ratified the U.N. treaty, so therefore they haven't been granted emigration rights. In fact, there's been little in the way of a formal relationship between the WHU and the Federation. We're even having trouble deporting a suspected terrorist whom we caught trying to pass through customs last year. They don't want to claim him as one of their own, and we don't have anything on him but a weapons charge, so all we've been able to do is keep him on probation and hope he doesn't . . ."

He shook his head. "Sorry. Getting off the subject there. Anyway, the WHU hasn't been able to establish any colonies here because they refused to recognize the Federation. But now the Union is falling apart, and from what we've heard, the reason why they're having a revolution is because living conditions have become so bad that their entire social structure has broken down . . . not that it ever worked well in the first place. So now they've got several million people on the verge of killing each other for a bag of potatoes, and the ones who are able to do so are getting out of there any way they can."

Carlos paused. "Any way they can," he said again, "and *anywhere* they can. Do you see what I mean?"

Suddenly, the fire wasn't warm enough to ease the chill that went through me. "They're coming here, aren't they?"

He shrugged. "Can't blame them. Not many other places for them to go. Europe and Asia are already overcrowded. Africa is a madhouse, and the Middle East is in ruins. The lunar and Mars colonies are stretched to the breaking point, and you'd have to be crazy to go to Jupiter . . ."

"But here?" I shook my head. "Sure, we've got enough room, but . . ."

"Sawyer . . ." He bent his head to rub the back of his neck. "My parents were among the D.I.s who hijacked the *Alabama*. My father risked public hanging just to get me and my sister out of the United Republic . . . and believe me, as bad as the Union may be, the URA was worse." He sighed. "Coyote has always been about second chances. We can't go slamming the door now, not when there are so many lives at stake. Like it or not, this place may be their best hope . . . their *only* hope."

"So that's why you're going back. To try to work something out for the refugees."

Carlos didn't reply, but instead pushed himself to his feet. Perhaps his legs had gone stiff from having sat so long, which was why he limped away from the fire, but at that moment he looked older than his years, like someone who was carrying the weight of the world. Perhaps he was.

"You want my advice? See as much of this world while you can, while it's still wild. Maybe even get that Corps of Exploration started. I might be able to help you there, if you want to take it seriously. But . . ." He glanced over his shoulder at me. "Keep doing what you're doing, while you're still able to, because Coyote is about to change. When it does, nothing will ever be the same again."

I started to say something, but didn't get a chance, for at that moment I heard something new: the distant clatter of rotors, as from an approaching aircraft. Carlos heard it the same time as I did, and we both looked around to see a gyro approaching from the west, flying in low above the treetops.

"Looks like our ride is here," Carlos said. "Better go wake up the others." Then he walked farther out into the clearing, raising his arms above his head to wave the pilot down. "And don't forget to put out the fire!" he called back. "Don't want to burn this place down, do we?"

By the end of the day, we were back in Liberty.

The rescue gyro touched down on Mt. Pesek just long enough for the four of us to climb aboard, and within minutes we were airborne, leaving behind the wrecked gyro and an extinguished campfire as the only evidence that we'd ever been there. En route to Hammerhead, a Colonial Militia medic looked us over; he was faintly surprised that we'd come away from the crash as well as we did. He replaced Charlie's makeshift neck brace with an inflatable version of the same, but when he chided our pilot about losing his aircraft, Carlos informed him that, if it hadn't been for Lieutenant Banks's flying skills, he'd probably be digging four graves just then.

A little more than an hour later, we touched down at Ft. Lopez, where Carlos, Lynn, and I transferred to a long-range gyro. I caught only a brief glimpse of the outpost; the hurricane had only made a near miss, but that was still enough to rip the shingles from several rooftops and overturn one of the solar farms. Luckily, the communications tower had remained standing, which was how the fort received both Charlie's mayday and our transponder signal.

Just before we left, the commandant came out to the flight line to greet the president. After apologizing for not having sent a search-and-rescue team sooner, he informed us that they'd just received a satphone message from the *LeMare*. Although the aft mast had sustained some minor damage and would have to be repaired, the ship had otherwise managed to ride out the storm, with no injuries reported among the crew. Carlos was visibly relieved; he thanked the commandant for telling us this, then led Lynn and me to the waiting aircraft. After what we'd just been through, I would've preferred a chance to change into some dry clothes and perhaps grab a hot meal, but Carlos was in a hurry. Ten minutes after we'd arrived at Ft. Lopez, we were in the sky again.

Lynn and I dozed off shortly after the gyro crossed the Highland Channel and was over Midland. She rested her head against my shoulder, and I propped my feet up against the back of the pilot's seat, but Carlos was still awake when I let my eyes close. We must have been more tired than we thought, because both of us slept through most of the flight; I didn't wake up until my ears popped, a sign that the gyro was on final approach. Gazing through the porthole beside me, I saw that it was almost dusk, the last light of day upon the East Channel. A brief glimpse of the docks of Bridgeton, which we'd last seen only a few weeks earlier, then the aircraft crossed the Eastern Divide, its landing gear coming down from its wells.

Carlos barely noticed, sitting on the other side of the passenger compartment, a pad propped up in his lap. It looked as if he'd spent the last several hours studying reports relayed to him from Government House. I tried to talk to him, but he clearly wasn't interested in idle chatter; his mind was on the refugee crisis, and the ExEx was something that no longer held his attention.

And indeed, the minute the gyro touched down in Shuttlefield, a subtle change came over him. He was no longer Carlos Montero, leader of the Exploratory Expedition, but former president Carlos Montero, point man in the high-level negotiations between the Coyote Federation and what was left of the Western Hemisphere Union. A sedan was waiting for him at the airstrip, a couple of proctors ready to escort him to Government House; a handshake, a brief smile, then he was gone.

So was Lynn. If I'd been hoping that we'd consummate our shipboard romance once we got back to civilization, I was sadly mistaken; my girlfriend had become a working journalist on the trail of the biggest story of her career. A hasty kiss on the cheek and a whispered promise to catch up with me later, and before I knew it she was jogging across the tarmac to catch up with Carlos. Apparently President Montero didn't mind having the press tagging along, because he let her climb into the back of the sedan with him, leaving me behind with the dumbstruck expression of a guy who'd just been jilted.

That was how the Exploratory Expedition ended for me. But the ExEx didn't come to a finish once Carlos, Lynn, and I left the ship. During the rest of the summer, after I returned to Leeport and prepared to relocate my business to Liberty, I continued to hear reports of the expedition's progress. How the *LeMare* sailed westward down the Great Equatorial River, making stops on Pocahontas, Mohawk, and Massasoit, before it crossed the Eastern Meridian and traveled along the Navajo coast until it reached the eastern coast of Great Dakota and, finally, New Florida again. Along the way, its scientists collected dozens of plant and animal specimens, and spotted creatures no one had ever seen before, most notably a heretofore unknown tribe of *chirreep* living in the deserts of Navajo and, on Apache, a related species of boid that was both vegetarian and remarkably docile.

When the *LeMare* returned to its home port, the ExEx entered the history books as the first successful circumnavigation of Coyote. Yet few people took notice of the achievement, let alone cared. By then, events had conspired to overshadow the Exploratory Expedition, despite all that it had accomplished.

As I walked away from the airfield, knapsack over my shoulder and gun beneath my arm, I had no way of knowing that something Carlos had said to me on Mt. Pesek would soon be proven correct.

Our world was about to change. When it did, nothing would ever be the same again.

Part 6

CARLOS'S PIZZA

The teacher came to Carlos's Pizza, bearing wisdom.

Established in c.y. 15, Carlos's Pizza was a relatively recent settlement with a population just under a thousand, mostly fishermen. Located on the southwest coast of Midland just east of the Montero Delta, the town derived its unusual name from a perhaps-apocryphal story about the first person to set foot there. When the teenage Carlos Montero set out on his own to explore the Great Equatorial River, the first place he set up camp was at that locale. He built a small tree house in a blackwood tree not far from the freshwater stream that still flowed just outside town, and when anyone from Liberty tried to call him on the satphone he'd carried with him, he would answer it by saying, "Carlos's Pizza."

Many years later, after commercial fishermen decided that they wanted to establish a port closer to the Great Equatorial than the one in Bridgeton, they discovered that same blackwood, the half-collapsed remnants of that tree house still hanging to its lower limbs. Someone realized that it had once been President Montero's camp, and so the name stuck.

The blackwood was long gone, cut down to make room for the processing plant that dominated the town center, but not before an enterprising soul carefully dismantled the tree house and sold its rotting timbers to the Colonial University as a historical artifact. Which was typical of the mind-set of the town's inhabitants. People didn't live there for the scenic beauty of the river or its place in Coyote history, but because they wanted to get away from everyone else, and becoming a fisherman was a reliable way of making a living while they hid from the rest of the world.

So Carlos's Pizza was an untidy collection of clapboard houses, log cabins, and shotgun shacks built along narrow, packed-dirt streets that radiated away from the waterfront, where barks, pirogues, and schooners were lined up at its docks, their masts forming a forest nearly as dense as that which once occupied this little corner of Midland. The village perpetually reeked of fish, not only from the commercial wharf, where they were unloaded from the boats, but also from the processing plant, where they were beheaded, cleaned, scaled, and either cut up as fillets and packed in ice for wholesale farther inland or, in the case of inedible varieties, boned for household implements, chopped up for fertilizer, or boiled down for lamp oil and lubricant. There were a few shops, to be sure, along with such necessities as a meetinghouse, a clinic, a sewage-treatment facility, and a one-room school for the handful of children who lived there, but even those existed only as afterthoughts. The business of Carlos's Pizza was business, and that business was fish.

Ironically, one thing Carlos's Pizza didn't have was a pizzeria. At the town's only public house, a waterfront inn called the Laughing Sailor, pizza was not on the menu, for reasons the owner never deigned to explain. Therefore, one could not get a pizza in Carlos's Pizza.

Like Nantucket before it, Carlos's Pizza was prosperous in its own hardscrabble way yet nonetheless isolated from the rest of civilization. Since the town didn't have an aircraft landing strip—voted down by the selectmen because they didn't want gyros bringing in tourists and other unwanted visitors—there were only two means by which to reach the place. The first, of course, was by water, which is how most people arrived there. The second was by the Midland Highway, the long road that meandered alongside the East Channel from New Boston to Forest Camp to Carlos's Pizza, where it turned northeast to lead travelers into the Pioneer Valley, where Defiance lay.

That was the way by which the teacher came to Carlos's Pizza. No one noticed him at first, aside from a handful of farmers whose fields lay on the northern outskirts of town, and even they barely paid attention to the shag wagon that moved down the Midland Highway past their lands. They looked up from their work only long enough to recognize this particular wagon as belonging to Yuri Scklovskii, a Russian immigrant who made his living by hauling casks of weirdling oil north to

Forest Camp and New Boston before coming home with whatever he could resell to the shops in town.

Yuri sometimes carried passengers. Most travelers preferred to buy passage on one of the riverboats that moved up and down the East Channel, but a four-day ride from New Boston to Carlos's Pizza was cheaper, if a bit more dangerous. The Midland Highway went through boid country, and although the creatures had learned to stay clear of human settlements, every so often they'd attack someone unwary enough to be caught alone on the road. But Yuri was a crack shot with the rifle he carried on the wagon's buckboard, and if you didn't mind having him talk your ear off—he always had something to complain about, in excruciating detail—there were worse ways to travel.

Yet this time, Yuri was oddly quiet as he drove his wagon the last few miles to town. If his friends had seen him, they might have noticed the preoccupied expression on his face, as if there was something on his mind that, for once, he didn't want to discuss. But before that, they probably would have first noticed the three people riding in the back of his wagon. Seated on duffel bags, backs propped against crates and barrels, were two men and a woman. Despite the warmth of the Hamaliel afternoon, each of them wore a long brown robe, and although their hoods were pulled up above their faces, their eyes restlessly moved back and forth, as if taking in their surroundings.

The wagon entered Carlos's Pizza, and Yuri clucked his tongue and pulled the reins slightly to the right, coaxing his shag to leave the Midland Highway for one of the side streets that would take them into the village. The stench from the processing plant became more powerful as the wagon drew closer to the town center, until the woman and the older of the two men raised their hands to cover their noses and mouths. Only the younger man seemed unperturbed; from his seat directly behind the buckboard, he continued to survey the town with calm curiosity.

The wagon rolled past the processing plant and the houses and shops surrounding it until it finally reached the waterfront, where Yuri yanked back on the reins to bring his wagon to a halt in front of the Laughing Sailor. "Here you are," he said. "The only inn in town, I'm afraid . . . but comfortable enough, if you're not too particular."

His three passengers gazed warily at the two-story clapboard building, but none of them complained. "This will be fine," the older man said, standing up in the back of the wagon. "We appreciate the courtesy."

"Yes. Thank you very much." The other man, who was several years younger than his companion, turned to help the woman to her feet. "And it's been a pleasure to meet you."

If anyone who knew Yuri had been seated in one of the bamboo chairs on the front porch, he might have been amused to hear this. Yuri Scklovskii was not known for either courtesy or charm. But the observer would have been utterly shocked by what he did next: climbing down from the buckboard, he helped his passengers off the wagon, and even went so far as to gallantly pick up the woman's bag and carry it up the front steps.

"Thank you," the young man said. "How much do we owe you?"

Yuri seemed to think about this for a moment. Then he shook his head. "Nothing," he said, his voice uncommonly quiet. "You've . . . given me a great deal to think about. The least I can do is offer you a ride."

"Again, many thanks." The young man lowered his head and shoulders as a bow to the drover. "Remember what we've talked about. Tell others, if you will. *Sa'Tong qo.*"

"*Sa'Tong qo,*" Yuri repeated. "And thank you."

Without another word, Yuri returned to his wagon. It was the first time he'd ever refused payment from passengers. But if that hadn't surprised any townspeople who knew him, even his wife—whom Yuri had abandoned three Earth-years ago, leaving her behind in St. Petersburg after secretly using their life savings to buy a ticket to 47 Ursae Majoris— would have been stunned by the uncharacteristic smile on his face and the tears in the corners of his eyes.

The young man watched him go, then picked up his bag. His companions were waiting for him by the front door. The three of them looked at one another; no one said anything, but after a few seconds the older man silently nodded, then turned to open the door.

Their arrival hadn't gone unobserved. From behind his desk inside the foyer, Owen McKay watched the newcomers as they disembarked from the wagon. As soon as he saw Yuri pull down their bags—and he thought it strange that he'd do this, but only for a moment—the innkeeper reached up to the wooden sign that hung above the desk and turned it around. As required by law, the sign posted the daily rates for the Laughing Sailor's upstairs rooms. What most people didn't know, though, was that those rooms had two different rates: one for itinerant fishermen and locals who needed a place to flop after they'd been drinking in his tavern all night, and another for folks who happened to pass through town. Since it was obvious that these three people weren't from around there, McKay decided to make them pay the higher rate. He also made a mental note to tell the barmaid to give them the tourist menu when they came downstairs to eat; it, too, was adjusted for inflation.

That done, McKay fixed a pleasant smile upon his bearded face. "Hello, there," he said as the trio approached the desk. "Welcome to the Laughing Sailor. Will you be wanting rooms for the night?"

"Yes, please." The young man was the one who spoke; his companions remained quiet. "Two next to each other, if possible."

McKay activated the registration pad and pretended to study its screen, even though he already knew that only one of the eight guest rooms upstairs was presently occupied, and that by a late-sleeping drunk he intended to evict soon. "Yes," he said slowly. "I think that can be done. We have a room with two beds and another next it to it with just one . . . Will those be suitable?"

When he didn't get a response, he looked up from the pad. The young man had lowered his robe's hood, and it was only then that McKay could clearly see his face. His head was completely shaved, save for a long, braided scalp lock that hung down the back of his neck. At the center of his forehead, between his eyebrows, was a small tattoo, a glyph that somewhat resembled the Greek symbol *pi* except that it was turned upside down and one leg was slightly longer than the other.

Yet what struck McKay the most were his eyes. Never before had he ever seen a gaze that was as direct, or as serene, as the one that was fastened upon him. It seemed as if the newcomer was peering directly into his soul and had found something there that he liked, even if it was a bit amusing. Instead of a stranger who'd just walked into his establishment, McKay immediately felt as if this person was a friend he never knew he had.

"That will be fine," the young man said. "How much do we owe you?"

Apparently he hadn't noticed the sign above his head. Either that, or he'd chosen to ignore it. "Fifty colonials a night for the double, forty for the single," the innkeeper said. "We also require a ninety-colonial deposit in advance . . ."

"No." The look in the young man's eyes changed to that of weary disappointment as he shook his head. "I'm sorry, but that's not your usual rate. It's thirty colonials a night for the double, twenty for the single." He paused. "And you never intend to repay that deposit, do you? You'll find something wrong with the rooms just before we leave, and will claim the deposit to cover the imagined expense of repairing it."

McKay's face became warm. Not meaning to do so, he found himself glancing up at his sign, making sure that he'd flipped it around. "No, no, that's what . . ."

"The other side of your sign has the true rates. No, you didn't forget to switch it just before we came in." A gentle smile appeared. "Owen, you shouldn't cheat people like that. It isn't good for you, and it only makes them want to cheat you as well."

McKay stared at him. His first impulse was to angrily deny that he'd ever do such a thing, that the visible rates really were the correct ones, yet there was no accusation in the young man's voice, and his eyes remained as placid as before. It never occurred to the innkeeper to ask how the young man knew his name; somehow, it just seemed natural that he would, as if they'd known each other for a long time.

"Yeah . . . yeah, you're right," he murmured, suddenly embarrassed. "Sorry. I just . . ."

"Fifty colonials for both rooms. That's fine, thank you." The young man spoke as if the disagreement had never occurred, and his companions nodded as well. "And, yes, I think we'll be staying a few nights," he added, as if anticipating McKay's next question. "One of us will pay you in advance every morning, at the same time we settle our tavern bill. Is this satisfactory?"

McKay was still stumbling for a response when the older man stepped forward. As he pulled back his hood and reached within his robe to produce a thick roll of colonials, the innkeeper noticed for the first time that he was a Native American. Not only that, but the woman standing behind them was pregnant; judging from the way her belly pushed against the front of her robe, she'd probably been expecting for at least the last two LeMarean months.

"That . . . Yeah, sure, that's fine." McKay was having trouble speaking. At a loss for words, he turned the pad around, then picked up a stylus and held it out to the young man. "If you'll just sign here . . ."

"Of course." He took the stylus and traced three names upon the screen. When he was done, he turned to the others. Without another word, they picked up their bags. The young man looked at McKay again. "You may show us to our rooms now, if you please . . . ?"

"Oh . . . right, sure." McKay fumbled for the keys hanging beneath his desk; without really thinking about it, he selected those for the two best rooms in the inn, which he normally reserved for fishing-boat captains and the higher-priced prostitutes who worked his tavern. "If you'll come this way, please."

The newcomers moved to follow him upstairs, but just before they left the foyer, McKay stole a glance at the registration pad. Upon the screen, he saw three names:

Joseph Cassidy.

Melissa Sanchez.

Chaaz'maha.

When he looked back at his guests, he saw that they'd paused at the foot of the stairs and were watching him. McKay hesitated. "Excuse me, but this"—he motioned to the bottom signature—"isn't a proper name."

"No, it wasn't." There was a whisper of a smile on the young man's face. "But it is now."

The rooms the innkeeper leased to his guests might have been the best available, but nonetheless they were still rough: bare plaster walls, unfinished wooden floors, bamboo furniture that looked as if it had been repaired many times. The newcomers didn't say anything as McKay nervously puttered about, showing them the closets where the spare linen was stored and how to get to the bathroom down the hall, and when he was finally gone, the woman sat down on one of the beds in the room she was sharing with the young man and slowly let out her breath.

"Not exactly the lap of luxury, is it?" Melissa murmured.

"It'll do." Cassidy strolled over to the window and pushed aside its curtain. The glass hadn't been cleaned in a while, but he still had a good view of the street in front of the building. A few pedestrians were on the raised wooden sidewalks; he waited, expecting to see something that he'd found in McKay's mind even as the innkeeper had been telling them when dinner would be served. "Not that we have much choice . . . do we, *chaaz'maha*?"

The *chaaz'maha* stood near the door, arms folded together within the sleeves of his robe, head bowed slightly. "Still think we should have gone to Liberty?" he asked. Receiving no answer from either of them, he shook his head. "No. I disagree. Liberty is too big. Too many people. We need to start small, in a place where we won't be ignored."

"I don't think we'll have to worry about that." From the window, Walking Star watched as the front door opened and McKay appeared directly below. The innkeeper glanced first one way, then the other; he seemed to hesitate for a moment, then he bustled across the street, heading away from the waterfront. "There he goes," he murmured. "Off to find the chief proctor . . ."

"And tell him about the people who just checked in." The *chaaz'maha* smiled. "Yes, I caught that, too. I'm afraid I really spooked the poor man."

"Are you really?" Melissa sighed as she lay back on the bed, resting her hands lightly upon her swollen belly. "Or did you do that deliberately?"

The *chaaz'maha* frowned. "He would've gouged us if I'd let him. Would you have preferred that I let him overcharge us?" He stopped, then added, "I think we'll be getting the regular menu as well, but we'd better search the barmaid, too. He might forget to give her the message."

"That's not what I mean . . ."

"I know what you mean. I don't have to search you to figure that out." The *chaaz'maha* walked over to a bamboo armchair; one of its legs was slightly shorter than the others, and it wobbled as he sat down. "If we're going to be successful, we're going to have to do this one person at a time, with whoever we happen to meet. Small steps, little lessons . . ."

"At least at the beginning, yes." Now that the innkeeper was gone, Cassidy moved away from the window. "But remember, a good teacher intrigues his students, not baffles them. Sooner or later, you're going to have to reveal all that you know."

"But surely not everything?" The *chaaz'maha* raised an eyebrow. "The Order, for instance. Or my name . . ."

"No doubt people have heard about the Order. Everyone who built The Sanctuary has gone home, and they've probably told their families and friends about where they were and what they were doing. That couldn't be helped." Walking Star absently ran a fingertip across the top of a bureau, scowled at the dust it collected. "As for you . . . well, that may or may not happen. Your appearance has changed a bit, and you're no longer using the name your mother gave you . . ."

"Hawk is too aggressive for what I mean to do. You said that yourself."

"Not to mention the fact that you're wanted by the law. But if you're successful, someone will eventually recognize you. That, too, is inevitable. However, your actions will determine just how long it'll be before your identity . . . your former identity, that is . . . becomes known."

Hawk Thompson was quiet for a few moments as he contemplated what his own teacher had said. "If I'm to be the *chaaz'maha*," he said at last, "I can't keep a low profile. Perhaps a good teacher doesn't baffle his students, but neither does he hide in a corner of his classroom and wait for them to come to him. Sooner or later, he has to stand and deliver . . ."

"And let 'em throw spitballs at him," Melissa added.

The two men stared at her for a second, then they broke down laughing, with Walking Star clutching the side of the bureau for support and the *chaaz'maha* doubled over in his chair. Melissa started to laugh at her own remark, then she abruptly gasped. "Aggh . . . I think the baby just kicked at that one!"

"Are you okay?" The *chaaz'maha* was on his feet in an instant, rushing to kneel by her side. "Was he too rough?"

"Not really . . . and I'm telling you, he's a she. A mother knows." Melissa took deep breaths, finally relaxed. "I'll be fine, just as long as I get something to eat soon." She grinned at the *chaaz'maha*. "I know we'll get plenty of fish here . . . but what I want with it is some chocolate ice cream."

Holding her hand, the *chaaz'maha* looked up at Walking Star. Neither of them said anything, but they didn't have to search each other's mind to know what the other person was thinking. By the LeMarean calendar, Melissa was due in less than a month; where the three of them would be by then, they didn't know, but it would have to be some place where there was a doctor, or at least a competent midwife. Not only that, but none of them had any idea what effect her initiation into the Order would have upon her pregnancy, which had occurred at nearly the same time she'd insisted upon crawling into the sweat lodge where the captive ball plant lay.

"Chocolate ice cream." The *chaaz'maha* regarded Melissa with loving eyes. "I'm sure someone here knows how to make it."

Melissa smiled and nodded, but Cassidy remained silent as he returned to the window. No sign of the innkeeper. He was probably talking to the law.

"We'll find out," he murmured. "Sooner or later."

As Walking Star expected, it wasn't long before they were paid a visit by the chief proctor.

Around twilight, the three of them went downstairs to the tavern, which opened for business as shadows began to lengthen upon the street outside. It was a large, wood-paneled room with beer-stained tables and a fireplace near the bar; like the guest rooms, it was comfortable, but hardly luxurious. A voluptuous woman who'd been stuffed into a low-cut dress had just finished opening the windows; she eyed them with suspicion as they came in, but nonetheless offered them a table near a window before going to the bar to fetch a pitcher of water and some crudely printed menus. The *chaaz'maha* searched her, and was satisfied to find that McKay had instructed her to give them the regular menu. He learned that her name was Bess, and it was rather sad to also discover that she'd gotten her job by sleeping with the innkeeper, whom she'd once loved but had since come secretly to despise.

The tavern fare was plain—sandwiches, soup, and stew, most of it made from one sort of fish or another—but they were too hungry to complain even had they been of a mind to do so. No chocolate ice cream, though; Melissa's craving for it would have to go unsatisfied. Bess's attitude softened a bit when she heard the request; she understood pregnancy, having once been knocked up in her younger days—the child, alas, had been lost in a miscarriage—and so she promised to bring Melissa a slice of rhubarb pie from the kitchen. Yet she was puzzled, even faintly annoyed, that none of her customers ordered ale; one of the few things she liked about her job was the Laughing Sailor's home brew, which she imbibed herself at every opportunity.

—*There goes an unhappy woman,* the *chaaz'maha* sent, once Bess had disappeared into the kitchen. As customary when there was a chance of being overheard, he spoke to the others with his mind, not his tongue. —*Such a miserable life . . . and she doesn't even realize it herself.*

—*She could learn much from you, I agree.* Melissa didn't look directly at him, but instead idly gazed out the window, relishing the cool evening breeze against her face.

—*So how do you intend to reach out to her?* Walking Star traced a finger across the tabletop, allowing the *chaaz'maha* and Melissa to feel the coarse texture of the wood grain.—*I don't think this is someone who's going to respond to a sermon about the wisdom of* Sa'Tong.

—*Patience. Patience.* The *chaaz'maha* poured water into a glass.—*We've just arrived. All in good time.*

So they sat in silence, speaking to one another only when necessary while sharing the small, tactile sensations that so many overlooked from moment to moment of ordinary human existence. Each was capable of blocking out the others, of course—one thing they'd learned from *Sa'Tong* was the sort of mental discipline they needed to keep from going mad—so Melissa was considerate enough not to send the occasional squirms and aches of the unborn child within her, just as Walking Star didn't ruin everyone else's appetite when Beth brought out their food by broadcasting his low opinion of the redfish stew he'd ordered.

They ate quietly, taking their time, while the tavern gradually filled with its regular customers. One or two at a time, they arrived, the people who came here every night after work: fishermen, shop owners, longshoremen, the people who worked in the processing plant, a school-teacher, a farmer, a mousy girl trying to find a guy who would buy her a drink. Hard-eyed men and women, for the most part, accustomed to living in a small town on the edge of civilization, vaguely dissatisfied with their existence yet not knowing what to do with it except eat, drink, screw, and get through another day without giving in to despera-tion.

The *chaaz'maha* knew how they felt. He'd once been just that way himself. Sitting with his back against the wall, hood raised above his head, he watched them with shrouded eyes. During the year he'd spent in The Sanctuary, he'd learned how to search thoughts of others with-out the irritating cerebral tickle that Walking Star's less-adept students sometimes caused. So no one in the tavern became aware of what he was doing as he opened his mind to theirs, allowing their stream of con-sciousness to cascade upon his like cool summer rain:

—*Goddamn captain won't gimme a raise ungrateful sunnabitch like I don't know the boat better than he does who needs this shit anyway should tie an an-chor around his neck kick his ass overboard . . .*

—*Wish I were anywhere but here why did I come here tonight all I'm gonna do is drink drink drink till I go home and fall down what the hell I'll get another brew maybe it'll be different tonight maybe I'll get laid or something . . .*

—*God I'm lonely god I wish I had someone I loved could really love I mean but all I do is have sex better than nothing but oh god I'm so lonely . . .*

—*Who's the spook over there why's he looking at me like that is he queer or something and what's the deal with that hood what's he trying to hide anyway hey you keep looking at me like that there's gonna be trouble boy I . . .*

—*Good beer good beer like beer love beer oops just farted did anyone notice who cares good beer . . .*

—*That must be them Owen wants me to have a word with them thinks they're weird yeah well they look harmless enough but if he wants me to talk to them I guess I should but hell I got better things to do . . .*

The last came from the stout, thickset young man who'd just walked into the tavern. The *chaaz'maha* didn't have to search him to know that he was the chief proctor; the blue shirt he wore, along with an air of quiet authority, was sufficient. The only surprise was that he was no older than the *chaaz'maha* himself; in his midtwenties, by Gregorian reckoning, he was almost too young for the job.

Pretending nonchalance, the proctor strolled over to their table. "Hi, folks. Understand you're new in town. Mind if I join you?"

"Not at all. Please do." Neither Walking Star nor Melissa said anything as the *chaaz'maha* beckoned him toward an empty chair.

"Thanks." The proctor sat down, then turned toward Bess and raised a finger. The barmaid was lighting the oil lamps; she nodded, then headed for the bar. "Can I get you anything?" the proctor asked, glancing at the half-empty glasses around the table. "Or are you not drinking?"

"Only water, thank you," the *chaaz'maha* replied.

—*Not drinking in a bar weird but at least I won't have to worry about them getting drunk will I?* "Just thought I'd ask."—*Go ahead introduce yourself.* "I'm Rhea Wolff, the chief proctor. Mr. McKay told me that he had some new guests. We don't get many visitors, so I thought I might drop by and . . . well, see if there's anything I could do for you."

"Thank you, Constable Wolff . . ."

"Rhea." A smile flickered across his face. "We're informal here in Carlos's Pizza."

"Of course." The *chaaz'maha* gazed back at him. "No, there's nothing you can do for us, but my friends and I appreciate the offer nonetheless."

"Uh-huh."—*Don't say much do you pal?* "So . . . who are you, anyway?"

The *chaaz'maha* gestured to the others. "My companions are Melissa Sanchez and Joseph Walking Star Cassidy. I am the *chaaz'maha*."

Wolff blinked.—*What did he say what the hell what kind of name is that?* "Chas . . . chas . . . I'm sorry, but I don't . . ."

"*Chaaz'maha.*" He repeated it slowly, drawing out the syllables. "It's a *hjadd* word. Roughly translated, it means 'spiritual teacher.' Which is what I am . . . or rather, what I have become."

—*What kind of nut is this guy oh boy . . .* "Uh-huh, I see." Wolff's expression remained neutral, trying to hide thoughts that the *chaaz'maha* could read as easily as if the proctor had written them on a piece of paper. "And . . . um, so what was your name before you became a *hjadd*?"

The *chaaz'maha* smiled. "I'm afraid you've misinterpreted what I just said. As you can clearly see, I'm not a *hjadd*, nor do I believe I am. See?" He reached up to lower the hood of his robe, revealing his face for the first time since he'd walked into the tavern. "I'm human, just as much as you are. As for my previous name . . ." He shrugged. "No longer important. I don't use it anymore. I am the *chaaz'maha*. That's all that matters."

—*This guy is missing a few pints from his keg what the hell is that on his forehead?*

Before Wolff could give voice to his next question, the *chaaz'maha* tapped a finger against the tattoo on his brow. "This is the *hjadd* symbol for *chaaz'maha*. It's customary for teachers of *Sa'Tong* to wear it so that anyone who mets them will know who they are."

—*How did he know I was going to ask that this guy is really giving me the creeps . . .* "Uh-huh, I see." The chief proctor peered more closely at the tattoo. "Nice, very nice indeed. You think I could get one just like it?"

The *chaaz'maha* shook his head. "I'm sorry, no. Not unless you become a disciple of *Sa'Tong* and learn to adhere to its codicils, and even then you couldn't become a *chaaz'maha* . . ."

"It's difficult to explain," Walking Star said, speaking for the first time. "You'll just have to trust him when he says that he is who he says he is."

—*Yeah right anything you say big guy.* "I see," Wolff said slowly, patronizing him. "So . . . um . . . let me get this straight. You call yourself the *chaaz'maha*, and you . . ."

"I don't *claim* to be a teacher of *Sa'Tong*." The *chaaz'maha* shook his head again. "I *am* a teacher of *Sa'Tong*."

—*How the hell does he know what I'm about to say this is really weird man . . .* "Pardon. Didn't mean to offend you."

"No offense taken." The *chaaz'maha* smiled. "And before you ask . . . *Sa'Tong* is a system of spiritual beliefs practiced by most of the intelligent races of the galaxy. The *hjadd* are but one race that has adopted it. Its book, the *Sa'Tong-tas*, was recently given to me by Jasahajahd Taf Sa-Fhadda, the cultural ambassador of the *hjadd*, with the intent of spreading its wisdom to humankind. I have undertaken the task of doing so . . . in other words, to become the *chaaz'maha* for the human race." He paused. "Do you understand now, Rhea?"

As he spoke, the *chaaz'maha* became aware that conversation around them had died, as all the tavern's patrons turned their attention toward him. A cacophony of thoughts flooded his awareness, some so distracting that they threatened to overwhelm him. He wasn't prepared for that, so he moved his left hand beneath the table to surreptitiously rub his thumb against the nail of his index finger, something that Walking Star had taught him to do as a way of blocking out unwelcome distractions. One by one, the unspoken voices of everyone else in the tavern faded away, until the only thoughts he heard were those of Rhea Wolff.

—Understand no not really but dunno this guy somehow I don't think he's such a nut after all what if he's telling the truth no that can't be he's obviously . . .

"This is difficult for you, I know," the *chaaz'maha* went on. "A lot to take in all at once. But you have to trust me when I tell you that I'm not crazy, that what I've said is the truth, and that my companions and I mean you no harm. I am a teacher, and I have come here to teach. No more, no less."

The proctor didn't respond. Looking away from the *chaaz'maha*, he seemed to notice for the first time that the room had gone quiet. Even Bess, who'd just then returned to the table with a pint of ale in hand, stopped what she was doing to listen to what the stranger had to say. Shifting his gaze toward her, the *chaaz'maha* opened his mind to hers.

—Oh my god who is this guy look at his eyes can't believe how beautiful they are wonder what he's like in bed no forget it Bess he's taken wonder if I can talk to him maybe he really is a teacher . . .

"All right," Wolff said at last, "I believe you . . . or at least the part about not wanting to do any harm." He didn't notice that Bess's hand trembled as she placed the ale on the table before him, or that she lingered for a second longer than necessary, bending over to let the *chaaz'maha* have a good look at her breasts. "Just so you know that I've got a low tolerance for troublemakers, and our jail is a lot less comfortable than the upstairs rooms."

The *chaaz'maha* paid no attention to Bess or her clumsy attempt to interest him sexually. "You'll have no trouble from us, Rhea. We appreciate your desire to maintain the peace." He paused, then added, "Perhaps you'd like to read the *Sa'Tong-tas* yourself. It may give you a better idea of who we are."

Wolff hesitated.—*Great just what I need another missionary oh what the hell take it be polite can't do any harm maybe worth a laugh right?* "Sure. I'd like to see it."

The *chaaz'maha* pulled out a pad, and the proctor did the same; it took only a few seconds to download the *Sa'Tong-tas* into Wolff's comp. The version that the *chaaz'maha* gave him wasn't identical to the one he'd received from Taf; pads didn't have sufficient power or memory to emulate the *hjadd* AI within the original *Sa'Tong-tas*, and he'd learned that it was incompatible with the operating systems of human-made comps. So he and Walking Star had spent most of the previous year transcribing the *Sa'Tong*, including the Codicils and the various Poems of Wisdom and Peace, into Anglo text that could be read easily by their fellow humans, with the pad itself translating it into other languages.

"If you like what you read," he said once they'd disconnected the pads, "feel free to pass it along to others."

"I'll do that."—*Like hell.* Wolff folded his pad and tucked it in his pocket. "So . . . how long do you think you'll be staying?"—*Not long I hope you guys are really strange.*

"Perhaps just a few days. As I said, you'll have no trouble from us." The *chaaz'maha* glanced at his companions; without a word, the three of them stood up as one, pushing back their chairs to leave the table. "Pleasure to meet you, Rhea. I hope we'll have a chance to talk again soon."

He blocked his mind from the proctor's thoughts, not wanting to hear more, but as he turned away from Wolff, he found Bess still hovering nearby. She hastily glanced away, but it wasn't hard to miss the blush that appeared on her face. The *chaaz'maha* didn't hesitate; stepping closer to her, he reached into his pocket and withdrew a colonial.

"This is for you," he said, offering the coin to her. "Thank you for your hospitality. I assume the cost of our meal will be added to our bill, yes?"

"Yeah . . . yes, of course." Flustered, Bess accepted the tip. "You . . . you can pay up in the . . . the morning."

"Thank you." He smiled, then moved a little closer. "Hate is not a substitute for love," he whispered, his voice so soft that only she could hear it. "If you can't love the one you're with, then don't hate him instead. Just find another who'll be willing to accept your gift."

Her eyes widened.—*God oh god oh god how does he know like he's looked into my soul and I dunno I need to talk to him I really need to talk to him* . . .

"I'll be around," he added. "Come see me anytime you want."

And then he walked away, with Melissa and Walking Star falling in behind him. No one stood in their way as they strolled through the crowded tavern, but nonetheless a tide of confused and conflicting thoughts swept them from the room. Smiling to himself, the *chaaz'maha* reached up to raise his hood. If he'd sought to make an impression, then . . .

—*I know him I know him I've heard that voice before back in Liberty the* Sa'Tong-tas *he told me about it* I know him!

From somewhere in the crowd, one thought came through as clearly as if it had been a shout from across the room. The *chaaz'maha* stopped, and for a second he had an impulse to turn and look back. He restrained himself, though, and instead continued to walk toward the door.

He recognized the individual to whom those thoughts belonged. But it would have to be up to him if they'd ever meet again.

The following morning, the *chaaz'maha* and his small entourage began making themselves visible in the community. They didn't linger in their rooms all day, but instead left the Laughing Sailor shortly after breakfast and set out to walk around town. Although they wore their robes, no longer did they keep their hoods raised; Walking Star advised the *chaaz'maha* that continuing to hide their faces would only cause suspicion, and that was the last thing they wanted to do. So everyone they encountered saw the *hjadd* symbol tattooed on the *chaaz'maha's* forehead, and that added to his mystique.

They made their way to the row of shops near the waterfront, where they found a grocery that sold homemade chocolate ice cream. Overjoyed, Melissa bought a couple of pints, even though the *chaaz'maha* laughingly reminded her that she probably wouldn't be able to eat one before the other melted. She responded by buying three spoons as well; the three of them sat on a bench overlooking the wharf, with the *chaaz'maha* and Walking Star sharing one carton while Melissa gorged herself on the other.

Once they were done, they continued their stroll, stopping now and then to see what few sights Carlos's Pizza had to offer: the processing plant, the school, the meetinghouse and the town hall next door, the various boat builders and nautical supply shops that catered to the local fishermen. They could have been no more than tourists who'd found an unlikely spot for a vacation, except that the locals were even more curious about them than they were about the village. Wherever they went, people stopped what they were doing to stare at them . . . or, more precisely, at the *chaaz'maha*. Carlos's Pizza was a small town, after all, and news traveled fast; rumors had circulated about the stranger staying at the Laughing Sailor who claimed to be a *hjadd* holy man, and even if the description wasn't wholly accurate, it was enough to rouse interest.

The *chaaz'maha* wasn't surprised. In fact, he was pleased. He wanted the townspeople to see him, meet him, talk to him. Even though he rarely had any direct questions—most of the time, he received innocuous queries like *where are you from?* and *how did you get here?* and *how long will you be staying?*—he found them in their minds nonetheless. *Who are you? Why are you here? Are you really what you say you are?*

Having made that initial sojourn, the three of them returned to the inn. Melissa was tired, so after lunch—once again, she ate heartily, feeding both herself and the baby inside her—she went upstairs to take a nap, while the *chaaz'maha* and his tall, silent companion went out on the front porch, where they took seats in the bamboo rocking chairs overlooking the street. And there they waited to see who would come to see them.

They didn't have long to wait. Not surprisingly, their first visitor was Bess. She'd apparently decided not to put on the low-cut dress that Mc-

Kay insisted that she wear for the titillation of his customers, but instead a more demure outfit that she saved for special occasions. As Walking Star sat quietly nearby, she and the *chaaz'maha* spoke for a little more than an hour, keeping their voices low so that her boss couldn't overhear them from inside. When they were done, the *chaaz'maha* downloaded a copy of the *Sa'Tong-tas* into the battered pad Bess had brought with her, then she left, going home to rest awhile before returning for work. Only the *chaaz'maha* knew that it would be her last night at the Laughing Sailor; she was already planning to tell McKay that he'd have to find another serving wench, and then burn that damn dress.

A little while later, someone else arrived, a tough-looking sailor who served as second mate on a fishing schooner. Upon searching him, the *chaaz'maha* recognized this person as the same individual who'd been idly contemplating lashing his captain to an anchor and throwing him overboard. The sailor was just as aggressive that afternoon as he'd been the previous evening; there was a lot of pent-up hostility deep inside, and he'd come to the inn with the half-formed notion of finding the weirdo who claimed to be a holy guy and picking a fight with him. As he stomped up the front steps, Walking Star rose from his chair to stand beside the *chaaz'maha*, his arms folded across his chest; that intimidated the sailor just enough to give the *chaaz'maha* a chance to start talking. Their conversation was a little longer than the one he'd had with Bess, but in the end, the sailor had come to see, albeit reluctantly, that violence wasn't only futile but in fact was ultimately self-destructive, and if he really wanted to show his captain that he knew what he was doing, he'd concentrate more on doing his job and less on thinking about ways to murder him. The sailor didn't own a pad, but he said that he'd come back later once he borrowed one from a friend; humbled, he shook the *chaaz'maha's* hand, then ambled away, feeling oddly at peace with himself.

Yuri reappeared. He'd spent the evening thinking about the things the *chaaz'maha* had told him during the long ride from New Boston, and he wanted to know more. They spoke for a little while, then the *chaaz'maha* copied the *Sa'Tong-tas* into the pad the drover had brought with him. Yuri left again, but not before telling the *chaaz'maha* that he thought he'd like to see his wife again, and perhaps the time had come for him to buy her passage to Coyote from Russia.

And so it went, not only for the rest of that day, but also the next day, and the day after that. One by one at first, and then in twos and threes, the people of Carlos's Pizza came to see the man with the odd tattoo on his forehead. Sometimes they were curious, other times they were skeptical, but more often than not they were desperate, scared, depressed, or angry at the way life had treated them. The only common factor was that they had questions for which they had no answers and were willing to listen to what the stranger had to say.

The *chaaz'maha* delivered no sermons, nor did he treat the inn's front porch as if it were a church. When he spoke, it was with only one person at a time, and often he spent more time listening to others than talking. Searching their minds, he was able to determine what troubled them even if they didn't articulate the problem themselves, and responded in kind. Sometimes Walking Star or Melissa joined him on the porch, but after a while he grew confident enough to be able to sit out there on his own, meeting with whoever happened to show up. He refused offers of money, politely saying that he didn't need any, although he was always grateful when someone was thoughtful enough to bring him some water or perhaps a snack.

He never claimed to know the mind of God, except to occasionally say that the only holy spirit was that which all beings carried within themselves. And that may have been what finally persuaded Grey Rice to pay him a visit.

Indeed, Rice had never been far from the *chaaz'maha*. From his very first day in Carlos's Pizza, the young Dominionist minister—or rather, former minister—had lurked nearby, often following him down the street or quietly standing at a corner of the porch, maintaining a discreet distance while staying just close enough that he could hear what the *chaaz'maha* had to say. Walking Star was wary of his presence, and Melissa didn't recognize him until the *chaaz'maha* reminded her of who he was; when Cassidy searched Rice, he didn't find any hostile thoughts, only a sense of curiosity. So the *chaaz'maha* continued to ignore him, giving Rice a chance to come to him if and when he felt like it.

It was late afternoon of their fourth day in Carlos's Pizza when Rice finally decided to approach the *chaaz'maha*. By then, it was almost din-nertime; the *chaaz'maha* had been talking to townspeople all day, and his throat was raw and his stomach was beginning to rumble. Melissa was taking a nap, and Walking Star was off on an errand. The *chaaz'maha* was about to get up from his chair when he heard footsteps on the porch, and when he looked around, he saw Rice strolling toward him.

"Hello, Reverend Rice," he said. "I was hoping you'd eventually come to see me."

That stopped Rice dead in his tracks. "So you remember me."

"Of course, I do," the *chaaz'maha* replied, although he didn't say how. In the year and a quarter since they'd last spoken to each other, Grey Rice's appearance had changed. No longer wearing the black vestments of a Dominionist minister, he'd also lost weight; his long hair had be-come shaggy, and an unkempt beard covered his lean face. But the most noticeable difference was his eyes; once confident and open, they were now shrouded and hollow, filled only by a deep sense of loss. The *chaaz'maha* didn't need to search him to know that Rice was in pain.

"Please, sit with me." The *chaaz'maha* gestured to the vacant chair next to him, still warm from his previous visitor. "I've been wondering if we'd ever meet again."

Rice hesitated. "I remember you," he said, coming closer but not sit-ting down. "You're the person who came to see me at my church . . . the one who said he'd met the *hjadd* ambassador." He paused, then added, "You didn't tell me your name, and you look a lot different now, but as you mentioned *Sa'Tong*, I knew who you were."

"You're very observant." The *chaaz'maha* settled back in his chair, ca-sually crossed his legs. "Yeah, I'm the same guy," he went on, briefly allowing himself to become Hawk Thompson again. "Kinda surprised you picked up on it. Guess I do look a bit different these days." A pause. "So do you, Reverend, if you don't mind me saying so . . ."

"I do mind." Rice's eyes narrowed, and there was an angry harshness in his voice. "I'm no longer a pastor. I've lost my church . . . Hell, be-cause of you, I've lost my religion . . ."

"Because of me?" The *chaaz'maha* shook his head. "Sorry you blame me for this, but the choices you've made are your own. They can't be the result of the few minutes we spent together."

Rice let out his breath. "Not directly, no . . . but because of you, I went to meet the *hjadd* ambassador myself. The things he told me, the things he said to me . . ."

"Heshe." The *chaaz'maha* was careful not to smile. "The *hjadd* share both genders."

"Don't change the subject." Rice glared at him. "That day, everything changed for me. Sure, it took a couple of weeks for it to really sink in, but when I finally had a chance to speak my mind to a deacon who came from Earth to meet with me, I realized that I no longer had faith in my own beliefs, that I couldn't function as a pastor. I abandoned my church, and when I found I couldn't even live in Liberty without being reminded every day of what I once was, I came here."

"And what have you been doing since?" The *chaaz'maha* refrained from searching him. He wanted to hear the truth from Rice himself, in his own words.

"I found work at the plant. Filleting brownhead and packing them in ice." A humorless smile. "It's a lousy job, but the smell keeps me from thinking too much. About you, about where you led me . . ."

"I'm sorry." The *chaaz'maha* briefly closed his eyes. "Really, I am. I never meant to harm you, or do anything that would cause you to lose your way. All I wanted to do was ask a few questions, see if you had any answers to the things I needed to know."

"Guess you found them yourself, didn't you?" Rice pointed to the tattoo on his forehead. "Now you're setting yourself up as some sort of messiah, starting your own religion . . ."

"No. There you're wrong." The *chaaz'maha* shook his head. "*Sa'Tong* isn't a religion so much as it is a system of spiritual beliefs. Sort of a higher form of ethics, if you will. And the last thing I want to be is a messiah. If you've listened to anything I've said these last few days, you'd know that my role is that of a teacher."

"Better hope that's your role." A cynical grin. "Coyote's had a messiah before, y'know. Zoltan Shirow, the Church of Universal Transformation . . ." He gestured in the direction of the Midland Range. "They ate each other alive way back when, up on Mt. Shaw. If you don't watch yourself . . ."

"I know all about Shirow. I was born and raised here. My parents . . ." Realizing that he was about to reveal more about himself than he meant to, the *chaaz'maha* changed the subject. "That's an experience I have no desire to repeat," he went on. "Shirow was a charlatan, someone who claimed to be a holy prophet but instead used his followers. That's not what I intend to do."

"So you say . . . you're a teacher, that's all." Leaning against the porch rail, Rice folded his arms together. "I've heard what you've told the others. That the only God is that which is within us, and if we are to truly worship Him, then we must learn to worship and respect each other."

"Essentially, yes." The *chaaz'maha* nodded. "The First and Second Codicils of *Sa'Tong*, although not exactly in those words . . ."

"Autotheism. The belief in self-deification, an idea that goes all the way back to the seventeenth century." Rice shook his head. "Nothing new, really. I learned this stuff in divinity school."

"Similar, yes, but not the same." The *chaaz'maha* raised a hand. "Again, you continue to insist that *Sa'Tong* is a religion. It isn't, or at least not the way you're accustomed to thinking of religion. As I've said, it's more like an ethical construct, or a philosophy. The major difference is that it doesn't recognize God as a divine entity but rather as something we invent ourselves. God didn't create us . . ."

" 'We created God.' Yes, I've heard you say that." Rice shrugged. "Old wine, new bottle."

"A different vintage entirely, if you'll only allow yourself to taste it." Bending forward to rest his elbows on his knees, the *chaaz'maha* gazed up at him. "Grey, if you'll stop blaming me for your loss of faith, I can show you something that's greater than Dominionism, more true than anything you heard before. No, it isn't the word of God, nor does it pretend to be. It's a way of thought . . . a way of living . . . that can ease your pain."

"The one, true path to Heaven." The same weary cynicism.

"There is no Heaven. There is no Hell. There's only the world that we make for ourselves, in this life . . . which is the only one we have." The *chaaz'maha* hesitated, then reached into his robe. "You've seen me do this," he said, holding up his pad. "You know what's in here. If you've got a pad, let me give you the *Sa'Tong-tas*. You can read it, then decide for yourself . . ."

"No." Grey shook his head. "I don't want the watered-down version you've given everyone else. When we met before, you told me about the one the *hjadd* gave you. That's what I want to see."

"I'm sorry, but I can't do that. We decided it was too valuable to carry along with us, so we left it behind." The *chaaz'maha* was careful not to say where they had come from. As Walking Star had said, people would inevitably learn about The Sanctuary, but the longer its existence was kept secret, the better.

Grey shrugged. "Then it's hard for me to accept it at face value. Sorry I have to be skeptical about this, but . . ."

"I understand . . . In fact, I agree. All forms of spiritualism should be treated skeptically." Grey's face turned red, but the *chaaz'maha* paid it no mind as he put the pad back in his robe. "Then you're welcome to hang around while I deliver my teachings. You can even sit beside me. Ask all the questions you like. Challenge me, if you feel the need to do so. This isn't church."

"No need to be insulting."

"My apologies. Didn't mean to offend you. I was only trying to point out the difference between *Sa'Tong* and most human religions. Religion insists upon its dogma being accepted at face value, no questions asked. But *Sa'Tong* isn't a religion, or at least not the way we usually define it, nor am I a priest, but rather a teacher . . . and only a mediocre teacher wouldn't allow his students to ask questions."

Grey scowled. "That's rather presumptuous of you. What makes you think I'm your student?"

The *chaaz'maha* rose from his seat. "You've come to listen to me, haven't you? I'd say that qualifies." He turned toward the door. "Now, if you'll excuse me . . . it's been a long day, and I think it's almost time for dinner."

Grey hesitated. "Would you mind company?"

The *chaaz'maha* stopped, looked back at him. "Not at all. You're always welcome at my table."

Over the course of the next week and a half, the *chaaz'maha's* life assumed a pattern. After breakfast, he and his companions would take their morning exercise by walking around town, visiting places where they were no longer strangers: the waterfront, the grocery and various shops, the clinic where a local physician had offered to monitor Melissa's pregnancy. He'd made friends with various townspeople, so he'd sometimes drop by for a cup of coffee; the *chaaz'maha* had become a familiar face in their homes, a caring friend to those who'd come to him with their problems.

In the afternoons, he resumed his place on the Laughing Sailor's front porch, where he spoke with whoever came to see him. By then, he was often drawing a small crowd, with some returning every day; whenever he sensed that someone needed to meet with him on some private matter, he'd take the individual to another side of the porch, where they could talk without being overheard. At first, Owen McKay had objected to having so many people crowded onto his porch; he was also irate that he'd lost his barmaid, although he hadn't yet connected Bess's abrupt departure with anything the *chaaz'maha* might have said to her. But when he noticed that the tavern was gaining revenue from people coming in for drinks and snacks, he came to realize that playing host to a spiritual teacher wasn't bad for business.

Grey Rice was always there. He never accepted the *chaaz'maha's* invitation to sit next to him, but he did frequently ask questions, often challenging him at one point or another. The *chaaz'maha* always answered him, candidly and without obfuscation, and after a few days Grey decided that perhaps he should read the *Sa'Tong-tas* himself, just as many of the regulars already had. And both men were amused when, not long after that, Grey found himself defending *Sa'Tong*, reciting the Codicils or Poems from memory when another person began making objections to their principles.

Yet the *chaaz'maha* didn't just hold forth. He listened, too, sometimes not speaking for a long time as he heard what people had to say. Very often, the afternoon meetings took the form of informal bull sessions, with townspeople discussing matters that had nothing to do with *Sa'Tong*. The falling wholesale price of weirdling oil, now that more homes and businesses in the colonies were being refitted with photovoltaic cells imported from Earth. Competition with Bridgeton's commercial fishing fleet and how it affected their share of the market, causing fishermen to bring home catches that they couldn't sell. Whether or not the town needed to build an expansion for its school. Which kind of sails were better, canvas or polymer, or the best ways to keep deck nails from rusting.

The subject that came up most often was increased immigration to Coyote. By then, it had become common knowledge that the Western Hemisphere Union had collapsed, with hundreds of thousands desperate to flee the riot-torn cities of North and South America. Word reached Carlos's Pizza that Carlos Montero was trying to negotiate an accord with the Union's provisional government that would remove the emigration barriers put in place by the Proletariat in exchange for formal recognition of the Coyote Federation and relinquishment of previous territorial claims. The U.N. treaty would finally be ratified by all of Earth's major superpowers, but it also raised the problem of a massive surge of refugees, with no obvious way to shelter or feed them.

Although the *chaaz'maha* shared their concerns, he was also pleased by the general tenor of the discussions. He was all too aware that, until recently, most of the townspeople would have reacted selfishly, deciding that it wasn't their problem and that the door should be slammed shut. Yet many had come to realize that, if they were to treat others as if they were manifestations of God, then they could not refuse them sanctuary in their time of need. So the talk wasn't about whether former citizens of the Union should be allowed to immigrate to Coyote, but rather how they would be cared for once they arrived. Indeed, there were even some who noted that the Carlos's Pizza fishing fleet often brought home more fish than the market could bear; perhaps the warehouse's frozen surplus could be sent across the channel to Albion, where the Colonial Militia was already beginning to set up a refugee camp.

Listening to all this, the *chaaz'maha* realized that there was a chance for him to guide his followers toward a positive purpose. Yet he had only begun to think about how to accomplish that when he received an unexpected visit from Rhea Wolff.

He and his companions had just finished breakfast and were about to leave the Laughing Sailor when they found the chief proctor waiting for them on the front steps. Aside from casual greetings now and then, none of them had spoken with Rhea since their first day in Carlos's Pizza. At first, the *chaaz'maha* was pleased to see him, but when he saw the look on Wolff's face, he realized that the proctor was there on official business.

"Good morning, Rhea," he said, walking down the steps. "Lovely day, isn't it?"

The fact of the matter was that the sky was overcast, promising rain by afternoon at the latest. But the proctor didn't seem to notice; his expression was grim, his arms folded together across his chest.

"Morning," he replied. "Got a minute? I need to talk to you about something."

"Of course. What's on your mind?" As he said this, the *chaaz'maha* glanced at Walking Star and Melissa. The question, so casually asked, was a private signal the three of them had worked out. Yet Cassidy had already searched Rhea, and when he looked back at the *chaaz'maha*, it was as if he were whispering in the teacher's ear.

—*He knows who you are.*

"Hate to put it to you like this," Rhea was saying, "but . . . well, something's come to my attention that I can't ignore."

"Is there a problem?" Melissa asked. She'd just suffered another bout of morning sickness; her face was sallow. Despite her appetite, which remained ravenous, it had become difficult for her to keep anything in her stomach. Yet she'd heard Walking Star as well.

"I'm afraid there is . . . or at least there may be, if what I've heard is true." Rhea pulled out his pad, unfolded it. "A year or so ago, I got a memo from Albion. Chief proctors send and receive a lot of stuff like this . . . it's our way of sharing information between jurisdictions . . . but most of the time they're pretty routine. Read it once, store it in memory, and forget about it. And that's what happened with the one I got from my colleague in New Brighton . . . until I happened to find it again yesterday."

As he spoke, he ran his index finger down the screen, pulling up a file from the menu. "Last year, someone went missing in New Brighton . . . a customs inspector who'd been working at the spaceport until he suddenly vanished. Wouldn't matter much except that this individual was currently on parole, having been previously convicted on charges of second-degree murder. But he decided to remove his inhibitor patch and monitor bracelet and skip town without informing his parole officer. The parole officer"—Rhea paused to read something on his pad—"name of Joe Bairns, eventually managed to track him as far as the fishing boat that carried him and an unidentified female companion across the channel to Bridgeton. And after that . . ."

"They vanished." The *chaaz'maha* tried to remain stoical, but he didn't have to search Rhea to know where he was going.

"Not entirely." The chief proctor didn't look up from his pad. "A few weeks later, there was an unconfirmed sighting in Liberty. But by the time Chief Levin over there heard about this, the two of 'em had left town. And they haven't been seen since."

Rhea raised his eyes to look straight at the *chaaz'maha*. "Until now, that is. May I ask . . . is this you?"

He turned the pad around in his hands so that the *chaaz'maha* could see the screen. Upon it was displayed a picture of himself, when he'd been known as Hawk Thompson and when he'd worn the uniform of a customs inspector.

"I can't be sure, of course," Rhea went on, watching the *chaaz'maha* carefully. "That is, he looks a bit like you, but . . ."

"You are correct. That's me." The *chaaz'maha* took a deep breath. "Or rather, that's the person I once was."

Rhea raised an eyebrow. "Sorry? Come again?"

Before he could reply, Melissa stepped forward. "Constable Wolff, if you know that he was originally Hawk Thompson, then you must also know that I'm Melissa Sanchez, the woman who left New Brighton with him." Rhea started to speak, but she held up her hand. "Listen to me, please. I've known him for almost a year and a half, and believe me when I tell you that this isn't the same person I first met in New Brighton. When he says he's changed, he doesn't just mean his name or his appearance. Hawk Thompson is the man he used to be. The *chaaz'maha* is who he is now."

"I can't accept that." Rhea shook his head; searching him, the *chaaz'maha* found determination mingled with regret. "Y'know, if you'd denied everything, I might have let it go at that, even though I know better. You've done a lot for this town while you've been here. I've also been reading the *Sa'Tong-tas* lately, and there's a lot to it that makes sense. But . . ."

"But you're an officer of the law, and have a sworn duty to uphold." Despite his efforts to remain calm, the *chaaz'maha* realized that his hands were trembling. "So I take it you're here to put me under arrest?"

"Let me finish, please." Wolff paused, then went on. "I haven't reported this matter to anyone yet. No one else knows about this except the four of us."

"I appreciate that."

"Uh-huh. I thought you would, considering the respect you've earned in this community. When you came here, I told you that you'd get no trouble from me if you didn't cause any yourself. You've kept your promise, which means the only thing I have on you is a charge of skipping parole. But still . . ."

—Just go get out of here don't make me do this I believe in Sa'Tong *I can't arrest my teacher just get out of here please . . .*

"What if we were to leave town?" the *chaaz'maha* asked. "Would that solve your problem?"

Wolff blinked, not quite believing what he'd just heard. "My thoughts exactly." He paused. "Y'know, I never know how you do that . . . I mean, figure out what people are going to say before they actually . . ."

"I'm a good listener, that's all." From the corner of his eye, he saw Melissa covering her mouth with her hand. "Just give us a day or two to make arrangements, and we'll go as quietly as we came. If you want to report seeing us after that . . ."

"No, no." Wolff shook his head. "Once you're gone, you'll be out of my jurisdiction. You won't be my problem anymore." He thought about it for a moment. "I'll give you twenty-seven hours to get out of town. Think that'll be enough?"

Walking Star started to say something, but the *chaaz'maha* looked at him and he kept his peace. "That will be sufficient, yes. It'll give us a chance to charter a boat ride." He paused, then added, "I'd also like to take care of some unfinished business before we go."

The chief proctor studied him. "What sort of business?"

"Now that we're done here, there's something I'd like to do next." The *chaaz'maha* smiled. "And I'm going to need help from some of your people, if you don't mind."

Wolff hesitated. "Depends."

"Here's what I'm thinking . . ."

The fishing boat was a twin-masted schooner, not much larger than the craft that had carried him from New Brighton over a year ago. This time, though, the *chaaz'maha* wasn't sneaking out of town at dawn; instead, he was leaving in the broad light of day.

The schooner's second mate was one of his students, the sailor who'd come to him the first morning the *chaaz'maha* sat on the inn's front porch. Now that he'd repaired his relationship with his captain, the second mate had been able to persuade him to take on passengers and cargo for a special trip across the channel. The captain was skeptical at first, but then the *chaaz'maha* passed him a handful of colonials and the bargain was made.

The *chaaz'maha* was returning to New Brighton, but he wouldn't be alone. During his last session on the Laughing Sailor's front porch, the *chaaz'maha* told his students where he was going, and what he intended to do once he got there. He wasn't surprised to find that he had volunteers. Yuri, Bess, a few other townspeople . . . even Grey, who'd decided that the *chaaz'maha's* new mission was more important than cutting up fish.

Indeed, Grey turned out to be instrumental in his plans. As the *chaaz'maha* stood on the dock, he watched as his small group helped the schooner's crew carry aboard barrels of ice-packed fish. Once Grey had explained to his employers what the *chaaz'maha* intended to do, the processing plant was glad to get rid of the surplus catch from its warehouse. Along with several kegs of fish oil, they would be welcome donations to the refugee relief effort, with more to come.

Yet the *chaaz'maha's* heart was heavy, and not only because he was about to leave a town he'd come to love. He was also leaving behind his companions.

"I'd still like to come with you." Melissa stood beside him on the dock, a shawl wrapped around her head. "The baby isn't due for another few weeks. I'm sure we could find a doctor over there who—"

"We've been over this before." The *chaaz'maha* shook his head. "I'm sorry, but the answer's still no. You've got a good doctor already, and he's willing to look after you while I'm gone."

Melissa nodded. As much as she wanted to remain by his side, they both knew that a refugee camp was no place for her to give birth. There was also the strong possibility that he might be arrested as soon as he set foot on Albion; indeed, the stress of the trip across the channel might complicate her pregnancy. So it was only for the best that she stay in Carlos's Pizza, at least for the time being.

The *chaaz'maha* didn't need to search her to see the sadness in her eyes. "Don't worry," he added, taking her hand. "Once I'm done over there, I'll be back."

"And when I have the baby . . . ?"

"Someone will let me know. We've got a satphone, remember?" He smiled as he let his hand fall to her swollen belly. "I want to see Inez, too, y'know."

She grinned, acknowledging that he'd finally lost the argument over whether they were going to have a son or a daughter. Nonetheless, there were tears in her eyes as she moved closer to him. "You better come back," she whispered. "She's going to want to meet her daddy."

A last kiss, one that lingered for a few seconds, before she reluctantly stepped away from him. The *chaaz'maha* let her go, then turned to Walking Star. "Still time to change your mind," he said. "We could use you over there."

Cassidy shook his head. "Believe me, I'd only get in your way." He nodded in the general direction of Albion. "Morgan's over there. If he finds out that I've returned, that could be trouble for you."

"I'm going to have trouble anyway, if Joe discovers who I am . . ."

"He might, or he might not." Cassidy paused. "Melissa was right . . . I mean, about what she said yesterday to Rhea. You have changed, and not just in appearance. The person I met last spring doesn't really exist anymore. You're no longer Hawk . . . you're the *chaaz'maha*."

"If that's so, it's because I had a good teacher."

"Maybe . . . but perhaps I've changed, too. Maybe I'm not your teacher any longer, but instead your student." Walking Star raised a hand before the *chaaz'maha* could object. "Look, we could argue about this all morning, but the truth of the matter is that you don't need my help anymore. My place is at The Sanctuary. Yours . . ."

"I know." The *chaaz'maha* let out his breath. "Take care of the *Sa'Tong-tas*, will you? I'll come back for it when . . ."

His voice trailed off as something caught in his throat. "When you come back," Walking Star finished. "I'm sure we'll see each other again before long." As he gazed at the schooner, a rare smile appeared on his face. "The next time we meet, you'll be a father as well as a teacher."

By then, the last of the barrels and kegs had been loaded aboard. The schooner's captain walked to the stern and looked at the *chaaz'maha*, not saying anything yet obviously impatient to set sail before the tide changed.

"I think you're wanted." Walking Star took a step back, then he clasped his hands together and bowed from the waist. "*Sa'Tong qo, chaaz'maha.*"

"*Sa'Tong qo*, Walking Star . . . and thank you." The *chaaz'maha* bowed as well . . . then, on impulse, he reached out to Cassidy. The two men embraced for a moment, then quietly let each other go. Nothing more needed to be said, nor was it necessary for either one of them to search the other's mind.

The *chaaz'maha* clasped Melissa's hand one last time, then he turned and walked away, heading for the waiting ship. He found a place on the aft deck as the sailors cast off the lines and raised the anchor. A shouted order from the captain, then the sails were raised and the schooner slipped away from the dock.

As the sails caught the morning wind, the *chaaz'maha* watched Carlos's Pizza until it gradually disappeared from sight, before turning to gaze at the channel. The past was only prelude. His destiny lay beyond the horizon, in the place where he'd begun his journey.

Part 7

THE NEW BRIGHTON STORY

COYOTE REFUGEE CRISIS DEEPENS
by Lynn Hu/Pan News Service

New Brighton, Albion, Coyote; June 22, 2352 (Hama. 79, c.y. 17)

With as many as 1,000 people arriving every day from Earth—most of them refugees from the Western Hemisphere Union—Coyote's refugee crisis has become worse, straining the resources of the colonies as they struggle to provide for so many homeless persons.

Now that the WHU's provisional government has agreed to ratify the United Nations treaty of 2340 that formally recognized the Coyote Federation as a sovereign nation, both the Union and the CF have rescinded the legal barriers that prohibited WHU citizens from traveling to the 47 Ursae Majoris system. In addition, the Federation has temporarily relaxed its immigration quotas and is no longer imposing limits on the number of people who wish to relocate to Coyote.

However, the humanitarian impulses that drove these political decisions may cost the new world dearly. Although Coyote has no shortage of land, the Federation is barely able to feed, shelter, and provide medical attention to the multitudes arriving every day at its spaceport on Albion. Food, building materials, and medicine have been donated by nearby colonies on New Florida, Midland, and Great Dakota, yet senior government officials express concern that this may not be sufficient to take care of everyone.

"We are doing our best to accommodate their needs," says Blair Kaye, spokeswoman for Coyote Federation President Garth Thompson. "However, the fact of the matter is that we've always had a hard time just taking care of our own. Having so many new people coming here at once is taxing the limits of what we can do."

A refugee camp has been established just outside New Brighton, where Coyote's principal spaceport is located. The vast majority of newly arrived immigrants have been located there, and an effort is being made to shelter them and provide food. But a senior government official, who declined to be identified for this story, has said . . .

"Oh, God. What a mess."

Although Carlos's voice was little more than a murmur, no one standing near the former president failed to hear him. The other Government House officials touring the refugee camp—Council representatives, for the most past, along with the heads of various ministries—looked in his direction, with most of them nodding in silent agreement. The former president had never been someone to be ignored, and now that he'd become one of the main figures in the crisis, every word he uttered was bound to be taken seriously.

Carlos seemed to realize that, for he glanced over his shoulder at Lynn. "That's off the record," he quietly added. "I don't want that showing up in your next story."

"Don't worry, Mr. President." Lynn held up her pad, letting him see that it wasn't in vox mode and that the only thing she was entering into it were handwritten notes. She knew that she was allowed to accompany Carlos because she'd agreed to his stipulation that nothing he said would be quoted for direct attribution. In fact, she'd described him so often already as "a senior government official" that her editors back home had lately asked her whether he'd ever say anything on the record.

Carlos nodded, then turned to the man walking beside him. "This is bad," he went on. "I mean, really bad. I haven't seen anything like this since Shuttlefield during the Union occupation . . . and even then, it was only a few thousand people. But this . . ."

He raised a hand toward the vast camp that sprawled around them. Mile upon mile of tents, sheds, shacks, and lean-to shelters, arranged in uneven rows along narrow paths that crisscrossed the settlement like a maze. The ground was littered with paper wrappers from the rations that had been airlifted in—what little there was, that is—while people

stood in line before bamboo water tanks, all of them holding whatever they could find to carry freshwater back to where they were living.
Even then, there was just enough for people to drink, and little else. A
handful of children ran past; they looked happy enough, but it wasn't
hard to miss the fact they looked like they hadn't bathed in days

Not far away, soldiers and volunteers labored to build barracks from
pallets of cheap faux birch donated by the Thompson Wood Company. A
dozen or more longhouses had been slapped together, but they were
already overcrowded; the lucky few hundred or so who'd moved into
them were hot-bunking, sleeping in shifts so that they could share their
beds with others, while still more curled up on the floors. Marie Thompson had told her older brother that the company would send more timber as soon as it could, but its warehouses on Great Dakota were depleted;
no one had anticipated such demand in so short a time, and the stock-
piles of faux birch, mountain briar, and blackwood were nearly exhausted.

"They're doing the best they can, but there are too many people and
too little material." Dieter Vogel, the European Alliance ambassador to
Coyote, surveyed the scene as well. "I've requested that my government
send relief, and they've said that they'll do what they can, but . . ."

"That's too many 'buts' here for my liking," Carlos growled.

"Mr. President, please remember we have our own problems back
home . . ."

"I know that. But the fact remains that your government has also sent
us people without giving us the means to support them. Now that we've
relaxed the quotas, they're loading refugees on whatever ships can carry
them. I don't know what it's going to take to make them listen to us,
but . . ." Carlos stopped, shook his head. "We can't be your dumping
ground. At least not without the Alliance contributing their fair share."

Vogel said nothing, but instead gazed at the distant rooftops of New
Brighton, rising above the bamboo fence that had been hastily erected
between the city and the camp. "I've asked people in New Brighton to
render assistance. A few have, but"—Carlos gave Vogel an annoyed
look, which he ignored—"I'm afraid there's a certain amount of ani-
mosity toward the immigrants. You know what they're called, don't
you?"

"Uh-huh. 'Gringos' . . . Americans who don't know what they're doing and can't fend for themselves." Carlos's mouth tightened into a dis-
tasteful frown. "Sort of overlooks the fact that Coyote was first settled
by Americans, me included." Vogel started to say something, but Carlos
shook his head. "Nothing you can do about that, I know. It's an old
story . . . earlier waves of immigrants resenting the ones who came after
them, while conveniently forgetting that they were once in the same
situation."

"Yes, well . . . that's why they insisted on putting up the fence." As
they strolled through the camp, their eyes were drawn toward a blueshirt
who walked past. "There's been no trouble so far . . . well, with one
exception . . . but nonetheless we've got . . ."

"What sort of trouble?" Carlos glanced at him. "I haven't heard anything about that."

"A minor incident, really . . . but rather unfortunate, since it happened with someone who's been trying to help." Vogel stopped to point
toward a large canvas tent a few hundred feet away; cook-fire smoke
rose from behind it, and several dozen people were lined up nearby,
waiting to go inside. "See that? It was set up a couple of weeks ago by a
group from Midland." An ironic smile. "From Carlos's Pizza, in fact . . ."

Carlos rolled his eyes, but said nothing. Lynn had noticed that he always seemed mildly embarrassed that a town had been named after
him. "Glad to hear that someone has stepped in, but I don't see how
they've been causing . . ."

"It's not them. They've been bringing in food on a regular basis and
using to it feed as many as possible. They've also pitched in with some of
the other jobs . . . building longhouses. digging latrines, taking care of
the sick, and so forth. But their leader . . . well, I'm afraid that he was
placed under arrest yesterday evening by the local authorities."

"Arrested?" Carlos raised an eyebrow. "Why? Who is he?"

"No name . . . or at least none that I've heard. But he calls himself the
chaaz'maha, and claims that he's a teacher of something called *Sa'Tong*.
According to him, it's the principal religion of . . ."

"The *hjadd*, yes. And also the Talus." Carlos became more interested.
"I've heard about it before. The Prime Emissary says that it's not a reli-

gion, per se, but rather sort of a spiritual philosophy." He regarded the tent with curiosity. "I wonder how he could've . . . ?"

"From what I've heard, he claims to have been given some sort of holy book by one of the *hjadd*." A crooked smile appeared on Vogel's face. "Sounds far-fetched, but apparently he's managed to attract quite a following in Carlos's Pizza. And now he's getting people here to listen to . . ."

"What does he look like?" Carlos looked at him sharply. "A young man, in his twenties?"

"I . . . I don't know." Vogel was obviously taken aback by the urgency of Carlos's question. Lynn quietly moved closer to listen in. "I haven't seen him myself, but I was told that a proctor recognized him as someone who's apparently wanted by the law. In any case, a couple of officers came into the camp yesterday to take him away . . ."

"Where is he now?"

"The local jail, probably." Vogel peered at him. "Why are you so . . . ?"

"Take me to him. Now." Without another word, Carlos turned to march back the way they'd come, toward the sedan that had brought his group in from the field where their airship had landed. Vogel glanced at the other officials. Everyone else was just as surprised as he was; no one had a clue as to why the former president wanted to see this person. Vogel hesitated, then hurried to catch up with Carlos, leaving the rest of their party behind . . . save for Lynn, who fell in with them.

She had a feeling that the New Brighton story had just taken an interesting twist.

RELIGIOUS LEADER ARRESTED IN NEW BRIGHTON

The leader of an as-yet-unnamed religious group has been arrested in New Brighton on charges that he is a convicted felon who violated the terms of his parole.

Hawk Thompson, who calls himself the "chaaz'maha," was picked up by local authorities while distributing food to immigrants in the Albion refugee camp. Thompson, 26, was convicted nine years earlier (Earth-time) of the

second-degree murder of his father, Lars Thompson. He was released on probation after serving eight years of his sentence in a rehabilitation farm in New
Florida, and had been working as a customs inspector at the New Brighton
spaceport before he abruptly vanished, thereby violating the terms of his parole.

According to sources, Thompson recently returned to New Brighton from
the nearby colony of Carlos's Pizza, where he had assumed the name
"chaaz'maha" and presented himself to local residents as a spiritual teacher,
advocating a quasi-religious practice he calls "Sa'Tong." While in Carlos's
Pizza, Thompson organized a relief effort to transport and distribute surplus
food from the fishing village to the refugee camp. It was while doing so that he
was recognized by New Brighton proctors, who had been on the lookout for
Thompson ever since his disappearance.

Thompson is the son of Marie Thompson, the owner of the Thompson Wood
Company, one of Coyote's largest private companies. His uncle is Garth Thomp-
son, the president of the Coyote Federation, and he is also related to Carlos
Montero, a former president of the Federation who has recently been involved
in high-level negotiations with the provisional government of the Western
Hemisphere Union.

Carlos's Pizza residents who came to New Brighton to assist with the effort
were shocked when they learned of Thompson's true identity, which until then
was unknown to them. However, they expressed support for Thompson, whom
they continue to refer to as the "chaaz'maha."

"It doesn't matter who he was or what he did," says Bess Cole, a volunteer
who witnessed Thompson's arrest. "So far as we're concerned, that's something that happened a long time ago. He's a different person now, and he's
made a difference in our lives, too."

Cole said that her group is petitioning for Thompson's release from the New
Brighton jail, where he is currently being held. They are also organizing a
public rally to protest . . .

"I always knew I'd see you again," Joe Bairns said. "I just didn't
think it'd be this way."

The parole officer stood outside the jail cell, gazing at the *chaaz'maha*
through the bars. The *chaaz'maha* noted that Joe had aged a bit since the
last time they'd seen each other; his grey hair had become thinner, and

he appeared to have lost some weight. Yet there was nothing smug in his attitude, and when the *chaaz'maha* searched his old friend, he found only bitter disappointment,

"In jail, you mean?" The *chaaz'maha* sat cross-legged on the cell bunk, hands folded together in his lap. The proctors had taken away his robe and boots, leaving him with only the homespun tunic and trousers he wore underneath. "If you were expecting to see me again, where else would I be?"

"No. I mean . . ." Bairns gestured toward his forehead. "What the hell is that, anyway? And what have you done with your hair? If you thought doing that would've kept anyone from recognizing you . . ."

"Not at all." The *chaaz'maha* smiled. "In fact, I'm surprised it took so long. My people and I were in the camp two weeks before a proctor spotted me . . . and even then, he had to come by our tent twice before he was sure," He shook his head. "So, no, I wasn't trying to hide from anyone. As you said, this was inevitable."

"Hawk . . ."

"*Chaaz'maha*, please." He pointed to the tattoo on his brow. "That's what this means. It's the *hjadd* symbol for a teacher of *Sa'Tong*, which is what I've become. Hawk Thompson is no more or less who I am now than is the shadow on the wall behind me."

Resting a shoulder against the bars, Joe closed his eyes. "Oh, man . . . you've really lost it, haven't you?"

"Joe . . ." The *chaaz'maha* sighed. "Joe, I haven't lost anything. When you knew me . . . when you knew Hawk Thompson, that is . . . he had nothing left to lose. He . . ."

"Knock if off. We both know who you are."

"As you wish . . . I was simply putting in time, waiting until the day I died. That's how hopeless I'd become." He uncrossed his legs, stood up from the bunk. "Since I left this place, I've found something new. A purpose to life, a direction that gives meaning to my existence. I couldn't have done that here, which is why I had to go. I apologize for disappointing you, and for the worry that I've caused, but please believe me when I say that I'm much happier now."

"I bet you are. Once you've got your own cult . . ."

"*Sa'Tong* is not a cult. It's . . ."

"Look, I really don't care. All I know is that I trusted you . . . hell, I even kept you out of jail, when I could have easily put you away . . . and this is how you've repaid me. I . . ."

They were interrupted by the creak of a door opening at the end of the cell block. Hearing this, other prisoners began to yell for attention, demanding food, attorneys, or extra blankets, yet the person who'd come in ignored them as he walked down the row to where Joe was standing. And the moment he appeared, the *chaaz'maha* recognized him.

"Mr. Bairns?" David Laird was properly deferential to the parole officer. "There's someone here to see the prisoner." He paused, then added, "I think it's President Montero."

Joe's eyes widened, and he glanced at the *chaaz'maha*. "Were you expecting him?"

"Not at all," he replied, as calmly as before. "I'm just as surprised as you are. But, yes, I'd like to see my uncle, if that's all right with you."

Joe seemed to think it over. "I want to talk to him first," he said at last. "Have you eaten yet today? I don't want you to say that we've been starving you."

"I haven't, no. Otherwise, the proctors have been quite hospitable."

"Get him some lunch," Joe said to Laird, then he looked back at the *chaaz'maha* again. "I'll bring him in, but not until he and I have had some words." Then he walked away, leaving Laird behind.

Laird watched him go, but it wasn't until the door shut behind Joe that he spoke to the *chaaz'maha*. "Hello, there," he said, his voice low. "Remember me?"

"Of course. I assisted in your arrest last year." The *chaaz'maha* noticed the control bracelet on Laird's left wrist. "Appears that you've done well with yourself since then . . . or at least as well as you could, under the circumstances. I take it you're wearing an inhibitor patch as well."

Laird's face reddened, but he forced a smile that was meant to be good-natured. The *chaaz'maha* knew otherwise. "Yeah, well . . . got lucky, I guess. The maggies don't have much on me . . . just that weapons charge, plus attempted assault . . . and they were still trying to figure out how to get rid of me when the Union collapsed. I behaved myself while I was in here, so they decided to put me on probation." He lifted his wrist. "Joe made me a trustee. I work the day shift, delivering meals and whatnot. That's why I haven't seen you till now. You didn't get in until last night, I hear."

"That is true. Seems you neglected to include me when you brought breakfast."

"Did I now? How thoughtless." Laird's smile became a gloating smirk. "Kinda ironic, isn't it. You . . ."

"Put you in here, and now I'm the one occupying a cell." While Laird had been speaking, the *chaaz'maha* had searched him. "You're particularly relishing the fact that I'm in the very same cell you occupied for over three months." He shrugged. "It's actually not all that uncomfortable. I even believe I could get used to it."

Laird's expression changed to one of bafflement. "Someone must have told you . . ."

"They didn't. You're just transparent, that's all." The *chaaz'maha* sighed as he resumed his seat on the bunk. "You think of yourself as a criminal genius, David, but that term is oxymoronic. Criminals are people who are too stupid to get what they want in an honest manner, which is why they resort to illegal acts. Truth is, you're little more than a common thug . . . and not even a very threatening thug at that."

Laird didn't respond, but the *chaaz'maha* didn't need to search him again to know the hateful thoughts coursing through his mind. Indeed, he had to rub his fingers together to keep the ugliness at bay. Finally, Laird regained control over his emotions.

"Remember what I said to you at the spaceport?" he asked, stepping closer to the bars. "That you'd made an enemy of Living Earth?"

"I do . . . and I have to admit it, it frightened me at the time." The *chaaz'maha* lifted his feet from the floor to cross his legs together again. "I know better now. You're the only Living Earth member on Coyote. In fact, the only reason why you came here in the first place is because you were desperate to get away from Earth before the law caught up with you. Your role in the bombing of the New Guinea space elevator . . ."

Laird's mouth fell open. "How could you . . . ?"

"Just a hunch." He tried not to smile. "Actually, if there's any irony to be found, it's that, for someone allegedly opposed to space travel, you had no problem with it when you found yourself on the run. But then, that's the same reason why there's no organization here to support you. You're on your own."

Astonished that the *chaaz'maha* could possibly know such things, Laird stared at him. "Maybe . . . or maybe not," he muttered, pulling himself together again. "But as long as you're in here . . ."

"I'm at your mercy." The *chaaz'maha* resumed his lotus position, his hands lightly resting upon his knees. "Yes, I'm sure you can make my stay here uncomfortable. You can withhold meals, or spit in my food, or deny me water, or take away my bedsheets and make me sleep on a bare mattress. And I have no doubt that you could come up with even more imaginative harassments . . ."

"You bet I can."

"Perhaps . . . although I should warn you about that inhibitor patch. I wore one once myself, and its effects are rather unpleasant." The *chaaz'maha* shrugged. "But your inability to do violence against me isn't the only thing you've overlooked."

"And what's that?"

"For me, this cell is only a physical form of incarceration. Sooner or later, I'll leave this place. But you're still in your own private prison." He paused, then sadly shook his head. "And I'm afraid nothing I could say would ever change that."

Laird glared at him for another moment or two, until the *chaaz'maha* closed his eyes and concentrated upon the friction between his thumb and forefinger. After a while, Laird stormed away, his heavy footsteps echoing off the concrete floor until they ended in the slamming of the cell-block door.

The *chaaz'maha* let out his breath as he sought to calm himself. The encounter with David Laird had been as unpleasant as it had been unexpected; even the few seconds he'd spent in the other man's mind had been enough to disturb his inner peace. He was about to recite the Poem of Acceptance to himself when a new sound reached his ears.

It came through the narrow window above his bunk, from some distant source beyond the jailhouse walls. Curious, the *chaaz'maha* listened more closely, and after a moment a smile crept across his face.

He'd heard his name, being chanted over and over again.

DOMINIONIST CLERGYMAN DENOUNCES
RELIGIOUS LEADER

The senior minister of the Church of the Holy Dominion mission on Coyote has publicly attacked the leader of the Sa'Tong spiritual group, stating that he represents an alien religion that is "godless, blasphemous, and dangerous."

The Reverend Alberto Cosenza, a Dominionist deacon who has been serving as acting pastor of the Church's mission in Liberty, New Florida, spoke out against Hawk Thompson, who calls himself the "chaaz'maha" and claims to be a teacher of a philosophy known as Sa'Tong, which he alleges to be the principal spiritual belief of most extraterrestrial races of the galaxy. Thompson, 26, was arrested in New Brighton, Albion, on charges of jumping parole in connection with the second-degree murder of his father, Lars Thompson, several years earlier.

"Thompson is a criminal and a charlatan," Rev. Cosenza says, speaking in New Brighton, where he traveled after learning of Thompson's arrest. "Anything he says is tainted by both past and present sins."

Rev. Cosenza said that he first learned of Sa'Tong from the mission's former pastor, Rev. Grey Rice, who resigned from the ministry shortly after Rev. Cosenza arrived on Coyote. The deacon admitted that he hasn't personally delved into the philosophy's teachings, but said that its central beliefs are contrary to what is taught by all human religions.

"Sa'Tong is nothing less than an assault on God," he says. "Regardless of its claim to be a philosophy, the fact remains that it is a religion that doesn't hold the existence of the Almighty at its core. That alone makes it a clear and present danger to the human race."

Rev. Cosenza refused to call Thompson by his chosen name, saying that "chaaz'maha" is only "a fictitious title." He expressed hope that the New Brighton authorities would hold Thompson indefinitely, and that he would face reincarceration for the slaying of his father . . .

The jail was located on the edge of New Brighton, close to the *torii* that marked the city limits. The bamboo fence separating the town from the nearby refugee camp had been erected at both ends of the Japanese gate, with a removable barrier blocking the gate itself. It was there, within sight of the jail, that the demonstrators held their rally. They were prevented by local proctors from coming any closer, but they could be clearly seen and heard for many blocks away.

Nonetheless, Grey Rice had managed to slip through the cordon. Upon his arrival two weeks earlier, the proctors had issued name badges to the group from Carlos's Pizza, identifying them as relief workers and thus allowing them to enter New Brighton for the purpose of bringing in supplies from the harbor. After the *chaaz'maha* was arrested, Grey volunteered to follow him into town and take up a post near the jail in order to keep an eye on him; the rest of the relief workers would stay behind, continuing to feed refugees while organizing a protest march in support of their leader. Although the others had been shaken by the news that the *chaaz'maha* had a dark past, it was a sign of their faith in their teacher that they remained loyal to him.

Grey had found a cheap room in a hostel a couple of blocks from the jail, but he'd only used the place to sleep and change clothes. He'd spent the previous evening, and the morning that followed, sitting on the low stone fence that surrounded the jail, the closest the proctors would allow him to come. They had already denied him permission to visit the *chaaz'maha*, stating that, for security reasons, none of his students would be allowed to see him. And although the *chaaz'maha* hadn't yet been arraigned, the Chief Magistrate had already sent word that he would be denied bail until further notice.

So Grey had spent long hours at the jail, waiting to see what would happen next. He'd used a satphone to keep in touch with the camp and learned that Bess had managed to enlist several hundred people to join the protest. That wasn't surprising; in the two weeks that the *chaaz'maha* and his people had been living and working among the refugees, they'd earned their respect and trust; many of them had accepted downloads of the *Sa'Tong-Tas* along with the hot meals served in their tent. When the *chaaz'maha* was taken away, it had been in full view of dozens who'd been waiting in line for dinner; word of the arrest had spread quickly, and by morning most of the camp knew that the soft-spoken young man who had come to take care of them had been dragged away by the authorities.

Bess had told Grey that the protesters were scheduled to meet shortly before noon, after which they would march to the *torii*, where they would stage a demonstration. No attempt would be made to pass through the gate; it was clear that the proctors didn't want any refugees to enter the city, and the last thing anyone wanted to do was take any actions that might compromise the *chaaz'maha's* chances of being released. So nonviolent civil disobedience was to be their way of expressing their outrage. And in the meantime, Grey was to remain where he was, watching the jail to see how the proctors would react to the protest.

Grey hadn't had anything to eat. He'd left the hostel almost as soon as the sun had come up, and by late morning his stomach was growling. The demonstration wasn't to begin for another hour, though, so he'd decided to take care of his hunger. He'd spotted a small cafe down the street from the jail, and it was there that he went to grab a quick breakfast. Two scrambled eggs and a cup of coffee later, he returned to his post, and it was then and there that he saw someone he'd thought—and hoped—he'd never see again.

The Reverend Alberto Cosenza stood outside the jail, his black suit lending him the appearance of a raven. Speaking to a young woman holding a pad, his back was half-turned toward the street. Cosenza glanced over his shoulder at Rice as he approached; apparently dismissing him as a passerby, he turned back to the woman . . . then he did a double take, his eyes widening in recognition.

"Reverend Rice?" he asked. "Is that you?"

"Yes, it is . . . although the title no longer applies." Grey tried to smile, but found that he couldn't. "Good to see you again," he added, as cordially as possible.

Curious, the woman moved a little closer, yet Cosenza didn't appear as if he wanted to share this exchange with her. "I think that'll be all," he said. "Is there's anything further you'd like to ask?"

"No . . . no, that's enough for now." She switched off her pad, put it back in her pocket. "Thank you for your time, Reverend." He nodded, and she walked away; Grey noticed that the proctor standing nearby allowed her to pass through the fence gate.

"Press," Cosenza murmured, watching her go. "Reporter for a news service back on Earth. She showed up the same time I did, with President Montero."

"Carlos Montero is here?" Now it was Grey's turn to be surprised. He glanced at the front door of the jail. "I didn't see him when I was here just a little . . ."

He stopped himself, but that was enough to raise Cosenza's attention. "You've been here already?" he asked, and Grey reluctantly nodded. "Why?"

No point in lying. "I'm with the relief effort from Carlos's Pizza. When the *chaaz'maha* was arrested, I came over to . . ."

"Oh, dear God." Horrified, Cosenza stared at the former minister. "Grey, you don't mean to tell me you're . . . that you're following this false prophet, do you?"

Grey felt his face grow warm, yet he refused to look away. "He's not a prophet, Rever . . . Alberto." Cosenza's eyes narrowed at the sound of his first name; he was not accustomed to junior clergymen addressing him with such familiarity, even those who'd left the Church. "I don't think he even considers himself to be particularly holy. He's a spiritual teacher, that's all."

"Do you know what you're saying?" A vein throbbed at Cosenza's temple; the older man was struggling to keep his temper in check. "Grey, you know even more about this than I do. You've met those damned aliens. You've heard their godless immorality . . ."

"Godless, yes . . . or at least the way you define God." Grey shook his head. "Immoral, no. But you're right about one thing . . . I do know more about *Sa'Tong* than you do. I've listened to the *chaaz'maha*, I've studied the *Sa'Tong-tas*, and I've come to the conclusion that theirs is a better . . ."

"Hush!" Cosenza angrily held up a hand. "Be quiet!" He let out his breath as a frustrated sigh. "Grey, I . . . I can't tell you how much I'm disappointed in you. I know you've suffered a crisis of faith, but I would've never thought . . . never even dreamed . . . that you'd fallen so far."

Despite himself, Grey found a certain satisfaction in being able to irritate Cosenza so easily. "I'd already fallen, Alberto. After I left the pulpit, I was a lost man. But the *chaaz'maha* helped me find myself again . . . not through piety, but by teaching me that the way we worship others, and not some invisible entity, is more important than all the empty words and rituals . . ."

Cosenza's hand darted forward, an attempt to slap Rice across the face. Rice saw it coming; he didn't quite know how, except perhaps the time he'd spent with the *chaaz'maha* had taught him something about anticipating the actions of others. He stepped back before the deacon's palm could connect with his cheek, causing Cosenza to lose his balance and fall forward. As Rice caught him in his arms, the nearby proctor hurried forward.

"Reverend," he said, laying a hand on Cosenza's shoulder, "I'm sorry, but you're under . . ."

"Please, no, don't do that." Still holding Cosenza, Rice helped the older man steady himself. "Just a minor misunderstanding, that's all. He didn't mean any . . ."

"Get away from me!" Cosenza's voice was a harsh croak as he yanked himself away from Rice. "I'll have nothing more to do with you! And once I return to Earth, I'll see to it that you're excommunicated!"

At one time, Rice would have been reduced to begging forgiveness. And even now, if only for a moment, he felt a cold hand grip the pit of his stomach. But the sensation quickly passed, to be replaced by something else: the peace of mind that comes with learning to live without fear, along with pity for the angry old man who glowered at him.

"If you must," he said. "It doesn't matter to me."

Cosenza's mouth fell open. For a second, it seemed as if he was having trouble breathing. "You'll go to Hell for . . ."

"Hardly the act of a loving and merciful God, is it?" Amused, Rice gently smiled. "In fact, I have to say, any religion that keeps its supplicants in line with threats of banishment to a nonexistent place is not one to which I'd choose to belong."

But Cosenza was no longer listening. Turning his back on Rice, he stalked away from the jail. Rice watched him go and shook his head. How odd that he'd once been intimidated by the poor gent. If only . . .

From behind him, he suddenly heard something new: a chorus of voices, chanting the *chaaz'maha's* name. Looking around, he saw that, unnoticed until that moment, a large crowd was gathered on the other side of the *torii*. Several hundred refugees, led by his fellow relief workers, had arrived to begin their rally.

Rice grinned, raised his hand to wave to them. If there was, indeed, such a thing as Hell, then the Reverend Alberto Cosenza was hearing the tolling of its bells.

FORMER COYOTE PRESIDENT MEETS
WITH SPIRITUAL LEADER

Carlos Montero, the former president of the Coyote Federation, met today with Hawk Thompson, the spiritual leader of a group that has embraced the alien philosophy of Sa'Tong, at the jail in New Brighton where Thompson is being held.

Authorities said that the meeting was private and was arranged at President Montero's request. Thompson, who calls himself the "chaaz'maha," is the former president's nephew, which proctors say is the principal reason President Montero asked to see him. Only Thompson's parole officer was present during the meeting.

While the meeting was taking place, an estimated crowd of four hundred held a protest rally near the jail. The demonstration was organized by relief workers from the nearby refugee camp and was comprised of newly arrived immigrants from Earth. The protest was nonviolent, and authorities say that no arrests were made . . .

The jail had a small interrogation room, with a door that locked from the outside and a reflective one-way window in one of its cinderblock walls. It wasn't the most comfortable place for Carlos to visit his nephew, but it was the best compromise he had been able to work out with the chief proctor. Although Hawk's parole officer was the only other person in the room, Carlos was all too aware that the chief was probably watching them from the other side of the window.

Joe Bairns had warned Carlos that Hawk had changed since the last time he'd seen him. Nonetheless, he was stunned when his nephew was led into the room. It wasn't just the shaved head or the odd tattoo on his brow, though, but also the look in his eyes. Where there had once been a detached and emotionally repressed void was now utter serenity, an implacable calm that was almost eerie. Despite the fact that his wrists were held together by magnetic cuffs, Hawk was at ease with himself and everyone around him; when he saw Carlos sitting at the table, his face broke into a welcoming smile.

"Uncle Carlos . . . what a pleasant surprise!" He radiated warmth as he ambled toward the empty chair on the other side of the table. "Good to see you again. I hope you had a good trip."

"Uhh . . . yes, I did, thank you." Carlos glanced at Bairns, who stood against a wall near the table. Although his arms were folded together against his chest, the parole officer's right hand wasn't far from the holstered stun gun on his belt. Bairns said nothing, and his expression remained neutral. "Joe, I don't think he's going to need . . ."

"Sorry, Mr. President." Bairns shook his head. "Rules say that all prisoners must be secured when they're outside their cells. No exceptions."

"Don't worry about it." Hawk sat down. "They're not uncomfortable . . . at least, not very . . . and if my wearing them makes everyone feel safer . . ."

He shrugged, then leaned back in his chair, patiently waiting for his uncle to go on. Never once did his steady gaze depart from Carlos's face. "Yes, well . . ." Carlos tried to find the right thing to say. "Are you . . . ?"

"Being treated well? Yes, or at least as much as circumstances will allow. One of the trustees is an old acquaintance. He just brought me lunch, so I've had something to eat." Hawk glanced at Bairns. "Thank David for me, will you? And tell him that I enjoyed our chat, and hope to talk with him again soon."

Bairns's lips pursed together, and even Carlos was taken aback. He'd learned that one of the trustees was the same individual whom Hawk had helped apprehend last year. The proctors had apparently forgotten that fact until after Laird entered the cell block, but by then it was too late to keep him away from Hawk. Yet his nephew didn't seem to mind, and Laird himself had stormed out a few minutes later, visibly upset by something that had been said between them.

"We'll . . . be sure to do that." Carlos hesitated, then went on. "Hawk . . ."

"*Chaaz'maha*, please." His nephew shook his head. "As Joe has doubtless told you already, I no longer go by my old name."

"Yes, he has . . . but it's not the *chaaz'maha* who jumped parole, but Hawk Thompson. That's the person who's been arrested."

"I understand that . . . or at least I acknowledge it. But what you must understand as well is that I'm no longer the man I used to be." As before, the *chaaz'maha's* voice remained calm, his gaze unwavering. "If the purpose of my parole was for me to atone for the things I did when I was younger, don't you think I've done that already?"

"Your parole was . . ." Bairns began.

"Years away from being served out, yes. But, Joe . . . do you really think I was doing society much good by working as a customs inspector? Do you honestly believe that wearing a patch and a bracelet was making me a better person?" He shook his head. "In the short time that I've been the *chaaz'maha*, I've accomplished more than in all the months I spent behind a desk. Perhaps it's a rather unconventional means of making amends, but it's in keeping with the Fifth Codicil of *Sa'Tong*."

"Is that why you came back?" Carlos asked, and the *chaaz'maha* nodded. "You knew you were wanted by the law. To tell the truth, we had no idea where you were. You could have stayed away, but instead . . ."

"I chose to return because this is where I'm needed. Caring for others is far more important than my personal freedom." Again, a dismissive shrug. "The *Sa'Tong-tas* teaches us that all risk is acceptable . . . even necessary . . . when the cause is worthy enough."

"The *Sa'Tong-tas* . . . that was the object Taf gave you when we met him at the spaceport, wasn't it?" The *chaaz'maha* nodded again, and Carlos searched his memory. "He called it a book. 'Speak to it, and it will speak to you' . . ."

"That is what I did." An ironic smile. "I know now that it was only fortuitous that I happened to be the one who received it. Taf could have just as easily given it to you, or a blueshirt, or a gyro pilot, or anyone else he happened to encounter that day. But another person might not have known what to do with it, or only treated it as a trinket . . . no offense intended."

"None taken. Go on . . . You took it home, and you . . ."

"I spoke to it, and it spoke to me." The *chaaz'maha* sighed as he folded his manacled hands together in his lap. "It's hard to describe what happened that night. The *Sa'Tong-tas* told me things that were so obvious but hadn't occurred to me before. Not only did I learn who I was, but also who I *could* be . . . but even then, I didn't have all the answers, and

I knew I couldn't get them if I stayed here." He looked at Bairns. "As I said, that was why I had to leave. I acknowledge that what I did was against the law . . . but it wasn't wrong."

Bairns didn't respond except to shake his head ever so slightly. "The *Sa'Tong-tas*," Carlos continued. "Where is it now? Do you have it?"

The *chaaz'maha* shook his head. "No. I decided that it was too valuable to carry around with me, so I left it in a place where I know it'll be safe. But before I did, a friend of mine and I transcribed its teachings and loaded them into my pad. Since then, I've copied it into other pads whenever possible, and encouraged those who've received it to do the same. I estimate I've done this"—he thought for a moment—"at least a hundred times now, and I can only imagine how many more times it's been copied since then."

Bairns shut his eyes. "Oh, my god . . ."

"Yes, exactly . . . although perhaps not the way you mean." A quiet laugh, then he became serious again. "You must believe me when I say that there's nothing to be afraid of, or that I wouldn't have done this if I even suspected that it might be harmful. *Sa'Tong* isn't a religion . . . I can't repeat that often enough . . . but instead a way of looking at ourselves and our relationship with the universe. One of my students tells me that it's actually a rather old way . . . just one that has been neglected for so long that it's been almost forgotten."

Carlos nodded. "So you're not trying to be a prophet or a messiah . . ."

"No." His nephew shook his head. "Merely a teacher, that's all. Even the role of being a leader is uncomfortable, although I've found it necessary to take it up."

"I've seen the work you've done in the refugee camp. I have to admit, it's impressive." The *chaaz'maha* accepted the compliment with a faint smile, and Carlos let out his breath. "You know, of course, that your arrest has upset quite a few of your followers . . ."

"I prefer to think of them as my students . . . but yes, I heard the demonstration from my cell. You needn't worry about them. If they abide by the *Sa'Tong* . . . and I have little doubt that they will . . . then their protest will be nonviolent." He paused. "But I wouldn't ignore them if I were you. There are ways of fighting injustice that are far more effective than throwing a fist or a stone."

"He's right," Bairns said quietly. "I hate to admit it, but there are al-most as many people in the camp as there are here in town . . . many more than the proctors and militia can control. Even if they do nothing more than refuse to cooperate . . ."

"Exactly." The *chaaz'maha* smiled. "Protest is only the first step. Civil disobedience is the next. And if the authorities were to use aggressive measures . . ."

"No." Carlos sighed, shook his head. "I don't want to see it come to that either." He looked at Bairns, and the parole officer nodded in agree-ment. Carlos glanced at the one-way glass, hoping that the chief proctor was listening and had comprehended the situation as well. "Well . . . that brings us back to you, doesn't it? Keeping you here just invites trouble . . . but the fact remains that you broke the law, even if it was for what you consider to be good reasons."

" 'There is a difference between law and justice. They are not always the same thing.' " The *chaaz'maha* grinned. "That's from the *Sa'Tong-tas.*"

"Yes, well . . . the magistrates might not see things the same way you do." Carlos frowned as a new thought occurred to him. "Of course, I could put in a good word for you, if I was sure that you mean no harm. The fact that you've organized a relief effort will probably go a long way. But even if I was able to have you released, I doubt they'll simply let you go back to what you were doing. They'd want some assurance that you'd be under control, or at least some form of supervision . . ."

"If you mean returning to the conditions of my parole"—the *chaaz'maha* frowned—"no. I'm sorry, but I must refuse. I will not wear a patch or a bracelet again. That would only mean that I'd become Hawk Thompson once more. And as I said, that person is no longer who I am."

"Was it really so bad?" Bairns asked.

The *chaaz'maha* said nothing, but only regarded him with sadness until Bairns looked away. "I understand," Carlos said. "And I suppose I agree. But there must be some way we can . . ."

"You know how." The *chaaz'maha* gazed deep into his eyes. " 'The so-lution to one problem can often be the solution to another.' Something else *Sa'Tong* teaches us . . . do you know what I mean?"

Carlos understood . . . and suddenly, a new thought occurred to him, one that seemed so far-fetched as to seem implausible, but nonetheless had a strange logic of its own.

"Yes . . . yes, I think I do." He hesitated. "Would you be willing to take another trip? A rather long one, I'm afraid, but . . . we may both find it useful."

Bairns stared at him. "Where? New Florida?"

"No." Carlos found himself smiling. "Much farther than that, I think."

SPIRITUAL LEADER RELEASED

Hawk Thompson, the leader of a spiritual group devoted to an extraterrestrial philosophy, was released from jail in New Brighton following a private meeting with his uncle, former Coyote Federation president Carlos Montero.

Thompson, who calls himself the "chaaz'maha," was escorted from jail by President Montero. Thompson didn't speak to anyone. Instead, he accompanied the president to the city gate, where a large crowd of supporters had gathered to protest Thompson's arrest and incarceration.

Authorities would not comment on the terms of Thompson's release, other than to say that President Montero had intervened on his nephew's behalf after discussing the matter with local magistrates . . .

David Laird watched as Thompson walked down the front steps of the jail, his uncle at his side. Although the protesters from the refugee camp hadn't been permitted to come any closer than the *torii*, a large number of townspeople had gathered on the street in front of the jail, drawn there by word of mouth and curiosity. Joe Bairns and the chief proctor went with the *chaaz'maha* and the former president as far as the sidewalk, where a couple of sawhorses had been put up to keep the crowd at bay.

Laird was standing just outside the front door, so he'd been only a few feet away from the *chaaz'maha* as he strode past him. He'd tried to make eye contact with Thompson, intending to give him a parting word or two, yet the *chaaz'maha* was wearing his robe again, its hood raised to hide his face, and there were too many people around for Laird to say anything that wouldn't have been overheard. So Laird could do little more than glare at him, but the *chaaz'maha* apparently didn't notice the scowling figure who, for a brief instant, had been within arm's reach.

Laird took a deep breath, forcing himself to remain calm. He'd already learned that anger could trigger the inhibitor patch beneath his left armpit. But if he'd only had a gun, or a knife . . .

The moment Thompson left the building, a cry rose from the nearby demonstrators. For hours, they'd been chanting his name over and over again—*chaaz'maha! chaaz'maha! chaaz'maha!*—and now that it was clear that he was being released, they began to shout even louder, their voices mixed with applause and whistles. Their joy was infectious; it quickly spread to the townspeople standing outside the jail, and even if they didn't know exactly who this person was, they picked up the chant as well. The *chaaz'maha* responded by briefly raising a hand, a gesture of both acknowledgment and benediction, and the tumult grew even louder.

Laird gnawed at his lower lip. Whoever Thompson was now, whatever he'd become, it was obvious that he was more popular than ever before. Laird didn't believe for an instant that he was a spiritual leader; for him, Thompson was little more than someone lucky enough to have a powerful relative who was able to talk his nephew out of a jail cell. Rumor had it that President Montero had reached some sort of agreement with the maggies that would allow the *chaaz'maha* to be placed in his custody pending further review of his case.

Whatever the reason, it meant that Thompson was beyond Laird's reach. Nonetheless, he still wanted revenge, however futile that desire might be. If it hadn't been for some goddamn government stooge, no one on Coyote would have ever learned that Peter Desilitz had once been another person. No patch, no bracelet. A free man, able to do whatever he pleased. And now . . .

A sedan was parked just outside the jail fence, a couple of proctors waiting to escort President Montero and the *chaaz'maha* through the crowd. The *chaaz'maha* didn't go straight to the vehicle, though, but paused for a moment to speak to his uncle. President Montero hesitated, then reluctantly nodded; he turned to say something to Bairns, who gave a helpless shrug but nodded as well. Then the three of them, with the proctors on either side, walked past the sawhorses and began to move through the crowd, heading toward the *torii*.

Apparently Thompson wished to address his supporters. No one was paying attention to Laird, so he fell in behind them, carefully maintaining his distance while keeping the *chaaz'maha's* hooded head within sight. It was hard to do, for as soon as the *chaaz'maha* and President Montero entered the street, townspeople formed a solid knot around them, walking with them as they approached the *torii*. Beyond the ornamental gate, the noise of the demonstration rose to a fever pitch, as . . .

"Blasphemy!"

From the edge of the crowd, a harsh voice rang out. Several people turned to look, trying to see to whom it belonged.

"He is a false prophet!" A black-suited man, wearing the crucifix of a Dominionist minister, raised his hands above his head, a Bible clutched in one of them. "Remember the words of the Lord! Exodus 34:14 . . . 'Do not worship any other god, for the Lord, whose name is Jealous, is an angry . . . !' "

Whatever else he was about to say, it was lost beneath a groundswell of laughter. Ridicule rose around the elderly minister as those around him pushed him aside. He fell back; nonetheless, he refused to relent. " 'Break down their altars!' " he shouted, still quoting Biblical verse. " 'Smash their sacred stones, and cut down their . . . !' "

Then he was left behind, ignored by those who'd chosen instead to follow the *chaaz'maha* toward the *torii*. Thompson himself didn't even seem to notice the interruption; he didn't look back, or even pause for a second. Yet if he had, he might have seen that Laird had broken away from the others, heading instead for the angry clergyman, who stood alone in the street, stubbornly denouncing the false prophet who walked among the good people of New Brighton.

David Laird tried not to smile as he approached the Dominionist minister. The *chaaz'maha* appeared to have only two enemies, but perhaps two would be enough.

Part 8

APOTHEOSIS

The *chaaz'maha* arrived at the spaceport, the first step of his journey to Earth.

As he climbed out of the sedan that had carried him and his uncle from the Federation consulate in New Brighton, he reflected that, although the terminal hadn't changed since he'd worked there, it seemed smaller. Once it had occupied the center of his world, but now it was what it always had been: just another building, neither more nor less remarkable than any other. Another indication of how much he'd changed in the last year and a quarter.

"Bet you didn't think you'd ever see this place again." Uncle Carlos watched as the proctor who'd driven them to the spaceport removed their bags from the trunk.

"Not like this, no." The *chaaz'maha* gazed at immigrants lined up outside the main entrance. Too many to fit inside the terminal, they shuffled toward the inspection tables where overworked customs inspectors would open the suitcases, knapsacks, and bags they carried with them. "That's what I used to do," he murmured. "Almost makes me want to give them a hand."

"Does it really?" Carlos peered at him, then slowly nodded. "Yes, I think you really would." Turning to the driver, he gestured toward a roped-off side door where another proctor was waiting for them. "But that's not your job anymore. You've got a more important one now."

The *chaaz'maha* gave a him sidelong look. " 'No task is menial so long as it helps another.' Something else the *Sa'Tong* teaches us."

"Yes, well . . . right now, our task is to get aboard the skiff before the pilot decides to leave without us." But the *chaaz'maha* was no longer listening. The driver was already heading for the private entrance; the *chaaz'maha* hastened to relieve the overburdened officer of his duffel bag. "You don't have to . . ." Carlos started to add, then shrugged. "Oh, never mind."

The terminal was just as crowded inside as it was outside; indeed, the *chaaz'maha* had never seen it quite so packed. Then again, never before had so many people come to Coyote all at once. Through its high windows, he could see shuttles parked alongside each other on the reinforced concrete; he'd become accustomed to hearing the constant roar of their liftoffs and landings, but it wasn't until then that he realized how much traffic had increased. It was as if floodgates had opened, permitting a river of men, women, and children to inundate the new world.

He didn't get a chance to contemplate this, though, before his uncle led him to a kiosk cordoned off from the others. On the other side of the window, a passport control officer regarded them with an all-too-familiar expression of boredom. The *chaaz'maha* recognized him immediately as a former coworker, one who'd been fond of whispering behind his back whenever he entered the room. The *chaaz'maha* remained stoical as he waited to take his turn; after Carlos went through, the official impatiently gestured for him to come forward.

"Name?"

"I am the *chaaz'maha*."

The official's eyes widened with sudden recognition. "Hawk Thompson . . . it really *is* you, isn't it?"

"Hello, Bill." The *chaaz'maha* searched the other man's mind while giving the pretense that he remembered his name. "Good to see you again."

"I . . . ah . . . yeah, same here." Bill's face went red; he, too, remembered all the casual insults. "I'd heard that you . . . um . . ."

"Found a new line of work." The *chaaz'maha* smiled, trying to ease the other man's discomfiture. "Sorry to leave you guys shorthanded, but . . . well, something came up."

The passport control officer didn't seem to know what to say. It was obvious that he knew all about the *chaaz'maha*, including the fact that he was someone with whom he'd once worked. In the weeks since his release from jail, his reputation had only increased, even though he'd seldom been seen in public. Carlos had insisted upon that; as much as the *chaaz'maha* wanted to return to the refugee camp, the magistrates had stipulated that he remain in custody until it was time for them to depart for Earth. Although he'd been sequestered at the consulate, he was permitted to have visitors, and they'd told him that his stature had reached heroic proportions. So of course Bill would've heard all about that, even if he hadn't recognized Hawk on sight.

"Yeah, sure . . . no problem. We just hired another . . ." Apparently remembering his duties, the official stopped himself. "Destination?" he asked, becoming formal again.

"Earth."

Watching the interchange, Carlos restrained a smile. An obvious question, with an equally obvious answer. The *Liberty Post* had long since reported that the *chaaz'maha* would be accompanying President Montero to Earth, where they would meet with representatives from both the European Alliance and the provisional government of the Western Hemisphere Union. Having observed his nephew's considerable powers of persuasion, Carlos hoped that, as someone with firsthand knowledge of Coyote's refugee crisis, the *chaaz'maha* might be able to convince Earth's major superpowers that they needed to assist in the relief effort, or at least stop sending Coyote every warm body they could pack aboard their spacecraft.

Taking his nephew to Earth was a long shot, but Carlos knew that he'd need all the help he could get. At least for time being, the only aid Coyote could hope to get would have to be from Earth. Morgan Goldstein had recently returned from Rho Coronae Borealis with news that, although the *hjadd* were sympathetic to their problems, there was little that the aliens were willing to do for them. And although the Talus had accepted humankind, at least on a provisional basis, Jasahajahd Taf Sa-Fhadda had reminded both Morgan and Carlos himself that the interstellar community customarily distanced itself from the internal affairs of its member races.

Ultimately, the solution to Coyote's immigration crisis would have to come from the very source of the problem itself. As he watched his nephew give his travel documents to the flustered customs official, though, Carlos reflected that he could do worse than to have a spiritual leader at his side. Indeed, once the passport officer scanned the *chaaz'maha's* passport and handed it back to him, he surprised Carlos by bowing.

"*Sa'Tong qo, chaaz'maha.*" His tone was respectful, without a trace of irony.

"*Sa'Tong qo,* Bill." The *chaaz'maha* reciprocated with a bow of his own. "Thank you. I hope to see you again soon." Then he walked over to where his uncle was waiting for him

"What does that mean?" Carlos asked as they walked out of the terminal. "*Sa'Tong qo,* that is."

"It's difficult to translate," the *chaaz'maha* replied. "Literally speaking, it means 'Follow the wisdom of *Sa'Tong*' . . . but it could also mean 'good-bye,' 'good luck,' 'safe journey,' or whatever else the occasion demands."

Outside the building, they surrendered their bags to a cargo handler, who loaded them onto a cart to be taken directly to their waiting craft. For outbound flights, there was no customs inspection; their luggage wouldn't be opened again until they reached Highgate, in Lagrangian orbit between Earth and the Moon. "So it's an all-purpose phrase," Carlos murmured as they watched the cart pull away. "I'm surprised your friend back there knows it."

The *chaaz'maha* shrugged. "The *Sa'Tong-tas* has found its way into quite a few hands lately." Then he smiled. "Bill may not know exactly what the expression means, but I'm sure he'll learn soon enough."

Again, Carlos was impressed by his nephew's self-confidence. How different he'd become in such a short time; where once there had been a troubled, insecure boy, now there was a young man at peace with himself and the world. Yet Carlos still couldn't help but wonder if the *chaaz'maha* was, in fact, who he claimed to be, a teacher dedicated to bringing a new form of spiritual enlightenment to humankind.

A tram arrived to carry them across the field. As it rolled across the tarmac, Carlos spotted the shuttle that would ferry the *Robert E. Lee's* remaining passengers to orbit. It wasn't scheduled to depart for another couple of hours, though, and in the meantime, Commodore Tereshkova had dispatched her personal skiff to pick up the VIPs. It was a gesture Carlos appreciated, even if he considered it unnecessary. However, the

Commodore had insisted that, for the sake of privacy, the president and the *chaaz'maha* should arrive earlier, in order for them to settle into their private cabin before anyone else boarded the starship.

Standing beside the skiff, familiar faces waited for them. Wendy had flown in from Liberty earlier that morning; it had been nearly three weeks since Carlos had last seen his wife; although it was not the first time they'd been apart from one another, it seemed as if it had been only yesterday that he'd returned from the Exploratory Expedition. He hated to have to leave her again, but it couldn't be helped. Unfortunately, Susan, Jon, and Jorge were still aboard the *LeMare*; according to the most recent report from the ExEx, the ship was off the coast of Navajo, nearly three-quarters of the way around the world. Although the *LeMare* was just close enough for the Colonial Militia to send out a gyro, everyone agreed that it was probably best that Susan and her family stay where they were.

Wendy wasn't alone. With her was the woman whom Carlos had met only the night before: Melissa Sanchez, the young lady whom the *chaaz'maha* had taken as his partner. And cradled in her arms, wrapped in a soft cotton blanket with her head carefully shaded against the morning sun, was Inez—their infant daughter, born only a few days ago in Carlos's Pizza.

Until after he was released from jail, the *chaaz'maha* had kept secret the fact that he had a companion—he refused to call Melissa his wife, even though it was obvious that she filled that role—or that she was pregnant. He'd told Carlos that he wanted to be certain that he wouldn't be prosecuted before he let anyone know that he had a family; no sense in potentially putting them in harm's way as well. Carlos was surprised to learn about Melissa and Inez, but not displeased; he was glad that his nephew had found someone. Nonetheless, he hadn't been able to get permission from the Chief Magistrate to let the *chaaz'maha* return to Midland in time to see his baby come into the world. But as soon as Melissa's doctor pronounced both mother and child fit to travel, a boat was sent across the Great Equatorial Channel to pick them up.

"Off again, I see." Wendy feigned a scowl even as she extended her hands to her husband. "A fine excuse for not mucking out the barn . . ."

"Nag, nag, nag." It was an old joke between them; Carlos's least favorite household chore was shoveling horse manure. "I'll get to it when I come home."

"You'd better." She couldn't keep up the pretense any longer. Taking his hands in her own, Wendy drew him closer. "Damn it," she whispered, "why does it always have to be you?"

"Because . . ." Not having an easy answer to that, he wrapped his arms around her. "This is the last time. I promise. After this, someone else gets to do all the hard work. I'm retiring."

"You should've retired already." Wendy laid her head against his chest; she was fighting back tears, and suddenly he felt ashamed of himself. She'd cried, too, when he'd told her that he was leading the ExEx. "You just won't stop, will you? Just the other day, there was a message from someone named"—a pause as she searched her memory—"Lee, Sawyer Lee. Something about a Corps of Exploration. What's this all . . . ?"

"Nothing." Carlos let out his breath; he'd all but forgotten the discussion he'd had with Sawyer Lee about forming a dedicated exploration team. One more thing that threatened to keep him apart from his wife when they should be spending their days together at Traveler's Rest. "A fellow I met on the ExEx. Wilderness guide, I'll talk to him when I get back, but . . . well, I think it's something he can handle by himself."

"I'm going to take that as a promise." Wendy looked him straight in the eye. "I mean it. The next time you come home . . ."

"I'm here to stay. That's a promise."

Wendy smiled, then gently pulled his face toward hers to give him a kiss. Then and there, Carlos resolved to himself to keep his word. She was right; the time had come for him to settle down. One last diplomatic mission to Earth, then he'd return to Coyote for good. He'd ride their horse, and learn how to garden, and sit out on the deck and watch his wife paint. Let younger men like Sawyer have all the adventures; his day was done.

Off to the side, the *chaaz'maha* was saying farewell to his own family. Again, Carlos noticed that few words were exchanged between him and Melissa. He'd observed the same thing the night before, the first time he'd met her at the consulate. Seeing that, a chill went down his back. He'd heard about the Order of the Eye; rumor had it they'd apparently

learned how to read minds. He didn't know if the stories were true, unlikely as they seemed, yet his nephew had been with them in Medsylvania for over a year. Had he become a telepath during that time? The
chaaz'maha wasn't saying, yet it was always possible . . .

"Pardon me, folks." From the top of the ladder, the skiff's pilot called
down to them. "Sorry to have to rush you, but I'm afraid we're on a
schedule here. If you'll please . . ."

"Certainly. By all means." Carlos turned toward Wendy again. "See
you in a couple of weeks," he said quietly. "Then I'll sleep with you for a
month."

"Better bring home some oysters, if you plan to do that." A sly wink,
then she became serious again. "Love you."

"Love you, too." A final embrace, a last kiss, and he let her go. The
chaaz'maha did the same for Melissa; he gently stroked the fine hair on
Inez's tiny head, then he turned to follow his uncle up the ladder.

A few minutes later, the skiff was airborne. With the pilot and copilot
at the controls, it slowly rose upon its vertical thrusters until it cleared
the field. Then its prow tilted upward, its main engines fired, and Carlos
felt himself pushed back into his seat.

They were on their way to Earth.

David Laird found the Reverend Alberto Cosenza just where the
deacon said he would be, in a small cafe across the street from the inn
where Cosenza had been staying. Why they couldn't have met in Cosenza's room, he didn't know. Perhaps Cosenza was afraid that he'd miss
his ride to the spaceport. Or maybe he just wanted to see the world one
last time.

In any case, Laird paused in the doorway to pull the bill of his cap a bit lower over his face. Cosenza was sitting alone at a table beside the window; outside, the street was busy with midmorning traffic, the good people of New Brighton going about their daily affairs. Laird decided that it probably wouldn't matter if the two of them were seen together; no one in the cafe seemed to be paying attention to them.

"Good morning." Cosenza looked up as Laird approached. "Care for some coffee?" He tapped a fingernail against the small clay pot on the table. "I had the waiter bring an extra cup, just in case you . . ."

"No thanks." Laird didn't intend to stay any longer than necessary. Sitting down next to Cosenza, he placed the suitcase he'd brought with him between them, making sure that it was upright. "I'm sure you're anxious to be on your way, so . . ."

"My cab won't be here for another few minutes." Cosenza appeared calm, yet Laird couldn't help but notice that his hand trembled slightly when he picked up his coffee. "I've been enjoying the view," he added, nodding toward the window. "What a lovely town this is. So many beautiful people. Seems a shame to . . ."

His voice trailed off, and he sighed. "Well. Such as it is." His gaze flickered toward the suitcase; oversized, its outer shell constructed of titanium alloy, it was the same one that he'd brought with him from Earth last year. "You've done as I've asked?"

Laird pulled his chair closer to the table. From the corner of his eye, he checked the room. Only a couple of other tables were occupied, and those were far enough away from their own that he felt safe that they wouldn't be overheard; the waiter was at the serving counter, chatting up a pretty cook.

"All taken care of," he murmured. "Took a while to get the stuff I needed, but . . ."

"I don't need to know the details. Only that it'll work." Cosenza shifted around in his chair so that he was able to pick up the suitcase by its handle. He grunted with the exertion. "Rather heavy, don't you think?"

"Can't be helped. There's a lot packed in there." Laird pointed to its lockplate. "It's been deactivated, of course, but as soon as you enter your thumbprint, it'll be sealed. No one but you will be able to open it."

Cosenza raised an eyebrow. "And if someone asks me to . . . ?"

"They won't." Laird shook his head. "I asked around, and it's the same procedure as when you came here, only in reverse. No customs inspections for outbound passengers. After you check it at the space-port, it'll be put into a freight container along with everyone else's lug-gage and taken straight out to the shuttle. Once the shuttle docks with the *Lee*, the container will be transferred to the cargo bay . . ."

"That's not something that will concern me. What about the detona-tor?"

Another glance around the room, then Laird reached into his jacket pocket to pull out the datapad he'd bought in a secondhand electronics shop. Along with the suitcase, he'd spent the last couple of weeks work-ing on it in the secrecy of his tiny apartment. The hard part hadn't been gathering the necessary materials—ammonium nitrate, aluminum powder, even the chemical components of trinitrotoluene; all had been available from local agriculture or construction-supply stores, where he'd paid cash for them, no questions asked—but assembling everything without becoming so nervous that he'd touch off his control bracelet. But he'd built things like it before, and he knew how to remain calm. The trick was pretending that it was just a toy . . .

"This is it," he said, flipping open the pad's cover. "Works like any other except that it now holds a high-frequency transmitter, effective range of three hundred yards. Don't worry, it'll send through bulkheads."

Cosenza took the pad from him "And the trigger itself . . . ?"

"Second function key on the menu bar." Careful not to touch the pad himself, Laird pointed to its tiny screen. "Push it once, and it's armed. Push it twice . . ."

"I see." Cosenza weighed the pad in his palm. "And the timer? How does that work?"

"Third function key. A clock will come up once you've armed the mechanism. All you have to do is set it for however long you want, then push the ENTER button to start the countdown." He paused. "Of course, if you decide to change your mind, all you have to do is close the pad. It'll turn off, and everything will reset to neutral position."

"Nice to know, but . . ." Cosenza let out his breath as he placed the pad on the table. "I sincerely doubt it."

"Well . . . all right, then." Laird pushed back his chair, prepared to stand up. The less time he spent with the Dominionist preacher, the better. It wasn't just for fear of being linked to what Cosenza intended to do. It was also that, in the years that Laird had been a member of Living Earth, he'd learned how to recognize a fanatic when he saw one. And Alberto Cosenza was as driven as they come.

"Yes. I think our business is concluded." Cosenza regarded him with unblinking eyes, and it seemed for a moment as if a certain sadness had come over him. "I know our motives aren't the same, David"—Laird hissed at the sound of his name, but the deacon didn't appear to notice—"but, all the same, I hope that you'll pray for me."

Laird stopped halfway out of his seat. From their first meeting outside the jail, he'd pretended to be a devout Dominionist, even going so far as to take communion with the clergyman. He thought his performance had been convincing, but it seemed that Cosenza had seen through him from the very beginning.

"I will," he said. It was a lie, of course, but it was the only way he could respond.

Cosenza nodded. "Thank you. And may the Lord . . ."

Laird didn't want to hear the rest. He hurried out of the cafe, hoping that no one there had seen him. But it wasn't until he was several blocks away that his heart stopped pounding.

"I can't believe you let me sleep late." Sitting beside him in the back of the rickshaw cab, Lynn glared at Sawyer. "If this is your way of trying to keep me here . . ."

"It's not! I swear!" Sawyer was trying not to laugh, but it was impossible to keep the grin off his face. "If I'd wanted to do that, I would have . . ."

He stopped, not knowing how to complete that sentence. Ordered more wine at dinner last night? Failed to set the alarm on his pad? While it was true that they'd been roaring drunk when the two of them had returned to her room, the latter had never occurred to him, or at least not as something he'd do deliberately. In any case, Lynn was positively livid when she woke up to discover that she had little more than an hour to get to the spaceport before her shuttle lifted off. And she was holding him to blame.

"You would've what?" Lynn clasped her shoulder bag closer to her chest as the rickshaw's left wheel hit a pothole, then she leaned forward in her seat. "Do you think you can go any faster?" she called out to the driver. "I'll throw in another five if you can get me there sooner."

The driver didn't say anything, but her muscular legs pumped a bit harder as she stood up on the pedals. The rickshaw bounced again as it found another pothole; they'd left the town behind, and now were traveling down the unpaved dirt road leading to the spaceport, weaving in and out between the seemingly endless procession of newly arrived immigrants making their way into the refugee camp. It was hard to look at them.

"Look, you're going to get there on time. Don't worry about it." Sawyer glanced over his shoulder to make sure her suitcase was still tied down. "I'm sorry, but it's not—"

A sudden boom from somewhere far above. Looking up, he caught a glimpse of a pair of contrails. An incoming shuttle, bringing in another boatload of refugees. When was it ever going to end . . . ?

"When is what ever going to end?" Lynn peered at him, and Sawyer suddenly realized that he'd spoken aloud.

"I dunno." He shrugged, reluctant to say more. "All these people, I guess."

"Yeah, well . . . can't blame them, you know." She gazed at the vast collection of shacks, tents, and sheds that sprawled around them. "You're lucky," she added, and there was no mistaking the edge in her voice. "You came here years ago, by your own choice. These people . . . most of them have left behind everything they had. And they're just the ones fortunate enough to be able to afford to."

"I know, I know . . . sorry." Sawyer let out his breath. He didn't want their time together to end this way. In fact, he didn't want it to end, period, but least of all with a one-night stand in a hotel room, followed the next morning by an argument.

When Lynn had called to tell him that she was leaving for Earth, he'd caught an airship from Liberty. He hadn't seen her since the ExEx, and his only intention had been to say good-bye, or at least bon voyage. But one thing led to another; one too many bottles of waterfruit wine, and they'd wound up in bed together, doing what they'd meant to do but couldn't when they were on the *LeMare*. It was hard to admit, even to himself, but he'd missed her. And now that she was going home, he knew that he'd miss her even more.

"So . . ." He hesitated, reluctant to ask again the same question he'd asked last night over dinner. "Do you think you're coming back?"

Lynn didn't respond, but instead stared straight ahead. "I don't know," she said at last. "I've been here longer than I thought I would be. It's been quite an experience, but there's not much reason for me to stay. At least not after I write about Carlos's trip . . ."

"You're not curious about the *chaaz'maha*?" He gave her a sidelong look. "I thought you were interested in him."

"Oh, I am. I've filed at least a dozen stories about him. I wish I could have gotten an interview, but . . ." She shrugged. "I'm not sure that's sufficient cause for my editors to let me come back here." A wry grin. "Besides, you've seen one messiah, you've seen 'em all . . . even if that's not what he claims to be."

"We've got a newspaper . . ."

"The *Liberty Post*?" The grin became a grimace. "That rag isn't worth the paper it's printed on. Hell, I can't believe you people even use paper."

"No shortage of wood pulp here. And it recycles just fine."

"Yes, well . . . look, I'm a writer. Pretty good one, too, if I say so myself. Working for Pan, I've got a global readership of nearly 500 million, plus a possible book contract once I rewrite the series. If I move here, I'd be covering . . ." She shrugged. "I dunno. Town council meetings, Farmer Brown losing all his pigs to ring disease . . . sort of a step down, if y'know what I mean."

"Maybe. At least you'd be alive."

Again, Lynn fell silent. "I can't believe . . . I won't believe . . . that the situation will get to that point," she said after a moment. "I know times are tough back home, but sooner or later they're going to get better. And I don't want to be one of the guys who jumps ship when it needs every able-bodied seaman it can get in order to stay afloat."

"But . . ."

"I'm going back, Sawyer. Case closed." She seemed to regret the harshness of her words, because she took his hand. "Look, I may be stubborn, but I'm not stupid. If things really do get bad, I'll grab the first ship back here I can, job or no job. You can live with that, can't you?"

He reluctantly nodded, then put his arm around her and pulled her close. The spaceport was in sight; it was impossible to ignore the refugees lined up outside. "If you do, you won't have to go through all that," he said softly. "You've got a place to stay."

Her smile reappeared. "If I didn't know better, I'd say that was a proposal."

Sawyer didn't say anything, but he couldn't help but grin. Perhaps it was . . .

The rickshaw came to a stop in front of the entrance, and the driver got off her bike to unfasten Lynn's bag from the back. Sawyer pulled out a money roll and peeled off ten colonials; the driver tucked them in her pocket, then waited while he followed Lynn to the door. "You don't have to see me off," she said. "In fact, I'd just as soon you didn't. Let's just say good-bye right here, okay?"

She didn't want to be sentimental, nor could he blame her. Nonetheless, he took her in his arms one last time. Their kiss lasted longer than he expected, but not as long as he wanted. "Come back soon," he whispered in her ear, and she nodded without saying whether she would or not. Then she picked up her luggage and, with a parting glance and a smile over her shoulder, walked through the door into the terminal.

As Sawyer climbed back aboard the rickshaw, he saw another cab pull up behind them. A Dominionist minister, sour-faced and dressed in black, sat in the rear; Sawyer guessed that he was another homeward-bound passenger, arriving to catch the shuttle to the *Lee*. Remembering that Lynn had interviewed a church deacon the day the *chaaz'maha* was released from jail, he wondered if it was the same person.

His own driver had just begun to pedal away when Sawyer noticed something peculiar. The minister insisted upon unloading his suitcase by himself, impatiently swatting the driver's hands away from its handle. But when he picked it up, his shoulders visibly sagged beneath its weight.

Souvenirs, Sawyer decided. Either that, or perhaps even a Dominionist minister wasn't above smuggling.

When Alberto Cosenza learned that Hawk Thompson had already departed from New Brighton, he almost canceled his reservation. He'd counted on being aboard the same shuttle as the false prophet; in fact, his entire plan depended upon it. But when he checked in at the spaceport, a casual inquiry to the ticket agent revealed the unexpected truth: Thompson, along with President Montero, had been aboard a private skiff that had lifted off over an hour earlier.

Cosenza cared little for the fact that the former Federation president was on the same flight. He had nothing against Montero, except, perhaps, that he was taking the heretic to Earth. Yet that alone was unforgivable. *Sa'Tong* was worse than sacrilegious; in its denial of the very existence of God, it was profoundly blasphemous. Cosenza had seen how its teachings had poisoned one mind already; Grey Rice was a lost soul, and the deacon was terrified by the notion that countless others back home might be swayed by this godless doctrine.

That simply could not be allowed to happen. The so-called *chaaz'maha* simply could not be allowed to set foot on Earth . . . even if Cosenza had to give up his own life, along with those of everyone aboard, to prevent it.

It was a regrettable sacrifice, but necessary.

And yet, as he rode the tram that carried him across the spaceport to the waiting shuttle, the deacon found himself forced to weigh his options. When he'd thought Thompson would be aboard the same spacecraft, the plan had been rather easy. Wait until the shuttle was about to lift off, then set the detonator's timer for sixty seconds. That would prohibit him from chickening out at the last second, and would also ensure that the bomb would go off when the shuttle was high enough off the ground. Although his suitcase would be in the shuttle's cargo hold, the explosion would doubtless destroy the spacecraft, and its altitude would preclude any survivors. With luck, the wreckage would have come down in the Great Equatorial River, where salvage would have been unlikely; no one would have seriously suspected that the cause was anything but the most unfortunate of accidents. An act of God.

But with Thompson no longer aboard the same shuttle . . . well, that changed everything, didn't it? Cosenza absently gazed at the spacecraft closely parked together on the landing field. He could wait until the *Lee* reached Highgate, then retrieve his suitcase and try to get close enough to Thompson that the explosion would kill him . . . but there were too many risks involved. Thompson might disembark just the same way as he'd been brought aboard, his contact with other passengers minimized as much as possible. Or a customs inspector might open the suitcase when the false prophet was nowhere in sight; Cosenza would immediately be arrested, and Thompson would escape once and for all. Either way, the odds of success would be diminished as soon as the *Lee* reached the station.

That left only one alternative: set off the bomb aboard the starship itself. But even that option—with its added cost of the lives of the *Lee*'s crew—had its uncertainties. Cosenza regretted not letting Laird tell him how he'd constructed the bomb; he could only guess that it was comprised of some sort of material that would detonate once an electrical charge was introduced. Whatever it was, though, it was probably only powerful enough to mortally wound a relatively small spacecraft. But the *Lee* was a much larger ship, and the bomb would be in its cargo bay, away from the passenger compartments. The explosion would undoubtedly cripple the vessel, maybe even cause a temporary loss of control . . . but it wouldn't destroy it.

Cosenza frowned. There had to be another way. The Lord wouldn't have let him come that far, only to . . .

"Something wrong, Reverend?"

In the seat in front of him, a young woman had turned to regard him with curious eyes. It took a second for Cosenza to recognize her: the journalist who'd interviewed him a couple of weeks ago, outside the New Brighton jail the day Thompson was released. He couldn't remember her name; indeed, he'd forgotten almost everything else about that afternoon, except his final encounter with Grey and his first meeting with David.

"No . . . no, nothing at all." He forced a smile. "I'm just . . ."

Not knowing what else to say, his voice trailed off. "Nervous?" she finished, giving him a sympathetic grin. "Can't blame you. I hate this whole hyperspace thing. Almost makes me wish I could take the slow boat instead."

"No, you don't." This from another passenger sitting nearby: well dressed, middle-aged, probably business traveler on his way home. "Those old ships took fifty-six years to get here. Hell, there's one that left after the Revolution that still hasn't made it back." Smug in his wisdom, he grinned. "Five minutes from here to Earth . . . that's fine with me."

"Yeah, well . . ." The woman shook her head. "Maybe so, but it's those five minutes that get me. Especially the one when we actually make the jump."

It was at that moment when the Lord presented a solution to Cosenza's problem.

There was a narrow window of opportunity. It would take careful timing, of course; he couldn't be off by more than a few seconds. Nor could he rely upon the timer. But if the *Lee* returned to Earth exactly the same way as it had come, then there was a chance . . .

"Yes," Cosenza murmured. "It's that one minute."

Carlos had been aboard the *Robert E. Lee*, but several years ago. Formerly the EASS *Francis Drake*, the starship belonged to the European Alliance until it was ceded to the Coyote Federation in the aftermath of Parson's Rebellion. He'd briefly toured the ship just prior to its rechristening ceremony, but he had never been a passenger during one of its voyages to Earth. His only previous journey to the planet of his birth had been aboard a smaller craft that, while adequate for hyperspace travel, was nowhere near as impressive.

So he'd forgotten just how large the *Lee* was. As the skiff came in on primary approach, he gazed at it through the porthole beside his seat. Nearly six hundred feet long, its sleek hull was gracefully streamlined from its tapered bow to the twin nacelles of its diametric-drive engines. Although primarily intended to be a military vessel, it had since been refitted to carry passengers and cargo as well, and now served as the flagship of the Federation Navy . . . which itself was as modest as an understatement could be, since the rest of the fleet consisted of only a small handful of freighters and shuttles. Nonetheless, Carlos couldn't help but feel a surge of pride when he saw the Federation flag against one of the ship's vertical stabilizers. The *Lee* might be a spoil of war, but all the same, it belonged to Coyote.

"Never thought I'd ever see this," the *chaaz'maha* said, and Carlos looked over to see him regarding the *Lee* with unabashed awe. "Just . . . amazing, isn't it?"

Carlos smiled. He'd all but forgotten that his nephew had never been in space. Indeed, he was surprised that the *chaaz'maha* hadn't become ill on the way up, as most first-time space travelers usually did. But the young man had remained calm the entire time, although at one point he'd briefly closed his eyes and chanted something under his breath that sounded somewhat like a mantra. After that, he'd stared through the porthole on his side of the cabin, obviously fascinated by the sight of Coyote from orbit.

"Yes, it is." Carlos hesitated. "Beats just watching it land and take off, doesn't it?"

The *chaaz'maha* shrugged, not taking his eyes away from the porthole. "Yes, but that was pretty amazing, too. Didn't happen very often, though. And this is the first time I've seen it . . . well, up here. Where it belongs."

Carlos was about to reply when there was a loud chime from the cockpit. The pilot silenced the annunciator, then glanced back at them. "We're on final approach, gentlemen. Could you please make sure that your harnesses are secure?"

"Wilco." Carlos tugged at his seat and shoulder straps, and ascertained that the *chaaz'maha* did the same. "Just a precaution," he said quietly. "Docking should be a lot easier than liftoff, but as soon as we're in the hangar bay . . ."

"The Millis-Clement Field will be reactivated, so there might be a bump or two when we land." The *chaaz'maha* grinned. "I didn't spend all that time at the spaceport without learning a thing or two."

"Of course . . . sorry." Carlos returned his attention to his porthole. Now that they were above the *Lee*, he could see that the ship's enormous hangar doors were wide open; directly below, a fluorescent circle had appeared on the hangar floor, red arrows around its circumference lit to help guide the skiff during its descent. There was a brief surge as RCRs fired to correct its trajectory, then the pilot carefully maneuvered the small craft down into the cavernous bay.

As the *chaaz'maha* predicted, they felt gravity return the moment the skiff entered the hangar. Carlos grasped his armrests and gritted his teeth, but there was only a mild jar as the landing gear touched down. Chimes rang again from the cockpit, and the pilot silenced them once more. "All right, gentlemen, we're down," he said, snapping toggles along his dashboard. "Give us a few minutes to close the doors and re-pressurize, and you'll be free to go as soon as . . ."

He paused, cocking his head as if to listen to his headset. Then he looked back at them again. "Mr. President, I've been requested to ask you to remain on board a little while longer. The Commodore will be receiving you in person, along with an honor guard."

"Oh, for the love of . . ." Hastily unclasping his harness, Carlos leaned forward to rest his elbows on the back of the pilot's seat. "Please inform the Commodore that I'll be happy to see her again, but an honor guard is unnecessary." He glanced back at his nephew. "Unless, of course, you want . . ."

"No. Not at all." The *chaaz'maha* shook his head.

"All right, then." Carlos turned to the pilot again. "Tell the Commodore that she's been overruled"—the pilot blanched—"or words to that effect," he added, trying to soften the blow a bit.

The pilot reluctantly nodded, then spoke quietly into his mike wand. "Well, we dodged that bullet," Carlos murmured, settling back in his seat, "but I'm afraid we're going to have to put up with this sort of thing, sooner or later, once we get to Earth."

"I hope you're wrong." The *chaaz'maha* was distinctly uncomfortable at the prospect. "I'm just a simple teacher, you know. Not . . ."

"Sure. And I'm just a simple passenger. But people like ceremonies, and they'll do whatever they can to make sure you suffer through them." He paused. "Better get used to it, especially since you're now the *chaaz'maha*."

He didn't intend for the last part to sound sarcastic, but it did. The *chaaz'maha* nodded, but remained quiet as he watched the hangar doors slowly lower back into place. A few seconds later, their portholes misted over as atmosphere was reintroduced to the vast space. The hangar crew had just emerged to push a ladder toward the skiff when the *chaaz'maha* leaned over toward Carlos.

"As I said, I prefer my new name," he said quietly, his voice low enough that only Carlos could hear him. "If it makes you more comfortable, though, you can call me Hawk . . . at least when we're alone."

Carlos blinked. "I thought you were pretty adamant about your title."

"I am, but"—an offhand shrug—"you still have doubts about who I am, so there's little purpose in my belaboring the point."

Carlos was surprised. He'd never spoken his thoughts aloud; more than ever before, he began to suspect that the stories about the Order were true. "Suppose that's true," he murmured, glancing at the pilot to make sure he wasn't eavesdropping. "Do you really believe it? What you say you are, I mean . . . or is this just a clever way of staying out of jail?"

Hawk gazed back at him, his expression neutral. "What do you think?"

"You already know the answer to that, don't you?" The *chaaz'maha* didn't reply, and his face remained stoical. "Besides," Carlos went on, "it doesn't really matter what I think. Other people believe you . . . and to tell the truth, that's all I really care about. You can be pretty persuasive, and I'm counting on that. So if this is just a con game . . ."

"It isn't." The slightest of smiles. "But as you said yourself, it doesn't really matter, now does it?"

Carlos had no ready answer for that. A moment later, his ears popped as the cabin pressure equalized and the skiff's hatch was opened from outside. The pilot stood up, but politely waited until President Montero and the *chaaz'maha* exited the spacecraft.

To Carlos's relief, there was no honor guard waiting for them, only a lone midshipman in dress uniform standing at stiff attention at the bottom of the ladder. Carlos returned his salute and the *chaaz'maha* bowed; behind them, the deck crew were already unloading their bags from the cargo hold. As soon as the pilot exited the craft, the ladder was pushed away and a small tractor moved in to pull the skiff toward another side of the deck, clearing the landing zone for the incoming passenger shuttle.

The midshipman led them to a bulkhead hatch. Commodore Anastasia Tereshkova awaited them in the corridor on the other side, another officer standing beside her. "President Montero," she said, offering a formal salute. "Welcome aboard. It's an honor to have you here again."

"And it's an honor to be here, Cap . . . Commodore, I mean." Tereshkova didn't seem to mind the slip of the tongue; they both remembered that she'd held the lesser rank when she was with the European Space Agency. Carlos returned the salute, but he couldn't keep a straight face any longer. "Hello, Ana," he added, ignoring the nearby crewmen as he opened his arms to her. "Good to see you."

"Good to see you, too, Carlos." Tereshkova relaxed, and allowed him to give her a quick hug. The two had been friends ever since he'd escorted her on a long river expedition across Barren Isle not long after her first ship, the *Columbus*, had reached 47 Ursae Majoris. Their relationship had become so close that, for a brief time, there had been a rumor that the two of them were having an affair. Completely untrue, of course, but it had caused a bit of embarrassment for everyone involved until it finally went away. Fortunately, their friendship had survived; indeed, if anything, it had become stronger.

Stepping back from her, Carlos remembered his nephew, still quietly standing nearby. "Allow me to introduce Hawk"—damn, another slip of the tongue!—"that is, the *chaaz'maha*. He's joining me on my mission as . . . ah, a senior advisor, you might say."

"Pleased to meet you, *chaaz'maha*." There was a wary look in Tereshkova's eyes as she stepped toward him; nonetheless, she offered her hand.

"Pleased to meet you, too, Commodore." The *chaaz'maha* briefly took her hand, then bowed. "Although I should say that we've met before . . . when I worked as a customs inspector at New Brighton. I doubt you remember me, though."

Tereshkova frowned, her left eyebrow rising ever so slightly. *Of course she doesn't remember,* Carlos thought. *But you already know that, don't you?* "Sorry, but I can't say that I do," she said. "However, your reputation precedes you. Welcome aboard."

This time, she didn't sound as if she meant it. Carlos hastened to ease the situation. "So, Commodore . . . an honor guard." He shook his head in mock disgust. "I'm flattered, but really, you should know better."

That returned the smile to her face. "I do, but . . ." She shrugged as she turned to lead them down the corridor, the two officers falling in behind their passengers. "I'm not joking when I say that it's an honor to have you aboard again. Call it a token of my respect."

"C'mon. It's just a diplomatic mission."

"'Just a . . .'?" She stared at him. "Finally, we're getting a chance to settle things with the Union, and you call it 'just a diplomatic mission'?" An appalled sigh. "I'll have you know that I was supposed to take a four-week shore leave when this came up, but I pushed it back just so that I'd have the privilege of escorting you to Earth."

"You didn't."

"I did . . . and you'd damned well better be appreciative, Mr. President. I have a rose garden that badly needs to be weeded." A wry grin, then she became serious again. "I have complete confidence in my crew, but for something as important as this, I decided that I needed to be aboard. Just to watch your back in case something should happen again."

Carlos nodded. They both remembered how his first mission to Earth had ended. Although he and Wendy had successfully negotiated the U.N. treaty that formally recognized Coyote's independence, the Western Hemisphere Union had been the sole holdout, going so far as attempting to spark an international incident that would have led to their detainment on Union soil. Had it not been for Morgan Goldstein's last-minute intervention, Coyote's diplomatic team might have become bargaining chips in a power play between the Federation and the Union. He wasn't expecting the same thing to occur twice, but Tereshkova was right. It would be prudent to have the *Lee* guarding his back, with its commanding officer at the helm.

"I suppose you're right," Carlos said. "Thank you."

"You're welcome." She paused to return the salute of a junior officer who passed them in the corridor, then went on. "Because of the priority nature of your mission, I've also instructed my crew to . . . what's the old saying? Not relieve the ponies . . . ?"

"Don't spare the horses."

"*Da.* Yes, that's it. What I mean is, we'll be engaging the differential drive as soon as we break orbit, thereby cutting our flight time by a little more than six hours."

Carlos looked at her askance. "That's not really necessary . . ."

"Perhaps not." Tereshkova shrugged. "But I'd rather spend fuel in braking maneuvers than have you arrive at your final destination any later than possible." There was a grim smile on her face as she returned the glance. "I know how important this is, my friend. And it's what little I can do, *nyet?*"

Knowing that it was impossible to argue with the Commodore aboard her own ship, Carlos simply nodded. By then they'd come to a ladder leading to the upper decks; Tereshkova halted there to step aside. "I have some business down here before I return to the bridge," she said, then gestured to the officer who'd been with her at the hangar. "This is Mr. Heflin, my chief petty officer. He'll escort you to your quarters . . . a first-class cabin in the passenger section."

"Pleased to meet you." Carlos nodded to Heflin, then looked at Anastasia again. "Perhaps we can have dinner sometime, if you're not too busy?"

"I'll have to check my schedule, but, yes, I'd like that very much." She grasped his hand again. "Again, welcome aboard, Mr. President . . . and see you soon."

A deferential nod to the *chaaz'maha*, then she turned to head farther down the corridor. As Heflin eased past to lead them up the ladder, the *chaaz'maha* stepped closer to Carlos. "I like her," he whispered, "even if she doesn't like me."

Carlos looked at him sharply. "And how would you know that?"

The *chaaz'maha* didn't reply, but Carlos had no remaining doubt that, although Tereshkova was very good at concealing her emotions, her thoughts couldn't stay hidden from his nephew for very long.

He was certain of it now. Hawk could read minds.

Four bells rang, followed a minute later by a brief surge as the *Lee*'s fusion secondary engines fired. Lynn felt herself being pushed back in her seat, but she looked up from her pad long enough to watch Coyote as it slowly drifted away. Departure was bittersweet; after over four Earth-years on this world, she was ready to go home, but she also regretted the things she was leaving behind. Nor was she altogether convinced that she'd never pass this way again.

Apparently, she wasn't the only person to have some regrets. Looking around the passenger compartment, Lynn couldn't help but notice the thoughtful expressions of her fellow travelers, or the fact that more than half of the seats were vacant. She'd even been able to put her shoulder bag on the empty seat beside her. The last time she'd been aboard the *Lee*, though, the second-class section had been full, and even the first-class cabins in the front of the compartment were booked solid. Now there weren't so many people returning to Earth as there were coming to Coyote, and even those who were homeward-bound seemed reluctant to be making the trip.

Maybe Sawyer was right. Perhaps the time had come for her to consider a change of scenery. She wouldn't be the first journalist to move to a place where they'd first visited to cover a story . . .

With that thought in mind, Lynn returned her attention to her work. She had one last dispatch to write, an update on President Montero's diplomatic mission. Her editors were expecting her to file before the *Lee* reached Highgate, and the steward had assured her that she'd be able to transmit it via the ship's hyperlink. With a little less than ten hours to go until the *Lee* rendezvoused with Starbridge Coyote, she had plenty of time to put something together.

Looking over her notes, though, she saw that the story was still thin. Carlos had granted her a brief interview the night before, when she'd dropped by the Federation consulate in New Brighton just before meeting Sawyer for dinner, and for once the former president had gone on the record instead of asking her to describe him as "a highly placed government source." But even then, Lynn had lost count of how many times she'd already interviewed him . . . and after her account of the crash landing on Vulcan, in which she'd depicted Carlos in frankly heroic terms, one of her editors had gone so far as to ask whether she'd become his press secretary.

So there was nothing new about another interview with President Montero. What she needed to cap off her long tenure as a foreign correspondent was a real, honest-to-God scoop, something that would blow the competition on Earth right out of the water . . . and, just maybe, persuade her editors that they ought to send her back to Coyote, perhaps to open a permanent PNS bureau. That would give her a reason to return—and she smiled at the thought of coming back to Sawyer as well; there *was* something special about their relationship, wasn't there?—but she knew that she'd have to do something outstanding to earn such a promotion.

Absently tapping a finger against her lips, she gazed toward the front of the cabin. Just past the second-class seats was the narrow passageway leading to the first-class cabins. A curtain had been pulled across the entrance, with a steward stationed just outside. It was obvious that measures were being taken to protect President Montero's privacy while he was in transit, just as he'd been brought aboard on the captain's skiff. It wasn't Carlos whom she wanted to see, though, but the person traveling with him.

No one had yet interviewed the *chaaz'maha*. Lynn hadn't even known who he was until he was arrested, and after he was released from jail, the magistrates had ordered him sequestered in the consulate, with no one allowed to visit him except family members. However, there was no question that, in a very short period of time, he had become a figure of enormous influence.

Not to mention controversial, or least potentially so. Lynn turned her head to gaze across the aisle. The Reverend Alberto Cosenza was seated on the starboard side of the cabin; a Bible lay open in his lap, but he stared out the porthole even though, now that the *Lee* had left orbit, there was little to be seen. His right hand tapped nervously at the cover of a datapad resting on the armrest. When he looked away from the porthole for a moment, Lynn noticed the tightness of his jaw, the angry look in his eyes, as he regarded the curtain behind which lay the cabin Carlos and the *chaaz'maha* were sharing.

An idea occurred to her. Ever since she'd come aboard, Lynn had been kicking herself for not having had the foresight to reserve first-class accommodations; PNS didn't budget her for such extravagances, but she could have shelled out the money on her own. And the steward had already made it clear to her that she wouldn't be allowed to go forward to see the president.

But maybe there was a way to get the *chaaz'maha* to visit her instead? And if she could persuade him to do so, how interesting it would be, to conduct an interview within earshot of a Dominionist clergyman so

virulently opposed to his teachings? Lynn normally didn't practice ambush journalism, considering it unethical to lay traps for interview sub-
jects. In this case, though, she could always claim that it had been sheer
coincidence that the two men happened to be in the same place at the
same time.

Lynn still had Carlos's private number stored in her pad's memory; he'd
given it to her when she started covering his early negotiations with
Earth, so that she'd keep informed of new developments as they occurred.
No doubt he would have his pad with him. Pulling up the text-message
function, she took a few minutes to compose a brief note, taking care to
make her request as respectful as possible. Once she was satisfied, she
tapped the SEND button, then settled back in her seat to wait.

Nothing might come of it. The *chaaz'maha* could always turn her
down. But it was worth a shot . . .

Carlos's pad beeped just as he and the *chaaz'maha* **were finishing**
lunch. Surprised by the interruption, he retrieved his jacket from where
he'd stashed it beneath his seat and fished the pad out of its pocket. The
chaaz'maha watched him from the other side of the fold-down table as
he read the message that appeared on its screen.

"Oh, dear . . ." Carlos chuckled, shook his head. "Should've known
this would happen." He looked up at his nephew. "Remember Lynn Hu,
the PNS reporter I was telling you about? She's here."

"Aboard the *Lee*?" The *chaaz'maha* spoke around a mouthful of teri-
yaki noodles.

"Uh-huh. I'd forgotten she was heading back to Earth today. Anyway,
she wants an interview . . . with you, for a change."

The *chaaz'maha* wiped his mouth and put aside his chopsticks. "About
what? Or does she say?"

"Read for yourself." Carlos pushed the pad across the table. "She's not
very specific, but it sounds like she'd like to talk to you about *Sa'Tong*
and your role in it."

The *chaaz'maha* picked up the pad, studied it for a moment. "That's
something I didn't expect. Didn't think I'd be speaking to the press anytime soon."

Carlos shrugged. Until less than two weeks ago, he'd been careful to keep Hawk out of sight after he'd bargained his release from jail, not authorizing public disclosure of the fact that the *chaaz'maha* would be accompanying him on the trip. "Like I said, it was bound to happen sooner or later."

The *chaaz'maha* looked up. "Think I should do it?"

"Well . . . the pope gives interviews. So does the Dalai Lama. No reason why you shouldn't. And Lynn is reasonably honest, at least so far as reporters go. When I've asked her not to quote me for the record, she's gone along with it." He paused, then added, "Not that you'd have the same liberty, I'm afraid. As a religious leader . . ."

"Spiritual teacher."

"Hawk . . ." Carlos sighed, rubbed his eyes. "Look, I know the difference, but most people aren't going to make that distinction. *Sa'Tong* is going to be viewed as a religion, no matter how you try to nuance it. Don't be surprised if you get a lot of resistance because of that."

"Oh, I know." The *chaaz'maha* smiled as he put down the pad. "One of my students is a former Dominionist minister. We've had quite a few interesting discussions." He gazed out the porthole; Coyote had vanished behind, to be replaced by Bear. "So . . . you think I should do this?"

"I don't see why not. You haven't done any interviews. Besides, it'll give you good practice for when we get to Earth." He looked at the message again, and frowned. "Says here that she'd like for you to go back to second class. I could always turn things around, invite her to come here instead."

The *chaaz'maha* shook his head. "Cabin's too small for three people," he said, and Carlos had to admit that he had a point. Although their accommodations were relatively luxurious, with brass rails, window curtains, a wall screen, and faux-leather seats that could be folded down to serve as bunks, the fact remained that it was not much larger than a closet. Big enough for two, but three would be a crowd. "And if I'm going to have to get used to doing interviews, perhaps I should also get used to doing them without your holding my hand."

"All right, then." Carlos tapped the REPLY button on the message bar. "I'll tell her that you . . ."

"Does it have to be right now?" The *chaaz'maha* sighed. "I mean . . . I want to do it, sure, but it's been a long morning already. I was looking forward to a nap."

Carlos glanced at the wall screen. It depicted a graphic display of the *Lee*'s projected course, with Starbridge Coyote as a tiny ring in trojan orbit around Bear. A chronometer at the bottom of the screen informed him that a little more than three hours remained until the ship rendezvoused with the starbridge. Normally the trip took ten hours, but once the differential drive was engaged, as Ana said it would, the flight time would be reduced by nearly two-thirds.

"Sure. I understand. I'll let her know that you'll come back in a little while." He grinned as he began to type in an appropriate response. "Anyway, maybe it'll do her good to let her sweat for a change. No point in jumping whenever she says frog."

"Frogs." The *chaaz'maha* rotated his chair away from the table, then reached down to the lever that cranked his seat back to horizontal position. "I'd like to see one once we get to Earth . . . if they're not extinct, that is."

Carlos smiled, watching his nephew as he closed his eyes. Sometimes, it was easy to forget that the he hadn't been born on Earth. He had many surprises waiting for him. Carlos hoped that few of them would be unpleasant.

The *chaaz'maha* awoke to the sound of bells: two sharp clangs, coming through the ceiling speaker. Opening his eyes, he turned his head to look up at his uncle. Carlos was calmly seated on the other side of the cabin, a pad open in his lap.

"Have a good nap?" Carlos asked.

"Yes, thank you." The *chaaz'maha* yawned, then raised his seat to its upright position. He glanced out the porthole, felt his breath catch: Bear was much closer, larger than he'd ever seen it, its rings filling the window. "How long have I . . . ?"

"About three hours." Carlos nodded toward the wall screen. "Those bells were the signal that we're on primary approach. The main drive has been shut down, and we're now in braking maneuvers."

If he'd had a mind to do so, the *chaaz'maha* might have cursed under his breath. Obviously, he'd been more tired than he thought, or he wouldn't have slept quite so long. "I suppose that means I won't be able to do that interview after all," he murmured, shaking his head to clear away the cobwebs.

"No . . . no, you've still got time." Carlos grinned. "You're not getting out of it that easy. In fact, Lynn just sent me another message, asking me to remind you about this."

"I suppose you're right. I did promise her, didn't I?" Sighing in resignation, he pushed himself out of his chair. Even though the differential drive had been shut down, the Millis-Clement field was still active; he'd be able to walk around, or at least until the field itself was shut off just prior to the ship's insertion into hyperspace. "Very well, then. Be back soon."

"Have a good time." The *chaaz'maha* was about to open the door when Carlos lifted a finger. "Want some advice? When you talk to the press, always tell them everything, but say nothing."

"That makes no sense whatsoever."

"Trust me, it will." Carlos gave him a wink, then returned his attention to his pad.

The *chaaz'maha* was still trying to figure out what his uncle meant as he pushed aside the curtain leading to the second-class section. He was mildly surprised to see that most of the seats were vacant; the lights had been lowered, and the majority of the passengers were napping, but the few who were awake looked up in astonishment as he made his way down the center aisle. The steward, surprised that he'd left his cabin, immediately came forward to ask if he needed anything. He smiled and shook his head, and the steward stepped aside to let him pass.

It wasn't hard to figure out who Lynn Hu was: a petite young woman, sitting alone in the rear of the compartment. Seeing him, she rose from her seat. *"Chaaz'maha,"* she said, offering her hand. "Thanks for coming back to see me."

"My pleasure, Ms. Hu. Thank you for inviting me." As he took her hand, the *chaaz'maha* opened his mind to hers.

—God better-looking than I thought look at his eyes so warm never thought I'd be so turned on wow get a grip dammit you got a job to do but damn . . .

Perhaps he was giving himself an unfair advantage by searching her mind, but this was the first time he'd met a reporter, and he didn't want to be caught off guard. So he fixed a smile upon his face as he moved toward the seat next to Lynn. She'd put her shoulder bag there, but she hastily pulled it aside, putting it in her lap as she sat down again.

"Many apologies for not coming back sooner," he went on, taking the empty seat. "The trip up took a lot out of me, and I needed to rest before we . . ."

"No, no. Not at all. I understand perfectly." A glance at the screen in the seatback in front of her, and she frowned. "Although we're probably going to have to make this short. We're about to rendezvous with the starbridge, and . . ."

—Cut the small talk this is your only chance skip the soft questions go straight to the hard stuff . . .

"Of course." The *chaaz'maha* folded his hands together. "Again, my apologies. I didn't . . ."

At that instant, violent emotion hit him like a cold, dark wave, its fury so unexpected that he involuntarily sucked in his breath as a new stream of consciousness invaded his mind:

—There he is there he is blasphemer false prophet Antichrist there he is here now I could reach out kill him with my bare hands end it all now . . .

The unspoken voice, harsh and menacing, rode the crest of a psychic surge so foul that it threatened to nauseate him. It clearly didn't belong to the smiling young woman beside him, but came from another source, yet one so near that it must have been almost as close to him as she was.

"No need to apologize." Lynn apparently didn't notice his discomfiture; distracted by her pad, she gazed at the screen as she switched it to vox mode. "But since we have just a few minutes, perhaps we should . . ."

—*You'll burn heretic you'll die die die today child of Satan by my hand your life will end oh Lord thy will shalt be done only a few minutes give me only a few . . .*

Ignoring Lynn, the *chaaz'maha* slowly turned his head, searching for the source of the terrible thoughts. Across the aisle, only a few feet away, was an elderly man. Dressed in the black outfit of a Dominionist minister, he stared directly at him, and there was no mistaking the unmitigated loathing in his face. And in that instant, as their eyes met, the *chaaz'maha* searched him, and found . . .

—*There now while he's looking at you arm the bomb open the pad press the menu key do it like Laird told you arm the bomb no wait arm the bomb but wait wait until we're about to go through the starbridge when the moment is right press the key again . . .*

"*Chaaz'maha?*" Although Lynn was only a few inches away, it seemed as if she were speaking to him from a much greater distance. "Are you all right? You . . ."

She laid a hand across his wrist, and he jerked at her touch. "No . . . no, I'm fine," he muttered, looking back at her. "It's just that . . ."

He couldn't finish, his mind still overwhelmed by the dark thoughts of the man seated on the other side of the aisle. Lynn was saying something else, but she was no longer the focus of his attention. Instead, he stared straight ahead, carefully avoiding looking directly at the clergyman even as he plunged deeper into his mind, searching for whatever horror this person had in store for him.

It took only a couple of seconds for him to discover the truth, but when he did, he almost gasped out loud. The bomb in the cargo bay, the detonator concealed in the datapad, the plan to activate it at the critical second . . . and above all else, the cold-blooded and utterly merciless determination to bring an end to his life, even if it also meant the destruction of the *Lee* and everyone on board.

"*Chaaz'maha?*" Lynn peered at him. "What's wrong? Is there something I can . . . ?"

"I'm . . . I'm sorry, but . . ." Wiping sweat from his face, he staggered to his feet, holding on to the seatback for support. "We're going to have to do this another time. Something has . . ."

—Get behind me scion of Lucifer leave you can't stop me my last pleasure will be the knowledge that you're dead . . .

"Just an upset stomach," he murmured, then turned away to lurch down the aisle. He did his best to pretend nothing was wrong, but as soon as he was on the other side of the curtain, he sagged against a bulkhead, fighting to keep from getting sick.

Then he pulled himself together and quickly headed for his cabin.

"You're sure?" Commodore Tereshkova regarded the *chaaz'maha* with an intensity Carlos had never seen before. "You're not mistaken, or . . . ?"

"Delusional?" In the cramped confines of the cabin, the *chaaz'maha* had no choice but to look her straight in the eye. "No. I wish I were, but"—he shook his head—"you have to believe me when I say the threat is real, and he fully intends to . . ."

"I still don't understand how you could know this." Although Tereshkova was concerned for the safety of her ship, her skepticism was obvious. "You haven't seen the bomb or the pad you claim he's using as a detonator. He didn't even say anything to you. So how is it possible for you to learn any of these things?"

"Ana . . ." Carlos let out his breath. "You're just going to have to trust Hawk . . . the *chaaz'maha*, I mean. He's . . . well, he's unusually perceptive. Let's just put it that way and leave it at that."

His nephew glanced at him, silently nodded. As soon as he'd returned to the cabin, the *chaaz'maha* had told him everything, including the way by which he'd come by the knowledge. It was only the fact that Carlos had already concluded—or at least strongly suspected beyond any reasonable doubt—that Hawk had somehow gained telepathic abilities that kept him from believing that the *chaaz'maha* had lost his mind. But even though Carlos had immediately summoned Anastasia to their cabin, he decided to keep that part of the story from her, if only because she might think that both of them were crazy.

"But . . ." Tereshkova began.

"Commodore, please . . . we simply don't have time to argue." The *chaaz'maha* held up a hand, and there was something in the way he spoke that caused her to go quiet. "If I'm wrong, then I'll be held fully accountable for my accusations. But"—he shook his head again—"I'm not wrong. Of that, I'm quite certain. There's a bomb in his bag, one powerful enough to cause serious damage to your vessel. It's triggered by a detonator concealed within the pad he's carrying . . . two simple keystrokes, and it goes off. He's doing this to kill me, and he simply does not care if he or anyone else dies as a result."

"And when do you say he intends to do this?"

"As soon as the *Lee* passes through the starbridge." Seeing the horrified look in her eyes, the *chaaz'maha* hesitated, then went on. "You know he can destroy the ship that way, don't you? If he set off the bomb anytime before then, the blast would be confined to the cargo bay, and that would probably be about it. But during those few seconds just before we enter hyperspace, when the *Lee* is under maximum stress . . ."

"*Da*. It would destroy the ship. No question about it." Carlos noticed that, as she spoke, her hands trembled ever so slightly at her sides. "And you're wrong about the cargo bay being the only part of the ship that would be affected. It's adjacent to the internal oxygen tanks, so a sufficiently powerful explosion would tear through the internal bulkheads and cause them to go up as well. And that . . ."

"So you can't chance it, can you?" The *chaaz'maha* stared at her. "Commodore, you must believe me. You have no other choice."

Once again, Carlos glanced at the wall screen. The *Lee* was less than fifty thousand miles from Starbridge Coyote; since braking maneuvers were complete, the vessel was only fourteen minutes away from hyperspace insertion. On the bridge, the crew was already linking the ship's

AI with the one aboard the nearby gatehouse, the prelude to an intricate ballet of quantum-level computations that would result in an artificial wormhole being created between 47 Ursae Majoris and Earth's solar system.

Fourteen minutes. Time was running out . . .

"Very well. I'll . . . trust you, even if I don't completely believe you." Tereshkova let out a breath; she'd also noticed the screen. "I'll summon Mr. Heflin, have him put the suspect under arrest."

She started to turn toward the door, but the *chaaz'maha* reached out to stop her. "No, don't do that. He's high-strung enough already. If he sees a member of your crew . . . especially a senior officer . . . coming toward him, he's liable to set off the bomb." He paused. "I didn't see him do so, but I believe he's already armed the detonator. The pad has a timer, but I don't think he's using it. Besides the fact that his timing is critical, he really wants to blow the thing himself. That way he can kill me with his own hand. If he thinks someone is going to stop him, or you put the ship on alert . . ."

"Can you jettison the cargo?" Carlos asked. "If you blow it out into space before . . ."

"No." Tereshkova shook her head. "Passenger baggage is sealed inside containers, which in turn are locked down inside the cargo bay. We can open the bay doors, certainly, but there's no mechanism for jettisoning the containers themselves."

"Then maybe we can find the bomb, disarm it."

"No. We can't open the canisters while they're in the bay. They're packed together too tightly." The Commodore's mouth pursed together. "No one ever anticipated this sort of emergency, I regret to say."

"So abort the jump." Carlos shrugged. "If we don't go through the starbridge, maybe he won't . . ."

"It won't make any difference." The *chaaz'maha* shook his head. "He's already committed himself. Even if we don't go through, he'll explode the bomb anyway . . . and as the Commodore says, chances are he won't need hyperspace to kill everyone aboard."

Carlos closed his eyes. "So we're going to have to deal with this guy . . ."

"Cosenza," the *chaaz'maha* said quietly. "The Reverend Alberto Cosenza. Deacon of the Church of the Holy Dominion." He glanced at his uncle. "If you intend to negotiate with him, you'd do well to know his name and who he is."

A Dominionist. Carlos quietly sighed. Although he considered the Church to be misguided, its tenets antiquated and archaic, he'd never thought it to be dangerous. And indeed, the institution itself probably wasn't to blame. Just one man, so fanatically determined to defend his religion that he's willing to commit mass murder in the name of God.

Uh-huh, he thought. *And how many times has that happened?*

"All right, then." He pushed himself out of his chair. "Let me go back there. Maybe I can talk to—"

"*Nyet!*" Tereshkova moved to block the door. "As commander of this vessel, I absolutely forbid it."

"But . . ."

"In fact, I'm doing exactly the opposite." She opened the door; her chief petty officer was standing just outside. "Mr. Heflin? Please escort President Montero and the *chaaz'maha* below and put them in a life-boat . . ."

"Ana!" Carlos stepped closer to her. "Dammit, don't . . . !"

Tereshkova laid a hand on his chest, started to push him back. Then, as if on second thought, she grabbed his arm and pulled him toward the door. "Take them below," she repeated, ignoring Carlos's objections. "Once they're aboard, rig the lifeboat for automatic jettison in the event of a general alarm."

Heflin's face went pale. He had no idea what was going on, but he knew better than to question his captain's orders. "Yes, ma'am," he murmured, then he held out a hand to Carlos. "Mr. President, if you will . . ."

Carlos wasn't about to be taken away without a fight. "Ana, you can't . . ."

"Mr. President, this is not open to discussion." No longer bothering with common courtesy, she shoved him out of the cabin. "We'll deal with him ourselves. Your safety . . . your nephew's . . . are my prime concern just now. *Chaaz'maha,* please . . . ?"

"As you insist." Apparently seeing the futility in offering any resistance, the *chaaz'maha* stepped past her. As he joined his uncle in the corridor, though, he turned to offer a solemn bow. "*Sa'Tong qo*, Commodore."

Tereshkova had no idea what that meant, but she gave him a quick nod in return. "Thanks. You, too." Then she pointed toward a hatch at the forward end of the corridor and snapped her fingers. "Go now."

Carlos reluctantly nodded, then turned to follow the *chaaz'maha*. Then he stopped and looked back at Ana. "So what are you going to do?"

"I'm . . . I'm afraid this is a situation where there are no good choices. Only ones less dangerous than others." She hesitated. "We're going to have to take him down."

Sitting in the back of the passenger section, the pad resting on the armrest beside his right hand, Alberto Cosenza felt a serenity that he'd never experienced. All at once, it seemed as if he perceived things with a certain clarity; he'd come to realize that his entire life had been leading up to this moment, that he was about to play a role that had been preordained since the moment of his birth. Nothing else mattered, save what he was about to do.

Cosenza was vaguely aware of a minor commotion on the other side of the curtain, but paid little attention. He'd noticed Thompson's reaction to him, how he'd abruptly rushed away. No doubt the false prophet had been sickened by the presence of a man of God; it was merely another indication that the deacon was being guided by a higher power.

Cosenza rested his fingertips lightly upon the pad. The detonator was armed, the timer disengaged; all he needed to do was tap the appropriate command into the menu bar, and it would all be over. Gazing at the screen on the seatback before him, he was satisfied to see that the *Lee* was only seven minutes away from its rendezvous with the starbridge.

Soon. Very soon . . .

Carlos knew that Ana was making the wrong decision. But he had to wait to make his own move.

The lifeboats were located on the deck below the passenger section, behind circular hatches tilted downward on both sides of a narrow passageway. Carlos let Heflin escort him and the *chaaz'maha* down the ladder, and quietly stood by while the chief petty officer opened the nearest lifeboat. The *chaaz'maha* climbed aboard, but Carlos paused to watch as Heflin opened a service panel beside the outer hatch, revealing a small keypad. Heflin tapped in a code number, then entered a series of commands, following instructions on the pad's tiny screen. A soft double *beep*, then Heflin shut the panel again.

"There. It's set to jettison the moment there's a general alarm." There was a grim smile on the chief petty officer's face as he turned toward Carlos. "All right, Mr. President . . . in you go."

"Of course." Carlos ducked his head as if to climb into the lifeboat, then he hesitated. "Umm . . . I'm not sure how this works. The seats, I mean. How do you . . . ?"

"They fold down from the bulkheads. Very easy to do." Heflin was becoming impatient. "Mr. President, please . . ."

"Certainly. Of course." Carlos put his shoulders through the hatch, but when he saw that Hawk was having trouble lowering one of the seats, he withdrew again. "Look, I'm sorry to be a pest, but . . ."

Heflin let out his breath in exasperation, but without another word he climbed into the lifeboat. The second he entered the small capsule, Carlos slammed the hatch behind him. Grabbing the lock-lever, he shoved it upward, sealing the lifeboat shut from outside. Heflin was already banging his fist against the hatch as the president sprinted back down the passageway to the ladder.

As expected, he found Tereshkova in the first-class section, standing beside the curtain. Two midshipmen were with her; all three had stun guns in their hands. The Commodore's eyes widened the moment she saw Carlos come through the forward hatch.

"What the hell are you . . . ?" she hissed, her voice an angry whisper.

"Shut up and listen." Keeping his voice low, Carlos held up a hand as he came closer. "That's not going to work. If he's already armed the detonator, he'll set it off as soon as he sees you . . ."

"I have two more men behind the hatch on the other end of the compartment." Tereshkova jerked her head toward the second-class section. "We're just the backup. On my signal, they're going to come in from behind and—"

"Ana, please." He shook his head. "You heard what Hawk said. Cosenza's got his finger on the trigger. If he sees anyone come in, either from the front or the rear . . ."

"We're just going to have to take that chance." Tereshkova pointed toward the hatch Carlos had just come through, which still lay open. "Now do as you're told. Go back where you belong."

Through the open hatch behind him, Carlos heard the hollow clang of footsteps running up the ladder. Heflin had managed to escape from the lifeboat and was pursuing him topside. "Look," he said, trying not to raise his voice, "there's a better way. Let me go in there . . ."

"Out of the question." Tereshkova gazed past him. "Mr. Heflin . . ."

"Listen!" Carlos pushed past one of the midshipmen until he was right in Tereshkova's face. "I'm with you on this. There's no way we can talk him out of it. We are just going to have to take him down . . . but let me do it."

Tereshkova raised an eyebrow; this wasn't what she expected to hear. She started to say something, but Carlos didn't let her. "Look, he won't suspect me . . . not if I go in to see someone else. There's another woman back there . . . a reporter, Lynn Hu. That's who Hawk was visiting in the first place. She's sitting directly across the aisle from him. If I sit down beside her . . ."

Heflin's hand came to rest on his shoulder, but Tereshkova surprised them both by shaking her head. Heflin reluctantly let go of him, and Carlos went on. "If you give me a stun gun, then I'll have a close shot. Way closer than any of your men." He paused, swallowing what felt like a dry lump in his throat. "And you know I can handle a gun. I've been doing this sort of thing all my life."

That wasn't exactly the truth, but Ana was fully aware of the years he'd spent as a guerrilla fighter. Long before he was President Montero, he'd been Rigil Kent, the man who'd led the fight to liberate the colonies. Yet Tereshkova still seemed uncertain. Her gaze flickered from him to the two midshipmen, then to the curtain, then back to Carlos again. "Time," she whispered, glancing at Heflin.

"Three minutes, twenty seconds," the chief petty officer replied.

Carlos understood. Hyperspace insertion would begin sixty seconds before the *Lee* entered the wormhole created by the giant ring of the starbridge. It would be at that one-minute mark when the Millis-Clement field would be deactivated and the ship would lose artificial gravity. He had to be seated by then.

"Commodore . . ." He held out his hand. "Please. I know what I'm—"

"All right." Tereshkova made up her mind. She slapped her stunner into his palm. "Go. Do it."

Carlos nodded, but said nothing as he tucked the small pistol in the waistband of his trousers, carefully positioning it on his right side where he could easily get to it with his right hand. He pulled the front of his jacket around the gun but didn't button it, instead letting his jacket hang open. So long as he kept his arms at his sides, the stun gun would remain hidden.

Heflin patted his shoulder, a silent gesture of good luck. Tereshkova was quiet, but the look in her eyes spoke volumes. Carlos took a deep breath, then, as the officers slipped behind him so that they wouldn't be spotted, he pushed aside the curtain and stepped out into the compartment.

The passengers were gazing out the portholes, trying to catch a glimpse of the starbridge that lay directly before them. A few of them looked up as Carlos walked down the aisle; their surprise at his sudden appearance was obvious from the way he heard his name being whispered. He ignored them as he sauntered toward the back of the compartment, trying to appear more relaxed than he actually was.

As he expected, Lynn was seated to his right, on the port side of the cabin. Across the aisle was Cosenza, seated on the starboard side. Although Lynn spotted him at once, the deacon barely seemed to notice him. Cosenza continued to stare straight ahead, his gaze fixed upon the seatback screen in front of him.

"Mr. President!" Lynn's mouth fell open. "I didn't . . . I'm sorry, but I wasn't expecting . . ."

"I know, I know." Carlos forced a congenial smile that he didn't feel. "Getting a little tired of first class, so I thought I'd come back, ride the rest of the way with you." He tried not to look at Cosenza. "Mind if I . . . ?"

"No . . . no, of course not." Startled, she started to reach down to the vacant seat beside her, and it was then that Carlos noticed that she'd placed her shoulder bag upon it, even taking care to pull a lapstrap around it so that it wouldn't float away when the Millis-Clement field was deactivated. "Just let me . . ."

"Oh, no. Don't bother." Carlos couldn't believe his luck; Lynn's bag in the seat next to her meant that he had an excuse to sit beside Cosenza, thereby putting him in arm's reach. "I'll just sit here."

Not bothering to ask permission, Carlos settled in the vacant seat next to Cosenza's. "Excuse me," he murmured, keeping the rigid smile on his face even as he turned his head to glance at the deacon. For the first time, Cosenza became aware of him. Regarding Carlos with a gaze that was unnaturally intense, he shrank away, avoiding even the most casual contact.

Carlos spotted the datapad. It was on the right armrest, Cosenza's hand lightly upon it. Close, so close . . .

A voice came over the ceiling speaker just then. *"Your attention, please. We are on final approach toward Starbridge Coyote, with hyperspace insertion in two minutes. In sixty seconds, the ship will disengage its Millis-Clement field. When this occurs, we will lose artificial gravity. Please make sure your seat belts are securely fastened, and all loose objects are safely stowed . . ."*

"I'm so glad you've decided to join me." Lynn was paying little attention to the announcement; she'd turned around in her seat as much as its straps would allow. "I really hate this part of the trip. Making the jump . . ."

"Nothing to worry about. It's perfectly safe, really." Carlos buckled his waist strap. He pretended to tighten it, while in fact making sure that it was loose enough that it wouldn't interfere with his movements. In that instant, he realized that he'd made a mistake; by sitting down next to Cosenza, he'd put himself in a position where he couldn't easily reach the stunner concealed beneath his jacket. At least not without jostling the priest with his right elbow, therefore tipping his hand. He was close, yes . . . but *too* close.

Perhaps he should first try to grab the pad, then go for his weapon? No. Forget the gun. The crewmen waiting for him to make his move would take care of Cosenza. The first priority was getting his hands on that goddamn pad.

"Yes, well . . . you're right, of course." Lynn continued to blather on, oblivious to what was happening beside her. "Anyway, I just want to thank you for reading the message I sent you, and asking your nephew if he'd be willing to do an interview."

"Forget it." Carlos prayed that Cosenza hadn't heard her words. From the corner of his eye, he saw that the minister was still watching his screen. Its image had changed from a course map to a real-time view of the starbridge, as seen from a camera in the ship's bow.

"No, really. I just wish that he'd stayed longer, but he said that he had an upset stomach . . ."

Cosenza looked sharply at her, then his gaze shifted toward Carlos. The deacon had caught that remark. Finally realizing who was sitting beside him, he'd become suspicious. *Dammit!* Carlos thought. *Can't that silly woman ever keep her mouth shut?*

"He'll be . . . he'll be fine," he said hastily, and found that he couldn't keep from stammering. "I'm sure he'll . . . I mean, that he . . ."

Four bells rang, the signal that the field was about to be shut down. A few seconds later, he felt his body rise from the seat cushion, held down only by the loosened strap. On the screen before him, the starbridge completely filled the view. Its broad silver torus was no longer empty at its center, though: a brilliant flash of defocused light, filtered slightly by the camera but nonetheless blinding, was replaced an instant later by a swirling haze of multicolored light.

The *Lee* surged forward, rushing toward the opened wormhole, and in that second, Cosenza raised the pad from his armrest. Holding it in his right hand, he lifted his left hand, extended a forefinger . . .

Now!

Twisting around in his seat, Carlos made a grab for Cosenza's left hand. He managed to get hold of the deacon's wrist. Cosenza snarled at him, an incoherent protest that sounded like an animal's angry growl, as Carlos yanked the priest's hand away from the pad. For an instant, Carlos thought he had him. He heard Lynn yell something, and behind them there was the sharp bang of the compartment's rear hatch being slammed open . . .

Cosenza wrenched his hand free. Desperately, Carlos tried to lunge across his seat, but the strap interfered with him. "Don't . . . !"

Cosenza stabbed his finger against the pad.

For a timeless moment, it appeared as if nothing was going to happen. Cosenza sagged back in his seat, letting out his breath even as he allowed the pad to fall from his grasp.

"Praise . . ." he whispered.

The rest was lost beneath an immense *thump!* as an explosion rocked the ship. Carlos heard the warbling shriek of the master alarm. On the screen, the image fuzzed and blurred. Another *thump*, harder, followed by a loud *wham!* as the oxygen tanks exploded.

The passengers screamed in terror as, several yards away, the immense rip appeared in the cabin fuselage. A cyclone tore through the compartment, tearing at loose objects and flinging them into space. Through the porthole, Carlos caught a glimpse of the starbridge hurtling toward them, the curving edge of its torus a vast silver wall.

He shut his eyes, took his last breath. His final living thought was of Wendy, and how beautiful she'd been the day he'd first met her.

The night was still, the city uncommonly quiet. It seemed to Wendy as if the world itself was holding its breath, waiting for a miracle that would never occur.

Pulling the curtains back in place, she moved away from the window, reluctantly returning to the suite on the second floor of the Federation consulate, where she'd spent her last night with her husband. Sometime during the morning—before she'd returned from the spaceport, before anyone had heard the awful news—someone from the housekeeping staff had come in here and made the bed: smoothing out the sheets, plumping the pillows, pulling the bedspread and comforter back in place. A thoughtful gesture, but one she wished hadn't been made. It was the last bed she would ever share with Carlos; she would've preferred to have it left undisturbed.

She wasn't alone. Melissa sat on the end of the bed, cuddling Inez in her arms as she quietly wept for . . . how many times had it been, for both women? Wendy had lost count, if she'd ever kept one in the first place. A staff member had brought mother and child to the guest suite shortly after they'd received word of the *Lee*'s destruction, and in hindsight Wendy realized that it was fortunate that Hawk's family had decided to spend the night in New Brighton before returning to Midland. After the skiff lifted off, Wendy herself had briefly considered catching an airship back to New Florida—but changed her mind; there was some minor government business in New Brighton that required the attention of a former president, and since Carlos wasn't available . . .

She let out her breath as a rattling sigh, laid a hand across the back of a wicker chair to steady herself. Government business. In the end, that was what had killed her husband. Not a boid, not his role as Rigil Kent during the Revolution, not any of the wilderness expeditions he'd participated in or led since his teenage years. A diplomatic mission, important yet hardly dangerous, that he shouldn't have even undertaken in the first place. The irony was . . .

A soft knock at the door. Wendy glanced at Melissa, but the other woman—the other widow in the room, she reminded herself, although they barely knew each other—didn't appear to notice. They'd already had quite a few visitors these last few hours. What was one more?

"Come in," she said, surprised by how hoarse her voice had become.

The door slowly opened, and Tomas Conseco came in. Her aide had caught a gyro from Liberty as soon as he'd heard the news. "Wendy?" he said, for once addressing her by her first name. "Someone here to see you." Seeing the look on her face, he quickly added, "I think you might like to talk to him."

Wendy hesitated. For the first several hours after she'd learned of the *Lee*'s destruction, she'd had to deal with a seemingly endless progression of government officials, most of whom were strangers, each coming by to express condolences. They'd meant well, of course, but after a while she welcomed Tomas's arrival, if only to have him run interference until the rest of her family made their way to New Brighton. But if her aide thought it was a person she ought to meet . . .

"All right," she murmured, trying not to sigh. "Let him in."

Tomas turned toward the open door, nodded to someone standing just outside. A moment later, a tall, dark-skinned man dressed in homespun clothing came in. Wendy had never seen him before, but he obviously knew who she was.

"Madam President?" he asked. "I'm . . . sorry to bother you at a time like this, but . . ."

"Go ahead." She hoped that, whatever he had to say, he'd be quick about it. "And you are . . . ?

"Sawyer Lee." He nervously shifted from one foot to another. "I'm a friend . . . I mean, I was a friend of your . . ."

"Yes, of course." Wendy remembered his name from the letter Carlos had received from him. "Carlos and I were talking about you only this morning. Something about a . . ."

Quietly clearing his throat, Tomas lifted a finger. Seeing that her aide was trying to get her attention, she raised a hand to Sawyer. "Just a second," she said, then looked at Tomas. "Yes?"

"Don't mean to interrupt, ma'am, but . . ." For the first time, Wendy noticed the papers under his arm. "We've just received a preliminary report from the gatehouse. A little more information about the"—an uncertain pause—"the accident."

Something in the way he chose his words made Wendy forget about her visitor. "What does it say?" she asked. Tomas pulled the pages from under his arm, but she shook her head. "Don't read it to me, please. Just sum it up."

Tomas reluctantly nodded. "There's not a lot here that we haven't heard already, but . . . well, two or three things you might want to know. First, the gatehouse is certain that there was an explosion aboard the *Lee* as it was entering the starbridge. They've reviewed remote imagery taken of the ship, and it appears that it came from the cargo bay, with a second explosion occurring just a few moments later from the oxygen tanks just below the passenger section."

From the corner of her eye, Wendy saw Melissa look up from Inez. Sawyer's mouth fell open in astonishment. "The cargo bay?" he asked. "So . . . you mean it wasn't the engines?"

"No, it wasn't." Wendy traded a glance with Tomas, then turned toward him. "Mr. Lee . . . Sawyer . . . what I'm about to tell you is classified, or at least for the time being. So I'm going to have to ask you to . . ."

"Keep my mouth shut. Sure, of course. I . . ."

"We received an earlier report from the gatehouse," Wendy went on. "A few minutes before the . . . well, we can't really call it an accident . . . the gatehouse received a final text message from the ship, stating that they had reason to believe that there was a bomb aboard. Apparently it was brought on by a passenger, a Dominionist minister . . ."

Sawyer's eyes went wide. "Oh, my god," he whispered. "I saw . . . when I was at the spaceport . . . I was there to bring a friend of mine who was . . ." He quickly shook his head. "What I'm trying to say is, I saw a Dominionist preacher get out of a cab, and he was carrying a suitcase that looked . . . I mean, it seemed like it was too heavy for him to . . ."

"We're going to want to hear more about that," Wendy said impatiently, "but not just now." Seeing the stricken expression on his face, she softened her tone. "You had a friend aboard the *Lee*?"

He nodded, and it was hard not to miss the tears at the corners of his eyes. "Yes . . . yes, I did. A lady by the name of Lynn Hu. She was a reporter. We were both on the ExEx with . . ."

"Carlos. Yes, I know." Wendy forced a smile. "I met her once, last year, when she came to our house to interview me." She hesitated. "I liked her. She was a good reporter. I'm very sorry for your loss."

Sawyer nodded, yet he appeared unable to speak. Wendy looked at Tomas again. "So we know for sure that it was a bomb. Any further word about the starbridge itself?"

"Yes, ma'am." The papers rattled softly in his hands. "They confirm that it's been destroyed. When the explosion . . . explosions, I mean . . . occurred, they had sufficient force to throw the *Lee* against the torus. So even if the ship had managed to survive the blasts themselves . . . well, the collision did the rest. There's not much left of the ring . . . just a few pieces that were thrown clear before the rest was sucked into the wormhole when it collapsed."

Feeling her legs grow weak, Wendy collapsed into the chair she'd been leaning against. There. That was it. With the starbridge destroyed, so was Coyote's hyperspace link with Earth, not to mention Hjarr and the rest of the galaxy. They might eventually be able to rebuild it—its inventor, Jonas Whittaker, was living in semiretirement just outside Leeport—and the *hjadd* might be able to help as well, if they were willing to do so. Yet the fact remained that the starbridge had been assembled from materials brought from Earth by the *Columbus*. Replacing it, or at least anytime soon . . .

"So we're cut off." Appreciating for the first time that the tragedy extended beyond her own personal loss, Wendy suddenly felt numb. "Whatever happens next, we're on our own."

"Yes, ma'am." Tomas didn't know quite what to say. "That seems to be . . ."

He stopped himself, and glanced at the report again. "One more item . . . something else the gatehouse noticed when they reviewed the images. Just after the first explosion . . . the one in the cargo bay, that is . . . but before the *Lee* collided with the starbridge, it appears as if something may have been ejected from the ship."

He hesitated. "Madam President . . . Wendy . . . they think it may have been a lifeboat."

Wendy felt her heart stop. "A lifeboat," she repeated, her voice little more than a whisper. "Did it . . . did it get away?"

"They're not sure. The explosion distorted the visual image, so they don't know for certain whether it entered the wormhole before it collapsed. And before you ask"—he shook his head—"no, they don't know who was aboard. It may have only been a misfire." He shrugged. "I mean, it's strange that there would only be one lifeboat, isn't it? If the crew was attempting to evacuate the ship, wouldn't there be more?"

Wendy knew that he was trying not to raise her hopes unjustifiably. She also realized that, even if a lifeboat had been jettisoned and it had managed to go through the wormhole before the starbridge was destroyed, they would never know who, if anyone, was aboard. And yet . . .

"Maybe someone got away." Sawyer had found his voice again.

She slowly nodded. Perhaps there was hope after all. She could only pray that it was true.

"Thank you, Tomas." Wendy found the strength to stand up again. "Is that all?" He nodded, and she turned to Sawyer once more. "Mr. Lee, thanks for stopping by. As I said, my husband mentioned you just this morning. Apparently he was quite impressed with you, so I appreciate the . . ."

"Yes, ma'am, but . . ." He paused, uncertain of what to say. "That's not the reason why I'm here. Not all of it anyway." Seeing that she was waiting for him to go on, he took a deep breath. "Some people I know, they were wondering . . . will you be able to attend the vigil?"

"Pardon me?" Wendy blinked. "Vigil? I haven't heard of any . . ."

Again, Tomas cleared his throat. "I didn't want to mention this to you, ma'am, but . . . yes, there's to be a public memorial this evening. A vigil, as it were. In fact . . ."

He glanced at his watch, but Sawyer was already ahead of him. "Ma'am, it should be getting started just about now." He took a couple of steps farther into the suite. "If you'll permit me . . . ?"

Not knowing what to expect, Wendy nodded. Sawyer walked over to the window where she'd been standing only a few minutes earlier. Pulling aside the curtains, he looked outside. A smile appeared on his face, then he stepped aside.

"There's something here you may want to see," he said, his voice low. "All of you, please."

Wendy hesitated, then went to the window. Behind her, Melissa rose from the bed; carrying Inez in her arms, she followed, Tomas close behind. As they gazed through the window, Wendy felt something catch in her throat.

Outside the consulate, where there had once only been darkness, there was light. A river of candles, fish-oil lamps, flashlights, and makeshift torches, flowing in a magnificent procession through the streets of New Brighton. Each light was held by an individual hand, yet there were so many—tens, perhaps even hundreds of thousands—that they couldn't have been carried by the city's inhabitants alone.

The refugees were there as well, she suddenly realized. The fence surrounding the camp must have been removed, the city gate opened. Which was only appropriate. There was no longer any difference between those who'd been on Coyote before and those who'd recently fled Earth. They all belonged to this world now.

The procession moved through the streets, the lights growing brighter and more numerous as townspeople emerged from the tenements to join in the vigil. As Wendy watched, awestruck by the majesty of the moment, she heard a new sound. A word, a single word, that came first from one throat, and then another, and then another, gradually rising in volume until it became a solemn and reverent chant.

"Chaaz'maha . . ."

"Chaaz'maha . . ."

"Chaaz'maha . . ."

Sawyer Lee shook his head. "For someone who said he was only a teacher, this is . . ." Not knowing what else to say, he fell silent.

"He was only a teacher, yes." When Melissa finally spoke, her voice was little more than a whisper. "But he's more than that now. He has become God."

COYOTE CALENDAR

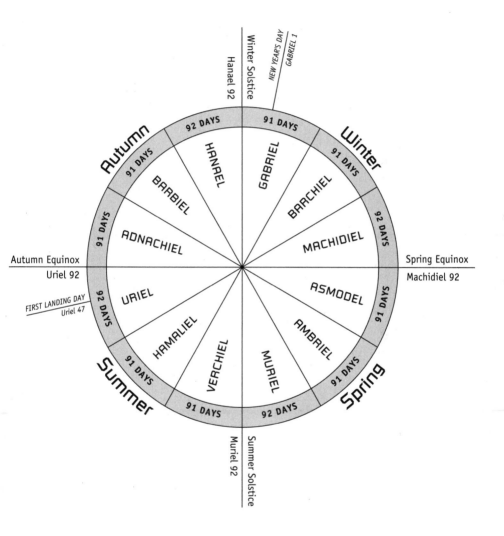

TIMELINE: COYOTE HISTORY

Earth Events:

JULY 5, 2070—URSS *Alabama* departs from Earth for 47 Ursae Majoris and Coyote.

APRIL–DECEMBER 2096—United Republic of America falls. Treaty of Havana cedes control of North America to the Western Hemisphere Union.

JUNE 16, 2256—WHSS *Seeking Glorious Destiny Among the Stars for Greater Good of Social Collectivism* leaves Earth for Coyote.

JANUARY 4, 2258—WHSS *Traveling Forth to Spread Social Collectivism to New Frontiers* leaves Earth for Coyote.

DECEMBER 10, 2258—WHSS *Long Journey to the Galaxy in the Spirit of Social Collectivism* leaves Earth for Coyote.

AUGUST 23, 2259—WHSS *Magnificent Voyage to the Stars in Search of Social Collectivism* leaves Earth for Coyote.

MARCH 4, 2260—WHSS *Spirit of Social Collectivism Carried to the Stars* leaves Earth for Coyote.

AUGUST 2270–JULY 2279—The Savant Genocide; 35,000 on Earth killed; mass extermination of savants, with the survivors fleeing the inner solar system.

APRIL 2288—First sighting of Spindrift by telescope array on the lunar farside.

JUNE 1, 2288—EASS *Galileo* leaves Earth for rendezvous with Spindrift; contact lost with Earth soon thereafter.

JANUARY 2291—EASS *Galileo* reaches Spindrift. First contact.

SEPTEMBER 18, 2291—EASS *Columbus* leaves for Coyote.

FEBRUARY 1, 2344—CFSS *Robert E. Lee* returns to Earth, transporting survivors of the *Galileo* expedition.

Coyote Events:

AUGUST 5, 2300—URSS *Alabama* arrives at 47 Ursae Majoris system.

SEPTEMBER 7, 2300 / URIEL 47, C.Y. 01—Colonists arrive on Coyote; later known as "First Landing Day."

URIEL 52, C.Y. 02—First child born on Coyote: Susan Gunther Montero.

GABRIEL 18, C.Y. 03—WHSS *Glorious Destiny* arrives. Original colonists flee Liberty; Western Hemisphere Union occupation of Coyote begins.

AMBRIEL 32, C.Y. 03—WHSS *New Frontiers* arrives.

HAMALIEL 2, C.Y. 04—WHSS *Long Journey* arrives.

BARCHIEL 6, C.Y. 05—WHSS *Magnificent Voyage* arrives.

BARBIEL 30, C.Y. 05—Thompson's Ferry Massacre; beginning of the Revolution.

GABRIEL 75, C.Y. 06—WHSS *Spirit* arrives.

ASMODEL 5, C.Y. 06—Liberty retaken by colonial rebels, Union forces evicted from Coyote; later known as "Liberation Day."

HAMALIEL C.Y. 13—EASS *Columbus* arrives; construction of starbridge begins.

NOVEMBER 2340 / HANAEL C.Y. 13—*Columbus* shuttle EAS *Isabella* returns to Earth via Starbridge Coyote; United Nations recognition of Coyote Federation.

MURIEL 45, C.Y. 15—*Galileo* shuttle EAS *Maria Celeste* returns to Coyote via alien starbridge.

ASMODEL 54, C.Y. 16—*Hjadd* cultural ambassador arrives on Coyote.

HAMALIEL 25, C.Y. 16—CFS *Pride of Cucamonga* departs for Rho Coronae Borealis via *hjadd* starbridge.

HAMALIEL 1, C.Y. 17—Exploratory Expedition departs Bridgeton for first circumnavigation of the Great Equatorial River.

ACKNOWLEDGMENTS

I'd like to express my appreciation to my editor, Ginjer Buchanan, and my literary agent, Martha Millard, for their continued support; to Marvin Kaye, whose request for a story for his anthology *Forbidden Planets* turned out to be the springboard for a new round of Coyote novels; and to Rob Caswell, Lesley Ham, Dr. Horace "Ace" Marchant, Jack McDevitt, Bob and Sara Schwager, Bud Sparhawk, and Kevin Weller for advice and assistance during the writing of this novel.

The religious and philosophical arguments posed in this novel were, in large part, inspired by *The God Delusion* by Richard Dawkins and *The Varieties of Scientific Experience* by Carl Sagan. On a more tangible level, the design of the *Ted LeMare* is adapted from the New Alchemy Institute's *Margaret Mead*, a hypothetical sailing ship described in "Ocean Arks" by John Todd (*CoEvolution Quarterly*, Fall 1979) and *Bioshelters, Ocean Arks, City Farming: Ecology As the Basis of Design* by Nancy Jack Todd and John Todd (Random House, 1984).

As always, my greatest thanks go to my wife, Linda, who encouraged me to return to Coyote.

August 2007–May 2008
Whately, Massachusetts